Advance Praise for

The N

"If you think humanity car   of
the aliens in The New Plan   ds
tension in a highly satisfyin

"Danger and suspense permeate every page in a gripping journey into a world teetering on the brink of collapse ... a tale of survival and redemption that is well-paced to deliver suspenseful moments of fear and big revelations with shocking twists ... a thought-provoking and immersive read that lingers long after the final page..." (K.C. Finn)

"The New Planet Policy will have lovers of science fiction with a touch of psychological thriller hooked and turning page after page. There is suspense, adventure, thrills, and spellbinding plot twists." (Keith Mbuya)

"The New Planet Policy is a thrilling sci-fi novel layered with mystery, intrigue, and suspense ... absolutely unpredictable ...a unique and refreshing take on alien invasions." (Pikasho Deka)

"... an exceptional job of integrating science fiction with real-world societal issues, blurring the lines between speculative fiction and contemporary crises." (Jamie Michele)

Fresh Blue Ink titles by
R. M. Kozan

Breakaway:1977 (2013)

The Voyages of Ralf, Vol. 1: The Arc of Purchaser (2020)

The New Planet Policy (2024)

THE NEW PLANET POLICY

R. M. Kozan

Fresh Blue Ink
Ottawa

Fresh Blue Ink
is an imprint of Fresh Blue, Inc.
Ottawa, ON

www.FreshBlueInk.ca

Paperback ISBN: 978-0-9920119-7-0
E-book ISBN: 978-0-9920119-6-3

Cover illustration © 2024 Fresh Blue Inc.

First edition: August 2024

For my parents,
Frank and Rose

THE NEW PLANET POLICY

PART 1: EARTH

Chapter One

Twenty years from the present day…

Ian Hesse, despite his clear intent and desire, would not be going home tonight. He had worked throughout this fine, long summer day.

Now the streets shone with a grey that portended the coming dark. Rush hour had faded to a forgotten pain as streetlamps flickered, flirting with illumination.

On the edge of Ottawa's western-most industrial area, the compact and nondescript building of Ian's employer, a custom industrial digital fabricator, was about to meet the desolation of night. This final man, a final representative of the day, was about to forsake his workplace of the light hours.

Ian Hesse's hair was an irreverent mop of pastel brown. He was cursed with pale skin, an invitation for skin cancer in extreme latitudes, but blessed with a quick wit and an infectious smile.

It is said brevity is the soul of wit, and Ian embraced that doctrine, but not voluntarily. His wit was often concise and carefully constructed for pragmatic viability as an inconvenient stutter often detoured his attempts at conversation. This had been his social burden since puberty.

Educated as an industrial engineer, yet having experience only in the petrochemical industry, Ian found himself, aged thirty-three, an under-appreciated anachronism in the emerging technological milieu of yet another decade of the new millennium. He had come to depend upon his easy and agreeable manner to brighten interviews and gain an advantage in the rapidly changing workforce of the third millennium.

Now, at the edge of dusk, work complete, he readied his exit from the small building that had been his place of employment for the last two years. He checked the building's back-up data receptacles and uninterruptible power supply and, after a final glance at the event log, made secure the glass door at the front of the building, himself on the outside.

Ian glanced towards the setting sun and grimaced, displeased. A day earlier, he had missed work due to a touch of toxicity syndrome, a common ailment of urban dwellers, and today his boss had insisted that Ian stay late to diminish his work backlog.

Two days of work in a day and an evening. Not one of the better ways to start a weekend. Almost dark now.

It was almost nine. The sunsets were getting later and later as the summer peaked. The final rays of the setting sun glinted on his battered and unwashed GE's dull plastic flank as he fumbled the emergency mechanical key in an attempt to gain entry.

How can the app have just suddenly failed? Everything else is fine.

Ian settled behind the wheel, closed the hatch and then, acting in the interests of maximum safety, activated the hatch locks.

They made no sound and nothing happened.

My battery is dead? That explains the app, but it's impossible! I was fully charged when I parked here.

Ian turned his attention to his phone again.

The sound barely registered as he heard the GE's hatch handle being tried by an unknown hand. Not quite believing the situation, Ian turned his head casually.

He saw only his filthy side window for a moment. Looking beyond that, a figure in torn white overalls. A heavily bearded, almost Neanderthal-like man carrying a large stained piece of wood. Miniature ice-cubes of safety glass flew into Ian's face just before he was struck by the wooden club.

The urgent high-pitched shattering noise of his driver's side window was followed by a deeper rending noise amplified within his own head. The wooden club was skidding along the side of his face, leaving a bloodied trench littered with slivers. Ian screamed in agony.

While one hand was held up in a weak effort to fend off the attacker, the other frantically tried the initiation panel, to bring the car to life and was rewarded only with silence.

It seemed to Ian that his car's death would precede his own by only a few moments.

A chilled hand clutched Ian's throat, and he was thrown out of the car onto the dusty ground. He looked up to see his attacker bellow in triumph.

The bearded wild man held the club high overhead, preparing to finish the vulnerable Ian. As the club streaked downwards, Ian rolled to one side. The club thumped dully on the ground and his attacker snarled in frustration.

Ian rolled a couple of meters away and scrambled to his feet. He swayed for a moment in disorientation, then barely managed to lift his arm in time to block another swing of the wooden club.

The jolt against his arm was tremendous and forced him back a step; he narrowly averted losing his balance and tumbling to the ground. Blood seeped through his white sleeve. His bones were shattered.

Another blow would render him completely helpless, and so, using his best knowledge of fighting, Ian decided to make one desperate offensive attempt. He stepped forward and kicked the bearded man in the groin with as much force as he could muster.

The attacker, howling in pain and surprised anger, doubled over and fell forward onto one knee. Realizing his advantage was temporary, Ian hobbled quickly past his attacker into his GE.

The hatch was open, window completely shattered. He fell into the GE, biting his lower lip fiercely and emitting an anguished whimper as a shard of plastic moulding cut into his thigh. He reached below the driver's seat with his one intact arm.

Ian had always been much interested in urban survival, and years earlier had secured a small .965 under the seat of his car. Now he praised his own thoughtfulness and relished his attention to the saying 'better safe than unidentifiable at the morgue'.

His hand found the gun, closed around its handle and, with a spasm of fear-accentuated pain, he fell out of the car.

The attacker was standing, albeit hunchback-like, again prepared to bludgeon him with the wooden stick.

Ian, sitting on the ground, back resting against the side of the GE, brought the gun up with his one undamaged arm. He looked into the eyes of his attacker and could still see no recognition there of approaching death nor flicker of fear. The taste of blood was in Ian's mouth; his lip now as well as his face, arm, and thigh bled freely.

The attacker again raised his club overhead. A repeat performance of his earlier attempt at homicide. Ian fired one shot into the behemoth's chest. The attacker bared his teeth.

Ian fired two shots into the left upper chest region. The force of the bullets caused the attacker to fall backwards onto the dirt, where he remained, apparently incapacitated.

Ian closed his eyes. For a few seconds he welcomed

4

unconsciousness. Then, just as he approached the point of no return in his blackout, he pulled back and cracked open his eyelids.

This was not the time to faint. He spit out a glob of blood, and blinked his eyes repeatedly.

Darkness had arrived in full bloom. In the north, across the river, the constellation Perseus was emerging from blackness. Ian reflected on its resemblance to a dog's head. Algol twinkled, rising to the ultimate brilliance of its cycle. The night smelled hot and claustrophobic with dust, a leftover of the petrochemical era.

Steadying himself against the car, Ian carefully leaned in and tried the initiator again. Nothing.

Ian staggered back to the door of his workplace from which he had exited only two minutes earlier. The lock worked smoothly and he was soon inside. He fumbled in the darkness for the switch. He found it, tried it, then cursed it. The small office remained dark.

Nothing works?? I need a cop.

Ian staggered to where the corporate landline should have been. It was still there, lying on the desk, a warm and secure connection with the order of the civilized world. Ian picked up the receiver and keyed 911. It didn't ring. He hung up and picked it up again. No dial tone.

With a strangled sob and without thinking, Ian groped his way out of the office into the warm dust-filled night.

Dark clouds were rolling in rapidly. The moon was absent. The few stars still visible over the edge of the city gave the night's blackness small argument.

Ian's sight could not penetrate very far down the deserted street. The local streetlamps seemed few and each now surprisingly defunct.

That's the first time I've ever shot someone.

Ian was alone. Only then did he begin to hear the many

sirens in the distance. He collapsed against the building, back on the concrete wall, knees in front of him, arms resting on his knees, head drooped, hope crushed, blood freely flowing, eyes fixed and seeing little hope for a future.

The sirens in the distance were not for Ian's emergency; he was somehow sure the gun shots had gone unnoticed.

Ian checked his still-warm gun. He had four, no three bullets left. The stars were beginning to blur over. The gun fell from his hand onto the ground beside him. One of the several sirens in the distance faded out, and soon, another had started up to replace it.

Chapter Two

The news of the treacherous alien attack slowly filtered through the fifth floor of the St. John's Rehabilitation Institute at the Royal Ottawa Medical Centre, never a convivial place to be working after a long night of heavy drinking.

Blythe clocked in, only dimly aware of the external drama in play.

"I think Penguin Deluxe is pissed at us for leaving the lady in 504 by herself in the john yesterday; she's already screamed at Katrina about it," was Darla's only greeting to her fellow nurse.

"She's down in dispatch now. Back in a minute. Wanna grab something?"

Blythe barely tolerated Darla and her stories at any time, but nodded and headed towards the elevator without protest.

"Tiberius and I really tore into each other last night at Whispers. I think I've finally had enough of him and his games."

"Yeah." Blythe was willing to talk to Darla only enough to end any conversation. She too was hung over. Part of her mind sought, without luck, the name of the plumbing apprentice she had met the previous night.

"Let's go somewhere tonight for a few drinks. I just want to forget about him," said Darla, wiping the invasive part of her earphones before pocketing them. "I've been patient with him too long, Bly."

The St. John's cafeteria was nearly full. Full of white and blue, the doctors and nurses, plus technicians, orderlies, housekeepers, and families of the rehabilitation institute's patients.

A St. John's breakfast required monastic composure on

the part of the eater; selection methodology was especially important for highly sensitive patrons, especially chronic ones. St. John's was notorious for its powdered eggs, especially when they left the powder out. Donuts were a safe bet however, and the women each took two.

"That penguin gives me any trouble this morning and I'm gonna leave. These cramps are killing me, and I forgot my heating pad," babbled Darla brusquely, squirting a container of something cream-like into her coffee. Darla was a constant complainer, deploring anything unworthy, which was approximately everything. Her period was a favourite millstone, and this time was no different.

"I think I'll take a couple of Zoomex when we get upstairs," she declared.

This statement went unheard by Blythe. Her empathy was on empty. A thousand-yard stare glazed her eyes and she dimly nodded, details of the previous night's revelry slowly coming back to her. She swallowed some coffee and forced down a bite of donut.

"What about this Centauran business?" Darla had finally disengaged her thoughts from her own personal woes and moved onto the more general crises afoot in the world. "Weird they'd just up and attack like that. I thought the scientists had been talking nice with them for years?"

"Yeah well. Maybe they were just drinking and don't really mean anything by it," croaked Blythe.

"You're funny." Darla glanced at the clock over the steam tables. "We better head back up."

Back on the fifth floor, there was relative quiet. Of the sixty beds, only fifty were occupied, most with patients transferred from the main ICU, or from 'the Garden', a unit housing patients with severe brain damage.

Blythe readied herself for her meeting with the nun. Sisters of Mercy, despite the name, had little mercy in dealing with lazy, incompetent nurses, although Blythe was not usually that. She would merely obey her own rules at times, and the floor nun would not tolerate any notions of free will in the workplace.

Yet Blythe got along relatively well with Sister Raymond, and they each expressed a mutual trust and liking for one another. Despite contention over minor issues, Sister Raymond had declared Blythe 'Charge' or head nurse the previous month after a brilliant performance during a full arrest in Room 552 when two interns had rendered completely useless medical treatment to a middle-aged man who had had a heart attack during a routine examination. Blythe saved him, although he did die twelve hours later from another cardiac arrest.

It was after nine o'clock and the nun still hadn't come back. All the nurses were busy dispensing drugs and updating reports, working hard and effectively during the early morning hours, preparing each patient for the coming physician rounds. Blythe's rooms, 550 through 552, each housed two patients, and each patient was connected to a respirator. None of Blythe's patients could talk, move, or breathe on their own. All were clinically dead, yet all were alive.

In Room 551, Blythe had two patients: one 19 years old, and the other, 34.

The teenager had blown his brains out two years ago but somehow remained alive, if only by a thread. Blythe injected a fructose solution into his IV and wiped the scum and mucous which had built up during the night from around his eyes.

His name was Juan Carlos and he had a large hole where his left eye used to be. This is where the barrel of the .965 sat when he had pulled the trigger. Blythe took extra time to swab the hole clean. Juan's uncle was to meet with the attending physician at bedside in about two hours, and nothing was worse than Juan's hole filled with crusty pus. She wanted him to look nice.

In the bed opposite Juan, lay Ian Hesse, a similar case in that he also had been unconscious for almost two years now.

Ian had been transferred from the Queensway Carleton ER unconscious and traumatized. Ongoing cardiac stimulation had been required since his admission. He had stopped breathing two days after that and was then provided a respirator. Although his trauma had long since healed, Ian had never emerged from coma.

Ian needed a shave. Blythe dropped the razor when she noticed Ian's support systems had undergone automatic shut-down. Ian's vital signs had returned.

Chapter Three

Ian's mind had swirled with dark curls of confusion for a time beyond his ability to maintain a grasp on any passage of time. Reality was a far-removed thing.

All of his memories had faded to senseless whispers and fogged images of unknown entities performing alien actions. He was alive, but alone in oblivion, his identity lost. All emotions had gone, for he had no use for them. Once he had believed that he had not always been as he was now, but long ago that thought had mutated into a blunted feeling that he was forever moving through fresh, unknown spaces.

Coherence requires a partial repetition of thought, and that was lost to Ian. Darkness and silence were not conditions of his existence, they were his existence.

A thought suddenly struck his brain cells, but he did not have the capacity to recognize it. Then another struck, then a barrage. Light and sound roared. A circle of light outlined consciousness. Not his own consciousness, but the consciousness of another who was beyond and apart from Ian. This was beyond Ian's comprehension as solitude was the primary symptom of his existence.

Despite the lack of understanding, Ian experienced a barrage of foreign internally guided motion: thoughts, communication. The foreign data found a suitable medium and broke through. The muted voice transmitted the emotion of fear to Ian. It was not understood. The Other chose a different, more structured medium, and a voice spoke into Ian's mind.

Ian finally recognized the meaning of the words: "Ian Hesse. You slumber with the concentration of the stillest fool. You hide, you seek escape, but it shall not be yours. You are saviour, but only as long as you remain motionless.

Motion shall destroy all that you love, and love is the only thing you have not destroyed within yourself. The time is ripe for a birth of the most restless terror. The Child shall emerge from you, to devour that which you seek most to escape. You are weak, and therefore safe. Your power is your death, and your love is your pain. Thus you are safe. To regain your life you shall seek to regain power. This is folly. Your love and your power are your highest folly. Do not approach them. Nothing is safe, and you must confine your actions to within your own darkness. This is your only alternative to …? For sake of your lost love, forget all words. Rest, let the Child expire".

A battle raged within Ian's body. The experience, which Ian was not conscious of nor would be able to freely recall, was simply his unconscious attempt to conceptualize and integrate a telepathic intrusion into his weakened mind.

The primal survival instinct was finally bringing the power to live back to his body as some external force was trying to subvert his mind, to circumnavigate his animal instinct for survival.

No one near Ian was aware of his inner battle. Some twenty feet down the corridor from Room 551, Blythe had already passed the news of Ian's improvement to Dr. Joberkt, an unusually sociable doctor who often chatted with staff near the nurses' station. Quite ordinarily, the conversations revolved around growing and fading relationships, and the mild but amusing incidents of horror and idiocy that occur innumerable times daily in hospital life.

A break in the conversation came when a phone rang. Blythe reached down and grasped the receiver. She had performed this action ten thousand times before, and each time the news imparted upon her varied. Most calls were insignificant searches for information, calls for help from the safe. Other times, they served as a first warning for misfortune and misdeeds necessitating medical or administrative attention.

The calls evoked the widest possible array of emotions, joy to fear to hate to pity, but Blythe reached calmly for the receiver and answered the phone in a bored voice. Later she would learn that the caller had specifically asked which floor Ian Hesse was on, and requested the call go to the nearest nurses' station.

The caller mumbled.

"Hello? Can I help you?" quoted Blythe from her memories of experiences with unclear phone inquiries.

"For the sake of life, I require a death." A gruff voice.

"I beg your pardon?"

"He must die. Within him are the seeds of time's end." Now the voice was clear but the message was incomprehensible.

"What?" asked Blythe loudly. The others at the station gave her a questioning glance. Looks like a strange one, a new thing to be marvelled at and discussed through endless tainted repetitions.

The voice was silent.

"Were you looking for a particular patient, sir?"

"The Saxon! The Saxon! He is corrupted with false love. His will has inspired a plague of tears. There can be no peace, should he find strength to close his eyes to his oblivion!"

"If you dial again, you can get the switchboard operator. I think you want the mental health unit. Okay?" asked Blythe.

A low rumbling sigh filled the receiver, and the line disconnected.

Blythe rolled her eyes as she replaced the old-fashioned phone handle on its grungy cradle.

13

"What was that about?"

"Some jerk. A crank. Nothing," muttered Blythe.

Outside, Darla, freshly freed from her shift, was raped, mugged, beaten, then fatally and repeatedly stabbed, all by different people.

Inside, Blythe, knowing as well as Darla how to circumvent the pharmaceutical inventory system, decided it was time for a Zoomex.

Chapter Four

S ister Raymond sat at her desk, occupied with the myriad detailed and depressingly familiar administrative tasks that were her domain. Somehow the information system had crashed some of the records in the pharmaceutical inventory system yet again and she was reconstructing the records on a best-guess basis.

If this was to continue much longer a new or overhauled software system would be necessary for pharmaceutical inventory was surely a critical subsystem of St. John's info system. It was an area where errors could quickly turn to allegations, and Sister Raymond, a fine administrator, wisely preferred monotony to misadventure.

A series of three short beeps sounded from her computer workstation, signifying the 10 AM coffee break. A barrage of keystrokes and her personal menu came on-line. Sister Raymond selected 'headline news' and began reading.

The Centaurans had apparently attacked. The hostility had not been anticipated. Key scientists who had been in radio communication with the aliens for the past ten years were dumbfounded.

It seemed that when the aliens had first noted Earth's attempts to communicate in the previous decade they had responded in a twofold manner: firstly by attempting to communicate with coded universal concepts such as binary numbers representing the predominant wavelength emitted by the fusion of hydrogen, calculated in electron diameters (as well as other still not-yet-deciphered messages); secondly, and simultaneously, by launching sub-light speed attack spaceships, or was it an invasion force?

The news service explained that while the radio messages had taken less than five years to arrive, the attacking ships must have taken considerably longer, and

15

therefore must have been launched nearly simultaneously with the onset of radio communication in order to have arrived in only fifteen years. Ten years of dialogue and all a sham.

Editorial leaning was toward immediate and massive retaliation. With the Catastrophic Asteroid Impact Prevention Program in operation, destruction of the alien ships would be swift. The CAIPP finally appeared to be paying dividends.

In the local news it appeared hysteria was ruling the streets. Although the local urban area had over the past couple of years experienced an unexplained upsurge of violent crimes, plus accidents and general mayhem of all forms, it had now been selected, it seemed, for a special level of hysteria far exceeding the world standard.

The streets weren't fit for walking, nor the road for driving. The number of vehicular accidents since the morning was astronomical, and the figures for violent incidents quite unbelievable. Sister Raymond reflected that the numbers could only be supported by a near mob mentality in the streets. She envisioned hordes of looters raping and pillaging their way throughout the city. Indeed there had already been three stabbings in the hospital this morning.

She had also noticed unrest in the patient wards. Like a corral of horses sensing a coming tornado, the hallways were abuzz with the sounds of fear and panic. The common area had been nearly deserted, card tables abandoned and television spewing entertainment to no-one. Most of the patients were cowering in their semi-private rooms or under forcible restraint and howling like hungry wolves.

Upon reflection, there did seem to be a whole new level of malcontent and malevolence washing over the hospital.

Disturbed, Sister Raymond moved to the window. The

scene outside was not reassuring.

Across the boulevard, a car lay on its side and a dog ran recklessly round and round it. Traffic was nonexistent. The Sony store across the way appeared to be undergoing general looting. A small knot of people stood on the corner with clubs and rifles. It wasn't clear if they were attempting to stop the looters or protecting them.

The local Schuldenhaus branch (an international collection agency) appeared to be undergoing some sort of crisis. One of the upper floors had its glass exterior walls smashed and apparent damage to some of the internal structure. A thin line of smoke reached upward from the mechanical equipment on the roof. Arson or some more natural type of fault?

Startled by the warble of her old-fashioned voicephone, Sister Raymond splashed hot coffee on her blouse front.

"My Goodness!" She set the mug down on one of the stacks of printouts covering her secondary desk and reseated herself as she snatched the handset from its cradle.

"Sister Raymond here."

It was the Bishop. A rare occurrence for such a personage to phone so low a functionary as Sister Raymond.

"Yes, your holiness, ma'am. I was just reading the news." The Bishop was undisputed liaison between top St. John's staff and church upper-ups outside the diocese.

"Quite shocking. I'm not sure what to make of it."

The Bishop had read the news too. And probably looked out her window.

"Of course. It wouldn't be good for our staff to head out into such mayhem. I'm sure arrangements can be made for their overnight accommodation within the facility..."

But the Bishop had already discussed that matter with the Chief Operational Administrator. The personal call to

17

Sister Raymond actually concerned humanity's putative special relationship with its creator.

"The Centaurans? Yes, well war is always a difficult issue for the Church to face..."

When the existence of the Centaurans had first become known ten years previously, the Church had, after some initial skepticism, pronounced the Centaurans of Divine origin, cousins of Man and to be considered human not animal. After all, which animals could encode the fundamental wavelength of hydrogen fusion expressed in electron diameters in binary other than Man? The Church's position was now being rapidly reversed.

"No, ma'am. I suppose there is no real evidence that these creatures should be considered the children of our Lord and not just brute animals. I must say that their behaviour..."

It had occurred to the Bishop's superiors that it is advantageous in war to consider one's enemy as less than human.

"Yes your Holiness, ma'am. Thank you for the ideological soundness update. No ma'am, not at all! I really don't have time to think about this type of thing anyway. You know, my duties here are quite substantial. Yes. I really appreciate your calling. When in Rome, right? Ha ha! Very nice talking with you. You too. Thanks again."

Chapter Five

After Darla's death, the St. John's staff did not offer any resistance to the idea of remaining within the facility after shift. Attacks on staff were quite common, but an actual death was not, especially a death that occurred outside the facility and which did not involve any intoxicated or disturbed patient.

Maxeen and Jeffory were trying to comfort Blythe in the ward's staff room. Maxeen was a listless middle-aged registered nurse with too-tight well-tanned skin, and Jeffory, a tall and slender diet tech with one too many piercings and a penchant for platitudes.

"It's no use grieving. There's nothing any of us could've done," continued Jeffory.

"What do you know? You never do anything for anyone you selfish oaf!" barked Blythe, red-eyed and slumped over the cheap and rather unstable table, her sleeve absorbing one of the plentiful coffee rings under constant cultivation there.

Jeffory rolled a dissipated look at Maxine, who flexed her skin and then opened her mouth.

"Now now honey. We all liked Darla as much as you."

"Yeah, that's right." Blythe guiltily absorbed the ambiguity of that statement.

Dr. Joberkt strolled into the staff room, clipboard absentmindedly tucked under his left arm. Patient status reports were not supposed to leave the immediate area of the patient or unit desk.

"Good news, Blythe." He smiled weakly. "You're 551? Hesse, right?" Blythe didn't dispute her designation, and simply nodded. "He's conscious! Incredible. After two months!"

"That's two years, Dr. Joberkt," corrected Blythe.

"More incredible. Incredibler and incredibler." Dr. Joberkt smiled again and shook his head, perhaps trying to get the idea to settle into his cranial area more comfortably. "I've annotated his record, and changed his orders. You can check it later. Take care of yourself." He patted Blythe on the shoulder and left.

A brief moment of silence followed.

"So you really can't blame yourself. It's all fate actually," continued Jeffory.

"Well, work is the best remedy," retorted Blythe responding with her own cliché. The irony was lost on Jeffory.

Blythe stood and excused herself, not able to bear any more sympathy or worthless conversation. She cared little for the opinions and sentiments of most of her co-workers, and was anxious to be out of the way of their social advances. True, she hadn't really liked Darla, but at least she could tolerate her. Darla's continual complaining had only been a symptom for her lack of social ingratiation, and Blythe had appreciated that lack.

Ian Hesse was indeed awake. From the door of 551, Blythe could see Ian was sitting upright in his bed, dazed and squinting.

"How're you doing?"

"I don't know. I think I'm dreaming."

"Not anymore. Now you're awake." Blythe smiled at her patient.

"The doctor said I've been out for two years. That can't be right..."

"You came in here, it was early June, two years ago. Today is July 4th, so yes it is twenty five months later. You're okay though. Come on, try to get up, just for a moment."

"Get up? After two years don't you think my muscles

would be about shot, like a Marsnaut? I'll need months of physiotherapy just to blink."

"This isn't the 20th Century!" Blythe laughed. "We've been giving your muscles nutrients directly ever since you were admitted. Induced physiotherapy once a week. Careful management of body chemical balances... Your health insurance was quite comprehensive. Lucky you. You could probably do a one-arm push-up. Come on. Try to get up."

Ian nodded grimly and slowly swung his feet over the edge of the bed. He made it to the bathroom door and back again to the bed.

"That wasn't too bad, but I still feel like it's 5 AM on a Monday morning."

"Well then, three more hours and we'll send you off to work," joked Blythe. She found something very appealing about Ian.

"Looters in the hospital!" screamed an intern through the door frame of 551 before continuing toward the fire exit stairwell. A loud clamour smashed the usual post-visiting-hours calm of the unit. Blythe could hear voices along the corridor. Some angry, some belligerent. Someone screamed in pain or horror.

"We'd better get out of here." Blythe grabbed Ian's arm and he allowed himself to be led out into the hall and towards the fire escape stairwell.

* *

Sister Raymond was going over the lists of books and magazines from the patient library that contained references to the Centaurans and tagging those with a positive slant for disposal.

Her concentration on her task allowed her to misinterpret the bustle in the corridor. She rose, furious, and strode to her door ready to chastise the unruly staff

21

behind the ruckus.

In the corridor, staff were fleeing towards the furthest wings of the facility while wild-looking hooligans brandishing clubs, knives and other weapons were advancing. They were just about at the staff-only demarcation point. One nurse, his face ashen, sat rigid in shock at the unit desk.

"What's going on here, Wyman?" demanded the nun.

"It's...the Centaurans! They're here!" Sweat poured down the man's neck and his lips twitched in feverish fear.

"Don't be silly, nurse. They're parked in solar orbit halfway to Mars... aren't they?"

Wyman stood and strode into the nun's office without responding.

"What's going on?"

"They're on the grounds!" Wyman stood at the window, eyes bulging. "There they are!! Giant! Horrible! Monsters!" He began to shake violently. His hands flew to his face and he moaned. "Nooo. Nooo."

"Take it easy." Sister Raymond glanced out the window. Much the same scene as in the afternoon. "It's okay." She touched his shoulder. Wyman moaned in panic, spun around to face the nun, clamped his eyes shut, and hurled himself backwards out her fifth storey office window.

Oddly enough, he didn't scream on the way down.

* *

Having not quite reached the stairwell, Blythe and Ian were huddled in a small supply room. They had heard strange, unhinged voices in the stairwell and decided to wait out whatever was going on in an inconspicuous place.

"This city has gotten worse since you went comatose. Crime has gone crazy, and now, with the Centaurans attacking, everyone is just mad with fear. There's looting and awful violence. I know it's been scary on the street, but

22

here in the hospital..." Blythe shook her head in disbelief at their situation.

Ian put his arm around her and she didn't resist. *Perhaps he is trying to comfort me,* she thought, amused at their role reversal.

"I don't understand. Twelve years ago the Centaurans were sending us formulae for complex organic molecules in the universal code that had been developed over, what, four years of two-way communication and eight years of, you know, even realizing each other was there. It doesn't make any sense." said Ian.

"Maybe they consider anything with more than nine carbons an insult." deadpanned Blythe.

"You're crazy." Ian squeezed her a bit to emphasize his point. "So, catch me up, please. Two years is a long time."

"Okay, let's see. Just after your admission, Korea re-united. Also, the UN recognized the cultural distinctiveness of the Roma, which was about time. And 3D video is big again. What else. Last year was a big asteroid gold rush, although India isn't recognizing some countries' claims. Nobody ever agrees to anything, right?"

"Right."

"So far this year: Health-net! On-line monitoring of vital signs for rich folks, with automatic nanobot configuration. We're involved in that. And a second aquafarm, this one in the Atlantic. And, of course, the new headline: Centauri attacks."

"What happened?"

"It's not clear. All we hear is that someone lobbed some missiles at us from half-way to Mars. CAIPP got most of them but one flattened Brasilia and one vapourized a chunk of the Mediterranean. We've never seen the Centaurans of course, but who else could it be?"

Ian nodded his head to contribute his own suspicions to

hers. Suddenly he sharpened: "Do you smell smoke?"

The unmistakable odour of combustion was seeping into the supply room. Blythe stood and Ian came up with her.

"Let's get out of here," she suggested.

Blythe peeked out the door then nodded back at Ian. The corridor was deserted. So was the fire stairwell. They made it all the way down and out onto the grounds of St. John's. Fire was evident in other parts of the sprawling complex that included the gargantuan Royal Ottawa Medical Centre. Thankfully there was a paucity of people, crazed and violent or otherwise.

"Maybe we could... my place is just a few blocks over there," Blythe motioned with a finger. "I know a way where we won't be seen. Looks pretty calm now but maybe we're in the eye of the hurricane."

"I hope the storm has passed us over entirely," added Ian. "Lousy world to wake up into."

Blythe put her arm around Ian and he felt a small twinge of doubt about his last statement. She was very attractive to him and her interest gifted him an incredible sense of possibility long absent.

Overhead, in the twilight sky, an incredibly large, dull shape blocked out a broad swath of starlight.

Chapter Six

The alien looked at the room key, a non-electronic key cut roughly from some steel alloy. The number system was easily understood, and the room it represented easily found.

Anonymity was achieved through enough high-quality synthetic cash and the technological wherewithal to appear as any humanoid shape it might require. The human who had supplied the key had appeared more concerned with the ubiquitous looters and lunatics loose than any suspicious cash-paying customer.

The motel unit was small and not recently painted, yet it did contain some amenities: an antiquated video receiver plus a single voice-only communication line. A nod to luxury, a printed newspaper, lay neatly folded on the desk. The alien recognized the date as the previous day. The headline was speculative and surely designed to induce panic and an impulse towards evacuation in the local humans:

ALIEN SHIP BEAMS MADNESS INTO CITY!

The smaller print directly below made a generous estimate as to the casualties, a five digit number.

The alien's suitcase lay on the bed, slowly metamorphosing, as was the alien who sat upon the only chair in the room. Soon the room contained only Sister Raymond and, on the bed, a large knitted shopping bag.

The motel clerk noted the middle-aged nun emerging from somewhere inside the motel perimeter and pausing at the curbside to hail a taxi. He wondered how such a frail-looking lady could handle so bulky a shopping bag. It seemed she was primed for tragedy. Carrying a full bag into the madness of the city! That was faith.

* *

Zarathustra Bruns was legally insane but, with the onslaught of madness in the city, he seemed to finally be in his element. The past few days had brought him periods of amazing lucidity mingled with his usual delusory episodes.

The only thing was that Zarathustra couldn't tell which was which. After all, he was mad.

As he slowly walked through the war-zone that had earlier been a major thoroughfare and fired his small button-stun at anyone who came too close to him, he tried to ignore the huge shape in the sky above. Delusions were easily ignored by the experienced and socially-minded madman.

It was a time to keep firmly anchored in reality; after all, he was on a mission to destroy the alien who was using Zarathustra's brain to store all manner of incomprehensible alien plans and information. If the alien could not be destroyed very soon, Zarathustra's head would be full and he would no longer have the will to free himself.

His madness had not helped matters either. When he should have been concentrating on destroying the mind-cluttering alien, he had instead foolishly been looking for some illusory character he had seen in a dream, a hospital patient who slept but yet contained an unimaginable horror.

It had seemed real, as the most persistent delusions always did, but now he realized his folly. Sleeping men do no harm. Harm comes from aliens having such insufficient data storage capacity as to necessitate the taking over the minds of living, intelligent beings for their own purposes.

Zarathustra's path angled out into the street and away from the teenagers crouched on the far side of a smashed and abandoned car that rested halfway up onto the sidewalk, his button-stun ready to emit a stream of noxious pellets at the earliest sign of malevolence. It was time to free himself from the alien and dispense with the delusion of Ian Hesse, hospital patient and apocalypse incarnate.

* *

Blythe was getting drunk. It was the best kind of drunk: naked drunk. Ian still lay on the bed where they had recently consummated their acquaintance. Previously, Ian had been more cautious in entering physical relationships; the threat of SIDAC and Herpes IX was ever-present. Yet under the current conditions, he had simply acquiesced to Blythe's desires.

Considering the tenuousness of existence in this violent new world, along with the fact that he was homeless, broke, and likely, by virtue of being a further two years beyond the peak petrochemical energy era, nearly unemployable, Ian realized he needed a friend and ally.

"More whisky?" offered Blythe. Ian retrieved his glass from the nightstand.

"Sure." He smiled at the naked Blythe who poured the whisky from a two litre bottle without looking at either container. She smiled at Ian, swaying a little to the music she had just programmed. Some rocking, but obscure Canadian band. Ian recognized it, so it couldn't have been that recent.

"Here's yer visky. I von't be stingy." she Greta Garboed.

Ian didn't get it, but didn't notice he didn't get it.

"You're really beautiful, you know?" Ian exaggerated only slightly. Blythe was indeed attractive. Not far north of thirty, the classic petite blonde-haired blue-eyed foxy lady. Maybe not model material, the lips a trifle too thin, some skin blemishes on her face, but certainly a major prize in any bar.

"Actions speak louder than words," said Blythe as she re-entered the bed and pressed her body against him.

"What the hell?" exclaimed Ian, bolting upright. A loud clanging was escalating just outside the window on the far

27

side of the room. They were on the second floor.

"Someone's on the fire escape!" explained Blythe. She reached behind a row of books at the head of the bed and produced a small handgun. The gun barrel wavered as she fiddled with the safety, her hand shaking.

"Here. I had a 965 before" admitted Ian.

She passed the gun to Ian who rose from the bed to slowly approach the window. The clamour continued. Between the half-drawn drapes Ian could see an old man on the fire escape looking in. He had a metal bar and was banging it against the metal railing.

Ian stood naked a few feet from the window, the gun gripped in both hands and pointed at the floor. He felt cold and despite the gun, defenceless. He had been armed two years ago, when he was attacked and he had not escaped unscathed.

The man outside had his back to Ian. He turned towards the window with his weapon held at eye level. Ian realized that he would shoot the man if he smashed the window. The man's gaze passed over the naked Ian without seeming to recognize his existence, then he slowly turned and continued climbing the fire escape stairs. His next victim would be someone from an upper floor.

Ian sagged and returned to the edge of the bed. Blythe slid to his side and peered around his shoulder.

"What was that?"

Ian exhaled noisily.

"A man. He's gone now I think."

Blythe could tell Ian was upset so she hugged him voluptuously, wrapping her upper legs and body around his back.

"It's okay for now." She stroked his hair. Ian shook his head, warding off her tenderness as if it were a bad luck charm.

"This is crazy. We've got to get out of here."

Blythe shook her head. "We've got nowhere to go. I know it's not safe here, but it's also not safe to leave. We should just wait this out."

Ian considered. A life could have a far less pleasant coda.

"More visky," prescribed Blythe.

* *

Zarathustra positioned himself directly beneath the huge saucer, or at least as directly beneath as he could approximate. Dawn was breaking. Soon the alien would return to his saucer and Zarathustra would confront him. The alien would not be able to defend himself from Zarathustra's attack. The information the alien had placed in Zarathustra's brain was irreplaceable and invaluable, so the alien could not destroy him or allow him to come to harm.

* *

The alien Sister Raymond entered the lobby of St. John's Rehabilitation Institute. The security guards had abandoned their posts. It was not unexpected. One wing of the massive health care complex was engulfed in flames and several others were severely vandalized. As the nun strode down a corridor, dazed patients lingering in front of their rooms looked imploringly to her.

"Nurse! My pills!" one emaciated male geriatric begged her.

Other voices: "I need my medicine too, please! Where're the rest of the staff? What's going on?"

Sister Raymond disintegrated the first old man with a weapon never seen before by human eyes. The other nearby patients rapidly retreated into their rooms.

Only the very elderly or immobile patients were left in the facility. The rest, along with the staff, were probably in hasty flight or hiding.

Sister Raymond came upon a nursing station and found what she sought: a video display terminal networked to the hospital information system. Struggling with the unfamiliar patient management system, she eventually found what she required. Ian Hesse was assigned to Room 551. A floorplan trapped under a clear plastic sheet that clothed a binder lay on the work surface. It indicated that Room 551 was in the wing that was currently on fire.

Not good. Sister Raymond uttered an alien curse. If the human she sought was indeed in that wing then quite possibly he would be dead, a burnt lump of flesh. Last night when she had checked the life-form EMF-signature monitor that was tuned to Hesse, and it had registered in the general direction of this location. Was it possible the target human had expired so soon after she had arrived?

She withdrew the monitor from her shopping bag and checked it again. The alien symbols danced briefly on the read-out window. Hesse was alive, and within walking distance. The direction was the same as St. John's was from the motel. It was possible he hadn't been at St. John's the previous night either. It was not material. All that mattered now was finding the Hesse before the 'accident' did.

* *

The human Sister Raymond sat barricaded in her office. When she had awoken, at dawn, her computer was down and the voice-line was dead. The smell of smoke permeated the room. When she went to listen at the door of her office, she noticed that it was warm to the touch. No matter, she had no plan to vacate the womb of her office. She felt reasonably safe here.

The view out her window was not encouraging. She could tell the west wing had been ravaged by fire, and no emergency services had been in attendance. The street still displayed no normal traffic, and she could see no evidence civil order had been restored. Worse yet, a large saucer-shaped spacecraft hung menacingly over the city.

What sort of propulsion system could possibly allow it maintain that state, motionless and completely quiet? The human race was in big trouble. Sure, they had their own spaceships, but what was in evidence outside Sister Raymond's window made the works of humankind appear the pasted colour paper collage of a preschooler.

The last news Sister Raymond had was that Ottawa had been declared a national disaster and sealed off. The media no longer spoke of CAIPP's attempts to destroy the alien spacecraft, and had been instead discussing methods of resistance for when the inevitable landing and occupation began. Key industrial areas on the Earth had been destroyed and there was speculation that an ultimatum had been received by the UN Security Council or the Secretary General.

* *

The madness in the city seemed to be an isolated phenomenon and the craft overhead had not been reported in the press by the time communication lines failed sometime in the night.

Sister Raymond felt her skin prickle and hair stand on end. Across the parking lot and toward the main entrance of St. John's, she could see herself carrying a bulging shopping bag and walking purposefully towards the inner city.

Chapter Seven

The alien Sister Raymond stood outside Blythe's apartment door. The building was very quiet and the corridor dark. For a moment, the nun thought the building completely deserted, then a cautious tread could be heard from an upper level. The occupants were subdued, but present.

Blythe's apartment was definitely not empty; Ian Hesse's EMF signature emanated from within. It seemed another of the humans was with him. For a moment the alien stood undecided. If Hesse was in no danger then it would be best not to reveal her presence. If, however, Hesse was in danger...

* *

Ian and Blythe had abandoned the convulsed sheets of Blythe's bed for the eating area. Ian, clad in a pair of almost uncomfortably undersized jogging pants (thank God for the new baggy women's fashions) was understandably famished. Blythe, faced with the problem of feeding someone who hadn't eaten solid food for two years and working with a kitchen bereft of electricity, stood to the challenge. She was making the world's most diverse Dagwood sandwiches.

Everything in her refrigerator was destined to spoil within hours so she portioned all foodstuffs vaguely resembling sandwich materiel onto the reserves from her luckily well-stocked bread cache. After Ian's second sandwich, she had joined him for one. Her stomach thanked her and she found it refreshingly easy to stand without leaning against the edge of the kitchen counter top. The third sandwich was enough to sate Ian's hunger.

"I think that'll do it. Thanks a lot." Ian cleared his palate with a swig from the half-emptied whisky bottle. "Nice to save some of this stuff. Who knows how long before we dare venture out to get more?"

Blythe nodded, despite not being sure whether he meant the food or the alcohol. She was a little hung-over yet somehow not feeling the usual regret of meeting her lover the morning after.

Surprisingly, he was still quite appealing. Perhaps it was his two-year lapse from the world that had conferred upon him some mark of innocence. He seemed a very gentle person and his dark eyes gave a quality of mystery to his appearance that compounded his existing Rip Van Winkle mystique.

"You live here long?"

Blythe shrugged. "Couple years. Used to cohab on Carlingwood. He was a jerk. Used to drink and then go all macho. After a few shots, the tobacco would come out. He's in AA now."

"Really? I tried tobacco once in college but it just made me sick. Must be the silliest contraband of all."

"Smoke weed?" Blythe already had a tea canister out and was extracting some cannabis paraphernalia.

"Couple times. Sure, go ahead."

Ian's compliance was beginning to surprise even himself. He rationalized that under the present conditions even if Blythe had wanted him to inject heroin he would've been hard pressed to raise any substantial objections beyond: is that needle really clean, are you sure you're completely healthy, and you do know how to use that needle, you are a nurse, right?

Blythe expertly rolled a small joint and immediately lit it with a candle lighter.

"Here."

Ian took the burning offering and sucked tentatively on the end. As he coughed out the first lungful, he noted

Blythe was only then slowly exhaling her first toke. A true expert.

"Some people see dope-smoking as a mystical thing, but I just think it makes life more interesting, like booze."

"Hmm." Ian again took the offering and this time managed to refrain from coughing for the few seconds his lungs held the intoxicating fumes.

"At this point, however, life may already be too interesting," noted Ian, and then immediately felt sorry for saying something which Blythe might have construed as a slur on her lifestyle. But Blythe only smiled and again extended the smoking bit of paper and leaf.

"'May you live in interesting times', right? The old Chinese curse."

"Right. 'When people lack a proper sense of awe, then some awful visitation will descend upon them.' From the book of the Taoists. Ancient Chinese religion," contributed Ian.

Blythe nodded sagely and placed the tiny hot remnant into a small glass bottle. Ian did not look comfortable, in fact he looked rather grey.

"Excuse me, my dear." Ian headed for the bathroom.

No doubt food, drink and cannabis together were a little much for his body to entertain after so long an absence. Blythe cursed her insensitivity.

* *

Zarathustra had absorbed more data. As he stood beneath the great disc, he suddenly could recall a set of experiences that were not his own. A set of strange, alien experiences.

'He' had been in a dark ancient chamber where he knew powerful and arcane rituals were frequently committed. This time, he was the one, a great sorcerer, who could call forth the power that dwelt here and simultaneously also somewhere vastly distant. There had been an agreement. He was to travel to a distant planet and protect an alien creature from harm. If he accomplished this task, he would be rewarded with great knowledge. If he failed, he would be destroyed. Eagerly, he accepted the challenge and all the details were given: the planet, the creature, and those dangers which would threaten the mission.

He had returned from the chamber and set to work preparing. Certain tools and weapons would be required. Some of it needed to be designed fresh and some could be modified from existing technology.

So much had to be learned. He had to move among the residents of that alien planet. There was the language to learn, the customs. A methodology of gathering data on specific locales and intelligent beings pertinent to the mission once he was in place also had to be carefully crafted. He was a great warrior and also a genius of technological application, but now he had to become a master of subterfuge, an undetected alien in an isolated and backward culture.

Plans for alien devices and a recollection of an accelerated learning regime tumbled through Zarathustra's mind. All normal human conventions and culture he saw through the eyes of an incredulous alien who had experienced these things only for the first time. Zarathustra did not experience any hostility emanating from the alien towards the people of the Earth, only a vague pity and mild academic interest. This seemed a strange attitude for an invader or conqueror.

Zarathustra entertained various interpretations of events in light of his new information. Was the one who was to be protected also an alien, perhaps the forward scout of the invasion force? And perhaps the one sent to protect him was actually a relatively benevolent being who did not realize the ends to which his actions would lead? If this was the case, then the focus of Zarathustra's mission should change: rather than eliminating the protector, he must eliminate the spy being protected.

Was it possible that, by eliminating the spy, the whole course of this alien attack could be waylaid? Could he indeed save the entire planet by destroying this alien mole? This seemed a very attractive idea to Zarathustra; megalomania was one of his best traits, he reflected.

His wait under the great disc would continue. Zarathustra awaited the return of the protector, or more information.

* *

The alien Sister Raymond's contemplation and indecisive loitering was interrupted by a shrieking that came from somewhere down the hall. A screaming woman suddenly appeared from the entrance of one of the living units. She was being pursued by a knife-wielding man. Blood already coursed down her chest from a neck wound.

* *

Blythe heard the screams from the hallway, then running feet. A sharp and unusual hum sounded from the hallway followed by a loud thump. Then only silence.

Curious, she moved to her front door and peered through the peep-hole. Unbelievably, there was Sister Raymond standing in the hallway, appearing somewhat stern but unafraid. Blythe opened the door.

"Sister Raymond! What are you doing? Come inside!" Blythe motioned her to enter with urgent gestures. Only then did Blythe notice the blood-stained woman sprawled on the floor.

Despite her injured and dishevelled appearance, Blythe recognized the woman as part of the friendly couple from two doors down that she often greeted in passing.

"Ramisa, come on!" Blythe helped the bleeding woman up and through the doorway. Sister Raymond had quickly thrust something back into her shopping bag and followed the other two back into the apartment. She secured the door once it was clear.

Blythe already had her first aid kit out and was examining Ramisa's wound. A superficial neck wound. Not destined to be a major blood spill. She applied sterile gauze and squeezed Ramisa's hand to keep her focused and reduce the risk of shock.

"My husband, Niranjan, gone, vaporized..." Obviously the woman was delirious. "Sister Raymond, what are you doing around here, and what's all that?" Blythe nodded at the nun's full shopping bag. "I can bet you weren't shopping."

The alien recognized Blythe as one of the nurses that worked under Sister Raymond. Thorough pre-insertion research pays off, it reflected.

"Well dear, I had to leave St. John's because of all the ... confusion. I thought I would take a few medical supplies and try to help out on the way over here. You're the only person I know that lives anywhere near the hospital and I thought, you know, this might be a safe haven until things calm down. I hope you don't mind."

Blythe thought of the half-naked man in her bathroom, the empty liquor bottles and the cannabis smoke that still hung in the air. She herself wore only panties. Why did the nun not recognize any of these behavioural anomalies?

"No no. I wouldn't dream of kicking you out into that ... whatever it is that's out there."

Blythe waited an awkward moment for the nun to take some appropriate action. The nun's eyes roamed freely over the apartment and Blythe's almost naked body without a glimmer of disapproval.

"You have some medical supplies, you say?"

"Yes. This should do the trick." Before Blythe could react, the nun had injected Ramisa with a needle-less hypodermic then turned abruptly away and stored her shopping bag in the coat closet adjacent to the apartment's front door.

Ian came out of the bathroom, looking improved but quite red-eyed. His mouth opened and his eyebrows began to climb as he saw the injured woman and the nun.

"It's alright, Ian. This is Sister Raymond from St. John's Rehab Institute, and this is my neighbour, Ramisa. She lives next door with her husband."

"What happened to her?" Ian peered over the now unconscious woman.

"I think her husband attacked her."

"Is she dead?" asked Ian.

"No. Sister Raymond just gave her a shot. Her wound isn't that bad. In fact, I don't know why she would be delirious from such a superficial wound."

"She was delirious?"

"She said her husband was vaporized." Blythe turned to the nun. "What happened out there, Sister Raymond?"

"Well. Her husband chased her into the hall. She fell down in front of me, and her husband ran off.

"Just ran off?"

"I think he saw the hypo I was holding and became frightened."

"Yeah, some people take a real fright to needles, don't they?" joked Ian.

The nun, visibly relieved, smiled in indulgence of human foible.

"If you will excuse us, Sister, Ian and I have to go have sex. You make yourself comfortable out here. Oh, and let us know if you need anything."

"Thank you, dear." The nun sat down on the couch, oblivious to the wounded woman slumped unconscious on the floor.

Blythe grabbed the half-empty bottle and her tin tea canister from the kitchen table. Ian, his cheeks doing a fine impression of a fire truck, allowed himself to be led into her bedroom.

Chapter Eight

Contrary to what Blythe had told Sister Raymond, she and Ian had not retreated to the clothing-strewn boudoir for libidinous purposes. Despite this, Ian and Blythe were under the sheets in Blythe's antiquated waterbed, now profoundly cold due to an extended lack of the electricity required to warm its liquid innards. They were both, however, fully dressed and secreted there only for the sake of appearances.

Ian, a good engineer and appraiser of heat sources, held Blythe against him and maintained the upper coverings in a repose optimally conducive to convective heat loss avoidance.

"Let's not rush this," Blythe whispered into Ian's ear. "I think if she suspects anything, she'll just kill us outright. Set your phasers on 'pudding'."

"How can you be sure she's a Centauran?" asked Ian.

"It's not that she doesn't look like Sister Raymond. She must be a shape changer, or maybe a robot!"

"Just because she acts a little strange? Maybe the poor woman has been through some kind of trauma worse than we imagine. She got here somehow, but maybe not without suffering some violence," mused Ian.

Blythe unconsciously shook her head slightly on the pillow and Ian felt the vibration. "Her clothes, though. Not a rip or tear. If she'd been through anything, she'd look like she had."

"Yeah. Good point," conceded Ian.

"Also, the shot she gave Ramisa. That wasn't a St. John's hypodermic. That was a Star Trek: The Twenty-Fifth Century hypodermic." Blythe moved her legs a bit to dispel the chill. "She's a tough old nun. I think that even if she chose to forego the lecture when she arrived, she would have at least made some kind of remark. It's like she didn't recognize that we weren't... you know."

"Pillars of virtue?"

"Hmm! It's pretty clear. She's a Centauran."

"It just doesn't explain why. Why is she here, with us?"

"Maybe we're flavour of the month and she's entrée procurement chef."

"Yow. She doesn't seem to be hostile, yet."

"You're an engineer, right? Maybe there's something that you were working on, something before you were comatose, that the aliens are after, and they don't want to damage the goods?"

"I didn't work for UNASA. I doubt they're after my n-d array loading utilities."

"Your what?"

"My stone axe."

"Not very useful stuff?"

"Not any more useful than the proprietary techniques of literally hundreds of digital fabrication companies. I graduated as a petroleum industry engineer and have been trying to catch up ever since."

"Sorry. I can't think of what she would be after, though, you know, if not something like that."

"Huh. Maybe we're too close to the problem."

"I'd agree to that."

"I mean maybe we weren't chosen because we're unique, but instead because we're, or they believe we are, non-unique or representative, like a point sample of the population."

"Why?"

"Perhaps by posing as someone who is trusted and familiar they can observe how we react to this crisis they've created. They want to observe our strengths and our weaknesses, our psychological capabilities."

"Yes. It's possible. Although she must not be in much of a rush to get her info if she's content to sit out there and let us hide in here."

"As you say, maybe she doesn't know our norms. Maybe she believes it's common for us humans to leave a guest waiting in the living room while we copulate."

"Yeah, maybe they were monitoring our TV from the late nineteen-sixties, the 'free love' years." Blythe caressed Ian's inner leg to emphasize her joke.

"Actually, contrary to popular myth," whispered Ian, "sex and violence in the media weren't rationalized until the zeroes. Nineteen-sixties TV was extremely staid."

"That makes sense, maybe more sense than us lying here, the unwitting experimental human guinea-pigs of bug-eyed creatures from Beta Centauri, discussing the evolution of human self-depiction in the media."

"Too many maybes." Ian held her closer, pleased with their easy rapport but still unbalanced by the unreality of current events.

* *

The alien nun in the living room was worried. Ian and the woman had gone into the sleeping room purportedly to engage in a sexual act, but by looking at the medical scanner pulled from the large shopping bag which was part of its costume, it could tell that their heartbeat frequencies had remained constant. This did not indicate sexual activity.

That they suspected the true nature of their visitor was a possibility, but luckily an irrelevant one. As long as Ian Hesse was kept physically intact, the mission objective could be completed. The many biological parameters the alien could measure from the living room all indicated that the two humans were resting comfortably.

* *

After an indefinite period in the bed, Ian grew restless

and extracted himself in favour of the view out the window. The sun was low on the horizon, a sorrowful god's eye closing on a post-apocalyptic city. The streets seemed empty of even the wandering mad who had seemed so common that afternoon.

Ian gave some thought to Blythe's earlier recommendation of an unhurried, carefully contrived escape.

Blythe pulled the thick quilt from the bed and, so wrapped, joined Ian at the window.

"Any sign of the cavalry?" she asked.

"Couple of road apples," he joked.

Blythe poked Ian with her elbow, then offered him a spot inside her wrap.

"Not really," amended Ian.

After a few moments silence, standing confronted with the desolate scene outside, their levity broke.

"Sunset." Blythe's voice indicated a feeling not of modern aesthetic appreciation, but rather the more primitive dread and apprehension associated with the phenomenon of Sol's daily disappearance.

* *

The Sun was about to slip over the horizon and the dusk threatened to smother sight in the public square where Zarathustra waited. Without any artificial lighting, the building facades surrounding the grassy green space faded to black-faced silhouettes. The belly of the alien spacecraft overhead shifted colours prettily.

Standing quite precisely near the juncture of the wide, paved pedways crisscrossing the square, Zarathustra grimly finished a meal of stale bread from a paper bag and tossed the looted remnants in a large green bin marked 'Make Trees, Not Eyesores'.

The affected, as he liked to think of them, were not

around. The square was quiet and afforded reflection. Somewhere in Zarathustra's mind was the identity of the traitor who would betray, or had betrayed, all humanity. The quantity of alien information was almost overwhelming and selecting one element from the garbled mass would prove a task requiring a degree of concentration Zarathustra had not summoned in some time.

He grimly remembered his grade school teacher explaining random versus ordered access and how he had not understood the video segment until several years later when, after he had experienced the gamut of state-operated parenting institutions, he began to live on his own and had to access the public databases himself. Random access the inherited alien hard drive in his brain was not.

Zarathustra accessed a few additional gigabytes.

He saw a progression of hospital staff. Nurses, doctors, nuns, and priests. Some kind of religious hospital. These people all shared an awareness of a certain patient, the target of this investigation.

Individual humans were cataloged, personalities demarcated for public and private characteristics. Physical data recorded in minute detail. Complete medical bios and physiological modelling information: a twisting scar on the abdomen of this one; a pattern of freckles non-symmetric and complex on another. Here was detailed analyses of individuals' voices, with special attention given to the correlation between emotional state and fundamental frequency.

More general material followed. Motion studies of humans walking, some generalities concerning biological processes: elimination and procreation. The garments of the people under study were also documented. Each individual contributed to the diverse apparel catalogue, some contributing over a dozen articles, and others, dressing literally in a more uniform manner, a substantially reduced number.

An array of animals paraded through Zarathustra's brain, from small shiny black beetles to birds and onto dogs. He remembered a stray pup he had once adopted in his childhood and was momentarily cheered.

Angered with himself, the lone occupant of the public square shook his head in visible disagreement. His head cleared and the zoo was gone.

Zarathustra re-examined his mental repository. It was in an almost dream-like manner that he now remembered the data access from moments ago. The hospital, the animals, the animals which hadn't posed danger, just the wild dogs, the not wild dogs...?

Behind the alien catalogue of information, Zarathustra now felt there were two sources. One which he had previously perceived, a neutral almost sympathetic consciousness, and now a new entity, one which cast the naked gaze of the treacherous enemy, appraising strength and taking an inventory of dangers posed. Zarathustra understood this was the second entity in the strange and great chamber, the distant entity which offered the arrangement to the first entity.

Zarathustra now felt that, discounting the glowing saucer bottom overhead, and even the chaos in the streets, his new intuition was evidence there would be no klaatu barado nikto. Gort was here, and he was mad as hell. The nurses in St. John's had said there were no monsters, but they had been far too early in their assessment.

The retrieval of the hospital data echoed strangely within Zarathustra. It was as if he were seeing it from two perspectives at once. In a few moments, he suddenly understood the cause for this. The hospital under alien scrutiny was St. John's, a place he knew very well himself,

45

having spent some time there receiving advanced treatments for his aberrant psychology.

A release from an enforced care facility in Smiths Falls had been conditional on his completion of certain experimental treatments. These involved biopsy and then direct chemical manipulation of those brain transmitter substances whose disproportionate composition had plagued Zarathustra with delusions and a propensity for fixed ideas since an early age. The results were mixed.

Many of his older ideas and obsessions seemed to abate, but a new set of unwelcome mental phenomena had replaced them. There was the obsession with Ian Hesse, a patient in a nearby ward whom Zarathustra had heard the nurses discuss in sympathetic tones, which was quickly followed by an explosion of strange ideas and perceptions that he soon came to understand as being extraterrestrial in origin.

With new motivation inspired by his freedom, Zarathustra had later been able to shake the first delusion, after some initial unease and that one strange interlude when he had actually phoned the St. John's ward where Ian was kept and, as best he could remember, delivered some type of warning to the staff there.

The other delusions he could not shake, but he refrained from talking about them, understanding clearly that such indiscretion would quickly reverse his new and preferred status as a free citizen. His new delusion was pernicious in that it was self-renewing. Just as he thought he could discount the veracity of what he had found in his mind, a new batch of data would arrive.

By only a few days after his release from the hospital, the alien ideas had come to occupy the greater part of his mind, and he feared losing his volition of thought, the possibility of thinking about the other more mundane but

46

nonetheless pressing matters of his only periodically monitored existence. Since the arrival of the Centaurans, those pressing matters were modified beyond recognition, and Zarathustra found himself again contemplating important thoughts regarding himself, unseen forces, and the fate of humanity.

Now it seemed the cache of alien information had reached a critical mass. It all fit. Everything was connected. His thoughts on the comatose Hesse were not just a residual symptom of his fading mental dysfunction. No, they had actually been the first of the alien transmissions.

It had become abundantly clear that the spy was Ian Hesse and it was Zarathustra's duty to snuff that one candle lighting the path to humanity's extinction.

Chapter Nine

The alien nun was at the window, still preoccupied, looking out into the fading light of day. Its belief in bad luck was being slowly de-occulted by a shining dark reality: a sole figure loitered in the public square at the end of the pedway that its position overlooked, and the scanner in its human-appearing hand indicated that the lone human was none other than the 'accident'.

The alien nun's visual acuity was far beyond the level of these bipeds and thus observing the 'accident', well over a hundred meters distant, was not difficult. At least not in the sense of alien physiology, the physics of optics, and the nature of visible electromagnetic energy as received by this particular planet.

More difficult was imagining the circumstances, or worse yet, the reasons, that could bring the 'accident' this close to Hesse, and further, in trying to face the unknown consequences of confrontation with this unknown element with any degree of equanimity.

Destruction of the 'accident' was a choice with an uncertain outcome. What was he doing anyway? The alien nun would have thought that the human was dead, unconscious or sleeping (so still was he) if not for the fact that he was standing. Possibilities. The alien searched its mind. Catatonic schizophrenia, sleep-walking, hypnosis, or just waiting? Insufficient background information was available to determine which of these explanations was most likely. In any case, further actions were entirely unpredictable.

The saucer bottom glimmered pleasantly with the dying rays of the Sun. Momentarily re-directing its scanner to the enormous, threatening, and also still body, the 'nun' grimaced strangely. Alien physiognomy misspeaks its truth, it had smiled. The saucer was apparently an energy field within a hologram. Not a real spacecraft or independent body of any sort, instead only an intimidating prop, pawn of some propaganda war in which the alien nun took no part and knew neither the strategy nor objective.

As its gaze returned to the rapidly darkening square, a series of worried glottal stops issued from the 'nun', who had reverted to its own language in a moment of extreme surprise. In less time than seemed likely, the 'accident' had abandoned his fixed stance and cleared the square. He was out of sight. He was also apparently out of scanner range. Not possible.

The alien nun checked the scanner for malfunction by checking the EMF signatures of Hesse and his companion in the next room. Both appeared nominal, just slightly more active than previously. The signature of the 'accident' was entirely absent. Either that human was now out of range, that is, tens of kilometres distant, or his brain function had entirely ceased. But if the 'accident' was dead, where was the carcass?

* *

Sister Raymond was again tending the sick. She had pushed the odd experience of seeing her double out of her mind. There was much madness about, but what still remained of St. John's was again serving the public. No part of the complex had survived unsullied by the recent cataclysmic events.

One wing was totally gutted by fire. The other four wings were all damaged and in disorder. Patients still mobile the previous evening had fled, and their fleeing, as well as the onslaught of those they had been fleeing from, had left the hallways and public areas of the medical center smashed and rubble-filled.

Slowly, floor by floor and corridor by corridor, Sister

Raymond and those few medical personnel still on hand attended to damaged stragglers, removed the dead, cleared equipment from traffic areas, and made a general attempt at restoring order and determining an agenda for the resuscitation of their medical services.

Following the suggestion of Dr. Joberkt, who had slept miraculously undisturbed in the doctor's 4B lounge through the worst of the conflagration, Sister Raymond was in the main pharmaceutical supply room looking for morphine and OxyContin. Someone had already been in the pharmastore and rummaged thoroughly and untidily for the street-favoured narcotics. Not a dose of morphine, Valium, or Zoomex was evident.

Dr. Joberkt shouted "Sister Raymond! Have a look outside! Help has arrived. I'm going to meet them" into the pharmastore as he passed the doorway, apparently on his way to the fire exit at the end of the wing.

It was true. A convoy of army trucks was snaking its way towards the main entrance of St. John's. A squad of helicopters escorted the convoy. Sister Raymond momentarily paused her work and moved closer to the window.

What would this bring? The alien spacecraft overhead, and now the army in the city. Was a swift and brutal confrontation of forces due at any moment? Their rescue and salvation might transform into a second and more savage deadly barrage of malevolent powers.

The lead helicopter was already landing on the swell of green space fronting St. John's main entrance, and Dr. Joberkt was approaching it. Two figures swiftly disembarked.

Dr. Joberkt stopped in his tracks, and took a couple of uncertain backward steps. One of the two rescuers was a white-haired, Caucasian man, stout of build and costumed in the best style of the UN's upper ranks. The other was a monstrosity: it wore an approximation of the other's UN uniform, but it had four arms, bright red skin and an elongated head. This, Sister Raymond thought, must be a Centauran.

*   *

Zarathustra awoke swimming. He gasped wildly, flailing his arms. The darkness was complete and only a faint echo could be heard. Something touched his head and he ducked convulsively. He regained control of his breathing in wonder: he was completely dry, his arms flew freely through the air, and his feet touched abyss. He had a momentary sensation of falling and straightened his arms above his head. His fingers reassuringly banged a solid surface and gently pushed it away. Nothing else was in reach.

Zarathustra tried to reconstruct his current thought. He noted his body was uninjured. Everything seemed entirely real and not at all dream-like; there was none of the panic or fear that had characterized all his previous hallucinations.

It was clear suddenly: he was in space, kidnapped by his tormentors. This was weightlessness and, yes, his feet touched and pushed away another solid surface.

How cruel were these creatures to leave him in a black chamber such as this, a premature burial for the abducted! Not that he expected mercy from these devils. Perhaps he would not be recognized as anything beyond an animal-like form of life.

Zarathustra wasn't long in waiting, thinking, and floating. Soon, the chamber revealed itself in light.

A room big enough for twenty coffins, he mused. The bottom, or that plane beneath his feet, had dropped out. Now his left ankle was snagged and he was pulled through the air into an adjacent space. Claustrophobia gripped his throat and lungs. This was indeed a coffin! His arms no longer had room to play, and the portal through which he had come snapped shut.

The walls of the new space were covered with a fine metal grid work. He reached out to touch the delicate pattern but, as his hand closely approached the shiny surface, it was delicately repelled. He began to twist and the other side of the chamber came into view: a glassy surface open to another dark chamber. The glass seemed nearly opaque.

The room beyond revealed its dimensions sketchily. The light source there seemed incredibly dim, and only silhouettes of some block-like shapes revealed themselves.

There was more. Larger bulbous forms seemed in motion. They were alive and purposeful, his malicious captors.

Zarathustra began to spasm as if electrocuted. His brain flooded with images. Smiths Falls, where he had lived as a child. Familiar faces, aunts, cousins, his mother, their friends, all the others he had met, first at the supervised school, then the youth housing project, the institutions, the hospitals, Toronto, Belleville, Ottawa, and finally the principals of his current life, living free in his new city: the neighbourhood people who hung out on the corner and tried banking on him for quarters; his irascible landlord; his upbeat social worker; his friend at the food bank; and finally the incredibly sharp vision of Ian Hesse.

Zarathustra possessed a comprehensive and incomprehensibly technical schematic of the human being Ian Hesse.

Zarathustra knew exactly where Ian's kidneys were, but could only make an educated guess on the location of his own based on that first knowledge. Data on the hospital staff followed, the animals, all the myriad pieces of the alien data cache that was threatening to overwhelm Zarathustra's consciousness. They are probing my brain, guessed Zarathustra.

* *

Outside the cylinder of one semi-opaque side, the aliens conferred in their own language.

"This planet has only one low-level outside contact, is that not correct?" Clerk One asked of its subordinate, the landing party overseer.

"We thought that light wave messaging with the Centaurans was their only contact beyond their world. I don't understand what we have found here. Perhaps this specimen is delusional?"

"It is not the place of landing staff to propose considerations, only to relay fact," snapped Clerk One. "Mission direction and planning lie solely with ship staff, as you are well aware."

"My apology, worthy one."

"Surely you have not been so long from a home planet to act in such a manner as this?"

"You are indeed correct, my worthy one. This is my first mission in the outer realm."

"If you wish to remain in your position I would remind you that out here we are not the same as the steaming rabble who inhabit the home planets. We respect order and status. One who mingles with inferior races, even as overseer, should never forget that it itself remains only a pawn in the great intergalactic crusade of ship staff." The previous a gentle reminder to the overseer. "Always let your elders speak without interruption and take care not to be an obstacle or distraction to one of the ship staff. Today you have distracted only a clerk; should you distract a supervisor, your return to a home planet would be certain."

And this more firmly.

"A cubic light year of gratitude, your worthiness," the overseer assumed a penitent posture. "From this examination we believe this specimen is worthless. Its recollection does not reflect the objective reality of this planet. We now seek your sign of continuance, exalted one."

"My sign is thus," began Clerk One. "Procure another specimen. Return this one. If your new specimen seems healthy and his recollection reflects objective reality, signal me your status. If not, repeat this process until you have a proper specimen. Once I am signalled, you will return to the target planet and resume your regular duties."

"Excellent, my worthiness."

Clerk One removed itself from the examination quarters to allow its underling to carry out its directive.

* *

Inside the cylinder where he was confined, Zarathustra's mind gradually came back under his control. His tormentor's probe had somehow improved the clarity of the alien information that was increasingly hijacking his consciousness. It seemed much had been added and updated.

Now that he was captured, would he become a piece of dedicated hardware, wired like add-on memory to some monstrous alien computer? Zarathustra felt his destiny was at hand. His confrontation had gone terribly wrong; he was completely in the control of his kidnappers, his body now as well as his brain.

He should have killed himself while he was still on Earth! That would have derailed the plans of these verminous creatures, or at least slowed them down as they sought another sucker.

Zarathustra's thoughts turned to Ian Hesse. More data

was available. Ian was with the nurse, Blythe, holed up in her apartment. They were being watched by another alien. Zarathustra wondered why.

If Ian was a traitor, why did he require supervision? Perhaps it was just a security arrangement, a body guard for the valuable alien asset. Was this Blythe another traitor? It was even possible the entire St. John's staff were some sort of advance party for the treacherous Centauran forces.

Inside the oppressive cylinder, Zarathustra's murderous intentions multiplied.

Chapter Ten

D r. Joberkt returned to St. John's escorted by the disembarked occupants of the UN helicopter: the general, the Centauran, and two lower rank UN soldiers who carried M-89s. This strange entourage entered St. John's by the fire exit where Dr. Joberkt had only a few minutes ago emerged to greet the UN force.

Sister Raymond stood perfectly still in the corridor as the group approached.

"Conference in the lounge. Come." Dr. Joberkt reverse nodded to indicate Sister Raymond was to fall in with his group.

Once inside the doctors' lounge, the members of the group made themselves comfortable on the leatherette sofas crammed into the small room. Dr. Joberkt busied himself at the sink.

"Coffee anyone?"

"Certainly and thank you," effused the UN general. The Centauran, sitting on a desk in one corner of the room near the window, eyed the general. Its facial expression meant nothing to the others in the room.

"Introductions are in order," continued the general. "I am General Pushkin. This is the esteemed emissary of the Centauran government, who may be addressed as 'worthy overseer'. My men here are RunningBear and Thurmeier, sergeants both." The general accepted his coffee. He was alone in his enjoyment of the freshly brewed beverage.

"Yes. As I said outside I am Dr. Nazmen Joberkt. This is Sister Raymond. We are the only staff presently in attendance at this facility."

General Pushkin nodded with raised eyebrows.

"You have your hands full so I'll make this as easy for you as possible. In the interests of simplicity, I hereby

56

assign you both as temporarily in charge of this facility."

"Thank you," said Dr. Joberkt dryly while Sister Raymond only nodded her acknowledgement.

"You may continue to perform your duties here, and I will remain long enough to explain the situation to you and to organize a garrison for this area. We hope to make the transition of power as easy as possible for everyone."

"Transition of power?" asked Sister Raymond.

The Centauran on the desk shifted its considerable weight in an agitated manner.

"I should tell you that the Centaurans are very status conscious and do not take well to conversation occurring between more than two entities at a time, more specifically, the two with the highest status in the room." Pushkin smiled as if explaining an aunt's dislike of children with dirty fingers. Sister Raymond crossed her arms in front of herself.

"But yes. A transition of power," continued Pushkin. "It seems the industrial countries of this planet will now be under joint UN/Centauran rule. The UN being the enforcement agency and the Centauran landing parties constituting the policy-making body. I know this is quite a shock for you both."

"Yes," agreed Dr. Joberkt evenly. "We are both quite surprised. This is a new role for the UN, is it not?"

Pushkin became stern. "Young doctor sir, this is a new role for Earth. We have had our choice presented to us: accept the role of a state governed by a foreign body for a limited period of time, or invite our immediate and complete destruction. I believe that we have chosen wisely, and that it would be in our best interests to attempt to allow this unfortunate turn of events proceed to a finish without undue tarrying or remonstration."

Dr. Joberkt looked uncomfortably around the room, but

refrained from interrupting the general.

"I am here speaking to you now only due to some very strange circumstances in this particular city. It seems you were in the midst of a disaster here irrespective of the Centauran, er, display of force. The usual means of mass communication have been inoperative since the beginning of the, uh, arrival of the Centaurans. In most of the cities on this continent, the UN forces were able to establish new patterns of order and a representative hierarchy for the people without significant bloodshed. Your city may well prove an exception. Unhappily.

Without being able to spread the news of the collaboration between the international bodies and the Centaurans, useless revolution and anarchy might well occur. I am here to prevent that. His worthy overseer will provide guidance in the new goals that will be set for the labour force of this city once order is established. Until then, I will command those forces available to me to restore constitutional government here, and prevent bloodshed. Those who assist the organs of order will be safeguarded, their human rights upheld."

"You refer to the UN Declaration of Human Rights, as amended last decade?" asked Dr. Joberkt.

"Actually, the New Agreement on Consolidation of Earth's Output, or NACEO, as signed by the heads of the UN and the Centauran representatives, uh, refers to some earlier legal documents such as the Geneva Convention Relative to the Treatment of Prisoners of War."

"We are considered prisoners of war, then?" Dr. Joberkt lowered his head to peer intensely at the General.

"For a period of five years after order has been established in the industrial areas. The NACEO will be in effect for that period only! After that, the Centaurans will leave, and Earth is left to its own devices, probably with a much improved technological base and a singular, consolidated political structure."

"To be succinct, General Pushkin, what is the punishment for not taking part in this grand scheme, for refusing work and escaping to the hills?"

"In all brevity, my young doctor sir, the punishment is death. Likely a bullet in the back of the head. But on a more pleasant subject, let me lay out the plans for the creation of the formal labour network and requisite political monitors that the Centaurans have put forward."

* *

Zarathustra felt his left ankle twist under him, as he collapsed onto his knees. He barked once in pain as he connected with the ground. Zarathustra then struggled back up as if it was important for him to be standing.

It was dusk. He was back on Earth again! Someone or perhaps two were standing far across the deepening gloom of the square outside the traitor's hold-out where Zarathustra had kept vigil.

Perhaps it was important to stand, remain attentive and somehow inconspicuous as he considered his strategy. Or even, thought Zarathustra, better to casually stroll in the direction of the strangers and see what dangers their presence might pose to the strategy under development.

The pair Zarathustra approached wore army fatigues, UN regulars apparently. They carried their M-89s loosely about the shoulder and appeared officious and self-possessed. Zarathustra noted they had fine nanofiber straps to support their rifles.

At the closest point of approach, the officer on the left unslung and brought his weapon diagonally across his chest as if he had just completed his training and wanted to remain well-practised in the dynamics of a really tight execution of such a manoeuvre.

But it was the one on the right spoke: "Identification, citizen."

Zarathustra peered into their faces as he vaguely patted his pockets. The well-practised one betrayed no enthusiasm; he stared at Zarathustra's mid-section and appeared not to breathe.

These are not humans, noted Zarathustra. They look like humans but they must be aliens, or robots. Their manner is totally inappropriate. How could the aliens obtain this dedicated a team so quickly, just days after the invasion?

"I... don't have much on me..." Zarathustra stalled, still patting more pockets, then some of the same pockets again as if he wouldn't want to have overlooked anything with a hasty initial once-through. "My prescription ..." Zarathustra offered, hand extending with a folded slip of white paper, the ends of which were curled and rumpled from a rough journey in his pants pocket.

"Photographic identification of all humans is required. You will come with us." The first officer snatched up the paper in an impatient, almost human-like gesture. It then blinked once in a distracted way and put the evidence in its shirt pocket without examining it.

There's no way this thing is human, thought Zarathustra, and now the interrogation is over and the incarceration is about to begin. Yes, progress reports would flow now.

Zarathustra resigned himself to the fact his custodians currently had the upper hand. The officer who had spoken pointed in the direction past his companion, while his companion seemed to point in the other direction, his rifle aimed back at the first fatigued figure.

Keystone Cops here we go, thought Zarathustra. Why are the people in charge always the ones most confused?

When the rifle discharged in the face of the first soldier, Zarathustra realized he had badly misinterpreted the intentions of the pointed rifle. The second officer was looking more human now; his face was contorted with rage as he bludgeoned the upper chest area and the pulpy mass that had been the first officer's head.

Zarathustra backed slowly away, not trusting his luck enough to turn his head from the grotesque sight of a rifle reverting to its baser use as a bludgeon. Without having completely analyzed the ramifications, he began to edge closer to his original target, the apartment building housing the only logical threat posed to humanity.

Invasions and armies and their attendant traitorous and debased he could understand, but this kind of random madness which had seemed to explode so forcefully of late throughout the streets of Ottawa was far removed from logic. Apparently the society which had so easily labelled him insane had a few glitches of its own to work out.

Zarathustra slipped into the small, walled garden in front of the target building, out of sight of the combatants in the square. They had ignored him as he had backed away. In a few minutes, the aggressor had finished his task and wandered off.

Zarathustra peeked over the dwarf wall fronting the apartment building and could see that the square was deserted save for one blue-helmeted soldier who lay unmoving at his station quite far down the block.

A rain of objects startled Zarathustra. Someone was throwing small items out of a high window. It was a rain of pets. Some hamsters, some goldfish, a cat, an oddly non-barking dog and then a limp bird plummeted into the courtyard. Zarathustra ran to shelter himself in the entrance alcove, a recessed brick space offering a sturdy overhead. He rubbed his head in confusion.

Were they after him or just killing pets? Killing pets? Maybe they were just discarding the bodies as a natural precaution. Perhaps the dead were the ones really doing all the random killing. Night of the Living Dead brought on by some alien bacteria introduced by the Centaurans. It was just too strange to figure.

Someone was shouting hysterically from above.

"Kill the killers! Destroy them all!"

Zarathustra hazarded a look skyward from his safe position. A much larger object accelerated towards the garden; a respectable-looking man in dark clothes landed with a sickening crunch.

This was beyond anything Zarathustra had seen in the past few days, an accelerated tumult of violent and twisted episodes. The fire alarm in the building began to wail, plain and mournful through the broken windows that punctuated the front of the building.

* *

In Blythe's apartment, the alien nun was hard at work. The holograph generator which controlled its physical appearance was suffering from strange transient noise impulses; the 'nun' manifestation was visually flickering at a rate slow enough to be visible to the human eye.

Several small metallic 'wands' had been carefully laid out on the thick arm of Blythe's couch and the seated alien nun attentively hunched over the coffee table, examining a small, shimmering metal box bristling with embellishments which obviously functioned as the complex user interface for the device.

The 'accident' had returned unexpectedly, seemingly instantaneously, and the 'nun' was tracking his approach on an automatic sensor tuned to his EMF signature; when the horizontal distance indicator set on the dining table emitted a beep indicating he had breached a roughly forty-three meter periphery (an even amount in the system of measurement used with that equipment) the 'nun'

62

abandoned the holograph generator on the coffee table and went to peer anxiously at some of the other instruments arranged on the dining table.

A quick glance revealed all background noise levels were up significantly. The existence of time-varying interference fields affecting the equipment was the obvious conclusion,but their source eluded the alien nun.

* *

Zarathustra thought to seek refuge in an abandoned apartment, something away from the dirty, naked ground and madness of the streets. He slipped into a stairwell. Then stopped. It was dark and comforting. His claustrophobic impulses had momentarily retreated, and he rested.

As his breathing settled, he noticed sounds of movement around him. It sounded like someone moving furniture with great energy and reckless aggression. The sound began to swell. Zarathustra moaned and began his ascent.

* *

The alien nun noted the proximity meter reading drop. There was agitated shouting in the hallway and someone was playing a saxophone loudly but atonally. Stereos were cranked. The 'nun' moved towards the hall door and further noticed that the loudest stereo was directly across the hall and blaring an incredible blast of static. Shouts came from the hallway and fire erupted on the coffee table. The smell of burning wire and plastic filled the living room and the alien nun suddenly realized her language protocol layer had failed her.

The shouts of the humans in the hall were incomprehensible. A warning indicator on its sleeve indicated that all external processing had ended. It was no longer in disguise!

The bedroom door banged open and Blythe screamed.

Ian called angrily to Christ and slammed the door again. Apparently they did not like the alien's natural appearance.

The alien nun understood that its charge was now escaping. The bedroom door was locked. It moved to the balcony to both escape the fire and try to maintain visual contact with its subject.

The two humans were already out of the building and had crossing the parking lot. Human-designed stairs were a challenge for the 'nun'. It would have no luck catching them by physical motion. It checked its instruments.

* *

Zarathustra had turned back and returned to the main level after being confronted by the increased sounds of destruction near Blythe's apartment. He pushed open the fire door at the stair landing.

People were in the street, so he headed for the small alley that cut across the backs of the adjacent house lots, where perhaps he might hide. He came upon a car surrounded by shattered safety glass, and suddenly saw Ian and Blythe running down the side street.

"You are free!?" shouted Zarathustra angrily after the retreating pair. The traitor was loose!

Ian jerked his head around but allowed his pace to slacken only momentarily. Zarathustra neglected to chase them, but instead carried out his original intent. He hid amid a group of recycling bins.

Their escape was clear confirmation to Zarathustra: Ian was collaborating with the Centaurans; Ian had dismissed his alien servant in the emergency and was fleeing to the arms of the traitors and those who had stolen Earth from humanity. For the moment Ian had the upper hand and Zarathustra had to bide his time, waiting for events to present an opportunity to serve his purpose in the great conflict that threatened all humanity.

Blythe and Ian cut through the parking lot of a Robo-Donut, the world-famous Canadian automated coffee and donut franchise.

"You don't see that every day," commented Blythe.

"The saucer?" asked Ian.

"No, I mean the Robo-Donut drive-thru is empty."

Ian was preparing to chuckle when a sudden, terrible panic overcame him. Everything glowed, and a prickly heat overcame his body. His clothes were drenched in sweat. Ian tried to look toward Blythe but she and her background dissolved into a shimmer of particles. Ian's body felt completely rigid.

Everything was gone and he was elsewhere.

PART 2: THE SAUCER

Chapter Eleven

Ian was paralyzed, floating or suspended in the middle of a dark chamber. To one side of him, some Centaurans conversed in their own language. Ian could not turn his head to see them. Their conversation served only to alert him to the fact that he was awake and captive. He noted cables attached to his head and torso.

"Medical scan complete? Has he been questioned?" The ship's primary clerk fired questions at the doctor.

"We have established consciousness in the subject, but translation is still disabled, exalted one."

"Enable translation," ordered Clerk One.

Ian heard English words superimposed over the alien's bizarre verbalisations: "You understand us and you can answer in this language? Agreed?"

Ian could now move his head. There were four aliens to his left. His throat, dry and dusty, was unresponsive. He rolled his tongue around his mouth, trying to lubricate his speaking apparatus.

The eyes of the closest alien seemed to widen and narrow repeatedly in some strange emotion as Ian cleared his throat. Perhaps it had never heard such a sound before.

"Yes. I understand. Where am I?" As Ian spoke a simultaneous translation of his words in the alien language emitted from the ceiling. It sounded rough and unpleasant.

The closest alien spoke again, and a simultaneous translation in English emitted from the ceiling. "What contact have you had with non-terrestrial powers?"

It took Ian a moment to digest the question. It must mean aliens, he thought.

"You're my first."

Ian listened to the alien translation, which seemed entirely too long for his response.

The same alien spoke again. "Falsehoods are disrespectful. If your responses are not faithful, you will be terminated. Do you understand?"

"I understand the truth. I don't think I understand your question."

The central eye of the alpha alien narrowed considerably before it began speaking again. "We are not from your planet. Detail all incidents of your communication with others who are not from your planet."

"I have not communicated with anyone not from my planet."

"Translation disable"

Ian felt his head again lock into position. He could no longer move it, but at least the aliens were still in his field of view. They began to converse with each other in their own language.

"There's something afoot here. This subject's K index signals the use of advanced technology. Either he is lying or he is not aware of what has been done to him. You ran the tests more than once?"

"Yes, most worthy executive. My team is completely satisfied our results are valid."

"Accepted. There may be malfeasance of other parties here, but no matter. Our plans are not disturbed. Prepare the subject for further testing."

"We will have the results within the next cycle."

When the alien chatter ended, the movement of a sliding panel abruptly revealed the exit and all four aliens departed.

Ian considered his situation. He was paralyzed and alone, kidnapped. He tried to move his fingers. No luck. If there was anything in his pockets that might aid his escape, it didn't matter. No doubt he was aboard the flying saucer, so there could be no escape regardless of the utility of his pocket contents.

Ian could move his tongue, but not his jaw. He surmised there must be a force field preventing any bodily movement.

A whirring noise caught his attention. A thin silvery robotic arm descended next to him and swivelled to align the point of an ovoid cylinder at his right arm. A hissing sound lasted only a second. Was this some type of non-contact intravenous injection system?

A great weight descended upon Ian's mind, smothering his thoughts with fuzzy grey wool. Even though he could not close his eyes, in a moment he was no longer conscious.

* *

Ian awoke sitting on a park bench in Hog's Back Park, a spot of natural beauty in the middle of Ottawa, where the Rideau Canal meets the Rideau River and this summation delivers a breathtaking waterfall over natural rock outcroppings.

A chipmunk was on the bench next to him. It looked at him expectantly but Ian had no peanuts or sunflower seeds to share. It scampered to the edge of the bench, then looked back at Ian. Last chance to feed me, it seemed to say, then jumped off and disappeared into the greenery beside the foot path.

Ian listened to the water rushing and the twitter of the local chickadees while he struggled to regain his continuity. Did he escape the saucer or was he freed?

His clothes did not make sense. He was wearing his favourite blue silk shirt and a pair of black Young Love shorts. When did he buy those? He had his wallet and keys. Did he drive here? He could not recall what happened to his car. Had it been moved to storage when he spent all those months in St. John's? Ian checked his phone. No calls in the memory. He did not remember ever erasing all his call data.

No saucer in the sky. Perhaps the Centaurans have left. Maybe they found a planet with easier pickings elsewhere. But the date on his phone was wrong. It indicated the current date as one month before the attack that had left Ian comatose. Ian pondered the robustness of his phone's clock source.

My phone synchronizes to the network clock signal provided by my telecom carrier, itself based on a Class 5 timing signal keyed to a system of satellites and nuclear timing sources (based upon decaying iridium, if I remember correctly). It would be impossible for it to display the wrong time, let alone the wrong date.

Ian's analysis was interrupted by a low growling sound. There was a large black dog behind the park bench, a black Labrador, a pit bull, or perhaps a mix. Somehow it had approached unheard and unseen. To avoid appearing threatening, Ian looked away from the dog's eyes, but not before its open mouth and sharp teeth made an impression on his adrenal gland.

Ian leaned forward, out of reach of any surprise snapping of jaws from behind the bench. With Ian now out of view of the dog, the growling still continued, but with small gaps where no sound issued. Ian was considering moving his legs from their vulnerable position, dangling in front of the bench. The dog could easily stick its head under the bench and mash a tibia or fibula into powder with its powerful jaws. Probably it could crush the upper leg bones in its mouth just as easily.

The growling started again. Then stopped. Still leaning forward and now being careful not to move his legs, Ian twisted to peer back between the gaps in the pitted wooden slats that made up the park bench. The pauses were the dog licking its chops, in an almost theatrically threatening exaggeration of hunger.

Ian withdrew his legs just in time as the dog's head popped forward from under the bench as if spring-loaded. The bony jaws snapped at the air.

Now Ian was standing on the bench. The dog circled, and with its palate sufficiently moistened, it now growled continuously. What could stop it from jumping upon the bench? Another split-second decision was needed.

A small trail led up through the dense forest area just behind the bench. Ian used the back of the bench as his elevated springboard and launched himself into the air in that direction.

As he scrambled up the path he noted a maple tree with a sturdy branch about shoulder height. Grasping it with one hand and the trunk with his other, he was off the ground when he felt the teeth on his ankle.

Kicking wildly with the injured leg was painful, and not very productive. With his good leg he landed a solid kick to the dog's head and felt its weight disappear. Ignoring the pain, he pulled himself up to a sitting position on the branch.

Safe for a moment.

The dog had not given up, however. It circled the tree, still growling, but now with a taste of his fear and blood.

Ian's left ankle was a sickening, glistening mess. It felt like wasps were inside his wound, biting him. Blood trickled down and stained his retro canvas sneakers.

So long favourite shirt.

Ian yanked the blue silk from his chest, buttons popping in eccentric trajectories like early rocket experiments. Then twisting the material to make it more rope-like, he tied it around his lower leg, just above the wound.

There was a crunching sound below. Was the dog eating the buttons? What kind of dog eats plastic buttons as well as people? One you want to stay very far away from, of course.

Ian's arms were going numb. Was he going into shock? *I haven't lose that much blood.*

There was a worse problem however. The branch he sat upon was starting to bow. It would not sustain his full weight for long. Arms wrapped around the rough trunk as a stabilizer, and using one leg as a piston to elevate himself, he might just make the next branch.

The pain was not helping his sense of balance. Without his shirt, the dense bough of the tree scratched his back and chest. Sweat trickled from his armpits, feeling like insects migrating down his sides. His hands were greasy with his own blood, but still managing to attract and accumulate bits of bark and dirt.

The growling was now punctuated with an occasional bark. Ian wished fervently for a passerby. Where was the owner of this delinquent cur? Its barking should attract someone eventually, but time was running out.

The branch had bowed so far down now that Ian worried the dog would leap up, clamp the far end in its mouth, and leverage its body weight to snap Ian's redoubt.

Properly motivated now, Ian ignored the pain and grasping a higher branch, dragged himself up the rough bark. As his weight came off the lower branch, it assumed its former equilibrium, now out of reach of the black dog.

Ian felt momentary relief. He was out of range of those jaws. Now if only he could use his phone to call for help. If he still had the phone, if he hadn't knocked it free of its belt clip during his initial leap for and scrabble up the tree.

Balancing on the higher branch with one foot and with

71

one arm wrapped around the tree trunk, Ian's hand carefully closed over his phone and removed it from its belt holster.

Only a foot or two above his head, a beautiful golden owl took that inopportune moment to decide to abandon the tree. With a great flap of wings causing a gust of wind, its departure startled Ian into dropping his phone. The black dog promptly found the phone and began chewing it, shaking its head like a cat capturing a feisty mouse.

High above, Ian cursed his clumsiness, the owl, the dog, various city bylaws, and the Universe in general.

His good leg was beginning to cramp and his sweaty skin was beginning to attract insects. Something was definitely crawling on his back. He tried to use his free hand to brush it off, but in the process inadvertently shifted his foot position causing his purchase on the branch to fail.

With only his arm around the trunk remained to support him, Ian began to slide down the trunk of the tree, the bark tearing at the skin on his chest. He swung his other hand towards a smaller branch, hoping to stop his descent.

For a moment Ian hung suspended, one arm grasping a thin subsidiary of the upper branch where he had earlier retreated, the other arm wrapped around the trunk as if it was an exhausted drinking companion.

He realized his position was unsustainable; he had slid down almost to the level of the first branch. Perhaps he could regain his balance there. As he tried to swing his body over to his previous position, the small overhead branch he had grasped tore free, and he slid down the trunk to the ground, leaving some skin along the way.

He struck the ground with his tailbone. It felt shattered. His chest was covered with blood.

Then the black dog was there, licking the blood streaks on his naked chest.

A plastic-eating vampire dog?

Fear constricted Ian's throat as he waited for the teeth. A terrible fetid smell forced his eyes open again. The dog's head was in his face, eyes glowering at him. Its breath was horrible.

Chapter Twelve

Ian was awake, and in the alien chamber again. This time his body felt less restricted by the force field. He could not lift his arms, but he could wiggle his fingers and move his head. The four aliens were back and the translator was on.

"Why do you fear creatures so much smaller than yourself?" Were they talking about his dream? It had seemed so real. "The snapping jaw black creature, we understand that fear, but why fall off your perch just because a caterpillar is crawling up your back?"

So it was a caterpillar. If Ian had known that, he would not have been as desperate to remove it. He was not pathologically neurotic; his insect phobias had reasonable limits. It was the fear of not knowing what type of bug was crawling up his back that he found intolerable. But he had no intention of educating these alien kidnappers.

"How do you know what was in my dream?"

"We know everything. You must answer our questions or you will die."

"I don't understand my own fears. If I did, then I could master them."

"Do all humans live in this type of mental fog?"

"I don't know. I only speak for myself. All humans are different."

"Impossible. You will speak for your type. Why do you fear these insignificant creatures?"

"Why do you fear humans? Why did you attack us?"

"We have no fear of humans." The alien behind the interrogator interrupted with an untranslated interjection. It sounded like a command in any language. The interrogator paused and changed tack.

"What aliens have you been in contact with?"

"Just you … things."

"On the Earth planet, what aliens have you been in contact with?"

"None whatsoever. I ran away from your soldiers."

"Translation disable."

The silver robotic arm descended again and Ian felt a pinch on his arm. This time I will not be fooled, Ian promised himself.

If I know I am in a dream, then I can control the dream.

* *

Logan came back from leave just in time. The new offensive was starting this very morning. Now was their chance to overrun the villages of the enemy. All their months of preparation had finally paid off and this final push would complete the defeat of the foe.

Logan's bunkmate Artoz was cleaning his boots.

"You're back just in time. In time to help me clean my boots!"

Logan guffawed at his comrade's unmitigated failure to persuade.

"If I were you, I'd wish my legs were longer, just to get me further from the stink!"

Artoz completed the guffaw cycle and turned serious for a moment.

"Do you have any of the new D10 foot powder?" An unpowdered foot after a long march and battle was not something wisely uncovered indoors.

As Logan rummaged through his gear locker seeking the foot elixir, an announcement came over the loudspeaker.

"Gamma Company moves out in ten minutes! Gamma Company to Deployment Area One. Gamma Company to Deployment Area One! Ten minutes, Gamma Company!!"

"Here's the powder, Artoz."

"Aren't you going to take that?" Artoz pointed at a small

metallic box inside Logan's foot locker.

Logan retrieved it and turned it over in his hands. A camera.

"No I don't think so…" What was it for? Had he ever even used it before?

"Your loss. You know what kill pics sell for. And the good stuff…" Artoz raised his eyebrow as if to intimate only a fool could not complete his sentence.

"Travel light I say."

"It's your bankruptcy, Logan."

Logan attached the rest of his gear to his uniform. Night-vision goggles, small knife, large knife, nutrition and water sterilization tabs, flash bombs, grenades, seam ripper, distress beacon. Ten kilograms heavier, Logan was ready.

Logan and Artoz boarded the very first helicopter. Artoz was very pleased by this and kept nudging him, but Logan could not recall what advantage their primacy conveyed. Logan's stomach lurched downward and then up as the helicopter bobbed toward the stratosphere.

A small island dwindled below them. This planet was mostly water. After a few minutes of travel, they dove back down through a cloud bank, and a chain of islands appeared. Their squadron of four helicopters landed on the pristine beach of the nearest island. They jumped ship and bee-lined for the green cover beyond the sandy shore.

Artoz gave the hand signal for follow. Logan and the two other soldiers from their helicopter used laser machetes to force a path through the inflexible underbrush. They emerged into the sunlight a hundred meters inland, in a clearing populated only with a few grass huts, some solar panels and a fresh water well clearly marked UPGD, for United Planets Galactic Development. Here was aid money gone wrong, hijacked by the enemy.

Logan could see his other squads emerging at the edge

of the clearing. They had sufficient forces to search each hut simultaneously. Artoz signalled for the other two soldiers to search the hut to his left, and then he and Logan entered the closer one, to his right.

The hut contained a family with several children, all clustered together in a group hug in the middle of the nearly-dark home. They were clearly scared.

Artoz barked orders at the civilians. The males stood to one side, the females opposite. Artoz mounted his camera on his helmet and activated it.

"Showtime!"

Artoz opened fire on the males, all collapsing into a bloody heap as the bullets struck them. The cries of the females struck Logan's ears. He stood frozen, as if uncertain where he was.

Artoz was laughing and smiling. He pulled the seam ripper from his belt and gracefully slit the tunic of the youngest post-pubescent female. He pulled the ruined clothing off and tossed it carelessly towards the pile of men.

The young female tried to cross her arms across her chest but Artoz pinned her hands behind her head and slipped plasti-cuffs on her wrists. Artoz flipped the girl over, yanked his Velcro fly open and began to rape her.

Logan remembered that sometimes Artoz was teased because he always flipped his rape victims over. He didn't like to see them cry.

This isn't right, thought Logan.

I have never been a soldier. There are no UP, there is only a UN. The armies of civilized nations do not rape or massacre, not generally. How did I get here and more importantly, how do I get out?

Logan could hear Artoz calling his name as he stumbled dazed from the hut. There was a narrow stone building that

77

he had not noticed before, protruding from the side of a embankment. Logan entered the double front doors and walked down a long corridor lit with ordinary fluorescent tube lights. The atmosphere was institutional. Logan stopped at one door and read the English text painted on the safety-wired glass panel: "Combatant Re-acclimation & Counselling".

All was quiet. He opened the door.

Logan was greeted by a short, blonde woman in her thirties who reminded him of someone. The familiarity was tantalizing, but remained unresolved as he stared at her.

"Come in! Don't be shy, not that you military types are very shy! Come sit over here. Okay let me just scan those dog tags and we won't have to fill out a bunch of forms."

The woman's name tag said 'Gale' and she smelled nice.

"Okay here's your file. You've got a lot of kills for one tour of duty but I don't see any deterrence actions. Is that why you're here?"

"Deterrence actions?"

"You know, we don't like to use the R word because these are enemy procreators. Do you have a problem with sexual aggression?"

Logan recalled Artoz, his camera, and the tears of his victim. "I think I do."

"Well really there's not much we can do about that. I mean there are some drugs, but the side effects can be problematic. Your best bet is to get into a different branch of the military, maybe the Bombardment Division."

"I'm not really sure I'm cut out for the military at all."

"Well we do have some re-training programs. Are you interested in a technical education?"

Logan was about to answer yes and was remembering university days as an undergraduate engineering student named Ian Hesse when two Centaurans flung open the door, strode in, and struck him hard in the face with an oblong object, perhaps an alien rifle or walking stick. Logan tasted his own blood as he fell from his chair onto the floor or nowhere.

* *

Clerk One stared angrily at Ian's body suspended in the test chamber. He had never seen this type of failure before. The medico had failed to explain how a test subject can override a new identity and access parts of the obscured personality to completely change the test scenario.

There were some associated failures in the control hardware, but the coincidental alignment of faults required to allow such a cascade of unexpected results was unthinkable. However, some adjustments in the anti-skew tracker should ensure that other tests would not spin out of control.

They must try again.

Chapter Thirteen

Logan awoke smelling Artoz' feet. They were worse than ever. He popped the plastic tabs that kept the window flaps in place. Soon, a very welcome breeze was flowing through their tent.

The day looked fresh and glorious. The mountains to the east were a misty blue, the tops obscured by puffs of corpulent clouds. The sea to the west sparkled like a green emerald; the only flaws in that gem were the multiple military ships restlessly patrolling the horizon. Today was a good day for the empire, regardless of the casualties, Logan understood.

Pulling on his boots with the stealth of a guerrilla fighter, Logan exited without waking Artoz.

The gravel of the footpath crunched under his feet. Logan felt like a patient taking his first walk after a long bed-ridden hospitalization. Nothing like casual encounters with death to illuminate the joy of life, thought Logan.

How many have died so that I could enjoy this early morning perambulation?

Beside the officer's mess stood the ACT, or Activity Co-ordination Tent, where schedules were distributed to officers and information was available for the enlisted troops. For security reasons, nothing was distributed electronically. To look ahead at the prospective schedule for your squad, a trip to ACT was required.

"Lieutenant Logan! It is good you are here. We have new orders for you. Some good news I think you'll be very happy to hear."

The co-ordination clerk was not usually effusive but the reason soon became clear as Logan examined his orders. He had been promoted to Captain and assigned to lead his own squad. Soon he would be smelling the feet of new people. He must report to Colonel Zander by oh seven hundred hours and then meet and deploy his new team by eight hundred. It was oh six forty-nine.

Now wide awake and energized by his status elevation, Logan was operating at peak efficiency. Colonel Zander was concise but complimentary as he handed Logan the new rank insignia for his dress uniform. Logan was an asset; Logan was on the right track; Logan was a man for the future.

Logan's new squad did not disappoint. They were experienced men whose previous team leader had been a desk jockey parachuted in from headquarters, no doubt as a punishment for an infraction against the mores of the moisturized, soft-buttocked elite that had no idea men were losing limbs to frostbite and gangrene as the offensive surged ever closer to the strangulation of this strategic but under-populated and under-evolved planet.

That leader had lasted only one operation, and the squad was clearly relieved that his replacement was someone with real combat experience. It was unlikely, but the higher-ups might have done something right finally.

Two of his men were from American Kurdistan so they had that in common with Logan. The others were ethnic Russians, but had very good English skills.

Logan was relieved they would not need to communicate via translator chip, which although officially classified as adequately accurate by command, was the subject of many hilarious anecdotes among the enlisted.

Their first operation would be to map and then destroy yet another newly discovered tunnel complex near the far southern coast of the continent where most of the local population was concentrated. By bivouacking around the entrance to the tunnel system, the primitive locals had given the game away to the surveillance drones and satellites staring down upon them.

The helicopter insertion ran perfectly. A diversion operation encouraged the enemy forces to abandon their nests near the tunnel entrance. Soon Logan and his team were peering down into the darkness of the smallest entrance.

"This is where we begin," declared Logan.

They set up the control equipment and manoeuvred their robots into the steep entrance shaft. The silent operation proceeded smoothly.

The first robot discovered a sentry after crawling only a dozen meters. A pinpoint laser burned through his left eyeball, snuffing him instantly. Logan grasped Sergeant Lviv's shoulder in silent congratulation for a moment. It was a high-quality kill.

After waiting twenty seconds for any alarm or reaction, the robot continued a few more meters before another alien was encountered. This one looked female and very human. It did not have the strange face paint or extravagantly uncut hair of the locals. She was dressed in a short white dress that would not be out of place on Earth. The woman was blond, mid-thirties, and tantalizingly familiar.

Logan belayed the kill order.

The woman looked directly at the camera on the robot and said distinctly: "I am coming out. I am unarmed. Please listen to me."

Although it was technically possible to do so, as the robot had a speaker as well as a microphone, Logan's team did not reply but instead sat in silence as the woman passed over the tiny robot. Her legs were very white and very long her panties pink.

Logan had an urge to replay the segment but immediately suppressed the thought as uncharacteristically unprofessional. As inappropriate and ill-advised as such a voyeuristic act might have been, bypassing the military imperative (to kill) and engaging in discussion with the enemy was perhaps worse.

"I am Gale. I represent the people of this planet. We must stop the killing and work together. There is no reason why we cannot combine our best attributes and create something better for both our peoples."

Lviv and the other three sergeants stood dumbfounded. They had no mandate to take prisoners. They could taser or sedate her but, if they left her here, the planned bombardment phase of the attack would certainly end her. Lviv fingered his seam-ripper.

"I am Captain Logan, representative of Earth. Why did you attack our trade delegation?"

"We intend no harm. It was not we who attacked. Your forces have much to answer for. But if you do not believe me, please, you must see the truth."

She extended a hand to Logan. Lviv exhaled noisily, in disbelief or displeasure, as Logan extended his own to her and their hands touched.

Warmth and knowledge flooded into Logan. The planet was a treasure trove of life. Useful animals and plants abounded. Her people were open and welcoming to strangers. They esteemed life and yearned to know more of the Universe, which they viewed as a benevolent place. Clearly, there had been misunderstandings. In his own head, Logan quoted drolly, "Mistakes were made."

Inside Logan's gut, his soul was folding, compacting. He was becoming very small, but hard and shiny. In a moment he rose free of his body, as a floating sense drone, tethered to his body by a thin silver cord, yet somehow unrestricted in his movements against gravity. The landscape shrank below him, the scale expanding until he could see his compatriots camped on the east shore. The feelings of the four-hundred humans concentrated there flowed up to him as freely as water trickling downhill.

The humans were marauders; they sought only victory for their empire, laurels, and arbitrary power awarded to the strongest, with no thought for collaboration or synergy with other civilizations. They dreamt of slaves.

Logan's yogic body recoiled from this unpleasant revelation, floating westward until it had passed over the massive mountain range near the center of the continent. He approached a high green plateau, a fertile and temperate micro-climate.

Again, the psychological gestalt of the occupants flowed up to Logan, no translation necessary.

Here multiple tribes of the aliens met and exchanged goods and ideas. Their minds were vibrant and optimistic. They found pride not in the defeat of their enemy, but in the combining of their and their friends' victory over chaos for the greater glory and advancement of all civilization.

Logan understood that his fight had been misguided. The true enemy was disorder and anti-reason. If these could be overcome, then true peace could be established throughout the galaxy.

As his floating yogic body followed the silver thread back to his corporeal body, he found himself once again staring at Gale, his hand still in hers. His heart filled with love for her.

"Traitor!" shouted Lviv, but the other soldiers were now Centaurans. Logan felt a bolt of fear electrify his nerves as they aimed their weapons at him. A giant noise blotted out his awareness, and he was floating in blackness.

* *

"You gave us quite a scare, Logan," admitted Dr. Ketz. "You're a very brave man. There aren't many who escape in such a situation. You look a little puzzled. Perhaps you don't remember it all. That's not unusual in trauma. Just relax, and take it easy. You need to heal, but you should be very proud of your actions."

"Okay." Logan's eyelids closed.

When Logan woke up again, the doctor was gone. The lights were a little lower in the hospital ward room, giving the impression of night. Some of the wounded snored, some wheezed. A gentle stream of beeps and clicks flowed as the automatic monitoring equipment probed, sampled, massaged, and generally maintained the immobile.

But Logan was feeling strong. My recovery must be nearly complete, he thought, as he sat up in his bed and examined his medical attachments, nothing but a couple of monitoring leads.

Logan experimentally flung his sheet away and swung his legs over the edge of the bed. No pain, no problem. He turned the audible signal down to the minimum before removing the sensing leads: one from his neck; one from his chest.

The flatline signal resulting from the disconnection was a soft monotone. A remote alarm might have been triggered, but in the ward it was quiet, with sufficient time for Logan to gain his legs.

His kit bag was beside the bed. He must have been evacuated from the planet, or at least from the camp. Walking carefully to the swing doors at the end of the ward, Logan noted that one of the injured was an alien. He found the bathroom down the corridor and after relieving himself, considered what he had seen.

Why would there be an alien in the recovery room? A shout distracted Logan before he could form any hypothesis.

"It's got Dr. Ketz and a needle laser!"

Some medical staff were gathered outside the recovery

room. Logan could hear the alien shout from inside.

"I want safe passage! I have a hostage!"

Its significant recovery mirrored Logan's own.

"There's no way," said the general. He was addressing the medical staff, none of whom were armed. "That's Garreto, their military leader. It took a thousand men to get him."

"I'm Captain Logan. Give me a sidearm and I'll take him out."

"We'll give you two minutes, then we're blowing the shit out of everything that moves." The general handed Logan his own side arm.

"Okay, I'm coming in to negotiate!" shouted Logan, tucking the pistol into his pants near his spine. "Don't shoot!" Ian entered the room slowly, with both hands up.

"I'm Captain Logan. I have the power to get you out of here. We don't want anyone getting hurt. I can make promises that you can count on. Do you understand?"

"Yes. What assurance do I have that you can be trusted?"

Pictures of Logan's family involuntarily flashed through his mind, his wife, a little blond boy, no, twins, a little blond boy and a little girl, their life in St. Alphonse Valley, a wonderful A-frame wooden house with a giant stone fireplace. His brother had already died in the war. If the aliens were stopped, his family would be safe. They were wily liars, never admitting they posed a risk of domination and destruction. Logan had heard of Garreto, the puppet master of the insurgency. He could not be allowed to go free.

"I intend you no harm. We need to communicate. Maybe this can be the opening to peace that we both seek. Let us discuss what needs to be done like reasonable people. May I put my hands down? My fingers are starting to tingle…" Logan smiled at the alien.

"Very slowly, and tell me more about what you offer," said Garreto.

Logan's arms descended slowly while his brain accelerated wildly ahead. What he was about to do was very risky, but there were thirty other wounded soldiers in the recovery room. If he failed, they would all perish in the conflagration that would surely follow. If he could take Garreto out, he would be a hero. Perhaps the war would end sooner, and no more of his kin would need to die. The end of the war was within sight, but only because of the capture of Garreto. It would be foolish to underestimate him.

There were rumours that an effectively cloaked tracking device had been implanted in the alien leader, for despite having been captured more than once by various forces of various strengths, Garreto would invariably summon help and escape while causing additional losses to the United Planetary Forces. Despite negotiations and various offers, the planet would not surrender to the forces of justice.

It was a shame and history would certainly say that Logan was on the side of truth but today only force would speak. The planet would be subjugated to reason and modernity. Still, deep inside Logan there was a twinge of doubt that something original and wonderful on the planet would be lost. When the enemy was defeated, their history would be lost forever.

Logan fell sideways on the floor retrieving and aiming his pistol at the same time. The first shot went astray, hitting Dr. Ketz, but the next five bullets traced a jagged red line across Garreto's chest and he collapsed without firing a shot.

Logan looked down at Dr. Ketz; he was now a Centauran. The others were all coming through the swinging doors now, the general, the medical staff. They

87

were all Centaurans.

Logan made a strangled noise in his throat and began shooting wildly around himself in all directions, but in a moment these explosive discharges stopped. Had he lost his weapon? Logan looked down and saw that he no longer had a right arm. No weapon either. His own blood soaked his right side but, mercifully, before the pain began, he fainted.

Chapter Fourteen

Clerk One gazed through the polarized wall and studied the subject suspended in the test chamber. Was it representative of all the humans? If so, the Centaurans had little to worry about.

"You may deliver your final interpretation for this subject now, medico."

"My most worthy mentor, after reviewing all the data regarding the subject, we can classify its reactions as a Class 7 non-aggressive pacifist. The subject suffers from neurotic fears and does not tolerate battle conditions well. Worse than that is the mental noise and disorientation that arises when it is confronted with stress or conflict. The subject relies upon internal experience and valuations to reach non-group ethical conclusions. The guidance of society or ruling powers can be overturned by this inner sense of correctness which can lead to unpredictability and …"

Ship Supervisor, the highest ranking Centauran on the ship, had accompanied Clerk One into the chamber. As the clerk, the penultimate power on the ship, turned to address his even higher status companion, the doctor halted his report.

"It seems our new planet is full of dangerous *individuals*." Clerk One's tone spared no venom for the word individuals.

"I do not see them as very dangerous. Certainly these traits are dangerous in citizens, but they do not elevate the quality of a warrior."

Ship Supervisor's words were not to be questioned. Clerk One blinked his agreement formally and offered the appropriate recommendation: "Based on our own two test subjects, plus the statements from the other ships, we are in accord and our plans can now advance to Stage Three without delay."

Ship Supervisor blinked in acknowledgement. Soon the ship would move close to the surface and the task of extinguishing dissent from their selected city, which the terrestrial humanoids called Ottawa, would advance. Only a few diurnal cycles would be required to complete their mission.

"You will implement." Ship Supervisor spoke but blinked an affirmation at the same time. His mood must be good to share such a familiarity with an underling.

"Understood, worthy one. I will carry this one to the final net." Clerk One took a bit of a risk with a netball metaphor but it paid off. Ship Supervisor blinked with amusement before stepping out of the chamber.

Clerk One ordered the doctor to resolve the issue of Ian's raised K index, something that did not pose a threat, but did present a mystery. K technology was outlawed throughout the galaxy.

* *

When Ian awoke, he was dispirited to find that of all the unpleasant dreams he had just endured, being kidnapped by Centaurans was not one of them. He still floated in that inky dark chamber. The only illumination was from one wall, to his left, which shimmered dully. That wall was a window and there were aliens are behind it, recalled Ian.

I can move my arms!

With a start he realized that a long black cable snaked down the ceiling and its tip, a metallic python head, was attached to his left forearm. Ian carefully grasped the silver python head and gently pried it away from his arm. He managed to retract it a few centimetres, enough to reveal that the tiny cables and ligaments that extended from it now travelled deep into his arm.

If he yanked the thing off, he might bleed to death, Ian feared, but leaving it on would also be difficult to stomach. He tried to convince himself it was a harmless feeder tube.

How long have I been here? I haven't eaten, and yet I'm not hungry. I'm not even thirsty. This thing must be keeping me alive.

Ian's hand played over the python's head, feeling for any button or release. No luck, but he found that each side of the head had a small, smooth depression. Ian applied his thumb and forefinger simultaneously at those points and the result was better than he could have imagined.

He immediately sensed a whirring and vibration. Before he had time to regret his intervention, Ian could feel the python's tentacles retract from inside his arm and move back into its silvery head. A small orange light activated on the python's nose and it slowly retracted half a meter from his side.

How long have I been here?

There was no way to tell. Ian had slept and had dreams, but not normal dreams. They were vivid and intense. He remembered the vicious dog, then the army dreams. Who was Logan? Not him, but during those dreams he was sure he had been Logan from American Kurdistan. But he had never been to Asia.

He had been totally paralyzed in this chamber at first, a horrible memory. Later he had been able to move his head and fingers minimally. Now he had succeeded in removing the feeding tube, or drug tube, or poison delivery system, or whatever the python was, and he could move his arms and legs quite freely. He contracted and then stretched his limbs.

Could he reach the wall? No. He felt weightless but there was still an invisible cocoon around him that prevented his straying from the center of the chamber.

What was the United Planets Federation? Hadn't he seen that in a movie lately? His dreams had been full of strange and half-familiar ideas. That woman, first in the counselling office and then in the tunnel, that was his ex-wife Gale.

He still loved her, but they had had their day and it had ended. Soon after the breakup he had gone into the coma that had robbed him of two years of his life. And now there was Blythe. Was she a pit stop along a quick road to death, or would he somehow return and take their romance further?

I'm locked up in an alien spaceship and I'm expending energy thinking about romance! I think I can forgive myself. There's no exit here, no plan I could come up with to free myself. Why shouldn't I spent my last few hours alive on the planet, or more accurately, near the planet, thinking about something hopeful?

Ian's eyes felt heavy. Maybe he could sleep.

* *

Ian crawled from the smoking wreckage of the alien shuttle. A wide scar marked the ground, describing the friction of his landing. The green women were upon him at once. They waved their spears in a manner not quite menacing, but clearly indicative of their wishes. Ian climbed to his feet and dusted off his suit. A brilliant orange sun glowed close to the horizon. The nearest green woman motioned him down a path.

"So, what's a nice girl like you doing in a place like this?"

No reply.

"What *is* your sign? Or is it even visible from Earth?"

"Chaktash."

"Ah." Ian nodded and continued along the path with his rescuers who now held their spears loosely at their sides.

The aliens' camp was a collection of small tents with dirt floors overlaid with animal furs. They brought Ian to the largest, which was scarcely the size of a small workstation cubicle.

The leader, or who Ian presumed to be leader, raised her spear and intoned an exotic incantation. The spear thumped the ground three times and the rest of the group dropped to their haunches. Ian paused only a moment before copying the green humanoids.

"Haba carme tseggi do wah," intoned the leader in a mocking tone of voice, looking heavily lidded upon Ian.

Ian smiled and the green leader returned the gesture while she slipped out of her thick animal hide. Ian noted that the leader had distinguishable tan zones, you couldn't quite call them lines, and thought she was quite perfectly beautiful in an uncivilized sort of way.

"Chaka chaka." The leader thumped the ground twice with her spear and two of her followers sprang up and shook two maraca-like instruments with a long sustaining agitation.

They then also disrobed, and fell silent. All eyes were on Ian.

Ian waited. The leader thumped the ground in an emphatic motion with her spear.

"Chaka tasha tasha tasha." At the third 'tasha' she dropped her spear onto the furs in front of Ian. This was definitely not a threat.

Ian, now excited, stood and began to disrobe. The leader moved forward to embrace him and he kissed her on the mouth.

She tasted exotic, vaguely of some strange spice, certainly not unpleasant. She stroked the side of his thighs as he followed the curve of her spine with his hands. She did not resist, but laid her head on his shoulder and whispered into his ear.

"Chaka do wah."

She pushed Ian back onto the fur-covered floor and sat astride him. Ian anticipated penetration as her smoky deep eyes shone a laser beam of carnal intent into his.

Suddenly his thigh pinched alarmingly. She had driven a knife deep into his thigh! What madness was this? Why would she pierce this perfect moment?

* *

Ian tried to roll on his side, but could not. Now he was awake in the dark alien chamber again. His green lover had been a dream, perhaps an actual human dream and not some inscrutable manipulation by his captors. A pleasant dream unfortunately interrupted by the persistent alien technology.

The silver metallic python was again attached to him, this time on his hip in the exact spot that he felt that green nymph stab him. It hurt.

Ian found the two depressions again and squeezed. The python retracted its multiple threads from his system and retreated half an arm's length. But how long until it randomly reached out and clamped him again? What if it clamped him in the genitals? Ian was hungry and thirsty. Maybe he did need the python.

Ian pulled the python head close to his left forearm. No reaction. He touched his skin with its mouth and the little orange light on its nose changed to a light blue colour. There was a slight vibration, then a soft tickling followed by a weak pinching sensation. In a moment it had reattached itself to the more comfortable and receptive spot on his arm.

As Ian considered that an alien feeding tube was the only thing keeping him alive, he oscillated between nausea and irrational hope. There was no way to tell what was being pumped into his body, or what removed by the python, but it had kept him well so far, or at least in a state where he felt no serious discomfort. If the aliens were purposely sustaining him, they must have a plan for him other than just disposal. This was at least a small thread of hope to which he could cling.

Also, the alien technology was not overwhelming. Sure they had amazing spaceflight capabilities, but his understanding of the python indicated that he could adapt and learn in the alien environment. This technology was not completely unintelligible or hopelessly beyond him.

My life is not over. I have a future. Someday I will escape.

But his eyes were heavy again, and this time it did again feel like real sleep coming on. How many days have I been in this chamber, wondered Ian, and will this be the first substantial real sleep I get, or another trap? He remembered his experiences as Logan. Did they span days or weeks?

Ian tried to resist the waves of fatigue, but it was futile and soon he was tumbling downwards through a warm black void. Surely far below a mattress awaited his landing.

* *

Ian awoke and immediately rose from his bed, his personal hygiene schedule kicking in automatically: shower and shave. The heat of the steam-soaked bathroom enveloped his drying body as he re-packed then closed his shaving kit.

A soft knocking on the door indicated he was not alone.

"Yes?" called Ian.

The door opened the minimal amount to allow Blythe to slip in.

"Finished dressing already?"

"Sorry," grinned Ian. "I'm just anxious to be out of here."

Blythe wrapped her arms around him. She did not

appear anxious to let him go.

"Can we afford to be late?" asked Ian.

Blythe smiled and stroked his chest.

"It wouldn't be the end of the world."

Ian smiled at her levity. Maybe the world could wait. She was beautiful and she wanted him. It would be easy to discard the towel and necessitate another shower. Her eyes were shining, and open wide in invitation and anticipation.

But Ian was on Earth. The aliens were still threatening the planet. How was he here again in his own bathroom? He remembered leaving Blythe's cramped and untidy apartment after seeing the true shape of the strange alien who had pretended to be Sister Raymond.

But when precisely did he and Blythe arrive back at his condominium? They had not, therefore this must be a dream.

Ian discarded his towel and ran his hands down Blythe's back, tracing the sculpture of her backside. No sense wasting a good dream.

As Ian fumbled with Blythe's skirt zipper his vision peripherally grazed the mirror, now clearing of steam. There was something strange there, and irresistibly his vision returned to check the detail: the face of the Rubbler reflected in Blythe's place.

Ian remembered the Rubbler from his battles with the aliens. He remembered crawling over the wreckage of a collapsed building, trying to ignore body parts and the slime of blood and bodily fluids that coated the destruction. He had hunted the Rubbler and had faced it. They had verbally sparred like foes in a old movie.

Why do you seek the destruction of the Earth, Ian had asked the Rubbler, who had introduced itself by name and then responded that it wished only the destruction of humanity, not Earth itself.

The aliens liked the planet very well, thank you, they just didn't care for the present occupants.

The aliens would help the planet revert to its natural beauty by turning all traces of human civilization into rubble. Hence the name of the alien, or more likely his nickname.

If Ian could kill the Rubbler, he would score a victory for the resistance on the order of shooting down the Red Baron in World War One. All this came back to Ian in a flash as he stood facing the bathroom mirror.

The alien's reflected face was tense; its mouth hung open and Ian could see the activity of the multiple tongues inside. This was what he had embraced, not Blythe. There was a monster in his arms, not bliss. Ian pushed it away in disgust.

"You're just not performing up to snuff, Ian Hesse. You will be terminated." The alien fully reverted to its authentic appearance and Ian noticed the tube-like instrument its lower left hand was slowly raising to point at him.

Ian thrashed in panic, kicking wildly in the small space. He managed to plant his foot on the frontal plate of the alien's clothing and shove it toward the shower.

The Rubbler fell backwards noisily and Ian propelled himself through the bathroom door, expecting to feel the wrath of the alien's tube weapon on his back any moment.

This is only a dream, Ian assured himself as he yanked open the front door and ran out into the hallway. His unit was at the far end of the floor and the elevators were in the middle. Too far. Already some of his neighbours' doors were opening to reveal other Centaurans observing him, their three eyes focused, calm and unblinking. Ian backed up and pushed through a fire door into the stairwell.

The fire exit was full of Centaurans, but there was no going back. Ian tried to push past the Centauran on the next lower landing, but could not. It grabbed him with all four arms and hoisted him in the air.

One wall in the stairwell was all glass and looked out on a green space next to Ian's high-rise building. The view was good from the seventeenth floor. Ian felt the glass break as his body slammed against it, and then he was falling to his death.

Chapter Fifteen

I am alive, thought Ian, again awake and suspended in the alien chamber. The silver python was still attached to his left arm but now a black python, previously unseen, had snaked from the ceiling on another black cable and attached to his right arm. How many more of these things would come to bite and poison him?

Ian was sure he had never met an alien like the Rubbler. Coming back to reality was a mixed bag, some relief, some despair. It seemed every time he slept in space he faced death and terror in scenarios that felt completely real and horrifying even when they started out as obvious dreams.

Unlike the rare nightmares he had suffered years ago on Earth, these episodes of alternate reality were exceptionally intense and seemed to recur whenever he was not awake. There was no escape into sweet dreams, no respite against the relentless tide of dark episodes. If he closed his eyes he could only expect that death would stalk him again.

If this madness continues, it may eat my mind and I will die, thought Ian.

There may be no escape at all. Should I even try to remove the black python? It will simply re-attach in its own time, next time I sleep, and probably to the most sensitive part or my body

Ian was still sleepy but fought to remain awake, biting his tongue at one point. The resulting alertness was short-lived and expensive. Now his tongue was very sore.

If I get a chance, I will get out of here, he thought.

Any chance, no matter how slim. Better to fight and be killed than to linger forever in this alien hell, tortured at the whim of inscrutable enemies, waking again and again in fear, as additional invasive mechanisms attach to my body.

A movement on his right side interrupted Ian's dark musings. The black python was vibrating. Now the orange light on its head had turned blue and Ian was sure he could feel its tendrils retreating from his arm. This was soon proven as it withdrew its head, now completely disengaged from his body, and the black cable retracted upwards. The mechanism disappeared into the darkness of the high ceiling.

Maybe the black python was the bringer of bad dreams. Maybe now Ian could sleep and rest, regain strength for the fight that lay ahead. Ian succumbed to the lethargy in his body and closed his eyes.

* *

Ian stood upon a mountain and surveyed the panorama, a valley thick with greenery, featuring a meandering river and a village at the far limit of his vision. It seemed idyllic. This was Earth. The sky was blue, interrupted by only a few banks of clouds.

The Sun was about to emerge from behind a tall cumulus cotton ball. Ian faced it, closed his eyes, anticipating letting the rays warm him.

"Ian…"

His eyes snapped open and he spun around. There was no one behind him. He had heard the voice distinctly but he was obviously alone.

What Ian saw in the sky almost caused him to lose control of his bowels. Where he expected the Sun to peek from behind a cloud, there was instead an intensely glowing body in the sky. It was white, luminous, and energetic. He could feel the heat radiating from it, like a sibling to the Sun. And it was approaching!

Ian heard a loud humming at first, which then resolved into a chorus of a thousand baritone voices repeating the traversal of some unfamiliar musical interval, harmonic but somehow threatening. The radiant entity travelled halfway from the cloud to Ian's high altitude perch, then halted mid-sky, and addressed him again.

"Ian. You are on the wrong planet."

"I am from Earth," replied Ian, reacting verbally instead of trying to reconcile his bizarre and unlikely situation with his last known waking location. The phrase Heavenly Host popped into his head. Was that who this was, or what did that even mean?

"I come on wings of great power and glory to give you truth."

"Who are you?"

"Listen and understand."

The angel moved closer but Ian could not look upon the blazing corona of its face.

"Your Bible is correct. Satan was the most beautiful of the angels. He ruled the world long ago and everything that came to pass was a reflection of his Satanic personality, creatures destroyed with impunity, savagery, the rule of the beasts, the greatest of which were dinosaurs and their souls were the souls of the angels of their time. You are a dinosaur."

"I am human!" Ian was agnostic, leaning towards atheistic. He could challenge an angel on so glaring an error.

"Listen well. When God decided to destroy all evil life upon Earth, He selected a great asteroid as the instrument of divine justice. Earth was smashed and your time ended. From that day, the nature of the Universe changed. God Himself changed and new souls arose, souls of perfect creatures who would take the responsibility of serving truth and reign over all animals.

To begin this new era, the greatest of the dinosaur souls, Satan, was thrown down to the lower realm and fragmented

101

into many creatures. This is your human race. You are the useless and toxic leftovers of an earlier era of corrupted life. It is the duty of the angels to reclaim Earth as a paradise for those deserving."

"How can that be? Aren't humans supposedly made in the image of God? That's what the Bible says." Ian knew this was an argument he could not win.

The angel was approaching nearer, and the temperature was rising. He felt paradoxically cool as the breeze robbed his heat via the liquid conduit of the sweat stream forming along his trunk.

"Your translations and interpretations are lacking. It is humanity that is brute animal. There is only one God and He is ours. Look upon me."

Ian did not look.

"Look upon me! I am perfection, the creator of worlds!"

The figure's white cloak blazed with light but the flickering energy that was its head began to coalesce into a solid form. The face was inhuman, the visage of his captors, the aliens in the saucer.

"No!" screamed Ian, raising his arms to ward off the terrible figure but it was still on a collision course with him, and closing fast.

Chapter Sixteen

Ian awoke in an agitated state. The angel was only a nightmare. Life was also a nightmare but, without the metaphysical twist, it at least had a probable end to suffering that could be envisioned.

Why should an angel frighten him so? Ian was not a believer, not quite an atheist but certainly a skeptic who viewed organized religions' purported histories as highly suspect. As an adult, he had read about the fall of the Jewish Temple in 70 A.D. and noted how this bellwether event for the region had been ignored and misinterpreted by self-proclaimed Christian historians.

The fact that an adult had tried to sexually assault him at a church camp when he was ten years old did much to attenuate his expectations of others based on their title or role. Luckily, Ian had been smart enough at the time to ask for help and his parents' church had been progressive enough to believe his version. The camp counsellor involved was summarily relieved of his duties.

Ian did not blame the church for this incident, but it highlighted to him at an early age that authorities and adults were not all equally deserving of respect and you had to follow your own mind when confronted with difficult scenarios.

A secondary effect of the incident came later. Once the summer camp concluded and Ian was again attending church each week with his family, rumours about what happened began to float around the church. Someone was not maintaining the confidentiality such a delicate incident demanded.

As it had back in the 20th Century, the tar brush of sexual abuse still painted both the accused and the accuser. The family of the counsellor, who also in the eyes of the law still a child, although a large and hormone-laden teenaged one, threatened Ian's family with a civil suit for defamation and false arrest. The atmosphere of their church was no longer welcoming.

Nothing came of the legal threats, but Ian absorbed the lesson that even if you are right, this is no guarantee you will completely succeed when opposing evil. You must take action only after very carefully considering the likely outcome and possible side effects. To do the right thing, only to have it backfire, makes you less action-oriented and more contemplation-oriented.

This characteristic served Ian well in his engineering career. He was known for his detailed analyses and careful answers. But it had not served him well when faced with the market collapse of his technological milieu.

While other engineers departed the oil industry, migrating to greener technologies in singles, pairs and sometimes whole v-shaped flocks (senior engineer at the front, leading entire workgroups across the corporate divide to new feeding grounds), Ian had stayed loyal to his company and remained behind to clean up the decades of irrationally exuberant expansion that had left the world with a glut of marginally-profitable but environmentally damaging operations.

His bosses had made it an attractive option for Ian but it was a career dead end and he was soon unemployed. The easy road had been a short journey into obsolescence.

The final insult was that, at the very end, when his employer declared bankruptcy, Ian was dismissed without the promised lucrative severance package, and his pension benefits were tied up in legal red tape.

His contract for working at Digifab had expired shortly after he went comatose. Now he floated, unemployed and kidnapped, in an alien saucer far above Earth.

Ian was exhausted. He felt like he had been woken up at two in the morning. He would fall back into sleep soon. No question. The black python was still gone. Ian closed his eyes and could not resist the darkness.

* *

I must have crashed on this planet, thought Ian as he dragged himself up another steep dune. His feet sank heavily into the sand with every step, multiplying the effort required to make progress across the desolate landscape.

The planet was obviously not Earth. The sky was blue but there were two satellites, both smaller than the Moon but equally grey and cratered.

Why wasn't I hurt in the crash? wondered Ian as he examined his tattered clothes. The insignia on his torn uniform was that of the United Planets. A small canteen was clipped to his belt. Ian unclipped and shook it, evaluating the resulting inertial variance.

Not very full.

Reaching the crest of the dune, the greater landscape was revealed. Mostly more dunes but off to the far right was an unusual dark spot, brownish green. Perhaps an oasis, or perhaps a wind-swept and tidied rock outcropping. But there was no other destination worthy of consideration. Ian stumbled and half slid down the far side of the dune, angling towards the dark anomaly.

As he approached, his hopes grew. It was not rock; it was indeed vegetation. He might rest in shade soon. Another half hour of struggling through the loose sand and he fell through a canopy of broad leaves that protected the modest valley, and down into a cooler, shady place.

The sound of trickling water teased his eardrums. The most pressing and immediate need for life as he knew it, and here it was in abundance. There must be an underground stream, thought Ian as he sat by the edge of the rocky pool at the very lowest point in the little valley.

The next sound that came to him bore no resemblance to anything one might reasonably find in such an oasis. It was a soft gurgling, not animal, definitely human. Ian took a few steps back from the edge of the pool and found the source of the gentle sounds was resting atop a pile of leaves: it was a baby.

The baby seemed glad to be found, making eye contact with Ian almost immediately and clapping its hands together as though approving its new prospective protector. The baby was not a newborn. but it did not look like it had too many kilometres on the crawl odometer.

Ian moved closer and began to stroke its arm, eliciting more gurgles and a friendly cooing. He picked the baby up and brought it back to the edge of the pond, keeping a close eye on it as he finished and then re-filled his canteen without drinking any of the alien water. If it was poison, he'd find out later, when he absolutely needed to hydrate again. It probably was not poison.

The baby seemed healthy. It was wrapped in a small blanket without any tag or marking to lessen the mystery of its origin.

Ian did not have much experience with babies, but he remembered the peek-a-boo game. Ian used one of the broad leaves from the oasis trees to hide his face. Revealing his face again after a few seconds continued to amuse the little tyke until the daylight began to fade.

"I shall call you Tycho, because you are the zeroth tyke I've found on this planet. Nothing to do with craters or acne, really, although you might suspect it once you get to be a teenager." Ian smiled at the scenario of an adolescent Tycho complaining about his name as he applied Derma-Dream cream before the big Grade 10 dance.

The alien sun now hugged the horizon, bloated and

blushing as its light refracted through the additional layers of atmosphere the low angle provided. The heat of the day had passed. Now they would find out how cold the nights became.

In another hour, Ian's tattered clothing had become inadequate. It was chilly. He gathered Tycho in his arms and settled into the insulation of a hastily created mattress of leaves.

A new sound entered the oasis valley: animals, people or both. When Ian looked behind him, he could see the newcomers. Torches were being lit and cargo-laden animals with being unburdened and led to the pond to drink.

It was time to reveal himself. Ian hoisted himself and his precious cargo up from the makeshift bed and approached the light of the torches.

"Hello! I am from planet Earth. I think I've crashed here, and I've found this baby."

Ian waited for a reply as everyone stopped talking and turned in his direction. I am so screwed, he thought.

What chance is there that they speak English?

There appeared to be about ten of the humanoids. They looked passably human except for their strange clothes and their alien pack mules. Tycho could easily be of their species. Ian noted the group was mostly men, but there were at least a couple of females as well.

One of the largest males carried a long wooden spear and cautiously approached. Ian fingered the reassuring heft of the repeater pistol clipped to his utility belt. He had little to fear from these people.

"Hola. Soy de planeta Earth. Esta tu bebida?" Ian tried some Spanish, but did not realize he had just asked them if Tycho was their beverage.

"Greetings fellow traveller! I am Caro, leader of the caravan. What have you there?" asked the alien male.

"My name is Ian. I'm not sure where I am, but I found this child among the leaves."

Caro looked at Ian expectantly. His spear might be just a walking stick.

Ian continued, "I don't know how to care for it. Do you know who his parents might be?"

"Ian. That is a wonderful child you have, but it clearly is not yours. You are not of this desert. Will you release him to us, his people?"

As Ian hesitated, Caro added, "You are welcome in our land as we always extend the hand of friendship to strangers."

"Thank you Caro. In the name of friendship then, I place this child in your care."

"We accept, Ian. Your generosity is proof of your friendly intent and be assured, it is for the best. On behalf of my caravan, I thank you."

Caro signalled and one of the females came forward to take little Tycho from Ian. Caro approached Ian and grasped him by the shoulders in close appraisal.

"Come, share a meal with us, weary traveller and new friend!"

The food was better than he expected, including some dried jerky, some root vegetables and a sweet tea warmed over the open fire. As to the source of the meat for the jerky, Ian did not inquire.

The caravan people explained to Ian that the great god Jrrak lived in the sky. He had created the world with the seed from His two giant testicles which had then become withered and empty. Hence the two moons.

Once the land had been fertile, and the people multiplied. But Jrrak had been tricked into fertilizing the planet to the point of His own desiccation. His balls hung over the sky eternally, and He could not still his anger. In

108

fact He was so jealous of the caravan people that He let the planet slowly dry out, until it was almost all desert. Jrrak had sacrificed His testicles for their world and the caravan people were therefore constantly tested and tormented by His demands for their suffering.

Only the cries of the innocent could assuage the great Jrrak's fury and that is where the children figured.

"Does Jrrak kill your children in revenge, then?" asked Ian, thinking that the diseases and accidents of such a marginal biosphere could easily be mistaken for divine retribution.

"No, no." replied Caro. "We must provide the suffering so that Jrrak spares us. For every child that is born, only one in ten is spared the suffering."

Ian wondered, could this mean that nine out of ten of their children died before reaching maturity? For a civilization without advanced technology or knowledge of medicine, that was not impossible.

Ian felt pity for the travails of the caravan people until he heard the first screams from Tycho. He ran to see what was being done and it was unthinkable.

The fragile infant was naked, tied onto a tiny wooden rack with only a bloodstained leather pillow supporting him. One of the females had already cut off one of his toes.

"Stop! Don't hurt him!"

"Ian, you do not understand. If we do not provide Jrrak the suffering He craves from our mortal flesh, then He will mortify us all. We will all suffer, including this little one, and no one will survive." Caro motioned to the two grey moons that had just risen again, in the opposite direction of their sun.

Another scream from Tycho squeezed Ian's stomach, driving bile into his throat. Another toe was gone. All the people of the caravan stood in a semi-circle as if absorbing some benefit from proximity to the torture they now continued.

Another toe; another scream. The other female daubed the bloody mess at the end of Tycho's left foot with a paste she continually stirred.

They were making this last as long as possible. Then another toe and Tycho's howls became a constant monsoon of agony.

"Jrrak does not profit from our happiness! He must be appeased," argued Caro but Ian had had enough. The repeater pistol had sixty rounds. That would be more than sufficient.

As Ian began firing at the caravan people, the female holding Tycho saw the others fall around her and rushed toward Ian, holding the child in front of her. Ian could not control his firing. He was shooting everyone. The female fell. Before he could stop firing, no one was left alive.

Ian lowered his weapon and slowly moved towards the pile of bodies. He toed the shoulder of the torturer with his foot and flipped her over. Tycho was underneath, blood spattered and dead. The blood was red.

If there is a God, thought Ian, he likes smiling faces, not screams of agony. Ian considered shooting himself.

Chapter Seventeen

Ian was awake again. The python must be working, he thought.

My thirst has diminished these last couple of hours and hunger no longer chews at my stomach. All quiet on the gastric front. How could a mechanical arm like the silver python relieve my bladder and bowels?

It was senseless to try to reverse engineer the alien technology Ian decided, but there was little else his brain wanted to do.

What type of propulsion system could keep a giant saucer floating in geosynchronous orbit, miles high above Ottawa?

There had been no chemical rockets firing, not any expulsion that could be indicative of mass reaction propulsion. The thing appeared stationary, inert, and silent, as comfortable resting on a cloud as on solid ground. Perhaps it was the same force that gave Ian the impression of weightlessness as he floated in his dim chamber. The saucer was in the upper thermosphere, but still inside Earth's gravity field.

If they can negate my gravity inside this chamber, perhaps they can apply the same force to negate the force of the Earth's gravity for the entire saucer.

Ian remembered that the first time he had been interrogated by the aliens they had been standing not floating. Ergo there was gravity outside his chamber and maybe, hopefully, he was still near the Earth, not on a long one-way flight to a torture chamber inside a black hole somewhere.

Really what was the end game here? If they have interrogated me, have tested me, and have sampled me (another function of the python?) then what further use am

111

I to them?

It seemed likely he would be killed soon.

Life has really taken a bizarre twist on me, thought Ian, then shook his head. His fate was not personal. The planet was surrounded by these saucers. The entire Earth was at risk of extinction. If Ian was to be killed by these aliens, then it seemed most probable that the fate of the Earth would closely match and follow his own.

I must escape, thought Ian.

I am the representative microcosm of this battle; if I can escape, then there is hope that all can survive.

Ian reached over and detached the python again. He felt its tiny tentacles crawl out from under his skin and back towards the silver head. Once fully detached, the python retreated slightly, but stayed within his reach.

Ian tested the limits of his cocoon. His feet were free to move but as he kicked out he could not create any momentum to move away from the gravity-free center of the chamber. He tested his arms with the same result. Now he tried moving his feet and arms at the same time. No progress. He was sweating. Even his own heat could not escape. It was useless.

As he paused to regain his calm, the orange light on the python head re-activated. The python began slowly moving towards him, like a dog sniffing his master's new friend. It had found his thigh and the light turned blue. Ian gasped in pain as it again attached itself against his hip bone. In a few seconds the sharp pain attenuated to a dull discomfort.

The python was attached to the ceiling with a thick black cable. Perhaps he could use it to dislodge himself from his antigravity cocoon. As Ian's right hand found the two depressions again and activated the disengagement mechanism. This time he did not let go. Instead, as the silver device retreated, Ian's right hand traced the black cable as high as possible, and then clasped it in an uncompromising life-or-death grip.

A grinding noise from the ceiling indicated that unexpected additional load on the cable retraction mechanism was significant. Ian was lifted an additional meter above the floor. The ceiling continued to buzz as he used his other arm to strengthen his grip on the cable and bring himself another meter higher.

The release came suddenly, as if by breaching the limits of the cocoon he had disabled it. Ian fell to the floor, landing on his back. He rolled over to relieve the pressure on his tailbone. It was bruised but not broken. He had fallen over two meters onto an unforgiving surface. If the gravity in the chamber had not been significantly less than Earth normal, he might have been incapacitated and his escape attempt halted.

Mindful that the cocoon might kick back in at any moment and snatch him off the floor like prey caught in a scoop-net trap, Ian crawled over to the glowing wall. His fingers investigated where floor met wall. It was perfectly smooth. No activation depressions as with the python.

Was this wall even the exit? He remembered that he had seen the aliens beyond this wall. It was probably acting as a one-way mirror even now, but Ian doubted he was being watched.

Now Ian stood and probed the corner by the window-wall. Floor to ceiling. Nothing on the left. He moved carefully to the right side, keeping flat against the wall to avoid being sucked into the antigravity cocoon again. Ceiling to floor. Nothing.

Last chance is the ceiling, thought Ian, as he stretched upwards, attempting to reach where the glowing wall met the ceiling. His arm length was insufficient, short about ten centimetres, but there did appear to be a small anomaly, a bump, up there.

Ian jumped and tried to grab the bump. There was something there, he felt it.

He jumped twice more, each time glancing the bump with his hand and creating a more detailed mental map of its surface. The topology was simple; it felt like two promontory buttons, close together.

How did these twin peaks work? Would one free him into a corridor and the other spit him into the deadly vacuum of space? There was no information upon which to base a guess.

Ian made another jump and tried to press the left button. It seemed solid. Another leap and he tried the right button. But it did not want to move either. Two buttons and neither accepting a direct frontal pressure.

How else could they work? Were they just sensors that read his fingerprints, his voice print, or the patterns on his optic nerve? Then all was lost, his effort futile. He jumped again.

The buttons were separated by a small but unusual space. They were not directly adjacent; there was perhaps a half cm between them. Why? Could it be that they were intended to slide towards each other and upon meeting up, activate their function?

There was no time to consider the downside of a wrong assumption or to consider alternatives. There was no upside of staying alive as a captive or co-operating with these aliens. He was sure any such concession would provide only a brief and temporary delay of his own death.

He jumped up and squeezed the two buttons together. They closed into a single rectangular form with a tactile snap.

The results were immediate. The glowing wall turned into a window.

He peered through the transparent material into the other chamber. It was full of banks of equipment littered with tiny lights, some flashing, some not lit. There were a couple of chairs with two arm rests per side so the aliens could rest all four of their arms at the same time. He was glad to see that the chairs were empty. This was the good news.

Before Ian could contemplate the bad news, the situation had changed. Two loud popping sounds were followed by a whirring sound and then the transparent panel that had been the glowing wall was retracting into the floor. When it reached thigh height, Ian clambered over it.

Now he was in the antechamber where his interrogators had stood. A large rectangle on the wall opposite the original chamber was obviously a door. There was a small panel next to it with buttons similar to what he had found at the edge of the ceiling in his isolation chamber.

His adrenaline began to spike as he glanced about the strange compartment. He rationalized that perhaps he should delay his inevitable next action in favour of accumulating extra intelligence on the aliens by examining their technology.

Ian identified the monitor first. The colourful fractal patterns mutating there would not have been out of place as a screensaver in his own lab. There was also a keyboard, but the symbols on it were indecipherable, a sort of space Hebrew with lots of extraneous dots and dashes. It had twice as many buttons as a human keyboard, which was not surprising, thought Ian, as the Centaurans had twice as many hands. On each side of the keyboard, there was a long bar with no symbol.

Ian pressed a random symbol in the middle of the keyboard. The fractal patterns on the monitor disappeared and a black box on a colourful background appeared. The order of the symbols was the same as for English; the latest symbol, the one on the key he had depressed, had appeared to the far right of a multi-symbol prompt, backlit with a brighter square of grey.

Ian pressed the blank bar on the right. The symbol he had input disappeared and the grey square moved left. Aha, the backspace button, thought Ian. When he pressed the blank bar on the left the grey square moved to the right. The space bar. For all the familiarity of keyboard operation and conventional left to right sequencing of symbols, Ian was no further ahead. He could not decipher the language. He might as well be operating a Mac in Japanese.

There were no weapons in the room, as far as he could tell. Ian's focus on calm inspection and analysis was beginning to buckle. He could be discovered at any moment. He was getting nowhere. It was time to try the door.

The top two studs on the panel next to the door strongly resembled what he had used to activate the window-wall. He pushed the two buttons together. Unlike his first experience, there was no detectable snap; these buttons moved together smoothly, easily, and sprang apart as soon as released.

The rectangular panel slid away and Ian faced a curving corridor. Multiple portholes on the outer wall streamed wide spectrum light into the ill-lit corridor. Sunlight! Ian moved to the nearest porthole, peering down as he let the warmth of his favourite star caress his face.

Far below was Earth. And they were moving towards it! If Ian could hide until they landed, perhaps he could escape. The portal he had passed through was the same on both sides: a flush panel that was the door plus a small rectangle, alongside at mid-height, containing pairs of buttons, just as he had seen and manipulated on the other side. There were many other such portals all down the

116

corridor. The portholes on the outer wall curved off in both directions with monotonous regularity.

Ian heard sounds emanate from far down the corridor to his left. A door was opening and creatures were emerging into the corridor. He moved down the corridor, away from the noise. Where could he hide? He wondered if the saucer had more than one level. His question was answered when he stopped in front of an unusual looking portal. It had a light above it that projected out a decimetre from its mounting. It was blue.

Blue is for caution or readiness, thought Ian. That was the colour that the python displayed when it was ready to attach. Just the colour you would use for an emergency exit. Ian manipulated the button pair on the suspect door and it slid open revealing a dark man-size tube. There was a colourful emblem or symbol on the rear of the tube.

Does this say, emergency exit, or please place trash in bag before depositing, wondered Ian. He hoped the former and carefully swung one foot into the tube. His foot felt weightless. This made it a little easier to convince himself to follow it with the rest of his body. It was dim inside the tube and once he had cleared the entry, the door panel snapped shut again.

If these aliens think anything like humans, they will likely have the command center at the apex of the craft and the less often occupied mechanical areas far below.

Having a head at the top of their body was something humans shared with these aliens. As Ian's eyes adjusted to the dimness, he noticed a silver rung on the back of the tube. Ian grasped the opportunity to propel himself downwards.

When he reached the bottom of the tube, he found another alien button pair. Squeezing it produced a portal opening into a long, straight corridor. Ian looked both ways down the corridor, failing to distinguish them as in any way unique, before stepping out. He was alone, safe for the moment.

This part of the alien saucer was warmer than the upper levels. A gentle humming permeated the air.

Where can I hide?

Ian examined the doors that lined each side of the corridor. None had the blue light except the portal he had just exited. Like they said in a classic SF video he had seen long ago: sometimes you have to roll a hard six. Ian chose the sixth door to his right. He squeezed the button pair adjacent and the portal slid open.

No aliens inside. So far so good.

The new chamber was narrow and long. Each of its long walls had breaks that crisscrossed from floor to ceiling in a rectangular grid. No doubt these indicated panels covering storage cubbyholes. Some other boxes and tubes were piled at the far end of the room, secured in place with cables.

These aliens are very advanced but they still can't design a UFO with sufficient storage.

Ian nursed this humorous thought like a soldier with an almost empty canteen as he sprawled on the floor.

How could he tell when they landed, and how would he get off the ship? It was unfortunate that the corridors did not provide floor plan diagrams like the building code back in Canada required of most workplaces.

If I had a weapon, I might be in a much better position to fight my way out, if and when we land, Ian reasoned as he began to examine the contents of the room. Each storage cubby could be accessed by simply pushing on the panel fronting it. This deactivated the electromagnets that kept each panel in place.

Most of what he found Ian could not recognize. There did not seem to be any weapons. One likely gun, upon closer inspection, seemed to be an injection system. Useless.

In the third compartment, Ian found a set of tools, including a two-headed axe made out of an unrecognizable black metal. One side of the business end had a sharp point, the other a flat chipping blade.

Could easily be a welder's slag hammer. Up here, it'll make a fine weapon.

Ian hefted it into his right hand. The handle was knurled for grip. He visually imagined the devastating effect of the tool puncturing one of a Centauran's three eyes. He assumed their blood was red.

Could I actually use this on someone?

A good reason not to carry a gun is that it is too dangerous a weapon to allow into your attacker's hands. If someone wrestled this hammer away from me in a fight, I would certainly regret bringing it, decided Ian.

These aliens could have killed me at any time during my seemingly endless incarceration. Do I want to introduce something so crude and potentially terminal to the struggle? Something I might not have the guts to use at all?

If I'd had this hammer when that black dog was threatening me, I might have used it, but I still don't think I'd go for an eye.

As Ian turned the deadly object over in his hands, the door to his hideaway snapped open and an alien pointed an oversized pistol in his direction. The heat-seeking plasti-ball struck his chest with insufficient force to knock him over. Ian's fingers touched the small plastic bead centred and affixed to his chest as its venom drowned his bloodstream and strangled his brain back to blackness.

* *

At the top of the saucer, in the command section, Clerk One was considering interrupting Ship Supervisor's lunch.

119

The medico's full report on the second human test subject contained some very disturbing elements. The human's K index was dangerously elevated. The resonance of this perturbation with the local space-time continuum, especially considering the level of K holes provided by the mass of planet Earth, pointed to extreme disruptions that would only grow worse as the K infiltration advanced.

This was no accident.

This unnatural state of affairs was an artificial manipulation that was clearly a very advanced but anonymous interference. There was another player in their game. This was worrisome in the extreme.

The ship had suffered numerous small breakdowns. The empathic testing gear had not achieved complete success with the last subject. The human had subverted identity revision and managed to take each successive programmed scenario beyond its intended parameters. For this reason the clerk doubted the medico's original assessment of human psychology as posing little threat.

The medical apparatus used to hold the test subjects had also malfunctioned, letting their most dangerous subject loose. If they could get the human far enough away from Earth, perhaps it could be destroyed. The hardest part would be telling the supervisor that their plans needed amendment.

"Report from the power deck. We have faults in inertial capacitors!" Helm Operator Two's stressed-out rumble accelerated the clerk's delicate considerations. They could not persist in atmosphere or land in such a condition. The helm operator understood this, but refrained from making it explicit, retaining hopes for eventual promotion.

"Helm! Prepare to initiate warp back to Position A." snapped Clerk One.

"Preparing warp initiation, worthy one" replied the

operator, clearly relieved its clerk had done the right thing to safeguard their lives.

The clerk started to move towards the supervisor's meditation cubicle. Disturbing the supervisor was as dangerous as facing a K imbalance, and the clerk moved slowly, brain racing to find the most inoffensive words to report the setback.

"Most valuable mentor and benefactor! There is something more."

The clerk paused and shot a warning look back at the operator, its middle eye narrowing. "Yes?"

"The test subject has been re-captured on the power deck."

"Have it sequestered in ER." The Emotional Recovery chamber was used to diagnose and rectify psychological problems for crew. It was a secure facility and had a perfect success rate because failure was not tolerated.

"ER, understood. Your order has been relayed."

"Anything else?"

"No, your worthiness."

Clerk One turned away and the operator detected some hesitancy in its superior as it restarted the pilgrimage to the supervisor's cubicle.

Chapter Eighteen

Ian's brain awoke before his body did. His limbs were unresponsive but his eyes were open and he could see his jailor exit this new cell.

The alien with the weapon had clamped Ian's left arm in both of its right hands, dragged him across the threshold, and roughly deposited him in the middle of the new chamber. One other alien stood beyond the door and waited for the first to rejoin it before sealing the cell.

Ian's head rested on the floor, facing a corner. He could not even blink. The view was of the closed portal and the junction of two walls. This room was brighter and more colourful than the force field chamber. No silver python extended from the ceiling, dangling into his field of vision. If there was anything else behind or above him, Ian would have to wait for the paralytic drug to wear off before he could pivot to see it.

Beyond Ian's view, just outside his cell, the armed alien shot its companion with another plasti-ball. Unfortunately for that unarmed alien, it was not shot in the chest but instead in the middle eye. It fell onto the deck and blue blood spilled from its head.

The first Centauran discarded its weapon and then its body covering. It began scampering down the corridor on all sixes, making a sound its shipmates would not recognize, perhaps a cross between an animal in heat and a monster in pain. Its eyes were rapidly blinking an asynchronous random pattern, a sure sign of madness.

* *

It might have been only a few minutes but it felt like an hour that Ian had lain helpless on the warm floor of the ER chamber before control of his body returned. First to recover were his eyes, sore and dry as he blinked for the

122

first time in far too long. Next came control of his neck and arms. His legs remained awkwardly stiff as he managed to sit up.

Every wall of the room was a different colour, or pattern, or both. The exit wall was the least interesting, a rectilinear pattern with squares of equal size but various shadings of monochromatic purple. The floor was an earthy brown, perhaps the darkest colour Ian had seen on the ship yet, and the ceiling was a light blue, reminiscent of terrestrial sky.

The walls to the left and right of the exit wall had line drawings with various shades and thicknesses of blue on the off-white background, the lines twisting and crossing each other, more akin to thread freed of its spool in zero gravity than any representation. The lines seemed almost blurry to Ian's eyes. Perhaps a 3D trick that worked well for three eyes, but not two.

The rear wall was plain in contrast, but the most tantalizing. A light shade of purple similar to those found on the exit wall formed the background, but the foreground attracted Ian's hopes: it was an arch, a luminous foggy white arch that promised escape. This apparent aperture was only a meter across at the widest point, near the floor, and the height of the arch was somewhere north of Ian's own one point nine meters.

His legs no longer numb, Ian managed to stand. He was thirsty now. This chamber was too warm for a human.

There was a button pair beside the exit, but nothing happened when Ian squeezed them together. He would not be going out the way he came in.

Moving close to the luminous archway, Ian extended his hand and it disappeared into the glow. Startled, he yanked it out. No damage. Try it again. As his hand entered the glow, fingers then palm disappeared, until only a truncated wrist

123

remained visible. There was a space behind the arch he could not see. His hand felt okay, slightly cool, but this was pleasant.

Despite some concern it might be a trap, Ian's decision to enter the arch was not difficult. Violence, fear, and thirst were the push factors. Hope and a more temperate room temperature were the pull factors. Action was the imperative. He would no longer float along, pulled by the current of fate. Ian stepped into the glowing fog.

* *

Clerk One had reached its Rubicon. The danger posed by delaying its recommendation regarding the human subject now outweighed the danger of presenting bad news to a superior. More than career advancement was at stake.

Clerk One had carefully reread the library files about K index and what its elevation in aliens might indicate. There were only a few reported cases but each was worse than the previous. One report likened it to radiation contamination, a deadly plague with a subtle but resilient transmission mechanism, making containment impossible. A second report related a correlation to mass hysteria. Another compared its effects on delicate electronic machinery to high-energy gamma rays. This was not something you wanted aboard your spaceship, and definitely not on the power deck. The n-dimensional magnetic fields used to contain the antimatter were not to be trifled with.

There was no escaping the difficult but correct decision. The ship must return to Point A immediately. The helm was ready to act. It was just a matter of getting approval for this radical departure from the expected mission parameters as laid out by the supervisor.

"Most worthy supervisor," began Clerk One, carefully pacing its words to camouflage its panic. "It has come to my attention that our human subject has an unexplained

124

elevated K index. My research indicates we might experience profound difficulty in escaping or containing the effect it radiates. Our best course of action is to remove ourselves from the vicinity of its original manifestation, this planet."

Ship Supervisor's middle eye narrowed to a linear squint, barely ovoid.

Involuntarily, the clerk's words began to spill more quickly. "If we do not act now then I am afraid our ship's contribution to the mission will be one of negative performance."

Ship Supervisor's middle eye had closed completely. It was defeated.

"That cannot be allowed. Alert the helm. We take action now. Return to Position A immediately," commanded the supervisor.

"Your ultimate worthiness has certainly safeguarded our mission and saved us all," asserted the clerk obsequiously but incorrectly.

The helm operator had an expression of stunned disbelief as it received the confirmation of the return order, its middle eye wide and the outer two eyes crossing, lids at half-mast. The calculations had already been checked and re-checked by the helm assistants who would have found the operator's expression amusing had the situation not been so serious. It was time to go.

The helm operator squeezed the initiation sequencer and the crash was instantaneous, flinging it free of its chair, with none of its four arms preventing it from bouncing off the ceiling.

Chapter Nineteen

I an awoke unusually refreshed and relaxed. He lay upon a clean bed of white sheets in an unfamiliar room, an enclave of unimpressive dimension and free of any personalizing features. A window opposite his bed greeted him with blazing sunshine and a waft of clear, pleasant air.

His sense of dislocation curiously aroused no concern in his thoughts. He lay for a moment, peaceful and content in the calm atmosphere of the room, thinking how well it boded for the day that he could linger here undisturbed by the necessities of life, unmindful of the clamour of work and city life.

Momentarily, a young woman with kind face appeared through an unsuspected sliding panel near the foot of Ian's comfortable bed. She carried a set of light garments, simple and pastel.

"You are awake. Well-rested, I hope."

Ian smiled at his respectful attendant.

"I have brought you some clothing. When you feel ready, come out and join us. There are some people waiting, and they will be pleased to see you again." She handed the garments to Ian and left without further instruction.

What is this place, and why do I not remember coming here?

Ian made up his mind to rise. Sliding out of the bed he noted his underwear, red boxers with little black oil wells. These were a gift from Gale, he remembered.

Where is she?

The fresh garments were well-fitted although likely not much protection against cold.

Ian stopped at the window. Balmy summer air flowed in,

proving the sufficiency of his fresh garments' material. The view was a naturalist's oil painting: a grassy slope leading down to a small river, with a far bank which supported great coniferous trees, towering pines and evergreens. The ground appeared pebbly and a few larger rocks were strewn about. This was glacier country. It struck Ian that he might not be far from home.

The exit panel slid away as he approached it, revealing a long dim corridor leading to a glowing rectangle, the doorway to some lighted chamber beyond. The corridor floor was cool and uncarpeted, but clean beneath his bare feet.

In a few steps, he passed into the bright rectangle and a larger room was revealed: a lounge, decorated in institutional style. Several faux-leather couches lined the walls. His attendant sat on one, hands clasped modestly on her lap, leaning forward and apparently just that moment breaking off a conversation as Ian entered the room. Upon another couch, familiar faces were evident. There sat Gale, his friend Orestes, and his sister Elynna.

"Ian!" cried Gale, and rose to embrace him. The others stood as well, waiting their turn to greet him.

"What has been going on? How did I get here?" Ian questioned his friends.

"They told us this could be a side effect," admitted Gale. Ian's attendant nodded sagely as Gale continued. "And that it would be best for us to be here when you woke to reassure and re-orient you. This is a Kobiashi Rest Centre. Yesterday was Easter Sunday. You came here for a forty-eight hour treatment. You're on vacation, remember? I thought this would be a good idea for your health, you know, living in the city, all the stress you've been under recently..."

The attendant broke in. "Kobiashi Rest Centres

specialize in induced sleep and chemical re-ordering of the body. We restore equilibrium and peak function through the management of body functions while inducing a prolonged period of REM sleep.

For city dwellers constantly exposed to polluted air and high stress levels, it is equivalent to an extended vacation in an unspoiled garden spot, without the video or photos, of course."

"My birthday gift to you, so you couldn't refuse it," explained Gale. "You'll feel normal when we get back to the city, and then you'll probably want to come back here!"

Orestes and Elynna laughed.

* *

The Smiths Falls Kobiashi Rest Centre provided helicopter service back to the city, where Gale took the wheel of the familiar GE and drove them home, to their ninety year old house on Granville Avenue. Orestes and Elynna stayed for a barbecue.

The back deck resounded with earnest but easy conversation and then general clownishness until the light failed and the two guests made their farewells.

Before Ian could tidy their deck, Gale caught him by the arm and kissed him languorously. "Happy birthday, lover. Maybe someday we won't need Kobiashi Rest Centres, when you finally finish your job."

Memory of his workaday life flooded back to Ian: his position with the decommissioning consultation service, New Paradigm Engineering. The nerve-fraying business of final abandonment for oilfield production and manufacturing facilities, the 're-positioning' of personnel and equipment which was turning the oil industry inside out, forcing a large segment of the workforce into re-thinking their careers or untimely retirement.

The UN Environmental Senate had allotted large sums

of capital to be diverted towards the redeployment of these workers, but many still felt hostility towards the emerging manufacturing and service sectors supporting electric vehicles.

Ian was lucky; he was 'redeploying' others rather than being redeployed himself. His work would likely continue well past his projected age of retirement and he would never know the anomie of irrevocable job disintegration.

"Yeah, nice thought. If it's not one thing..."

"It's two others," Gale finished his usual complaint. Ian nodded.

"Next it'll be satellite rain and the El Nino undersea volcanoes ripping up the weather patterns, dust storms in the west, and new seas in the arctic."

"El means the," corrected Gale.

"Hmm? Oh. I'm worried about the heavy-handed threat of environmental destruction dangling over our heads like the sword of Damocles, and you're correcting indefinite articles," scolded Ian, laughing and holding her tighter.

"Definite articles," corrected Gale, smiling over her shoulder as she released herself and turned away from Ian to seek the pile of dishes in the kitchen. Ian shook his head and returned to cleaning the barbecue.

The next morning Gale left early for the long commute to her veterinary practice far across the city. Ian passed the first hours of the day reading and then, as eleven o'clock approached, readied himself for the drive downtown to meet Orestes for lunch.

The freeway was a delight, its nature so different from that during rush hour. Traffic congestion became an obstacle only as he exited the main artery and began creeping along the four-lane streets adjacent to the city core.

Orestes was already in the restaurant and halfway

through his first cocktail when Ian arrived.

"Eight years of friendship," toasted Ian after his rye and coke had arrived.

Ian felt a special bond with Orestes. There was something about his friend that allowed Ian a rare fluency, and he greatly enjoyed the chance to express himself fully.

"And eighty more," affirmed Orestes. They contemplated the flavour of their drinks for a moment before Ian spoke up.

"You know, Orestes, throughout my life my friendships have usually lasted two, maybe three, years then somehow dissipated. I mean, even Gale has been with me for, what, five years now, and factoring in the nature of the relationship, that's some extreme longevity."

"Do I get a medal now?" asked Orestes "For putting up with your idiosyncrasies and maniacal mood swings?"

"Ha!" Ian shook his head in amusement. "Seriously, do you ever wonder what friendship really consists of? Can it be more than the transient paralleling of interests or the meeting of habitués? Certainly all of our voluntary relationships stem from some sort of self-interest, the need to orient ourselves in groups, to find people who can support our aspirations, give us advice and provide a mirror for our actions..."

"So this is what happens when you turn thirty!" laughed Orestes before then leaning forward over his cocktail. "Listen, you're sounding a bit cynical here, Ian. Sure we look out for our own self-interest, but that's only one component. You value my friendship but I'd say you value it more with your heart than your head, as you would have it.

You're not at work here. You don't have to analyze everything with such strict rationality. Although people use rationality as a tool, that doesn't mean they're at bottom completely rational themselves. Be that good or bad." Orestes shrugged. "As you yourself said, you're impressed with the longevity of our friendship. This points to sentiment overcoming pure rationality.

You value not the most immediately valuable relationship you now possess, I don't know, some B-level manager at your firm you feel might be in your pocket. No, instead you value most highly those relationships that have lasted through time, despite whatever shortcomings and deficiencies that might've become evident."

"Yeah. Maybe," nodded Ian. "Perhaps though, sentiment is based in rationality. Our friendship coming through eight years points to its lasting power and therefore its ultimate value. For example, my university friends. Our paths crossed and we understood that our interests and even our fates to some degree were intertwined and this drew us together. We spent time together. Sometimes accomplishing much, sometimes not so much. But our experience was common, shared.

This is where your 'sentiment' comes in. Those who can share memories should be able to share sentiment. Yet, in four or two years, or even less time, when life took us down separate paths, communication was lost. We seemed to lose the sense of each other and again became strangers. This doesn't seem to raise much hope for sentiment over self-interest, does it?"

"Well," began Orestes, pushing the ice cubes around in his drink, "let's assume a larger theoretical framework for the phenomenon. Do I speak your language? Let us define terms.

Now friendship should not be so loosely used as to describe the acquaintances one makes by default when pursuing particular ends. It's too strong a term! And likewise it's almost too weak a term to define the bonds that last throughout life.

We need nomenclature to delineate this quality from the others. Somewhere beyond acquaintances or friends, and closer toward cohab or family, lies an undefined region for which your analysis of quote friendship proves inadequate.

Is it possible that those college friends who later seemed to be strangers did not in fact share your experience, but only your time? Certainly your activities and interests coincided for a time, but what of your interpretation of those activities and interests?

Perhaps it's that we who're more than acquaintances possess not only an overlap of interests and the sharing of time and activities, but also a common philosophy of what we experience."

"Indeed you are correct my friend!" Ian raised another toast to Orestes. "Forgive my mechanistic views of human affairs. The engineer, it seems, must always concede to the artist on these issues."

"Especially if the artist is me!" agreed Orestes.

The chicken primavera was delicious and Orestes seemed in no hurry to leave the table at the conclusion of the repast.

"What are you working on these days?" Ian inquired of his friend as a second rye and coke arrived.

"A new genre, really," admitted Orestes looking suspiciously about himself, ever the writer jealous for his ideas and paranoid of plagiarists. "Sort of the reverse of science fiction. Rather than setting my story in the future, I'm now contemplating a sketchily distant past. Primitive fiction, you might call it.

Rather than tracing the effects of future technology and social development on the human psyche, I am exploring the primitive mind and its first grappling with abstraction and rationality. I'm finding the combination of the limits of their knowledge, their fear-based belief systems and yet limitless imagination, a sublime joy to expose and detail."

"Anything complete yet?"

"One story only needs a bit of polish and then I'm aiming it at New Story."

"That's a good market, isn't it?"

"Yes," sighed Orestes. "They've yet to publish anything of mine, but I still feel there's room for hope. My first novel went to four publishers before it was accepted."

"I remember," nodded Ian.

"Now I'm struggling to keep it out of the web libraries!"

"Hey!" Ian suddenly had an idea for his friend. "Maybe you could write something extrapolating the arrival of the Centaurans."

"The what?"

"The Centaurans, the alien race we've been receiving transmissions from for the last seven years!"

Orestes shook his head. "I don't know what you're talking about."

Ian sat dumbfounded. Transmission to Beta Centauri from Earth had started when he was eighteen. The first Centauran responses had arrived when he was twenty-three. Ian concentrated on his scant memory of the events that had followed. A code to communicate had slowly and painstakingly been established over the next ten years then, for no reason, the aliens had attacked.

Ian suddenly remembered Blythe's comment: more than nine carbons was an insult... Was he really only thirty years old? That was impossible.

He was either dreaming or dead.

Ian realized how comforting and anaesthetizing his surroundings were. His friend Orestes lived across the border, in New York. How could he be here for lunch? More explanation was required. And what of Gale? She was allergic to animals; it was impossible for her to be a veterinarian. Had she not left him for that irrational demagogue from GreenEarth, Miguel, just before Ian's twenty-seventh birthday?

Reality seemed to retreat from all the details of Ian's life. The house on Granville Avenue: it would be impossible for them to afford such a home, unless his job paid him an executive wage.

And what of that job? A decommissioning service? Not too likely. The majority of oil companies had diverted their investment toward new endeavours and left their capital equipment in the field for the creditors who swarmed like angry locusts around the many bankruptcies of the collapsing hydrocarbon empire.

At age twenty-six Ian had considered entering a master's program in engineering. It seemed the only course of action available to him considering the stifling new employment mindset which stigmatized workers of the fading petroleum industry. His unemployment was adding stress to his relationship with Gale. Orestes and his other friends were either far away or not interested in a down-and-out Ian. Nothing in his memories matched the reality of the restaurant and the exquisite chicken primavera he had just consumed.

Returning from these thoughts, Ian looked at Orestes and was surprised to see his friend gazing fixedly at the waitress across the room. The room was eerily silent. No one moved. Ian slowly stood up, his alarm increasing with every heartbeat.

A hole in the wall appeared quite close to him, and through it could be seen an impossible yet strangely familiar room. Ian felt compelled to step through the gap in the wall. He did not want to leave this comfortable world, but the opening pulled him irresistibly. Ian entered the gap

134

and his senses were enveloped by a luminous emptiness as he momentarily passed through some strange middle non-space.

He was back in the ER chamber, his current cell aboard the saucer, but the room was in disarray. Ceiling panels had detached, revealing hidden space between decks crammed with strange conduits and piping. Hanging suspended from a clump of strands, probably fibre optics, was a previously unseen red python.

The archway through which he had returned was now dark and solid, impassable. The ER chamber door, however, was open. An unpleasant dusty smell filled the air. Everything was coated with a white slippery substance.

Fire suppression foam?

Something had gone very wrong with his ride.

Chapter Twenty

Blythe looked about herself, bewildered. Ian was gone. A moment ago they had been running across the parking lot and far away from the alien nun in Blythe's apartment.

Now she was alone.

A destitute-looking man shouted at her from the edge of the parking lot. Blythe was acutely aware that violence and madness had been exploding throughout Ottawa since the arrival of the Centaurans. This was not a good time to meet new people. She strode towards the Robo-Donut but after only a few steps she could see that the fast food establishment was completely deserted.

The shabby figure called her again, this time by name. There was no escape. She would have to confront him.

"Who are you?"

The man was beyond the trailing edge of middle age. His clothes indicated poverty or disregard for convention. He did not smell very nice.

"I am Zarathustra and I have knowledge of Ian Hesse."

"Where is Ian? Is he hurt?"

"I believe he's been taken up to the saucer. I've recently come from there."

"How do you know Ian?"

"I know him very well. Better than I know anything. He is missing a tooth on the left side of his lower jaw, second spot from the back. There are ridges still on the bones he broke in his right foot when he was very young. There are three bones with these ridges. He suffers from a mild astigmatism in his right eye."

"How do you know these things?"

"I've intercepted a transmission that was intended for the alien that is monitoring you, the nun who came to your apartment."

"What do you want?" asked Blythe, taken aback by the stranger's knowledge.

"I need to understand who Ian really is. At first, I thought he was a traitor to our planet and I believed he had to be destroyed. Now I'm not so sure."

"You know about Sister Raymond's imposter?"

"I saw her true face, if you can call that a face."

"It was horrifying," admitted Blythe.

"Yes but think. It didn't look like a Centauran. It's an entirely different type of alien. I believe that it is here to fight the Centaurans."

"Then why was it after us?"

Zarathustra did not have an answer. He just shook his head and managed to look concerned, abandoned, hungry and harmless all at the same time.

Blythe understood they could not stay out in the open for long. They were bound to attract UN forces or out-of-control citizens. Zarathustra denied knowing of anywhere safe, but offered to reconnoiter Blythe's apartment. Perhaps the alien nun had gone. Unable to think of an alternate plan, Blythe agreed.

She waited in the stairwell for Zarathustra, and he was not gone long. The alien nun had departed and now she was stuck with this hobo. She gave him some food and let him stay the night. Unlike Ian, he did not get anywhere near her bedroom. Blythe slept deeply that night, her bedroom door locked. After the mayhem of the past few days, the night seemed absolutely still, as if the city was empty. No screams. No sirens or car alarms. The deluge had passed.

The next day, order resumed on the streets. UN soldiers patrolled in force but no one resisted their searches and orders. Blythe returned to her job at St. John's. There were many new patients but the influx of the freshly wounded had stopped during the night.

The great saucer remained overhead, reminding the city dwellers that they were at the mercy of insuperable forces. No one noticed when its image flickered for a millisecond.

PART 3: PLANETFALL

Chapter Twenty-One

I an consolidated his thoughts. It was possible the saucer had crashed but not exploded. There was evidence of damage but some systems still functioned. A series of small blue lights embedded in the floor ran from the center of the room out into the corridor. Ian followed the weakly lit trail. Blue was the colour of caution, he recalled.

If these are emergency lights, they might lead me out.

The corridor was straight and short, terminating in a T-junction with a longer corridor that curved along an exterior wall of the saucer, replete with windows, which were now black.

Those are not optical windows at all, surmised Ian.

Or else we are in a space of perfect blackness. They must be display screens that show what is outside the saucer, faux windows.

This seemed likely as Ian understood it would be difficult to engineer a truly transparent material with low optical distortion, strong radiation opacity, and the strength of regular hull materials.

Ian followed the curving corridor to his right. The blue lights dotting the center of the deck branched off at every portal. The white foam was less prevalent in the corridor than in his last cell. There were occasional streaks on the wall panels where it appeared the foam had bubbled up from under. Also, some small puddles remained on the floor. Ian carefully sidestepped these.

Whatever was ahead smelled bad, the same reek that had assaulted his nostrils when he had come out of the archway, but more intense. Another portal was open and Ian carefully peeked around the edge, trying to see but remain unseen.

At first glance, the large room was only full of disorganized and upended furniture, four-armed alien chairs and many small tables. No movement. Ian stepped inside. The stench intensified. There were large purple stains on one wall, near the side where most of the furniture had been piled. As Ian moved closer, he suddenly understood and his throat clenched, trying to pinch off the rising bile.

The smell and the stains were from alien blood flung free of now inanimate alien bodies which, along with the furniture, had impacted devastatingly along the interior wall. One alien was fatally intertwined with a chair and crushed almost flat. It reminded Ian of a car crash victim; the alien had been impaled not with a steering column but the legs of a chair. Other crew members were similarly crushed and splattered against the far wall.

This *is* a crash, thought Ian.

Maybe we are back on Earth and safe.

The stench was overwhelming near the bodies. Ian backed out of the room and continued along the curved corridor until he had travelled almost halfway around the saucer.

One doorway that stood open along the inside wall spilled cooler air into the corridor. There might be an exit nearby. The opening had the small blue light above it that Ian recognized; this was access to other deck levels.

He stuck his head inside the tube and sampled the air. It was cool, fresh, and free of extraterrestrial death stink. The silver rungs on the sides of the tube shone with reflected blue light.

Ian grasped one and swung himself into the tube. He immediately began to lose his grip as his full weight pulled him downwards.

The little blue lights embedded in the floor and this tube must be part of the emergency system; the antigravity in the access tubes sure isn't.

Ian grabbed the rung with his other hand and stabilized his position by moving both feet onto a lower rung. The cooler air was coming from below. He descended hand over hand, careful to first seek footholds for each increment of his descent.

He passed two deck levels, their portals wide open, pausing at each to check for the source of the fresh air inflow, and then carrying on. The third deck was the source of the air: a susurration that tickled Ian's ears with the long absent and very welcome presence of air movement.

Ian swung himself onto the lower deck. He could still feel a slight breeze. More whispers of air flow drew him along another curving corridor. This deck was different than those he had already seen, somehow more utilitarian. Also, every ten meters or so there were isolation doors that could seal off the corridor, each halfway open, as if failed. They did look sturdy, like blast doors. Ian examined the rubbery seals along their edges, and concluded the doors were also airtight.

He passed three sets of doors before he came to the exit, a portal located on the outer edge of the curving corridor, similar to the isolation doors in both design and status. The dual doors were partly open, wide enough to slip through, if he dared.

Beyond the portal was blackness and fresh air. Ian could make out a few stars in the sky. It was a dark, moonless night and Ian was blind to the surrounding landscape. But it was definitely a planet, and judging by the compatible air, quite possibly his own.

Ian sat on the edge of the portal and waited for his eyes to adjust. Soon he could discern a bumpy horizon and some questionable shadows nearer his location. He was in the middle of a forest or some type of dense vegetation.

Ian remembered the baby, little Tycho, and was glad this was not a desert. He did not want to meet the rest of the caravan civilization. Unlike in that dream or experience, or whatever it was, Ian was not armed. Perhaps he could find that storage room again and the welder's hammer, but he did not want to go back into the saucer at all.

There might still be a Centauran or two left, and I definitely do not want to risk bumping into one.

His eyes fully adjusted, Ian could now see that there was a long strip of plastic-like material extending from the edge of the exit and very far down into the blackness. It reminded him of the inflatable chutes used for airplane passenger emergency evacuation. In fact, he was quite sure this was a similar system, except that it had failed to inflate.

Ian grabbed the edge of the flaccid plastic ramp and eased himself off the edge of the portal. He had underestimated his weakness, however, and managed to lower himself only a few meters, hand over hand, before he lost his grip and slid the rest of the way, landing heavily on the ground where the final few meters of the chute lay piled in a tangle.

One small step for an alien, a hell of an impromptu luge for a human, thought Ian. Not going back for the hammer weapon was probably the correct decision as it would likely have injured him during this final tumble to the ground, Ian realized. Now he was back on firm ground and alive, uninjured even. This was cause for hope.

The night was very dark. Ian remained squatting by the exit chute trying to orient himself. Soon, a heavy disappointment set upon him.

The stars were wrong. None of the constellations were familiar. This was not Earth. Perhaps it was Beta Centauri, the home of the invaders, but that was only four light years from the Solar System, so shouldn't some of the constellations look familiar from such a similar, in galactic terms, perspective? Worse yet, the Milky Way was nowhere to be seen. Without the light pollution of any nearby city, the luminous grains of the billion stars nearer the galactic center should have been blazingly evident.

And if this was the home planet of the Centaurans, then where was the rescue squad for this crashed saucer? Why was there no ambulance, no fire department, no police force, no National Transportation Safety Board or whoever? It seemed improbable that the alien craft could cross the vastness of interstellar space to find the tiny speck of a habitable planet, but then botch the landing by selecting a location where no one would come to rescue them.

Very dark forest surrounded Ian on all sides except for a long break in front of him, ground cleared by the final moments of the saucer's deceleration as it slid to rest. The saucer must be made of sturdy material not to have broken up as it struck the ground. Ian revisited his evaluation of the landing as a crash, now re-assessing it as a mere hard landing with casualties. After all, he knew of at least one survivor.

There was no way to tell how long the night might last or how cold it might become. At present, it was still not uncomfortably cool and Ian sucked in the fresh air with pleasure. He was alive and free, for the moment. There was no movement around him, no animals to stalk him, no insects to harass him, and no aliens to screw with his mind. Peace. Maybe he would live in this forest for the rest of his days, hiding from the enemy.

Ian yawned. He did not understand why he was still so tired. All the experiences and dreams he had suffered aboard the saucer did not seem to count as sleep. The aliens had probably used drugs on him to manipulate his mind. He felt as if he had spent days without any real sleep. He badly needed some shut-eye.

Any predators would have been scared off by the hard landing, reasoned Ian. He touched the hull of the saucer. Still warm.

If Centaurans come to investigate they will no doubt start with this exit, and then the interior of the craft. If I at least move around to the other side of the saucer, I have a better chance of hearing them before they notice me.

Some twenty meters around the curve, travelling to his left from the exit, there was an extensive thicket of prickly bush half-crushed by the saucer.

Impassable.

Ian backtracked to the exit and followed the curve of the hull in the other direction. After about forty meters, which he estimated was one quarter of the vessel's circumference, Ian again found his way blocked, but this time by the ripped and shattered trunks of large trees. Not having a good idea, but having several imaginatively bad ideas, about what might live in such huge trees, Ian decided against a tree-sheltered rest.

He doubled back toward the exit and found a recess in the hull which provided a large enough surface for him to lay on. But when Ian touched the hull it was still warm and the word radiation mentally materialized, blinking and flashing a warning in his brain. Sleeping here was not a good idea.

Ian stumbled ten meters away from the hull. The ground had been churned by the landing and was relatively soft. He sat down, then curled into a ball and lay on his side. He could resist sleep no longer.

Chapter Twenty-Two

Today is Gale's thirtieth birthday, which should be a time to celebrate her many achievements but she seems preoccupied. It is evening and I am making my famous sautéed mushroom barbecue steak and my sister Elynna is in the kitchen helping Gale prepare the salad.

Miguel is standing next to me, lecturing about the delicate nature of the Arctic Ocean and what else the Canadian government had better start doing if they want to avoid ecological Armageddon. I've heard his argument before, but it will take years before the new fusion reactors make any dent in our energy demands, and therefore the trans-arctic gas pipelines are essential for the short-term stability of the world economy.

Of course, as always, Miguel disagrees, demanding immediate and radical action.

What non-technical people don't understand is that radical means unstable, at least in chemistry. Not the type of thing to advocate, not when six billion Asians are spewing twice as much carbon dioxide as North America did during its peak, which was almost five years ago.

But Miguel is with GreenEarth and opposes fusion power based on dogmatic fears. He ignores the real, measurable, positive impact fusion is starting to have on the true costs of energy.

Miguel is Gale's newest office friend. She works at Environment Canada as a meteorologist but her outgoing, driven personality allows her to meet all sorts of people, some of whom are not necessarily of a scientific bent. Some of them just bent, apparently.

Miguel for instance is a public finance graduate, counting the tax-payer devolved beans that power his corner of big government. This does not prevent him, however, from wading in on technical discussions brandishing political arguments.

His ideas do not concur with mine, to put it mildly. This was evident from our very first meeting. I enjoy a good debate and respect the opinions of others, but what I found so disturbing about Miguel's presence is the way that Gale hangs on his every word, jumping in to protest whenever I land a body blow on his weak arguments.

I don't do this very often as I dislike conflict and so try to avoid it. But I do come from a background of respectful and thoughtful discussion and will support a position if it is unfairly maligned, or its promulgators' motives slandered, as Miguel tends to do.

That is why we are discussing space-based solar power, again. Miguel seems to think that the thermosphere is a delicate ecosystem that we must respect on moral grounds. I view it as a resource to be managed and utilized. Hence our disagreement about how many thousands of solar power satellites would be appropriate in high orbit to harness the power of the Sun for the use of good old Homo sapiens, my favourite animal.

Miguel's argument seems to be that space junk is a threat to wildlife and therefore morally wrong. It would be better for humankind to reduce its own population, probably starting with those from the most immoral and greedy of countries, the democracies.

Miguel sees a beatitude in poverty. If we could unleash the creativity of the under-developed world, all problems would be solved. He rides to work on his bicycle every day, through rain and snow. This explains his excellent physique. Whether the extra time and energy he burns up proclaiming his moral superiority over all who prefer or require a conventional vehicle, be it fossil fuel burning, electric or hybrid, actually surpassed the amount of waste saved by his own transportation choice, feels very questionable right now. I find him similar to, and as annoying as those religious zealots, bigots really, who must convert everyone within earshot.

A couple of the steaks are ready. I try to give one to Miguel but Thursday is a vegetarian day for him. No problem, he can have salad. I pass the steak to Orestes who is being sidelined by Miguel's crazy wife, Aliana. She is monopolizing Orestes, who looks almost comically uncomfortable.

This is the first time I have met Aliana. Gale has never mentioned her, and I suspect it is because Miguel himself never does, but not for a lack of talking apparently. I look at her more closely. She has a weird skin tone and a strange deformity that we all are being very careful not to over-inspect. She has three eyes and four arms. She is able to hold her drink and a plate and still have two arms left over for cutlery and a napkin. She samples her salad as she waits for her steak. If she had more than one mouth she could also eat and talk at the same time, but I doubt anyone here wishes for this.

Now Gale and Elynna pass through the patio door to join the rest of the guests in the backyard. Gale still looks preoccupied and Elynna looks positively grim, shooting me a pained glance that I cannot decipher.

I am still trying to cook the steaks, but they do not seem to be cooking properly. It is physically impossible for slabs of cow to sit in a four-hundred degree barbecue for so many minutes and not cook. I check the temperature gauge again, but it does not admit any fault. This is like a bad dream.

"Ian." Gale is by my side, addressing me, but her hand is on Miguel's shoulder. "It is time."

"Time for what?" I ask but the answer that comes is not

verbal; a giant flying saucer emerges from behind the clouds directly above us.

Some of the guests scream and run while others remain where they are, shocked and still, staring upward. Miguel has sprouted a third eye and a second set of arms, matching the weirdness of Aliana's defects. He grabs Gale and they seem to embrace.

I am about to protest when Aliana grabs me in her four arms. I cannot shake free. Overhead the saucer is losing altitude, threatening to land right on top of us.

The majority of Aliana's eyes look into mine and she says something, but I cannot understand it because I am mesmerized, horrified at the sight of her open mouth, the sharp animal teeth and multiple discoloured tongues swirling inside that foul cavity.

Chapter Twenty-Three

When Ian awoke, the sun was clear of the horizon. Daylight destroyed any hope Ian retained that this was planet Earth. The sun was slightly too small and the landscape was beyond doubt alien; none of the plants were familiar. Also, the gravity was weaker than on Earth, Ian finally realized.

Then his dream came back to him. The memory of Aliana's embrace made him shudder. The barbecue had happened, but Miguel's wife had not attended. She would never accompany Miguel anywhere again, except for the court proceedings that would finalize their marriage endgame much later. But that barbecue was the last time Ian had been with Gale and not known about her affair with Miguel.

It was a painful memory, morphed by stressful sleep into a monster movie. But his present reality was the same monster movie and demanded his full attention if he wanted to live.

Now he could hear some sounds that might be animal chatter. This forest was alive. A giant brown spider, with a body the size of Ian's foot, crawled across the smashed tree trunk next to him. Ian backed away, his fear of insects resurging.

No rescue team had yet arrived, and no other survivor had emerged from the downed saucer. Ian returned to the exit slide and, grasping one edge, began to pull himself up towards the open portal ten meters above. The lighter gravity did help; Ian estimated his body weighed only half what it did on Earth.

The smell inside the saucer had intensified and there was still no sign of any other survivor. I must have that hammer, thought Ian. All the portals were half-open, allowing easy access to all the chambers of the saucer. Ian assumed a safety protocol for crash situations had cut in at the critical moment after landing to ensure that no one would be trapped aboard. We may be very different species, thought Ian, but our engineers still think alike.

Ian moved quickly through the dim corridor and entered the access tube. He found the storage room more easily than he had anticipated, and was soon examining the hammer again. It would be a formidable weapon, especially as compared to his bare hands. The air in the saucer was warm, and Ian was sweating profusely. Was there anything else worth taking with him?

The only other item with a recognizable function was an alien garment. It had four arms, but was clean. Ian's own shirt was ripped and filthy. He discarded it. This would be a worthwhile trade. The upper sleeves worked for his arms, and he turned the inner sleeves inside out, letting them hang down along his side, inside the garment, forming long vents.

What if a bug crawled inside through there?

Ian pulled the extra sleeves out, tied each end in a knot, and then again reversed and inserted them back inside the garment. No longer bottomless, they might serve as substantial pockets.

There was no reason to linger any longer. If a rescue team was coming, Ian would prefer to observe from a distance. He was certain it would be unpleasant to be surprised by whoever eventually showed up. And if a giant towing saucer materialized, he did not want to be stuck helpless inside this wreck as it was removed to some alien scrap yard.

Ian released the hammer to let it drop somewhat slowly to the ground before climbing down the escape chute again. The sun was higher in the sky now, but the air was cooler than inside the saucer. He took a deep breath, dusted himself off, and picked up the hammer. It fit neatly inside one of the pockets he had fashioned from an unused sleeve.

Now it was time to move away from the saucer. Ian needed water and food soon. Away from the reek of death permeating the saucer, Ian noted that he himself was beyond ripe. The new Centauran shirt helped his look but not his smell. All the rest of his clothes he had been wearing since before he left Earth, and although the silver python had kept him watered and fed, it did nothing for hygiene.

The pattern of crushed foliage extending behind the saucer provided the easiest path for Ian to navigate. He kept to the edge and started moving toward the direction where the sun had risen, a slight upward slope. As the sun moved overhead, the temperature likewise rose higher and higher. Soon Ian needed to move into the shade and rest. The thick trees did provide shelter from the sun and Ian found a large rock to sit on.

There he heard a very welcome sound, running water. He followed the trickle of sound farther from the crash clearing deeper into the woods until he found the source. At the bottom of a sloping bank of broken rocks, a small creek gurgled invitingly. Ian moved into the stream with little regard for danger. There might be alien piranhas, electric eels, or leeches, but his thirst did not allow any recognition of these possibilities. If he did not die of thirst, no doubt some alien predator would soon be able to smell him from kilometres away.

The creek bottom was not very steep. Ian waded in just above his knees, and cupped his hands to sample the clear liquid. It was water. Good enough. After a few mouthfuls, Ian laughed. There was now at least a chance of survival. He began to splash himself. Once he was fully soaked, he retreated to his resting rock to drip dry.

There were no animals at the watering hole. Perhaps there were no predators in this forest. A couple of times he had noted underbrush movement and heard the scampering of a small animal, but he had yet to spot any creatures other than insects.

Once dry, Ian decided to have another look at the crash site. Surely someone would come to investigate, and he needed information about the inhabitants of this planet. Gaining the edge of the open area created by the saucer's sliding arrival, Ian looked down the scraped slope toward the silvery bulk of the downed craft.

There were birds on it! They must have been very large, at least man-sized, because their shape was clearly defined even from his substantial distance. They looked rather like budgies and there were about ten of them. Perhaps they had smelled the dead aliens and had come for the carrion, or maybe they were just curious about the shiny hull. One of the birds emerged from the portal and flew up to the summit of the saucer where a small knot of its fellow investigators had congregated. They were too far away for any sound to reach Ian.

As he considered possible explanations for their interest in the saucer, Ian felt like he had been slapped in the face with a feather blanket and the ground began to recede beneath him. He had been captured by one of the giant budgies! Its claws dug into his shoulder, talons curling around into his armpits, pinching tightly enough that he could not escape but not quite drawing blood either.

Ian tried to get a good look at his kidnapper. The beating of its wings made it difficult for Ian to look up. Everything beyond the claws was a blur of blue and white motion. Ian noticed with amazement that, around what could be considered the budgie's ankle was a metallic band, an oval device covered with buttons and controls.

A telecommunications device? A virtual assistant?

His captor wasn't an animal; it was a subscriber.

Chapter Twenty-Four

As his avian kidnapper lifted him high above the forest, Ian tried to keep his panic muted and his brain engaged. Here was his first chance to see the wider layout of this strange planet.

Behind the saucer, a long scar stretched back into the forest, a rumple of torn ground and uprooted trees. Almost parallel to this trail of destruction, ran the little river where Ian had drunk and bathed.

Now they were headed further down the slope, over the downed saucer and away from the rising sun, west in Earth terms. Looking back, Ian noted a substantial mountain range far to the east, rising dramatically above the densely forested slope.

The velocity of the bird was substantial. In a couple of minutes they had travelled perhaps two kilometres and reached the end of the sloping foothills. A few thick patches of tall trees stood among less impressive tangles of bushes. A scattering of oddly-shaped sandy regions dominated the flat land. The creek met up with a larger river on the plain and Ian began to notice spots of development, small adobe-like structures with open-air atriums.

The ground was still too distant for Ian to see these compounds or any possible inhabitants clearly, but soon they were descending toward a huge structure close to the bank of the great river. The building covered thousands of square meters and contained dozens of octagon-shaped cells.

As they approached ground level, more details emerged. Each cell had a central open-air atrium of perhaps one-hundred square meters. The atriums comprised almost half of the structure's area; the remainder, the covered spaces of the boundaries between cells, must be the interior space of the alien apartments, Ian assumed.

The absurd thought that they would crash crossed Ian's mind but, at the last available moment, as their velocity reached zero and Ian's legs dangled just short of the ground, the bird let go.

Golden bird, that direction, two cells, Ian noted as he landed on the ground. This was data he must not forget. On one wall inside the atrium of his destination cell was a life-size picture of an alien bird, with golden feathers and wings extended. This was the direction closest to the edge of the habitat. Only one additional cell separated this cell from the outer boundary. This was the way out.

Ian felt for but did not reveal his hammer. It was still secure in the improvised pocket of his unused lower left sleeve. Meanwhile, the bird had landed behind him. Ian turned around just in time to see it disappear into a doorway on the opposite side of the octagonal atrium.

There was a small clear glass orb embedded in the wall above the doorway, and Ian had the impression that the bird had opened the portal by looking into the glassy orb. The twin half-doors had swung securely shut behind the bird.

Ian walked over and tested them with a slight push. No give. He stared into the glass eye and tried again. No luck. He was locked out on the patio. He assumed he would not be allowed into the house nor tolerated on the furniture. This bird was no wild animal. I might actually be okay for a while here, thought Ian.

If I was its food, it would already have killed me.

Half of the atrium walls displayed artwork. There was a blue bird, a red bird, and the golden bird, each monopolizing one wall. There was also a picture of a group of five colourful birds, at a much smaller scale, on another wall. Of the four non-art-bearing walls, one was occupied by the doorway and glass orb, and one other, directly opposite the doorway wall, had a large, black rectangular panel near the center and then three rectangular protrusions below it. Another glass orb or eye stared down from the top of the centred black panel.

Some small fruit bushes obscured the lower half of most of the eight walls. The floor in the compound was made of an unrecognizable material, resilient yet slightly spongy.

Before Ian could absorb the implications of the patio's amenities, the panels of the doorway swung open and the giant bird re-emerged. It approached slowly, pushing an enormous bowl. Ian froze as the bird passed in front of him and moved towards the wall where the large black rectangle hung.

With one claw, it touched one of the three smaller rectangles, and then pulled free one end of a long flexible tube concealed there. The bird looked up at the glass orb and gave what could only be a command, a short series of melodic chirps, and then water began to flow through the hose and into the bowl it had brought.

When the bowl was about half full, it turned the hose onto the nearby fruit bushes. After another riff of chirps, the flow ceased. The hose retracted neatly as the bird pushed it back into the rectangular receptacle.

The avian alien turned its back and re-entered its home, returning after a few seconds carrying a large sack in its mouth, which it dropped on the ground near Ian.

It turned to the fruit bushes and plucked a small blackish purple fruit with one claw. Turning so that Ian could not miss what it was doing, it tossed the fruit into its mouth and chewed ecstatically, rolling its head. It pulled another piece of fruit loose and tossed it at Ian's feet. Ian picked it up and sniffed it. Maybe he could eat this food.

As Ian examined the fruit carefully, a surge of noise struck him. The black rectangle on the wall was now awash with colour and action; it was a video display. Ian watched dumbfounded as bird talking-heads chirped on the screen and then the view cut away to a large group of birds on a beach, all chirping at once and hopping about excitedly. It looked like one hell of a party. A strange graphic composed of a blue diamond shape with an interior yellow circle followed. Inside the circle were clusters of little arcs, some stacked, some interlocked, each combined in various ways.

This had to be the written language of the birds. After the graphic disappeared, the talking, or actually chirping, head returned. Another set of graphics appeared on the screen, this time sectioned into eight areas, each with symbols that looked like clouds with bits of the bird script alongside. The weather forecast?

What is this? Bird Network News?

In another minute, the screen changed back to the diamond/circle graphic and Ian heard what sounded like several birds chirping the same phrase in unison. Ian's captor was manipulating its wrist device with one claw. The sound on the video rectangle dropped off and the picture went black. The show was over.

The bird hopped near the black rectangle and manipulated one of the lower rectangles. Ian heard a soft humming noise. The bird extended a wing tip and moved it in a circular fashion to emphasize a particular spot on the ground near the black rectangle wall. Ian moved closer to see the spot on the ground that the bird had indicated. It was a hole, perhaps half a meter wide. Too small to escape through. It smelled terrible and Ian quickly backed away.

Just missing the toilet paper now.

The bird emitted another set of chirps and touched one of its wing tips to its nose in a bizarre salute. Ian imitated the bird by touching his own nose with his right arm. The bird seemed to like that. It chirped a blue streak and rolled its head around in a way that would no doubt be very expressive if Ian knew anything about this species.

"Pleased to meet you Admiral Byrd" said Ian, performing the salute once more. Byrd didn't seem to mind the new moniker; it hopped around momentarily examining the fruit bushes and then, with a backward glance at Ian, returned into the covered part of its homey octagon.

The sunlight was starting to fade. Ian could see an intensely ruddy sunset progressing in the west. Even if the actual line of the horizon was blocked by the height of the patio walls, the patch of colour on the visible fraction of the sky was itself breathtakingly beautiful.

Ian's attention turned to the sack Byrd had brought. There was no opening on any side and it smelled of bird, not food. The contents were small lumps that although somewhat compressible did not break apart as he manipulated them through the textile covering. What use was a sack you could not open and didn't know what it contained?

Ian tested the water brought by Byrd. Better to drink now before it attracts bugs or somebody flies overhead and poops in it, he reasoned. And the water was good, cool and clear of grit, and nearly tasteless.

Probably even has fluoride.

When he looked at the sack again, its purpose was suddenly obvious. It was a pillow. Ian drank some more water and then lay on the ground, his upper body sprawled on the pillow. Surely this was a safer place to sleep than the forest.

Only a couple of minutes later, Ian was already proving this.

Chapter Twenty-Five

Ian opened his eyes. Byrd was standing over him, peering down curiously at the shape curled like a fetus around the pillow. Ian unwound himself and carefully stood up, maintaining Byrd in his field of vision.

"How was your night in my courtyard?"

Ian couldn't believe his ears. The giant budgie knew English.

"I slept well. Thank you for your hospitality. What planet am I on?"

"This is" Byrd began, and then followed with a string of rapid chirps. Apparently the name of the planet sounded the same in English as in the native tongue. "But you can call it Chirp-Chirp."

"Do your people on Chirp-Chirp know of others called the Centaurans?"

Byrd shook his head. "That word means nothing to me."

Ian fell silent. If there was no connection between this world and the Centaurans, then it was likely no one on Chirp-Chirp knew of Earth. Perhaps he was irretrievably lost.

"Why did you rescue me?"

"I am a scientist. I study rare animals. You are the rarest one I have ever seen. Obviously you are intelligent, but just as obviously you do not belong here. If you agree, I will look after you while we work together to determine your origin."

"May I touch your wing?" Ian extended his hand towards Byrd.

"Certainly." Byrd opened a wing and Ian felt the smooth feathers against his palm.

Ian looked around the atrium. These birds were clearly a civilized group. He could work with this creature and it would be an historic exchange between two previously isolated cultures. In time, the Birds might discover Earth's location and Ian could return. With the help of these curious-minded creatures, perhaps the Centauran occupation might also be reversed.

With a sudden flurry of wings that inspired Ian to dive to the ground and clutch his pillow, two other birds arrived. They were slightly smaller than Byrd and wore silver body armour.

"Admiral Byrd! The Lochhim have arrived and they have new allies. We need to evacuate this nest group immediately!"

"Very well. Evacuate the civilians to the emergency sanctuary and contact-"

Byrd's words were cut off by the second new arrival lunging at the first, pecking his eyes. Blood splattered on the seamless flooring of the atrium and the first arrival made a horrible noise, a terrible slurred single chirp that seemed like a death moan to Ian. It fell onto the ground and thrashed in pain, its wings spreading and contracting in agony.

Byrd stepped back from the struggle and used one claw to produce a small hand weapon that he used effectively against the attacking bird, driving it into its own death thrash. Byrd aimed his second shot at the innocent bird, putting it out of its misery.

"My poor Bandolerias..." Byrd stood over the bird with empty eye sockets. "We were of the same feather and flocked together..."

A humming vibration began to build inside Ian. Something was coming. He looked up and coming to cover the entire nest was a giant silver saucer. The Centaurans!

A great ruffling noise also arose, and the view upward was blocked by a mass of birds erupting from the group

160

nest, wings beating loudly in panic. They seemed to be attacking each other as much as fleeing. One enormous bird came down into Byrd's atrium and began sparring with Ian's host, lurching at his eyes, intending to peck, but only landing glancing blows against Byrd's body. Spots of blood appeared on Byrd's feathers.

"Get inside! Chirp chirp chirp!" shouted Byrd, but it was too late. Ian again felt the claws of a giant bird digging into his shoulders and watched helplessly as surface of the planet shrank below him.

Kidnapped yet again!

Ian felt for his hammer. It was gone. This entire world had gone mad. Bird was attacking bird. The Centaurans had landed and were battling the natives with various weapons. Puffs of smoke dotted the horizon. Dead birds lay on the ground. Others still struggled in bloody battle against their own kind. The saucers seemed to move closer. Was his captor taking him up to a saucer, or was the saucer coming to kill both him and his captor? Either way, death was likely the short-term result.

Ian smelled burning feathers and heard his captor squawk. Then he was falling through the air.

This is the end, thought Ian.

Even if my acceleration due to gravity is half that of Earth, I will still become a bloody lifeless smudge on the ground in a very few moments.

Chapter Twenty-Six

Ian opened his mouth and moaned in panic, tasting a mouthful of bird-smelling pillow. It was night and he had awoken from a frightful dream. There were no Centaurans on the bird planet. Byrd had not addressed him in English. He was alone in the atrium and the night was very dark.

Ian held his breath for a moment and listened intently. Only the faint sound of the river eventually registered. Ian exhaled.

The night sky was fantastic. Once his eyes adjusted, Ian marvelled again at the spray of stars overhead. Although there was no distinct band of Milky Way stars, the quantity of stars was still great, and many were concentrated in clusters. To an observer on Earth, most stars appeared an undistinguished white, but here blues and reds abounded.

The beauty might have inspired a peaceful feeling in Ian had he been able to shake the feeling that each of those stars was home to a potential threat to his own planet. How could an innocuous conversation about hydrogen fusion wavelengths and other mathematical matters turn into a bloody surprise attack? Clearly aliens could not be trusted. Greater technology did not signify greater wisdom, just deeper greed and wider aggression.

The hammer was still in his makeshift pocket. Ian uncovered it and contemplated its pointy end. The atrium walls were high, at least twice his height. Ian moved to the wall with the illustration of the golden bird then selected the blank wall just to the left of it.

No sense messing up Byrd's artwork.

He struck a spot as high above his head as possible with his hammer. The sharp point sank deeply into the smooth wall. The sound of the blow was muted by the plaster-like wall material. Ian removed the hammer and examined the hole. Large enough for two fingers. He paused to listen again. No alarm raised; no irate neighbour.

This might work.

Ian jammed the left index and middle fingers of his left hand into the hole and pulled himself up. He created another hole above his head, clamped the hammer between his teeth, and pulled himself up another arm length to a higher position.

Now he was halfway up the wall. His climbing skills evidently benefited from the weaker gravity. A third hole, then a fourth. In less than two minutes he was pulling himself up onto the top of the structure.

The group nest was huge. On the far side of Byrd's home, a sea of dark octagonal cavities disappeared into the darkness.

Ian stood up and turned towards the river. There was only one living unit to pass over and he would be at the edge of the structure. Ian moved slowly over the roof, ensuring his tread was gentle. He followed the edge of the neighbour's unit around the pit of their atrium. The outer edge of the nest offered no parapet.

Ian sat at the precipice, legs dangling. The river was louder now and he could see flashes of reflected starlight amid the moving water. The drop from the roof to the river level was significantly farther than into Byrd's atrium. Descent would not be easy and he could easily break a bone, putting him on a path to infection and certain death.

Did he really need to jump? Was escape critical right now? He had food and water. His captor did not seem to have a hostile intent. Was Byrd even a captor? By climbing onto the roof of this bizarre birdhouse, Ian had proven that escape was possible. But was it necessary?

Now that he had the option, it no longer seemed to be his top priority. It might be better to try to communicate

163

with Byrd and to learn as much as possible about this planet before he made any irreversible decisions.

The night seemed peaceful on this planet. Unlike on Earth, there was no one around at night. All the birds were sleeping. No shift-workers here. No students or malcontents up all night drinking. It would be easy to leave here during the night.

No, there is no reason to leave tonight.

With his decision made, Ian returned to Byrd's atrium much relieved. He had some time to think. He carefully descended using as holds the holes he had created earlier. His pillow awaited.

* *

This time, Ian dreamed of Blythe. They walked along a sandy beach, hand in hand, their bare feet tickled by the crash of the surf. They paused to kiss. Her face was warm against his cheek as she whispered encouraging words into his ear. He knew what to do. He would get them home. She believed in him. His plan would work.

Ian's mind struggled to recall the plan. Where was he escaping from and when? If he was with her, didn't that mean he had already escaped? But she did smell a bit like wet bird and an incessant chirping was distracting him from her words.

* *

Byrd was chirping at him. It was morning. The sunlight burst through his eyelids and Ian raised his head from the pillow. No, it was not Blythe's cheek.

Now Byrd was refilling his water bowl. The big bird had brought a second bowl. It was smaller and contained an array of nuts and seeds. Solid food.

Ian's stomach heard the rumour from his brain and immediately began to agitate for action. It growled.

Meanwhile Byrd was facing the video screen, which was

164

again alive with images and sound. A talking head was chirping without pause on the screen. The sound dropped to a whisper and Byrd turned to Ian.

It looked at him a moment without saying anything, then its eyes widened and it gave a squawk as it noticed the fresh holes in the wall beside the image of the golden bird. It hopped on one spot for a few seconds, then poked a claw into the first hole, seemingly to test for depth.

It turned its head to stare accusingly at Ian who tried to look apologetic by keeping his hands at his sides but turning them out. He dropped his head and his gaze diverted to the ground. In a few seconds, Byrd relaxed its wings, emitted some short chirps, and winked oddly.

Byrd hopped toward the door and disappeared for a few moments. When it re-emerged it pulled something from under its wing and showed it to Ian. It was a sheaf of paper and a large black crayon.

Byrd made some marks on the paper with the crayon, similar to the bird script Ian had seen earlier on the screen, and then handed it to Ian, who gratefully accepted it. Byrd knew he was intelligent, Ian realized. Here was his chance to communicate.

Ian quickly wrote his name on the paper and showed it to Byrd, who promptly tore off the sheet and kept it, tucking it away somewhere under its wing. Byrd raised a wingtip to the sky and traced a circle while chirping and looking directly at Ian. It was a question: where do you come from?

Ian sketched a sun with blaze spikes at the center of the page. Four inner planets. Dots for an asteroid belt. Two gas giants. Two more moderately sized outer planets.

He drew a square box around the third planet and tapped it with the black crayon as he showed it to Byrd. He tore off the sheet and handed it over.

165

On a third page, he drew a large circle, and within it sketched the shape of familiar continents: North America, South America, a bit of Europe and Africa peeking around the right edge of the circle. He drew an X where he hoped Ottawa still was, tapped it meaningfully while looking at Byrd, and then tore off and handed over the sheet. Byrd looked at it carefully before also stowing it underneath a wing.

Byrd indicated with a wingtip one of the smaller rectangles underneath the video screen, chirped twice in rapid succession, then launched into the air.

Ian was again alone and unsupervised.

Chapter Twenty-Seven

Ian was famished. While the ministrations of the silver python had kept his body fuelled during his stay on the saucer, he had been on the bird planet for two nights now and had eaten only that one piece of fruit Byrd had tossed him the previous evening.

He first now gorged on the large, oblong blackish berries supplied by Byrd's bushes. They were sweet, seedless, and tasted better than anything Ian could remember. They were not very symmetric, basically ovoid, but the stem side was slightly narrower than the bottom. Based on their haphazard geometry, Ian dubbed them blobberries.

Next, his attention turned to the bowl of nuts and seeds that Byrd had pushed into the atrium before flying away. One hand-sized, yellowish nut was too tough for Ian's teeth to do much more than leave furrows scarring its resilient spheroid surface and deliver some very meagre shavings onto his tongue for consideration.

For the amount of effort necessary to acquire this taste, it was disappointingly bitter.

He found another type of nut, pale and crescent shaped, that was more easily chewed. These he found delicious, slightly reminiscent of Brazil nuts. There were several types of smaller seeds near the bottom, the Bird Planet equivalents of sunflower and pumpkin seeds.

Ian enjoyed his meal and the empty pangs within his stomach were rapidly replaced with fullness. A few gulps of water clarified the situation. He needed a toilet. A familiarity with squat toilets gleaned from his international travels rendered Byrd's atrium toilet less formidable.

The weather was excellent again today. Ian had arrived during a clement season. He wondered what would have happened if he had arrived in winter, if they even had winter here. Would Byrd have left him out on the patio in a cardboard box? Ian resolved to be kinder to feathered creatures if and when he managed to return to Earth.

The video screen continued to make soft whistling and chirping sounds. Ian was missing the program. Here was a chance to learn about this planet. The content was not so different from Earth: a talking head delivers a stream of verbiage, cut to shots of whatever was being discussed with the monologue continuing on the audio track, additional information or captions appear along the top of the picture, some of it scrolling past. The fact that the captions were at the top of the screen was the reverse of Earth, otherwise the similarities were striking.

The bird script and sounds meant nothing to Ian, but the views of the planet and its civilization on the screen were enlightening. Birds congregated on beaches, in trees, amidst great buildings in an urban setting. The view of the bird city was a surprise; it was a very dense cluster of perch-laden towers.

Many of the birds flying there carried a sizable bag attached to their feet with a cord. Bird purses, briefcases, or cargo to be delivered? Maybe all three. Some of the birds did not appear to be carrying anything, but Ian recalled that Byrd seemed to have some storage capacity under each wing. A few birds carried very small bags, others mid-sized ones, and occasionally Ian saw a group of four or six birds all attached to some large cargo they transported as a group.

Truckers.

The next story was a forest fire. Birds carried containers high above the plumes of smoke, and dumped a liquid retardant, probably water, onto the flames.

Birds in a vast chamber with walls covered in electronic displays crammed with tiny bird script chirped excitedly.

Traders? Politicians?

A great number of birds crowded along the edge of a large building that had only a few entrance perches evident on that side. Access was controlled and a long lineup of grounded birds extended far out of frame. Ian noted there were some birds that seemed to be in control of the crowd; they paced along the side of the line and occasionally flew above those waiting. No other birds were in flight. Anyone wanting to join or leave the line had to walk or at least hop in a very restrained way.

The control birds wore a mark of authority: a small pointed black hat resting on their crown. Barely discernible, far overhead, a large mesh net let through sunlight but no queue breakers or escapees.

One segment even Ian could decipher as a humorous commercial. A bird with feathers ruffled and mottled due to age is standing in a crowd. Suddenly the other birds leap into flight and leave it behind. The bird blinks and then reluctantly hurtles into the air. A loud thump is heard and we see two feathers are left, plastered against a reflective wall as the bird slowly slides down the vertical surface like a cartoon character. In the next scene, the same older bird is wearing a pair of optical lenses. It leaps into the air, swerves at the last moment to avoid an obstacle and then, tilting its body, its wing span vertical, glides through a narrow opening between two trees. It lands in a forest and performs a brief victory hop.

After that segment, Ian watched for another hour but little else made sense. Birds talking to birds. Lots of bird script flashing by on the screen. Most of the activities on display probably had an analogue in the human world, Ian reflected but, for much of it, he was unable to make the connection.

Byrd had indicated the rightmost rectangle under the video screen before it left. Before *he* left, assumed Ian.

To think of Byrd as male humanizes it. Byrd is an individual, a person, definitely not a low order of animal. Anybody who pays their own stream access fees deserves at least a name and a sex.

Ian pressed the rectangle. Nothing happened. He pressed harder and it yielded a very slight retreat, but enough. The video screen went blank and the incessant soft chirping that accompanied the picture also disappeared. Then the only sound was the gentle breeze rolling across the group nest roof line.

Ian pressed the button again and the screen sprang back to life. Satisfied with his mastery of the controls, he activated the button a third time to reintroduce silence. Ian suspected Byrd would be gone all day. He would have time to study these broadcasts later. Right now he needed time to think.

Events had gotten far ahead of Ian's anticipation or analysis. He had not yet entirely recovered from the original attack that had left him in a coma these last two years. Having lost his wife, Gale, to the unspeakable Miguel, and then seen his career shipwrecked due to the Energy Transformation Act, he had thought he was at a personal nadir. But then came the attack and its aftermath.

When Ian had emerged from his long coma, the world was in turmoil. People were going mad all around him, a wave of senseless violence springing from the most unexpected quarters. Then came the alien invasion, but the aliens were not the cause of the violence. In large part, the invaders were the victims of the contagion just as much as the humans. Ergo they were not the cause.

As Ian hid with Blythe in her apartment, they had been confronted with another alien, one disguised as a nun who was known to Blythe. Certainly that alien was not part of the invasion force. It had not tried to harm either Ian or

Blythe, but the insane violence that Ian had first heard about and then witnessed upon waking at the hospital had followed them to Blythe's.

It was as if all the luck in the Universe had been drained and all that remained were the worst case scenarios, and these all arrived at once, piling up, re-enforcing and amplifying each other.

Perhaps I am cursed. But what does that even mean?

After Ian was aboard the saucer, he had experienced no further evidence of his deadly curse, but how many humans had been captured by these aliens? There were no others on the saucer. His luck had been singularly extreme and bad. What were the odds of being the only human whisked off the planet and then having your saucer crash?

Air and space craft were some of the most highly engineered, tested, and safe modes of conveyance on planet Earth. What were the odds a craft designed to travel between stars and engage in military operations would be so prone to failure? The odds of his misfortune boggled Ian's mind.

But his luck had changed since leaving Earth. Sure the saucer had crashed, but he had survived. The only survivor. And he had been rescued by a caring entity. Now he was being fed, watered and entertained, a guest in what appeared to be a safe environment.

Such a reversal of fortune was staggering to the reasonable mind, but there was an alternate explanation. If something is too fantastic to be true, perhaps it isn't true. Since his incarceration on the saucer, Ian had been plagued by a series of scintillating dreams. Which were real dreams and which were drug- or mechanically-induced hallucinations, and finally, which, if any, were real?

His dream of Admiral Byrd talking to him in English could not have been real. He was awake now and reality

171

contradicted that experience. Maybe he would wake again and be back at St. John's. Perhaps he had never recovered from the coma at all.

Like Plato's allegory of the cave, was he seeing only a stirring of shadows on a cave wall, and letting his brain present a wildly incorrect extrapolation of what was happening outside, in the sunlight? However, he realized, it is a futile premise to discount the data of one's own senses.

The dream in which the birds attacked each other as the Centaurans arrived had been just that: a dream. It had not occurred. Everything on this bird planet so far has agreed with physics and the generally agreed upon constraints of reality. If Ian was mad and hallucinating, then the symptoms were gradually moderating. He might still be delusional, but at least the violent edge had been removed.

There must be a kernel of reality in all this. I know I was attacked in my car. If I assume I actually woke up in the hospital, then I accept that it is now two years later and Earth has been invaded by aliens. Perhaps the shock of that invasion pushed me into a psychotic state.

But I got close to Blythe after the invasion began, when we fled the hospital together. Was that a delusion? Blythe did seem a bit like wish fulfillment. Why exactly did she hook up with me? And in her apartment, when she gave me the wine and cannabis, might that have been the point of departure? Possibly the joint had been laced with something nasty. Or maybe I still have a concussion and my brain is firing randomly, the stuff of nightmares and dreams slipping over the protective mental levees and spilling into my conscious mind.

Everything since leaving terra firma has been more and more fantastic. At what point do I simply stop believing in what I am experiencing?

172

Chapter Twenty-Eight

S ister Raymond appeared unexpectedly at Blythe's station accompanied by one of the re-purposed UN peacekeepers. The soldier's blue helmet still said United Nations but the UN was now only a proxy, supervising the Earth on behalf of the Centaurans.

"Blythe, this is Captain Sanjay Vendamarasamy."

The soldier allowed Sister Raymond only this introduction before he took over.

"I am investigating some of the violence from last month. Have you seen this man?"

The Captain offered Blythe a sheet of paper bearing two pictures. One was a young man, perhaps twenty, with dark features, intense eyes and unkempt brown hair. The other photo was slightly blurry, probably the same man, but now showing the ravages of decades of life, his hair shot through with grey and face beset with wrinkles.

"Don't think so. Sorry," lied Blythe.

"Have a good look. His name is Zarathustra Bruns. He's got schizophrenia. He's been treated at the Royal Ottawa in the past. We believe he might be responsible for attacking two of my men. One was shot dead, and the other is, well, incoherent. You know the troubles we've had."

Blythe nodded and made a show of examining the pictures more closely. It was true that the incredible storm of violence that accompanied the Centauran invasion could not be explained simply as the collateral damage of military actions. Human-on-human violence had spiked incredibly, with many bizarre murders and suicides as well as other destructive behaviour erupting from otherwise ordinary people. Blythe had treated the victims from countless acts of random and irrational violence in the days following the start of the Centauran takeover.

173

"No. Pretty sure I haven't seen them."

"Him. It's one person. The same person. Zarathustra Bruns."

"Oh, okay. Why do you think he killed your man?"

"We found Mr. Bruns prescription for anti-psychotics on our officer. We suspect he attacked when they examined his identification."

"Well he doesn't look familiar. And with a name like that, I think I would remember. Sorry."

The captain reluctantly accepted the glossy photo sheet back into his care.

"All right. Thanks for your help."

As Sister Raymond and the captain walked away, Blythe forced herself to stare down at her paperwork. A few seconds more and they would be gone.

Blythe remembered her first face-to-face meeting with Zarathustra. One moment she had been running across a parking lot with Ian, escaping from the unspeakably ugly alien who had disguised itself as Sister Raymond and now showed no sign of vacating her apartment, and then the next moment, Blythe was all alone. Ian had vanished. It was then that Zarathustra had presented himself.

* *

Dr. Joberkt was pulling an extra shift. The flow of victims had slackened since Red Tuesday, the day that the mass insanity had ebbed and everyone had crawled out of their hiding places to be confronted with scores of bloody victims strewn about. Some had been killed resisting the NACEO forces, but many more had died as the result of inexplicable human-on-human violence.

The Centaurans spun Red Tuesday as the day the resistance of the general population collapsed, but Dr. Joberkt realized it was a much more local phenomenon. The madness and arbitrary violence that had shaken Ottawa was confined to a relatively small area surrounding the St. John's Rehabilitation Institute and its co-located parent, the Royal Ottawa Medical Centre.

Now the casualties were coming from a wider region and were usually the result of people inadvertently getting in the way of the Centaurans. If you did not work directly for the Centaurans, they did not know your function and therefore ascribed you no value; you were considered a second-class citizen and so could be injured or killed with impunity.

Dr. Joberkt had just finished applying some steri-strips to the sliced finger of a prep cook when Blythe pulled him into an empty examination room with the whisper "Code White Two". That meant insurgency business.

"They're looking for Zarathustra," she said without preamble once the door was closed.

"You denied knowing him?"

"Of course."

"Where is he?"

"Still at my place," admitted Blythe.

"Do you think they suspect you?"

"No. I think they were showing his picture to every nurse in the entire complex."

"Okay, good. Then he'll stay with you until we can move him somewhere safer. I'm sure the Cents have great optical surveillance so don't let him go outside, and make sure he keeps the curtains drawn."

* *

Zarathustra knew his own madness. This was his advantage. He had seen unreal things, some horrible and some wonderful, but he always kept his reaction to a minimum until he could sort and decipher his thoughts, gather supporting or contradictory evidence, and make a decision based on as rational a frame of mind as he could manage. His madness had allowed him to refine an attitude of careful skepticism to things both external and internal.

The invasion had pushed his equanimity to a new level. While everyone else around him were losing their heads, leaping into conflict and violence, Zarathustra stayed calm and tried to understand the real situation.

By the time he was captured and then released from the saucer, Zarathustra considered himself an expert on aliens *sine pari*. The amount of information in his head regarding Ian Hesse was phenomenal and the source was, without doubt, alien. His brief incarceration aboard the Centauran saucer was another unique qualification.

When Zarathustra had introduced himself and shared some bizarrely detailed anatomical facts about Ian, including dental history and an old leg injury, Blythe thought he might be confabulating. But when she returned to St. John's the next day and accessed Ian's records, she was baffled to find that everything Zarathustra had said was collaborated by the medical records. Perhaps this mad man was not so mad after all.

It was clear that Zarathustra hated the Centaurans. He had spent his life nursing grudges against imaginary foes, endlessly replaying any perceived slight and innuendo delivered against him while sifting for clues about the nature of his tormentors' powers, dodging any contact with authority due to a deep distrust for those who did not see the same world as he.

The world was under attack and had been for a very long time. Only now was the realization starting to dawn on both the sheep and the wolves who kept them in place. The conflict between rulers and ruled could no longer be rendered invisible, painless, indeed even gentle and reassuring by the manipulation of the political, education and economic systems.

When the Centaurans had arrived, the cat was out of the bag. Finally it was clear that an attack was underway. The existence of Illuminati and space reptile Overlords could never be proven, but the mask had now been ripped away and, although the details were different, the outline was the same. Earth versus them. And some on Earth, those who sought to smooth over everything and anything, including even the genocide and enslavement of their own people, had capitulated for some small advantage in these end times, or perhaps a small mercy in the delay and manner of their execution.

Today Zarathustra smelled better than he had in a long, long time. The coconut body wash smelled delicious and he had not scrimped on its application. Nurses make good money and Blythe seemed very prosperous to him.

After his initial discussion with her, on the evening when Ian was snatched, Blythe had still seemed unsure of him. It wasn't until two days later, when he approached her again, this time with a request for a few dollars, that she seemed to believe he in fact did possess alien information.

She had taken him to Robo-Donut for a coffee and they discussed some of the details of his trip into the saucer. They agreed to meet again and, over the course of their next two meetings, found a convergence of purpose.

For Blythe, her hatred of the Centaurans was both personal and global.

There was Ian's disappearance. She believed Zarathustra when he said that Ian had been taken aboard the saucer. Despite or perhaps because of the dangers they had faced together, the initial feeling of rightness between her and Ian had been strong and grown further in remembrance.

Also, the Centaurans had slowly infiltrated St. John's, taking over a few rooms here and there, performing strange procedures on their own kind and occasionally even taking humans and turning them into something useful perhaps to them but horrifyingly subhuman. You did not confront or question the Centaurans or you risked undergoing their 'robotomy' as the medical staff called it, but always in furtive, hushed tones. You were robbed of your humanity but your body lived on.

She had seen Dr. Bergemon, their top neurologist, confront a Centauran who had annexed some of her clinical trial space. The next day, Dr. Bergemon was gone. Days later Blythe recognized the doctor as one of the UN uniformed staff protecting a shipment of equipment arriving at the hospital. Her eyes were dead and robotic, scanning for threats but recognizing nothing of her previous domain. Blythe did not approach her.

Zarathustra shared Blythe's hatred for the Centaurans. He blamed his disease on alien intervention. With his brain constantly bombarded by strange ideas and images, impossibilities presenting themselves as memories, how could he function normally?

His was the opposite problem of those who had undergone robotomy. He had not been robbed of his mind; it had been sublet against his will as an alien warehouse and the stored materials were toxic and disruptive. At first he had blamed Ian as a conduit between the aliens and himself, but now he agreed with Blythe that Ian was as much a victim as he.

Zarathustra doubted the Centaurans would honour their promise to depart in five years, as did Blythe. While many on Earth were content to keep their heads down and not question their new masters, preferring to believe their hollow promises instead of risking all in a conflagration, others had started to consider insurgency. The first steps were organization of resources and intelligence gathering. Action would come later.

Zarathustra sprawled on Blythe's couch, surfing news sites. He would share whatever information he obtained only with Blythe. He would scan the news streams for any sign of insurgency. He would do what he could to free Earth. For the first time in as long as he could remember, his goals aligned with the majority of his kind.

Zarathustra had been called dysfunctional, unemployable, sick, and worthless. He had always believed that the line between madness and genius was a social invention. Those with lucrative or socially useful outlier ideas were geniuses. Those with unique views that did not generate economic activity or support the status quo were simple mad. Zarathustra felt he was now approaching that line.

INSURGENCY FAILS

The headline caught his attention. A major news site was reporting that the sudden decline in violent incidents since last Tuesday indicated that the human insurgents had given up and were waiting for the five-year plan to run its course before taking further action. Perhaps it is time to trust our new masters and complete our agreements before losing the moral high ground by the use of violence, the site suggested. In fact, it claimed, the crime rate had actually gone down since the Centauran arrival. With the influx of new technology and a more stable social order, the Centauran-Human alliance was providing exemplary governance, so why would anyone resist the NACEO?

That is not what is happened at all, thought Zarathustra.

The crime rate had spiked when the Centaurans arrived, but abated shortly after Ian had gone missing. Perhaps the aliens turned off their 'crazy beam' or whatever was causing all the random mayhem at that time. In any case, the report described the opposite of the likely reality: the Centaurans were the cause of problems, not the solution. And most importantly, the insurgency was not terminating or even pausing, it was gestating.

A small green spider crawled out onto the great plain of Blythe's coffee table. It paused at the edge of an almost dry coffee ring. Zarathustra did not hesitate to casually squish it with his empty mug.

Chapter Twenty-Nine

Ian raised his face to the alien sun. Warm. Everything here was so real. The taste of the blobberries, the smell of his pillow. If he had to discount everything he knew to be improbable, there would be nothing left. If he could not admit he was on this alien world, if he must disallow everything unfamiliar, then he would be left without any anchor, adrift in sensory revisionism, a miasma of impenetrable shadow. If he was mad, there was no hope at all.

No, thought Ian.

I am sane. It's possible that this is all some type of alien simulation or virtual reality, but that won't change my reactions or my determination to understand and master my new reality. Just because I can't perceive the order in the system doesn't mean the system doesn't have order.

There are underlying principles and reasons for everything. Something caused that saucer to crash. Something caused all the mayhem on the Earth, which coincidentally started the first day I woke from my coma.

If I can learn to communicate with Byrd's kind, perhaps they have the technology to return me home.

But what is their relationship with the Centaurans? Are they foes, allies, trading partners? Maybe there is no relationship. Perhaps the Centaurans are using Byrd's planet as an unwitting staging ground for their war against the Earth.

Byrd's civilization seemed well-ordered, peaceful. But in the complex of international or interstellar politics an empire could, in the name of its own interest, attack innocents far away. Citizens of the powerful empire would be fooled by their own propaganda into consent or inaction. This had been the history on Earth. If alien birds had video

181

new streams, then why not the interstellar equivalent of blood for oil?

The unpleasant possibility that the bird planet and the Centaurans were in collusion walked across Ian's brain as if in golf shoes. This could be a fatal blow to his hope. Was Byrd contacting the authorities and even now was his handover being arranged?

Ian shook his head. The pieces did not fit.

Byrd had not put him in a cage. Byrd must know Ian could escape; he had seen the line of fresh holes punched into his patio walls and been upset, but he had not fixed the holes. His objection was therefore aesthetic, not functional. You don't replace the carpets until after the children are grown.

Byrd had never searched Ian. The hammer, his only weapon, was still nestled inside his stolen Centauran tunic. If Ian was a captive, Byrd was a rank amateur.

And what of the crash site? If the Centaurans and the Birds were allies, there should have been a rescue effort at the crash site. The few birds that Ian had seen on the downed saucer were not a rescue team. More like curious passersby. This might mean that the Centaurans were unknown to them, or a crashed saucer was so commonplace as to not elicit any wonder. Certainly if the first Centauran saucer to land on Earth had crashed, there would have been substantial attention and resources given to investigating such a bizarre arrival.

The psychology of the birds might be very different from that of humans, but the evidence so far did not suggest this. Ian was being cared for in a manner very similar to a bird with a broken wing might be cared for in the backyard of a human. But Ian was no wounded bird. He was an intelligent creature. Byrd knew this. Byrd had given Ian paper and a writing instrument. Byrd had left the video screen on for him. If Ian had found an intelligent bird creature, he would have done more than keep it as a pet. What was really going on here?

Ian's thoughts were forming a funnel cloud in his mind and all his energy was being drowned by whirling gray dervish of uncertainty.

This planet is real. Real confusing.

Ian approached the blobberry bushes along the wall with the five-bird mural and scanned for an appropriately plump specimen. There on the back wall sat a grotesquely large brown spider.

A shiver ran up Ian's spine. The spider was immobile, perhaps long dead and desiccated. Ian reached for a particularly symmetrical blobberry in front of him, but as his hand touched the bush, the spider began to wiggle its legs, threatening to launch itself at him. Ian withdrew his hand and backed away.

The spider had successfully defended its blobberry bush. Ian returned to his pillow which lay near the golden bird picture, on the side of the patio without any vegetation, to reconsider his situation.

This is ridiculous. I need to eat.

Ian extracted the hammer from inside his shirt.

I didn't survive crossing the interstellar void and escaping from an advanced alien invasion force only to go hungry because of my fear of insects.

Ian approached the bush again. There were more spiders apparent now. They liked to stay along the back wall where the bushes provided a little cover. Ian reached toward the previously selected piece of fruit but as soon as his hand entered the vicinity of the bushes, the spider began to flex its legs. Ian withdrew his hand.

How will I ever sleep on this planet again?

The spider was still. Ian brought the hammer up slowly,

inhaled to steel himself, and then jabbed at the overgrown arachnid with the head of the hammer. The damage was done, the spider's body had been pierced.

As Ian pulled the hammer back, the spider's body came with it, stuck to the tool with a coating of its internal slime. The long legs twitched, one tip brushing against Ian's hand.

"Gah!" shouted Ian as he dropped the hammer. As it tumbled onto the ground, the spider came loose. It was no longer moving.

"Yes!" Ian hissed through his teeth. He retrieved the hammer and cleaned it with some blobberry leaves and re-sleeved it. The other spiders did not react to their fallen comrade. Ian plucked another couple of blobberries, enough for lunch, and retreated to his pillow to eat, perhaps feeling more optimistic than his small victory warranted.

More information about this world was what he needed. Ian got up to push the rectangle that activated the view screen.

The image that formed was a shock. There was a second saucer in the forest! The image was a bit jerky, as if taken by an amateur. Bird script scrolled along the top of the screen. If only he could read it, what might he discover about this planet and its relationship with Centaurans? As it was, he could only watch the images of four-armed aliens carrying equipment from one saucer to the other.

At one point, they also appeared to be removing a body. In a few minutes, the montage began to repeat. The birds were finding this news story, whatever it meant, worthy of repetition.

The news continued with the usual stream of confusing bird-life images. Ian continued to watch, hoping for enlightenment.

Much later in the day, the saucer story was repeated a second time. The clip of Centauran activity near the saucers was repeated several times and the bird script at the top of the screen continued to roll as the voice over chirped insistently. The story was exciting, whatever it was.

All this video watching had given Ian enough information for a first draft impression of Bird society. They had an ordered civilization. There was no indication of wars or conflicts. They had technology, including electronics, and the ability to build large structures.

Unfortunately there was no indication of transportation technology. Birds flew and carried what they needed, sometimes as a group. Without the development of the automobile or the airplane, why would they develop space flight? And there was no indication that they had. Nothing he had seen on the view screen gave Ian any hope that Byrd or his people could help him leave this planet.

Slowly the unpleasant but inescapable conclusion formed in Ian's mind. The only way off this planet was aboard a Centauran saucer.

Chapter Thirty

At 2:30 in the afternoon, bright sunlight leaked through the thin material of Blythe's living room curtain. Zarathustra was fast asleep on the couch and dreaming when the 'nun' returned.

The creature that closely resembled Sister Raymond was not hindered by mechanical locks. Knowing its target was asleep, it entered the apartment swiftly and immediately began to scan Zarathustra's brain.

It would be leaving this planet for the last time soon, and now would be the best chance to correct the earlier 'accident'. Although this act was outside its mandate, the alien was intent upon additional measures in the interest of interstellar justice for this little planet.

* *

I sleep in a warm place. My mind is at ease. Where is this? Womb-like. Black velvet bed, no, there is a light, now there is much, I am a galactic cluster. My mental tendrils touch the farthest corners of creation. Force at a distance, creation at a distance.

I can taste the nebula, a sweet orange milkshake that is so good but now, suddenly, I move at the speed of light, back to Earth, to observe many things happening simultaneously: a man leaps from a window, a woman is stabbed, a building collapses, a church congregation erupts into a bloody brawling mass that spills onto a street where road rage has become the organizing force, cars slamming into buildings, pedestrians, and each other.

I see a sinew of energy flowing from each person in each situation, it is a dirty tobacco brown colour but there are swirls of golden specks inside, floating brightly, like diamonds in sewage.

I feel like I am supervising a slaughter. I can almost

hear the lamb bleats of fear. I hope it is not me. There is a rising feeling of panic all around and I vow to escape from these events. I will find those responsible. Nothing is by accident and I will not be an accident. I will be an actor on the stage of life, with a role to play and a particular end with a particular meaning.

I force my eyes to follow the stream of foul glitter rising from a woman who is smashing the furniture in her living room. My mind sees her clearly and then I follow the stream back towards its source.

I see NACEO soldiers everywhere. They seem unaware of the brown strands that twist into the sky from so many roots, like a malevolent tree. As this single branch merges into another, and then larger and larger branches, I see a nexus form in the thickening trunk of golden plasma transmission. It reaches higher and higher into the sky. What is it? It glows now, as the atmosphere drops away and darkness envelopes my perspective. There is no sound in a vacuum but I can still hear humming, like a power line.

There are so many of these bizarre power cables sprouting up into the sky, but they all curve in towards a particularly luminous hub of the strands, suspended by a massive central conduit. Everything converges and then flows into the top of the central conduit and, as a single channel, falls back toward the ground. I follow, tracing the conduit's path down through the clouds. Brightness. It is daytime.

Now I am the alien nun. I sit in my protective travel capsule in my original form. My tentacles play over the control grid. I am absorbing the planetary data while travelling toward its subject. The language-learning sequence passes as quickly as a flare that lights my mind with a matrix of symbols and sounds, and leaves its careful curves and intonations shaped upon the back wall of my brain, brilliantly contrasted one moment, then gone the next.

Next comes information about my target, the human known as Ian Hesse. His physiological details begin to stream into my mind, then suddenly the stream ends, incomplete, truncated. I wave a tentacle over the control grid. The data transfer process has gone astray. There is something inherently problematic about my target, something I know well and should have already compensated for. This type of error could jeopardize the clandestine nature of my mission.

This is a so-called lucid dream, thought Zarathustra.

Or I am being contacted by something far beyond this Earth. The information this alien is receiving, or trying to receive, is what wound up in my own brain by accident. I am seeing all this from the alien nun's perspective, and much of what I already suspected is being confirmed.

Zarathustra was himself again, lying in the black velvet abyss, comfortable but alert. There was new information pouring into his brain. The invaders had plans. They were not who they said they were. They had strengths, but they also had weaknesses. Therefore there was a chance they could be repelled.

* *

The poor creature, thought the alien nun.

His mind is overflowing with my data. No wonder he cannot operate properly.

Carefully, the disguised nun excised the older, accidental content and replaced it with something more compact, more focused, and much more useful.

Chapter Thirty-One

Ian spent the afternoon drawing. A single picture would be worth a thousand chirps, or perhaps a lot more than that. If Ian could render visually what he desired, then Byrd might be willing to assist him in enacting it.

The first picture was a bird carrying a man in its claws, a dotted line following the pair as they soared above the group nest. Far to one side was the saucer.

On another sheet, Ian drew the bird/man pair high above a saucer. A line extended down from the pair to the midst of a group of four-armed humanoids near the saucer.

On a final sheet, he drew the same bird/man pair high above the saucer and its nearby humanoids. The difference was, in this case, a line extended down from the pair to a cluster of trees that were drawn to one side, slightly separated from the saucer site. A more discreet landing zone.

When Byrd finally returned to the nest that evening, he was not alone. Three birds landed at once, creating a unnerving tumult as Ian tried to determine if Byrd was one of the arrivals. Two of the birds wore little black hats and were considerably smaller than Byrd. Ian hid his drawings. Yes, it was Byrd, hopping toward him, taking a buffer position between Ian and the other two.

The two new visitors began to chirp, an unbroken stream of vitriol created between the two of them and aimed at Byrd. These two officials had apparently worked together before and were comfortable with finishing each other's songs. Byrd hopped from side to side as he responded with very short phrases. Even to Ian it was clear these birds were not on a social call.

As the conversation progressed, Ian realized that the two officials differed physically. One was shorter than Byrd, but of similar size. The third bird was half the size of the second, slightly shorter than Ian. The taller visitor had more red in its wings while the smaller official was nearly identical to Byrd's own mix of blue and white feathers. Gradually the larger official began to hog the conversation. His assistant and Byrd grew silent. I am the first human to observe an alien harangue, mused Ian, but he already had too many firsts to be much impressed.

The larger official, whom Ian dubbed Pecker, hopped closer to Ian, bringing his head lower to inspect him. Byrd stayed close and even extended a wing towards Pecker. It was unclear whether it was meant as a friendly, arm on the shoulder gesture, or as a means to restrain Pecker from touching Ian.

Ian retreated backward until he was against the wall with the depiction of the golden bird and sat down, making himself as small and non-confrontational as possible. Pecker wasn't just a funny name to give this interrogator, it was what Ian hoped it wouldn't be doing to his eyes.

Pecker straightened up and withdrew from Ian's personal space, turning around and silently pacing the perimeter of the patio. It paused at Ian's pillow and began another rant, kicking the pillow for emphasis. Ian and Byrd remained motionless.

Pecker then moved near the toilet hole. It pushed the open button with one talon and briefly peered down into the foul recess before turning back to Byrd and continuing what Ian was pretty sure was verbal abuse.

Ian had an involuntary memory recall: he was in a restaurant in Guadalajara and one of the staff was coming out of the bathroom, muttering obscenities about whomever had tried to flush toilet paper in ignorance of the limitations of the local plumbing. As in that case, Ian considered himself blameless. He had not dropped anything except

190

excrement into this hole. Well, maybe a few blobberry leaves.

Meanwhile, Pecker's assistant had produced a piece of paper from under one of its wings. As Pecker continued its tirade, the assistant pushed the symbol-covered paper across the floor to Byrd, who peered down to read it, either multi-tasking or ignoring Pecker's continuous song.

Unable to decipher the progress of the conversation, Ian was startled as the two birds suddenly launched themselves into the air and disappeared. Byrd stuffed the paper under one wing and turned to look at Ian. Byrd chirped a short phrase quite slowly, and then repeated it. Although Ian had not yet distinguished any emotional component in the bird song of this planet, this time there did seem to be some melancholy apparent in the tones used.

This is my eviction notice. I have one chance to explain my plan.

Ian removed the three sheets from his pad of paper and waved his hand in front of them to direct Byrd's attention. Byrd rolled his head around in a circle, as if amused. Ian laid the three sheets flat on the ground and indicated the first one.

Your home. Far above, you carrying me. The saucer way over there.

Byrd hopped closer and tapped the crude drawing of the saucer with one talon. He had not forgotten where he had found Ian.

Ian moved on to the second drawing.

Humanoids with four arms, near the saucer. You carrying me there.

Ian drew a large X obliterating the second drawing as Byrd watched, then moved on to the third.

The forest near the saucer. No humanoids around.

Ian reinforced the dotted line from the human-carrying

191

bird figure down to the forest not quite beside the saucer.

We land here.

Ian drew another X through the second drawing, and returned to the third drawing to tap it repeatedly with his crayon.

Take me here, not there.

Byrd tapped the cluster of trees drawn on the third sheet.

"Yes! Away from the saucer, in the trees! That's it!" he exclaimed involuntarily.

Ian nodded vigorously. Byrd had understood! Now Byrd was imitating him, nodding back. Ian laughed and rolled his head, imitating Byrd's earlier act.

Byrd stepped back and spread his wings, preparing to take flight.

"Wait! Please!" Ian pushed his open palms towards his host, and Byrd's wings relaxed.

Ian moved to the blobberry bushes and began to fill one of his extra sleeves with firm specimens of the staple fruit. Byrd waited until Ian had turned back to face him, and raised his arms in what he hoped was an invitation to secure him for flight.

Byrd leapt into the air above Ian's head. Ian felt the talons clasp his shoulders tightly for a second time as his feet left the ground. Ian saw Byrd's neighbours look up from their adjacent cell as they flew overhead. This flying duo was surely a bizarre sight.

Byrd's apartment had been a very quiet place to live. Ian had not seen any of the neighbours until now, but perhaps they had smelled or heard him. Someone blew the whistle on Byrd and now the No Pets rule was being enforced.

Far below, the river and then the foothills passed by. Now treetops came closer and closer as they descended. Byrd was on a stealth approach. Their flight path followed the same creek that Ian had drunk from on his first night.

They dipped below the tree line, the space above the creek providing their low-altitude air corridor.

The return flight seemed shorter than the original journey. Also much less terrifying. Now he had confidence in his pilot. Byrd found the exact spot where Ian had first been scooped up and they landed gently in the shade.

"I'm not sure how to thank you, my friend."

Byrd could not understand Ian's words but perhaps he would understand a gesture. Ian extended his hand towards Byrd. The avian giant cocked his head, and extended one claw towards Ian while he perched on his other.

Marvelling at the massive bird's sense of balance, Ian took the claw in his own hand and very gently oscillated the joined limbs a short distance up and down four times, then released his grip.

Byrd withdrew his claw, hopped back and puked up some semi-digested material on the ground in front of Ian. It seemed impossible for a bird to have motion sickness, so probably this was a friendly gesture. Ian raised his hand, palm open, and gave a final smile and nod. Byrd nodded once and flew away.

Now comes the part of the plan where I don't have a plan.

Ian moved carefully to the edge of the crash wake, where the trees and bushes had been flattened. The second saucer had landed on the twisted mess that the first had created. There were no birds or Centaurans to be seen. Some of the innards of the first saucer had been extracted from the wreck and lay discarded nearby. Evidently, there was a salvage operation going on.

Staying hidden, moving from behind one flattened clump of vegetation to another, Ian approached the second saucer. When a Centauran emerged from the base of the original saucer, Ian paused his approach, and hid behind a smashed tree trunk. The Centauran had not climbed the emergency slide as Ian had. Instead, it was using a new unsuspected and much larger portal through which larger equipment could be moved. The Centauran was carrying a bag that appeared full. It approached the second saucer and extended one hand towards a personnel-sized door, which promptly opened and accepted the alien.

The second saucer was smaller than the first, the hull circumference two thirds as great. Multiple individual-sized ramps stuck out from the lowest level of the salvagers' craft, each one signifying another way in. As Ian watched, forty-five degrees further down the arc of the saucer hull and almost beyond his viewing angle, another door opened. A team of four Centaurans strode out of the portal, down the ramp, and towards the wreck, walking single file.

The lead Centauran stopped and examined something from the ground. Instead of continuing past him, the others halted and remained motionless. After a moment, the entire team began to move again. Ian waited until they disappeared through the large cargo door of the crashed saucer.

Still maintaining his stealth, Ian manoeuvred around to the side of the new saucer, out of the line-of-sight of the wreck. There were ramps on the far side, and therefore doors. These would be less conspicuous to inspect and attempt to subvert.

Ian selected a ramp within a few feet of a tangle of bushes that had been compressed and ground into a giant tumbleweed by the violent arrival of the first saucer. He eyed the outline of the man-sized door crowning the ramp. There was also a small black dot next to the door. Possibly a button or a sensor. Hopefully a button.

Ian extracted a blobberry from one redundant sleeve and bit into it. He removed the hammer from another redundant sleeve and hefted it, wasting a few seconds.

This is the irrevocable leap. Last chance to chicken out. Last chance to go back to Byrd's civilization. Last chance to say goodbye forever to the Centaurans.

Ian finished his blobberry and wiped his hand on a sleeve.

No, this is my last chance to get back home. Only the Centaurans know where Earth is.

Ian stepped onto the ramp and examined the black dot next to the door. He prodded it gently with the flat end of his hammer. The dot was round and firm, and did not yield to direct, reverse, or lateral pressure. The door remained closed.

Ian shifted the hammer to his left hand and ran the bare index finger of his right hand around the edge of the nub. No reaction. The surface was smoothly bland and featureless. No moving parts.

He squeezed both sides together using index finger and thumb, hoping that the enigmatic control would respond to the approach that had worked aboard the other saucer. He squeezed it side to side, top to bottom, as well as a few other intermediate angles.

The door remained shut.

If this is a fingerprint reader, I'm toast.

How had the Centauran activated the other control? Ian recalled that it had just reached up toward the control and the door had opened. But it had used its lower right arm! Ian grabbed the redundant lower right sleeve of his Centauran tunic and held it up to the black nub.

A hum broke the stillness, and the bulkhead slid open.

Some sort of embedded transceiver for near-field or low-power wireless communication!

Ian stepped inside.

Chapter Thirty-Two

Ian was relieved to find the inner hatch of the airlock open. The curving corridor just beyond resembled the lower level of the first saucer, a utilitarian space filled with multi-sourced humming and warm air.

Ian quickly moved into the corridor and followed its arc to the left. The first door he passed had a blue light above it, which he recognized as an inter-level access tube. He quickened his pace to get away from that potential source of company, passing several more doors, noting each one was accompanied by the familiar button pair control he had encountered on the first saucer.

A noise! The sound of a door opening. Ian squeezed the button pair on the door in front of him. It slid open and he retreated inside.

The room was long and narrow, perhaps two by six meters. A rectangular grid covered the wall to his left. This compartment was similar to the storage room where he had found the hammer. There were some crates made of a smooth plastic-like material along the other wall. Ian squeezed in past the last one. There was just enough room to sit with his legs out and not be seen from the doorway.

Good enough. I'll stay here.

The odds of making it this far without being discovered had been low, and Ian congratulated himself by eating another blobberry from his sleeve larder.

But just one. No idea where the bathroom is around here.

After completing his repast, Ian sat completely still and tried to detect movement or noises from other parts of the ship. There was a slight whisper from the ventilation system, but otherwise all was quiet. If the aliens were moving about the corridor outside his refuge, he could not hear them. Ian was a little alarmed when the lights went out, but he stifled any reaction and did not move.

If the lights are motion-activated, I don't want them signalling my presence.

After a couple more minutes Ian accepted that there was no light in the room for his eyes to adjust too. There was little he could do but give in to sleep. The days on Byrd's planet were very long and he had been awake since sunrise. Ian closed his eyes.

*   *

The audience was excited about the new contestant. Even after they had stopped clapping, Ian could sense they were restive. The stage manager shot dirty glances towards the sectors where murmuring had outlasted the applause signal.

Ian remembered watching the antics of this show as a freshman, reclining amid the fortification of books he had stacked along the perimeter of his dorm room bed. Perhaps he should have left the remote control outside his fortress of learning a little more often but today he was watching 'Primp My Life', a show about ordinary people who were offered the chance to go back in their lives and change fateful decisions that had echoed sourly right up to their current, regret-filled situation.

The hostess, Sparkle Rivers, was gorgeous and required little clothing, but Ian's eyes were drawn to the new contestant, a short, blond woman, who was tantalizingly familiar.

"You've made your choice. You've seized the day and made it your own. Let's show the audience what you did with your second chance."

Ian watched as the screen transitioned to an exterior shot, a leafy sidewalk. Two students were walking together, their knapsacks almost touching, their conversation low and intimate.

"The vector summation is laborious, but it's not actually difficult once you know the method. The important thing is to not make silly arithmetic mistakes during the calculation."

"I suppose you engineers need all that calculus, but I'll be glad to be done with it," said Gale.

"You environmental science people." Ian touched her arm. It was the farthest he had gotten with her so far.

They were stopped at the intersection along with a knot of similarly knapsack-burdened students, waiting for the walk light. A gasoline-powered automobile approached, slowing to a crawl as it eased its way through the crosswalk and turned the corner. Some of the students pointedly held their noses as it rolled past.

"It's not the smell that bugs me so much, more the noise," complained Gale.

"Well, the complete transition from petrochemical fuels to other sources will take time."

"We may not have that much time," cautioned Gale.

"I believe the world is robust, more robust than us puny humans. If we can survive the economic and political shocks, the physical world will be here for us."

"Your faith in humanity's future is touching." Gale was already stepping away from him. Weren't they going in the same direction? "But I don't think it is justified. Mother Earth first, fat cats later."

"Is it fat cats who run economies in the undeveloped world, where economic stagnation means starvation and war?"

"Yes, I think they do actually. And if you can't see that then I don't think you deserve that iron ring."

Ian fingered the iron ring on his left pinky. Why did he have it already? The iron ring ceremony, in which the professional engineering society bestows the symbol of integrity and ethical responsibility on graduate engineers, did not occur until fourth year. He was in second year.

"We all have to choose in this life, Ian, and I choose a life without passionless calculation and dirty compromise. Wasn't it that great paragon of right wing virtue, Ayn Rand herself, who said that compromise with evil was capitulation?"

Ian did not have time to respond, or he could not. The camera had fixed on Gale and now she turned around and stepped deliberately toward a tall, dreadlocked student. She slipped her arm through the triangle of Miguel's extended elbow.

"Compromise can be poison, but awareness is the antidote," pronounced Miguel.

Awareness, thought Ian, or perception?

His glib simplifications are just propaganda to politicize the ill-informed. Just another type of power grab.

"We cannot allow our will to be diluted by the old power structures and the comfortable status quo!" added Miguel.

Why is this guy talking? No one asked him anything.

"I'm sorry, Ian. I choose life. I choose Miguel."

Ian held the remote control in his hand but could not bring himself to end the program.

Sparkle was congratulating Gale on her choice, walking her to another giant view screen where they could watch the ripple of change evolving from her new choice as it spread down the timeline and into her later years. Yes, she would still work at Environment Canada, but her relationship with Miguel had started much earlier, that day at the crosswalk when Ian refused to hold his nose in symbolic protest, and now they had two perfect little children.

The additional responsibility had softened Miguel's

outlook, his rabid political views had morphed into concern for parental rights and taxation of the middle class. He still wanted to save the world, but that world had been simplified to the root biological imperative: the well-being of his mate and offspring. Miguel exuded confidence and untroubled focus as he pursued these new priorities. Gale had absorbed his worldview and shared his enthusiasm.

Beside the giant screen, Gale clapped along with the audience. Everyone was happy. Sparkle embraced Gale and offered her for one final round of applause before allowing her to walk, beaming, off the stage.

Now the stage manager was gesturing for Ian to take the stage. Was he in his bed, surrounded by books? No, he was part of the studio audience. The boisterous crowd, clapping and whistling, was unnerving but Ian obeyed the manager and presented himself at the edge of the stage.

"Ian Hesse! You also have a choice to make. Are you ready to primp your life?"

"Okay," said Ian, and he was instantly back in his dorm room.

The audience watched Ian as he stood up from his book-strewn bed and retrieved his computer. In a moment, he had printed the document he needed. He grabbed a pen to sign the form and headed for the basement. The printer farm was next to the laundry room. This was it. He was changing his major. To sign and deliver these forms was the first but irrevocable step.

He could re-arrange his classes for next semester and perhaps his graduation date might not even be delayed. Many of the classes for the first two years of Industrial Engineering and Robotics Engineering were the same. He would graduate and he would not work in the petrochemical industry.

"Congratulations Ian! You have selected a better future

for yourself. Let's see how it turns out for you."

Sparkle Rivers led Ian to the second giant screen. The audience hushed as Ian's larger-than-life-size image confronted them.

It was several years later and Ian was daydreaming at work. He had not thought of Gale since they had argued and split up in their last semester of university together.

The new production run was progressing smoothly. All the carefully choreographed shared activities among his robots were interfacing properly. The design changes were completely implemented. The red droid, as Ian called the robot that performed the final assembly operation, was correctly placing packaging-ready units on the conveyor belt. The quality assurance team was busy exercising their sets of test cases against the newly assembled units.

Ian was thinking of Blythe. Last night at Bassline Music Hall had been their best date yet. Ian had not danced since his freshman year at university but there was something about Blythe that made him less self-conscious. It was a very welcome feeling.

He knew they were on the verge of intimacy. If it had not been a weeknight, his invitation back to her place and into her bed late last night would have been assured. Now her latest email invited him to come over that very night for a romantic home-cooked meal.

I'm in.

This was Ian's last complacent thought. The headline news was full of images of saucers. Earth was being invaded.

It's a hoax. The Centaurans are mathematicians, not soldiers.

The power went out, draining Ian's hopeful theory of its chance at life.

Next, twenty-four hours had passed and things were

much worse. Earth's asteroid defences were powerless against the enemy ships. The UN had caved in, both literally and figuratively. New York was in full havoc as its citizens struggled to escape the dusty mess of the collapse of UN Headquarters. It was the World Trade Center twin towers all over again, but much worse. New York was not the extent of the attack.

All of the hospitals in the Ottawa area had been pulverized. There was nowhere to go for help.

Worse yet, he could not contact Blythe. He knew she had been on duty at St. John's when it had been destroyed. Right in the middle of her shift. She could be dead. His brain turned away from the thought, repulsed.

Now the UN had surrendered. There was an agreement; the NACEO was signed. Everyone would be working for the Centaurans for the next five years. If you didn't like it, you didn't have to stick around. Execution was the other available choice.

Ian's laptop was fading rapidly, the power warning icon flashing. He would have to go outside again and let the Sun coax it back to life.

The Imhotep Robotics facility was an immense building, but Ian spent most of his time in the design offices on the second floor overlooking the front grounds. There was a small balcony where the staff often enjoyed a coffee break or a moment of fresh air on a temperate day. Ian planted himself at one of the cheap plastic tables and switched his laptop to solar charge mode.

Below him, a squad of UN trucks and jeeps had arrived, parking in the drop-off zone directly in front of the formal entrance to Imhotep. Some UN soldiers, rifles at the ready, and accompanied by strange creatures with four arms, red skin and elongated heads, were spreading out like a pool of spilled filth. Nothing would be the same after mixing with this foul combination of misdirected forces.

Ian sat frozen.

Those are Centaurans. What do they want here?

Ian did not have to wait long for an answer. Two soldiers flung open the glass doors and faced Ian, who responded by putting his hands in the air very slowly.

"Identify yourself," the soldier on point demanded of him.

"I'm Ian Hesse. I work here as a design engineer."

There were others behind the two soldiers now, a ruddy Centauran and a human wearing the uniform of a UN general. The general waved the soldiers away and approached.

"I am General Pushkin, and this is Worthy Overseer." He gestured at the red alien beside him. "We are taking command of this facility in the name of the NACEO. You will assist Worthy Overseer in refitting your equipment to their specifications."

"I see." Ian hesitated to mention the obvious. "But the power is out here."

"That will be corrected. Here are the specifications. You will analyze them. Any additional requirements must be stated now."

Pushkin handed Ian a memory stick. The laptop power was back to 60%. Ian inserted the memory stick and scanned its contents.

"Our equipment here is not nano-capable. We assemble physical components with micrometer tolerances, at best. Parts of this device will require a more advanced fabrication technique."

Pushkin's mouth worked for a few seconds without any sound coming out.

"Well you can build most of it, can't you? Which parts require nanotech?"

"This. Probably this." Ian zoomed in to one convoluted section of the schematic and then circled his cursor around one, then another tiny subsystem.

"Our tolerances are not that strict. You are dissembling," objected the Centauran. Its crimson skin was intrinsically off-putting, as if it had lost its temper long ago and never recovered.

"We specialize in small runs of custom goods. Our equipment is highly reconfigurable and accurate, but we simply do not produce at nano tolerances."

"Worthy overseer, call it Worthy Overseer," cautioned Pushkin, but the overseer uncharacteristically ignored Ian's lapse in protocol.

"If you are lying, you must recant. If you are telling the truth, then you are of no use to us." The upper arms of the alien swung over and those hands clamped around Ian's neck. The grip was extraordinarily strong and Ian felt his feet leave the ground. The flow of blood to his head was blocked. He would not remain conscious for long.

"Recant. Admit. Agree."

Ian grabbed the alien's forearms but they were immovable, as solid as high grade carbon steel. Resistance was futile.

The giant screen went blank and the audience groaned sympathetically. Sparkle Rivers placed a consolatory hand on Ian's shoulder.

"Oh, Ian. Looks like it didn't work out for you. You *died* just then. I'm sorry but you won't be coming back next week. But let's hear it for Ian anyway!"

The applause burst from the audience like a dam bursting. A froth of whistling and cheers inundated Ian on the stage. The sound swelled and echoed around the giant set like rolling thunder.

* *

A sustained roar and strong vibration woke Ian. He recalled that he was a stowaway on the second saucer. In complete darkness, he struggled to identify the auditory stimulus.

Rockets! Are we manoeuvring or landing?

Perhaps his journey was nearing an end.

Chapter Thirty-Three

Ian had no idea how long he had slept or how much time had passed since the noise had begun. There was nothing else to hear but the steady-state drone that accompanied the vibration of the floor and walls. The floor was hard but warm, not an ideal sleeping surface. The arm Ian had rested his head upon was stiff and tingling as he pulled himself up into a seated position with his back against the wall.

There were almost three blobberries left in his sleeve. One was rather squished, leaving sticky pulp and juice on his hand as he felt his way around his larder. Ian ate the two intact blobberries and then scraped the bits of the damaged one up with his fingers and finished that as well. Now more thirsty than hungry, he inverted his storage sleeve and sucked at the fabric.

How long have I been wearing this shirt? I hope, at the very least, it was laundered before I borrowed it.

The sleeve did not smell very good and once he had ingested the debris of the crushed blobberry, his sucking did not yield any further liquid.

Ian recalled pieces of his dream. The name Sparkle Rivers invoked an image of a flowing river, which only reminded him again of his thirst. Some strange game show where you can go back into the past and change your life.

By travelling back to his university days, Ian had avoided both becoming involved with Gale and a career in petrochemical engineering, and things had seemed better, at least until the Centaurans came.

In that alternate timeline, rather than being stuck in his current predicament, he would have been strangled to death ignominiously upon his first meeting with the aliens. Not a better outcome.

Some things you can't escape, although they may come

*at different times, in different contexts or manifestations.
Eventually they will resurface and you will still need to
confront the underlying syndrome. Perhaps avoidance is
folly and the best approach is to be direct.*

*If this saucer was similar to the previous one, there
might be view screens, acting as virtual portholes, along
the deck. If I can see where we are, then I can decide on my
plan of action more effectively.*

The minuscule chance that the saucer had landed on
Earth was Ian's lifeline to his hope and sanity. Ian feared if
that was not the case, and he knew he was lost among
nameless creatures in an unknown corner of the galaxy, he
might go mad. But he had to find out.

Whether from the increased gravity (the Centaurans
seemed to maintain an almost Earth-normal gravity aboard
their ships) or from his weak, dehydrated condition, rising
to his feet required more exertion than expected. His knees
straightened only with difficulty and he took a few
moments to massage his petrified thighs and back.

The absence of light was total, without even the tiniest
reflection or dimmest glow to allay it. His eyes blinked
nervously, trying futilely to clear away the dark. Swirls of
light specks, rising like hordes of insects, flowed across his
field of vision.

*Not insects. My optic nerve is under-stimulated; that is
all.*

Ian felt his way along the back wall to the corner of the
compartment, and then forward until he was at the entry
bulkhead. The wall was very smooth and Ian struggled to
remain calm as he sought the double-button that he knew
must be next to the door.

*It has to be here. Around this high. There's the edge of
the door.*

Then he had it, his fingers curling around it almost

lovingly. His fate was under his control again, at least for the next few seconds. Ian pressed his ear against the door. Nothing was audible. Either the corridor was quiet or the door was soundproof. Not a conclusive test. The risk of opening the door was great but so was the payoff, and the longer he waited the greater the chance someone would wander into his vicinity.

Ian took a deep breath and squeezed the double-button. The door slid open rather quietly, the noise of the ship manoeuvring drowning out the gentle hum of the door mechanism.

Two-edged sword. They won't hear the door, but I won't hear them.

The lights in the storage room sprang back to life, temporarily blinding Ian. He blinked rapidly, clearing away some protective tears. He could not afford to be second in the game of Spot The Alien.

Ian eased his head a few inches beyond the portal to peer into the corridor. One side curved away, perfectly deserted; the other side at first appeared empty, but then the bulk of a Centauran came into view, emerging from a portal maybe ten meters away. Luck was on Ian's side; the alien's back was in his direction. It seemed to be engrossed in conversation with someone still out of sight.

Jerking his head back into the room, Ian squeezed the buttons again and launched himself back towards his hiding spot.

Did it see me??

Sitting again on the hard floor, Ian brought his knees up to his chest, pulling his feet clear of the traffic area beyond the crate that acted as his hideout.

I need to remain perfectly still. No sound at all.

Ian struggled to get his breathing under control, slowing and deepening the cycle.

Did I leave purple-black hand prints all over everything?

The thought worried Ian, but the danger of leaving his hidden position far outweighed any chance he could do something about the potential telltale stains. He had no way to remove them, if they existed, even if he had time. Which he didn't.

The sound of the compartment door opening jabbed his eardrums; it was as if the delicate membrane had ruptured and sounds from inside his body were now louder than those outside it. His heart hammered as it forced blood through his veins. Ian ignored the physiological noise and listened intently, far in the background, to the sound of two Centaurans stepping inside his compartment.

The two aliens murmured to each other in their strange language. They did not seem upset or excited. Ian heard a small click and some gentle noises of material being handled. They had not raised an alarm. They were there on other business.

Their conversation continued for several minutes. At one point Ian thought he detected laughter from one of them, but it could just as easily have been some emotion other than levity.

The small click repeated itself. Perhaps they were tidying up, almost done. Then the lights died, drowning the room in pure blackness once again.

"Luta!" cried one of the Centaurans, and the lights re-activated. They exchanged a few more words as Ian heard the door slide open again. Their conversation was truncated by the door sliding shut.

Ian peeked around the crate. They were definitely gone. Standing was easier this time. With the lights on, he could see that there was little evidence remaining of his feast of blobberries. One smear of black discoloured the wall right next to the door, but was noticeable only if you looked directly above the control plate. They had missed it this time.

Now that the lights were on, it was possible to inventory the contents of the room. The wall of storage cubbyholes was Ian's first target. Here he found additional Centauran tunics of various styles, but made of a material substantially heavier than his earlier acquisition and rendering them useless as replacement garb.

Guess I didn't made it to the summer sale.

Another storage recess contained various pills and small bottles of fluid, obviously medicines, as well as gauze and bandages. Also, there were several unfamiliar electronic devices, somewhat gun-shaped, but given their proximity to the medical supplies, likely not weapons.

I don't need to inadvertently fire stimulants at anyone chasing me.

The lights died suddenly.

"Luta!" said Ian firmly. Nothing happened. He tried again, emphasizing the glottal stop and spitting out each syllable. The light returned.

My first Centauran word!

Ian spied a small cutting device, similar to scissors but designed without the leveraging effect of finger holes as on human models. It might produce a usable blade if disassembled but, as it was, would provide no advantage in combat.

Another of the cupboards contained a further sub-compartmentalized storage array. Tiny electronic components, blobs of condensed manufactured logic, some with wire, some with fibre optic connectors.

The next cupboard contained boxes of what was perhaps some type of memory chip, fingernail-size rectangles with a strip of metal along the bottom. Another box contained small round items, coin-like but not made of metal, their function mysterious.

The final cupboard contained some tools, sets of tiny screwdrivers, magnetic prods, an eyepiece similar to a jeweller's loupe, a hammer similar to the one Ian had already appropriated, and a small mirror. This last item held his attention.

Ian peered into the reflective surface and was stunned by what he saw. He had aged. Since coming out of the coma, he had continually been on the run. His last proper shower had been at Blythe's.

Ian remembered the smell of her coconut shampoo wistfully. That shower had been accomplished in a hurry, with the fear that their guest, the alien nun, might turn hostile at any moment.

Apart from that, he had washed in the stream on Byrd's planet, and then tried to suppress his funk with the bowls of water Byrd had given him. It had not been very successful because he had no way to properly clean the Centauran tunic or the Earth clothes that still clad the lower part of his body.

His hair was longer than he remembered, having not been trimmed aggressively while he was in the hospital. Now it was very unruly. Worse yet, it was shot through with streaks of grey. The leathery red skin of the Centaurans did not produce scalp hair and therefore Ian would not be finding a hairbrush aboard the saucer.

There were new, deep wrinkles around his eyes, partially obscured by black circles that implied exhaustion. His cheeks looked caved in, making his face gaunt.

For the first time ever, the reflection that confronted Ian was a face at the leading edge of middle age. This was not the moisturized, well-fed, and comfortable transition into maturity displayed by bankers and management; this was

211

the decrepitude of a man who had been ejected from his community and forced to make do living in the woods, sharing Nature's meagre bounty with insects and predators.

It occurred to Ian that the best parts of his life might already have passed him by and all that remained was a short and violent final chapter in which he would struggle senselessly against ridiculous odds in an attempt to return home. Ian inhaled sharply and returned the mirror to its box.

Is it possible to be so far away from home that your home no longer has any meaning and you are no longer a product of its conditioning and experience but instead a new creature, wholly defined by your new situation?

This thought rose unchallenged in Ian's mind. All his life he had been careful to choose a path that would provide immediate payoff while minimizing the risk of a worst case scenario.

He had chosen to study engineering because his innate talents for math and science made it an easy path to a lucrative career, not out of a heartfelt fascination with technology. He had chosen to specialize in petrochemical processing because family connections within the industry should have provided a ready-made path to an attractive position had the entire industry not collapsed due to heavy government investment in alternative technologies.

He had chosen to date and then marry Gale because, well, there really was no factual reason. The reality is that Gale had chosen him and he had acquiesced. Certainly he had been happy to date the lovely Gale as a lowly freshman.

She saw his value early on, although much later as that value deflated along with his career prospects, she was again keen and proactive, but this time in terminating his role. He had avoided being alone in his school years but in doing so had missed the bigger risk and danger posed by the innate weakness of his approach. Avoiding risk is not a good long-term strategy.

I will not make the same mistakes here that I have made all my life.

Ian considered that his least risky short-term strategy was to remain hidden. This might extend his life, but it would not change the final outcome. He would be found and killed if not within the next twenty-four hours, then no doubt within forty-eight.

Another option would be to leave his hideaway and explore the ship. This strategy risked immediate capture but offered at least a chance to improve his situation. If Ian could find out where he was, there was at least some chance he could determine a path home.

I will not wait passively.

Ian shifted the alien hammer to his left hand and squeezed the door buttons with his right. The corridor was clear in both directions. Ian moved off to his left, the opposite direction to that from which the previous visitors had approached. Ian switched the hammer back to his right hand, his left shoulder nearly grazing the inner bulkhead as he followed the curve of the passageway, moving slowly and listening intently for any indication of company.

There were many more doors along the inside bulkhead. Ian counted them as he passed. No blue lights indicated emergency access tubes. He was almost halfway around the ship when the Holy Grail appeared, a virtual porthole, but the news it presented was not good. Ian moved his head closer to the view screen, trying to increase its field of vision. It was useless. The virtual porthole provided a single angle and did not emulate the 3D nature of an actual physical perspective. Ian saw a lot of spaceships, but no planet.

Is this the invasion fleet - is Earth below, just out of sight?

The spaceships were heterogeneous, a mix of small and large, saucer-shaped, cigar-shaped, and other completely non-aerodynamic designs, webbed and spindly vehicles that looked incapable of withstanding gentle acceleration, much less the gravitational well of a planet-sized body. The pattern of the stars did not seem familiar and Ian confirmed his worst fear again, looking carefully for even a small disc which might be obscured by the hull of a nearby ship. No, there was no planet anywhere in sight.

How do I see out the other side of the ship?

It was possible there was a porthole on the opposite side of the ship and it might provide the crucial perspective. Ian could venture far down the corridor to the other side of the ship but there had to be a safer way.

Ian touched the screen and dragged his finger right. The image shifted with it.

Now that's an intuitive interface!

The shift of perspective revealed more spaceships encompassing even more divergent designs scattered around the area. There was a yellow star dominating the view from the top. Many of the ships were oriented to point solar panels toward it. Any surface not facing that direction was dull and indistinct, illuminated only by the backdrop of interstellar pinpricks.

Ian shifted the image as far as it could go in every direction, seeing a silvery strip of metal, the hull edge of his present vehicle, each time he hit the limit. Lots of spaceships. No planets. He was nowhere near Earth.

Fighting a rising sense of panic, Ian retreated to his hideout once more. He had gambled but not won. Still, he had not lost, for he remained in the game, but very little had been gained in the way of useful information despite the great risk in performing his reconnaissance. What few options he could still consider were not good.

Chapter Thirty-Four

Ian's need was urgent now. There could be no further delay. His final blobberries had worked their way through his under-utilized digestive system and now sought immediate release. How to cover up traces of a bowel movement aboard a hostile alien spaceship?

Ian clawed his way through the contents of the rectangular storage grid again before selecting the alien scissors and a round container with a slip-on lid that seemed reasonably airtight.

Talk about working under pressure, intestinal pressure.

Ian used the scissors to detach the redundant sleeve that had been his blobberry larder. He cut several small squares from the sleeve material, then opened the round container and squatted over it. The bowel movement was mixed and foul, liquid followed by uncomfortably dense solids. He had not over-estimated the required capacity of the container.

Ian wiped himself with a few of the squares cut from his sleeve material, dropped them on top of the excrement, and sealed the container. He hoped the smell would dissipate rapidly.

He rubbed his hand vigorously on his pant leg. There was no water to wash it, and worse, no water to drink. The warmth of the ship only exacerbated his fatigue. He pushed the doors closed on the equipment compartments.

Everything back in place. Nothing to see here. No stowaway here.

Ian lowered himself to the floor and leaned back against the wall, hidden again by the crate. In a couple of minutes, the lights automatically extinguished. Ian closed his eyes, trying to visualize a new plan, some way to salvage this remnant of his existence.

* *

Ian was in a deep hole. He looked up the side of the ravine at the twisted strands of roots evident along the steep incline.

This is a fresh surface.

A mudslide had probably calved the previous layer free, leaving the roots of formerly secure vegetation exposed and vulnerable. The sound of running water lapped maddeningly at his ears but the ground under his feet was sandy, a dry creek bed.

"Ian!"

He turned around to see Blythe on a dirty white horse. She had an infant tucked under one arm and controlled the reins with the other. Ian approached them, mouth open, but hope clamping his throat closed, paralyzing his speech.

"Ian! We have to get out of here. Why don't you help us?"

The accusation speared him like a javelin. He would do anything for Blythe and little Tycho. He turned back to his challenge. He must scale the embankment and reach the water that existed somewhere up there.

He grabbed a handful of the exposed roots just above his eye level and pulled himself up. The gurgling of the exigent fluid far above increased in volume, driving him to greater exertion. Bits of dirt, stones and plant material worked loose as he climbed, most of it landing on his face and in his mouth. The climb was burying him alive. Ian tried to spit out dirt.

Then he noticed the spiders. Small brown spiders were running all about the exposed roots. Using the flat head of the hammer as a scoop, he swept the insects off the one hand that held him aloft and then cleared another root for his next grip above.

Two more moves and I'm at the top. I'm almost there.

Ian pulled himself up onto the edge of the precipice. A strong feeling of victory enveloped him. He had conquered his fear of insects and in doing so, saved three lives. But where were they?

Looking down into the ravine, he could no longer see the horse. Hundreds of meters away, the red skull of a Centauran was visible. It had Blythe. A cry of an infant was faintly discernible. They had Tycho too.

His climb was all for nothing. Reluctantly he turned his attention away from the drama below. The source of the gurgling was visible now, an ornate fountain only a few paces from the eroded bluff edge. Ian stumbled to the fountain and plunged his hands into the clear water.

I couldn't help them but I can't let grief overwhelm me. Besides, Tycho isn't real anyway.

The recognition of Tycho's unreality broke the spell of the dream. Nothing here was real, including the water. Ian stirred his hands in the fountain but they found no cool fluid, no resistance to movement that the density of water would provide.

Now Ian was awake again, painfully dehydrated, and still trapped in the dark belly of the saucer.

* *

Two levels above Ian, one of the alien functionaries was having a rough cycle. A large quantity of operational and security data from the ship had been transferred to a data analysis operation back on the base planet. The low-status operatives that combed the reams of information for anomalous conditions and early indicators of malfunction usually sent their reports twice a cycle. For each shift aboard the saucer, therefore, the data auditor on duty was responsible for vetting issues before driving them up the ship's hierarchy.

If the two-reports-per-cycle limit was ignored, there had

to be a very good reason, such as imminent disaster. With this in mind, Data Auditor Two was considering sending a behaviour correction order in response to this off-schedule priority report. Clearly someone was over-reacting.

The security access data stream had contained an unexpected datum. On their last mission, a salvage job of a no-survivor saucer crash on a non-aligned planet, one of their auxiliary airlocks had been opened by someone using a sleeve chip from the crashed saucer.

It was possible that someone had looted a fresh suit from the crash site and not changed the sleeve chip ID before using it to re-enter the ship, but it was more likely that the event data was corrupted or one of their suits had the wrong ID tagged to it.

Irritated, Data Auditor Two made a note in the incident log. This report would now have to be reviewed with Data Coordinator Three.

* *

Data Coordinator Three was not impressed with the recent work of the auditors. Not only did they report that a ghost crew member had boarded the ship, they compounded this folly with what they termed 'additional evidence' which was in fact only anecdotal statements from crew members about a strange smell in a first level compartment and a clump of dirt found along the first level corridor.

Medical Assistant Two had been tending a small wound on one of Mechanical Operative Four's upper arms using the supplies in compartment 7.17 when they noticed a strange, vaguely animal odour. At the time they did not log their concerns, but later when another mechanical operative found a clump of alien soil along the Level 7 corridor they suspected that an animal had somehow managed to come aboard.

The clump of dirt was analyzed and found to be from their recent planetfall. The crew were questioned but no one would admit any laxity regarding decontamination procedures, an offence punishable by forfeiture of wages. If someone was obscuring their own carelessness with false protestations of innocence, they should know that it is very unwise to dissemble to the hierarchy.

Such disloyalty was punishable by termination. Yet every voyage there was some rookie who had made it off a home world and into a valuable expeditionary position only to lose it all through a momentary lack of self-control. Theirs was a one-way journey into the void.

Animals, and ghosts! The stories and fears of the lower classifications reflected the primitive mindset of the planet-bound. Salvaging a rogue saucer had also stressed out the crew. It was a disillusioning experience surely, being exposed for the first time to the fact that ruthless pirates had emerged from their own community, The Domain of the Invincible Eight Arms.

All were siblings in biology and history, but some had gone beyond the pale to live the empty lives of criminals, condemned to never return home, and to spend their lives looting the outer moons or the foreign space far beyond. The psychological dysfunction that could separate a creature from its home was awesome in its depravity.

Data Coordinator Three sighed heavily and turned full attention to one last issue, a malfunction in the motion detectors in compartment 7.17, the same compartment where the smell had been reported.

Was it possible an animal or injured crewman from the rogue saucer had hidden itself there? The compartment contained some weapons storage and was considered high security; motion detectors, therefore, monitored for inappropriate activity. In this case, there were two detectors in the room but only one had noted a problem.

The officer clasped and unclasped both pairs of hands, wringing them across the same level, upper with upper, and then across levels, upper with lower. Was there something here that required action or were these data just noise?

If there really was something in 7.17, then both detectors should be registering movement. If the detectors do not agree, then they should not be relied upon. Thus, Data Coordinator Three discounted the final data anomaly and went for lunch.

Ian still had a few hours before he would be discovered.

Chapter Thirty-Five

Ian awoke with thirst his first thought. His throat was dry and his tongue felt swollen. He tried to swallow but there was no saliva present and his throat muscles protested against the futile order.

Now Ian understood that it had been a mistake to urinate in the same container where he had hidden his feces. Urine drinking was a common practice for nomadic desert people, a final lifeline against the cruel, slow death of dehydration. By mixing his liquid output with the bacteria-laden solid waste, he had wasted his final reservoir of bodily fluid.

Ian had been through every one of the storage cubbyholes. There was water nowhere. Zero.

This is my last day.

The water in the blobberries was the last that Ian had ingested since entering this second saucer and that had totalled only a few millilitres.

My brain is drying out.

Blood pounded through the veins in Ian's skull, pulsing in time with his heart, that organ itself convulsing much more rapidly than normal. The throb of cranial agony was reminiscent of the denouement after early experiments with alcohol in high school.

The room was dark again. He did not have the energy or a reason to reverse the inky opacity within the too-warm chamber. Specks of white floated in his vision, a snowy field that drifted to one side then the other.

Ian shook his head but the impression that the air molecules themselves were dancing in front of him did not dissipate. There was little time left before he would be unfit for any challenge, be it infiltrating the hostile ship or just standing up. There had to be something he had overlooked.

Of course. It is too obvious. How could I miss them?

"Luta!" croaked Ian and the light returned. He dragged himself from his hiding spot and pulled himself almost upright using one of the crates that blocked his view of the doorway. He had not yet looked inside these large containers.

It took a minute to figure out the locking mechanism. While fumbling with the alien latches, Ian struggled to remain focused. His legs were almost too weak to maintain his weight and the visual snow had not disappeared with the darkness.

Ian managed to undo the latches, but the lid still would not lift. He found two more latches on the sides of the crate and then shoved the cover upward. It tumbled free and fell heavily onto the floor with a thump, barely missing one of his feet. Ian cursed weakly under his breath. The last thing he needed was any blood loss to exacerbate his already critically low fluid level.

Ian pulled back the thin filmy cover and found a set of four identical items embedded in form-fitted foam. The items had pair-based anti-symmetry: two were designed for the right hands, and the other two for lefts. The pistol shape gave Ian hope.

These might very well be weapons.

But could he hold the entire ship hostage and demand safe passage back to Earth with only this little arsenal? It was a long shot.

The devices seemed relatively simple. The trigger was familiar. There was a simple two-way switch on the inner side of each pistol, accessible to the thumb. The safety. There was also a non-locking push button next to a four centimetre square screen along its back, facing the user.

Ian tapped the button and the screen came to life, indicating the charge level of unit was high. All the units were in a similar state.

223

Ian selected one pair for use, and then pocketed the other. Some sort of test was in order before he launched himself into a battle where he would be completely dependent on these alien tools. The idea that they might simply be soldering guns or some kind of scanner scratched uncomfortably inside his dry brain.

If this is a radar gun, then I don't want to be standing there, clocking the speed at which the aliens are approaching me.

Ian flipped the safety off on his right hand weapon and aimed it at the exit, but then paused to reconsider. He did not want to damage the door and get stuck inside this compartment. The aliens could pump in poison gas, or just suck all the air out. It would be a little more risky to make his stand in the corridor, but the chances of obtaining hostages could be well worth it.

He shuffled unsteadily to the door and squeezed the double button. The corridor was just as oppressively warm as his hiding spot. No Centaurans in sight.

Where to shoot this thing? If I aim inwards, I might hit some critical part of the drive system and cause a devastating explosion. If I aim outward, I might breach the hull and get sucked into space.

Ian stepped back into the storage compartment and put his hand on the double button again.

If the corridor starts to lose atmosphere, I will close this hatch. I have to try.

Ian aimed at a spot on the curved outer wall of the corridor and very slowly squeezed the trigger. It was a sensitive trigger and the results were spectacular, not only regarding the damage done but the immediate reaction of the automatic protection systems aboard the ship.

The sound the gun made was a teeth-rattling but short-lived hum. A visible ray emanated from its tip and

224

contacted the target surface, melting a hole a few centimetres across. Ian felt and heard the air rushing towards the fresh hole. The lights in the corridor immediately turned blue, flashing rapidly and insistently.

In another second, the doorway slid shut, almost biting Ian's nose. He had not activated the double button himself. This was the ship reflexively isolating the damaged area.

Ian backed away from the now closed door, pistols still drawn and aimed in that direction.

Yup. It's definitely a weapon.

A small smile curled Ian's lips for the first time since leaving Byrd's planet. It didn't last long. He had no idea what was going on outside in the corridor. Were the Centaurans busy fixing the hole or planning to eliminate him? The most likely case was both. The weapon test had succeeded extravagantly, but he might not get another chance to use his powerful new persuaders.

Chapter Thirty-Six

Data Coordinator Three was standing near the clerk when the alert sounded. The Command Section flashed blue in sync with the klaxons.

"Hull breach on Level 7! Directly across from 7.17!" shouted the helm operator.

"Isolation?" demanded Clerk One, well aware of the protocol to be followed.

"Positive, exquisite leader. Protective shields engaged immediately. Pressure loss contained and non-critical."

"Silence the alarm. Did we collide with something?"

"No, your worthiness. Nothing was approaching us. The damage must have come from inside, and wait, yes, I do see an indication of blaster fire," reported Helm Operator One.

"Inside…" mused Clerk One, "Isn't 7.17 where we put the military equipment from the salvage site?"

"You are correct as expected, sublime director. Several sets of assault blasters with complete field packaging were recovered, and then stored there."

"Were they not completely discharged?"

"It is unfortunate, worthy leader, but I see no record of that action."

"Yes it will be unfortunate indeed. Pull the name of the stevedore responsible and have the idiot sent to ER for re-adjustment." Helm Operator One was already pulling up the loading record and issuing the new orders for the unlucky and allegedly reckless cargo handler while the clerk continued to spout orders. "…and send a team down to Level 7 to check the damage and the cause. I want to know how that blaster discharged!"

"Issuing orders now, sagacious one."

Helm Operator One's middle eye opened wide and the

outer two closed tightly in shock while listening to updates via headphones. It shot a nervous glance at Data Coordinator Three. The rumours and gossip they had discredited a few minutes ago were now condensing into a coherent threat. Their ship was under attack.

Clerk One noticed the glance. It was inappropriate for information to be passed in this manner. "Report!" the clerk cried.

"Exalted leader, there is an armed alien in compartment 7.17."

* *

When the portal to the compartment opened again, unbidden, Ian was confronted with two unarmed Centaurans. Ian convinced the first to step into his compartment by waving the blaster pistols meaningfully. Ian's view of the second Centauran was blocked somewhat by the first and it managed to bolt before he could likewise convince it to step inside.

The captive Centauran looked frightened or at least nervous. Its middle eye was blinking rapidly and the outer two eyes were almost closed. It kept all four hands in front of its body, open, empty, and clearly visible to Ian.

"I want water. I need water. Do you understand? Where is the translator you had before?"

The Centauran did not react. Clearly it did not understand. Ian recalled his interrogation aboard the original saucer near Earth. The Centaurans had translation technology there, so surely they must have the same capability here.

I can't stand up much longer.

Ian's knees felt like they could buckle at any second. His head still throbbed and his eyes felt completely dry. The snow effect plaguing his vision continued, very likely a sign of his imminent collapse. Trying to look like it was a choice, Ian lowered himself to the floor and crossed his legs, tucking them under himself.

This posture will help me remain conscious a little longer.

His gaze did not waver from the Centauran, whose three eyes now all blinked randomly and at a much reduced rate. It had regained its composure.

"Don't even think of trying anything."

The admonishment was more to evince an active and purposeful demeanour than to communicate with his hostage. Ian hoped that his hostage's superiors valued the lives of their crew sufficiently to prefer negotiation to attack. This was his only hope if he wanted to survive this standoff.

* *

Ship Supervisor frowned at Clerk One. Things had gotten way out of hands. How could this unknown alien sneak aboard their ship during the salvage operation? The Branch planet had only one intelligent species: they were avian and not space-faring. The hostage-taker must have originated elsewhere, and been aboard the crashed ship for some reason.

"You have information regarding the attacker?"

"We have focused each scanner on the alien, but its type is unknown to the Domain. We do have information on the weapon used, one of our own Mark IV blaster pistol sets, military grade and capable of burning a hole from one end of our ship to the other. Depending how the two-arm thing aims, our protection systems might very well not be able to contain the damage. And if the beam hits the antimatter chamber, we will end."

"What about transfer? Can we dematerialize this creature?"

"No, my great benefactor, I am told this is impossible

within the confined space there. Also, the process is not instantaneous, so if the creature senses the process beginning, it might react and we would still end."

"How ironic that the power of our weapons would be used against us by something as primitive as this anemic, two-armed hominid."

"Your sense of irony is precise, worthy one."

"My decision is that we will placate this interloper for now. Send it food and water and await further orders."

"Understood."

Clerk One backed out of the supervisor's chamber, grateful that the discussion had remained constructive and not devolved into a barrage of punitive commands. The clerk had punished the stevedore, and perhaps that would be deemed a sufficient sanction against the crew laxity which had allowed this ridiculous scenario to unfold.

Ship Supervisor faced a difficult decision. The present location, among the cluster of spaceships and habitats known as Trade Nexus Four, was a special zone governed by intergalactic agreements. The enforcers of those agreements were the mysterious Far Galactans, a seemingly benevolent race with an insatiable curiosity about strange life forms and their cultures.

The supervisor could request their assistance, but the loss of face would negatively impact its own career. Of course the loss of the ship, or any of its contents, would also have a damaging impact. The supervisor held the ultimate authority to weigh these possibilities against the odds of losing its own or any subordinate life.

* *

Ian heard a noise from the corridor. The doorway was still open but all had been quiet since his hostage's compatriot had fled. Someone else was coming.

The second blaster pistol lay beside Ian. He needed both

hands now to hold even a single blaster upright and aimed at his hostage. Two more pistols remained mostly hidden in the ripped pockets of his filthy Centauran tunic.

Sweat dripped down his forehead and Ian freed one hand momentarily to sweep up the droplets which he then licked off his finger. His hand shook under the weight of the pistol.

Careful. That is a hair trigger.

The sound outside grew louder. Someone was approaching very slowly and making a clucking noise. It did not want its arrival to startle the dangerous alien trespasser.

Ian's eyes swept back and forth from his hostage to the doorway. A tiny scraping sound could be heard and he saw a tray with some small bowls slide into view. The red arm that had propelled it paused, then pushed the tray decisively into the room. A red Centauran head could not avoid appearing briefly before immediately retreating.

Ian rolled onto his side and pushed himself along the floor until he reached the tray. There were two bowls of water and two bowls of a warm red mush. Ian smelled the water first. No smell. He stuck his tongue in. No taste.

It was possible it was poison, but the Centaurans seemed to have thought of a clever way to reassure him. There were two bowls of each item, so Ian could easily share with his hostage and observe the effect before consuming any himself. Ian calculated his odds and then gulped the entire contents of one of the water bowls.

He gagged, almost vomited, and struggled to compose himself. The Centauran was looking at him and its eyes were not blinking.

Does that mean it is calm, or planning to attack?

Ian took the other water bowl and one food bowl off the tray and then shoved the tray with its remaining food bowl at his captive. It contemplated the bowl but did not eat until Ian waved the pistol and made an agitated comment.

"How can you have any pudding if you don't eat your meat?" demanded Ian, menacingly.

The hostage began to eat the red mush slowly, sticking an index finger in, then licking its digit. Ian sipped on the remaining water bowl and struggled to remain awake. His hands shook.

Mustn't spill.

Ian's stomach felt like it was full of bubbles. He struggled, choking momentarily, trying to keep the water down. His pistol, still in his right grip, now rested on the floor, pointing only vaguely at his prisoner.

Ian dropped the water bowl, precious water spilling, as a heavy projectile contacted forcefully with his head. It was the food bowl he had offered his captive. The sudden pain distracted Ian and the Centauran knocked the pistol from Ian's hand before he could react.

Now it grabbed him by the neck and, lifting him to a standing position, started pummelling Ian's body with its lower fists. Ian lost control of his digestive tract, expelling some of the valuable water through his mouth. This did not repel the Centauran but instead infuriated it. Its two upper hands now controlled Ian's only two as blows from its lower fists cracked more of Ian's ribs.

PART 4: THE NEXUS

Chapter Thirty-Seven

Ian did not see the strange creature materialize behind him. It resembled a biped evolved from a rodent species. More squirrel than mouse, it was a dark chocolate brown and almost two meters tall, not counting the fluffy, crimson tail.

Ian was swooning from exhaustion and the pain induced from his struggle with the Centauran. When the pressure around his neck suddenly moderated, and the blows raining down on his midsection ceased, Ian's first reaction was to reach for one of the two pistols still in his makeshift pockets. When he found he could not move, could not control any of his voluntary muscles, Ian's attention shifted to his surroundings.

The Centauran still grappled him, but appeared to be similarly paralyzed. And now there was a giant squirrel entering Ian's field of vision. It examined Ian closely, cocking its head as it considered his filthy clothing. Obviously an intelligent creature familiar with technology, it examined then gently prodded a small device held in one of its well-articulated paws. Ian felt his whole body tingle and his vision ceased to register any light.

* *

Ship Supervisor was already regretting its decision. The Far Galactans had removed the menace from the ship but now the supervisor was drowning in a flood of procedural requirements. Ship Supervisor had no proof that its crew had not kidnapped the alien instead of it stowing away. The two-arm had endangered the supervisor's ship and crew, but no one had been seriously injured. The damage to the

232

ship had been remarkably slight despite the enormous destructive potential of the Domain weapons that this two-arm had purloined. Probably the two-arm was something the recently salvaged rogue ship had taken from a primitive planet.

Now Ship Supervisor's next few cycles would be filled with statements and document filing. The ship's mission would be on hold until the mess regarding this terrorist refugee was sorted out. The idea of dumping the problem of the two-arm on the Trans-Galactic Tribunal was appealing, but unrealistic. The guarantors of peace in Trade Nexus Four had more rules than sense.

If Ship Supervisor did not pursue prosecution against the stowaway, the so-called justice system of Trade Nexus Four would allow the two-arm to turn the tables and sue its own victims. It would be imperative, therefore, to drive this prosecution to its logical end despite the considerable cost and effort required.

* *

Ian opened his eyes slowly. Brain awash in pain from bodily neglect and abuse, he was uncertain what had just happened. His new environment was a room unlike anything he had seen on either saucer.

The rectangular area in front of him sported two stainless steel doors, large but not inhuman in scale, and a clean white floor. The walls were off-white but covered with a band of textured detail that covered the middle two-thirds of the surface area.

Some of the bas relief patterns appeared to repeat, especially along the top and bottom of the strip, but the middle contained an intricate pattern that appeared random yet carefully balanced and considered. Perhaps this was a culture that cared about beauty and comfort.

Ian could not see what was behind himself, or move his

233

body. He hung suspended in a bubble. He could not feel any torque of gravity upon his body. His thirst had abated somewhat and his ribs had ceased to feel like organ-puncturing daggers. He was alive and out of immediate danger. This was an unexpected but welcome result.

One of the silver doors opened and another of the giant squirrel creatures entered. This one was smaller, thinner, and quite a bit redder than the first. It fiddled with a device in its paw for a moment, then looked up at Ian.

"How are you?"

The squirrel's mouth had not moved. The words had come from its paw-held device. Ian found he could now move his mouth.

"I'm thirsty. Hungry. I need medical help. I've got broken bones."

The squirrel's head was bobbing gently sideways, listening to the little chips and chirps its translator made as Ian spoke. With one paw, it slipped something inside its mouth and began to chew. It crinkled the wrapper that remained in its paw, nudged a point on the wall carving, and pushed the wrapper into a small rectangular slot that opened nearby.

It then appeared to choke as if in pain. Bits of whatever it was eating spewed out of its mouth, the bulk of which were launched as a gritty mist into the air. Then it squealed, an alarmed tone, rising and rising. With its paw still jammed inside the wall slot, it momentarily defied gravity by running up the wall, over the ceiling, and down onto the floor again.

As it repeated its circular journey, its distressed squeal rising in intensity, its thick crimson tail smacked Ian like a velvet baseball bat and knocked him into a spin. The room revolved as Ian rotated in his floating bubble.

After several more gravity-defying complete

234

revolutions, its paw came free and the squirrel dropped to the floor beside Ian. Floating bits of fur and foodstuff zigzagged slowly towards the floor.

"Sorry about that. My paw got pinched in there somehow. I didn't hit you, did I?"

"Nothing serious. I'm fine."

"I must apologize. Very unprofessional of me."

The giant squirrel reached toward Ian and removed one of its long reddish hairs that had settled on Ian.

"Let's see. Yes. We mended your bones and rebalanced your body chemistry. You are being hydrated and fed right now. You can't see the care line because it is behind you. Do you know why you are here?"

"I don't know where I am."

"You are safely aboard the administration node for this trade nexus. My people enforce order here. You were removed from the ship of the DogStars and pacified because of your violent actions."

"DogStars? Who is that? I thought I was aboard a Centauran spaceship. Aren't those four-armed red creatures from Beta Centauri?"

"That is not what we call them. The designation 'Centauran' is unknown to us."

"Whoever they are, they attacked my planet and kidnapped me."

"That is what we need to verify. If you were acting in self-defence then you will be set free. If not, you may have some real problems."

"I am not a violent or dangerous person. My planet was attacked."

"That could be hard to prove. We do agree that you are a person, despite your unknown type. The rest is to be adjudicated. Can you tell me more about your kidnapping?"

235

"My home planet is Earth, in the Solar System. The Centaurans, or DogStars, or whatever you call them, arrived at my planet with a fleet of giant spaceships and forced us to surrender. There was a peace deal, signed under duress, that stated my planet would provide labour and materials for five years to these invaders. Supposedly, after that time, they would leave and we would be free.

I was basically on the run from the mayhem of the invasion when the aliens beamed me aboard their ship. You know about this type of instant transportation; isn't that how you got me here?"

"Yes and no. You were tranquilized and then physically removed by our intervention team. We do have similar technology but there are strict limits on how it can be used safely and ethically. Please continue."

"Okay. They kept me in a room with a hose attached to me, but I escaped when their ship crashed on a planet of birds. I was the only survivor. When a second ship came along, same saucer design, same aliens, I stowed away in the hope it would take me back to Earth."

"But then you attacked the crew with military weapons?"

"I was hungry, dying of thirst. I had to do something. I found the weapons, their weapons not mine, and used them only with the thought of forcing them to take me home."

"They were carrying these weapons? That is interesting. It could be useful."

"Do you believe me? That I only intended to defend myself?"

"Certainly."

"But why would you believe me instead of these other creatures who you seem to be quite familiar with?"

"Apart from the fact that your story makes more sense than theirs, I believe you because it is my job. I am your

representative."

"Thank you. I am in your debt. Can you get me down from here?"

The giant squirrel hesitated for a moment, staring into Ian's eyes.

"There will be no further violence?"

"Not from me."

"You may call me Nut-beard."

"I am very pleased to meet you, Nut-beard. My name is Ian Hesse. Please call me Ian."

Nut-beard manipulated the small device in its paw and Ian slowly descended the half meter until his feet were touching the floor. Better yet, he could feel his feet as they contacted the floor. Feeling and control were returning to his whole body.

"Be careful not to disengage the care line in your left arm. There is a rest chair behind you. I suggest you use it. You are still weak."

Ian shuffled backwards weakly until his posterior bumped the promised soft platform. He hoisted himself onto its comfortable flat surface. The line attached to his arm tugged a bit painfully and he cursed in pain.

"Are you all right?"

"This thing is painful."

"We can remove it. Please don't move."

A much smaller squirrel, not much more than a meter tall, entered the room and approached Ian slowly. It chattered a bit with Nut-beard.

"It's not dangerous. It's intelligent, a kidnapping victim. It'll need water and solid food."

The translator did not clarify the second creature's chattering response to Nut-beard.

"No, we're not sure what it is."

More chatter.

"Yes, most unpleasant. If you could find some new coverings, I'd appreciate that. I will show it the hygiene chamber."

The second squirrel gingerly removed the line from Ian's arm and rubbed the puncture hole with a purple jelly that tingled in a pleasant way. It chattered again at Nut-beard as it exited the room.

"Thank you! I will stop by to talk with you before I go."

Nut-beard turned back to Ian.

"You can get rid of those dirty coverings. This is for discarded material."

Nut-beard pressed one of the carved wall patterns and a slot appeared below it.

"Also, this is for cleaning your body, and eliminating wastes."

Nut-beard pressed another pattern on the wall and a sizable panel disappeared revealing another chamber, smaller and with smooth walls.

"Push these toggles up and down to initiate warm and cold water streams. You can remove the water spray handle by pulling on it. Push this button for some mild cleaning liquid. It is safe. I think you'll like it."

Nut-beard pointed to a familiar-looking toilet in the hygiene closet.

"This receptacle is for bodily waste elimination. Remain seated and the fixture will clean you. When you are clean, the little blue light goes off."

Ian nodded, blinked heavily, and leaned back on the rest chair.

"We will get you some clean coverings soon, but in the meantime, you can wrap yourself in these."

Nut-beard touched another panel which promptly retreated exposing a small linen cupboard filled with white fluffy towels.

"The next time I come back we can..."

But Ian was already asleep on his clean rest chair. Nut-beard left the room feeling optimistic.

I'm pretty sure this one is innocent, thought Nut-beard. *Surely this time I will finally win a case.*

Chapter Thirty-Eight

Blythe looked beautiful and relaxed. She stood among beds of variously coloured tulips in full bloom. Her starched, plain nurse attire had been left behind. Today she wore a short black skirt and a trendy gold foil blouse. As Ian admired her, she laid her head on his shoulder next to his ear.

"I'm not wearing any panties," she confided, and then laughed, a beautifully self-contained giggle of mischief.

She led him deeper into the arboretum. A bee buzzed by on its way to important business. Birds idled in the trees, deciding their next move. They selected a shady spot, sheltered from the wrath of the Sun at apogee.

Ian spread out their blanket, smoothing the rumples and flicking away a too-inquisitive ant. Her bare arm contacted Ian's, sending an electric shock of sensual energy into his body. He leaned in towards her warmth, expecting a kiss but instead received the poor substitution of a surprised shout.

"Look, Ian!"

High above them, a silvery grey flying saucer was rapidly approaching. They watched the circle of its belly grow and grow until just as it appeared they were about to be crushed, the saucer veered toward an open area closer to the road. The silent landing portended menace to Ian, but Blythe was enthusiastic.

"This is incredible! Let's go meet them!"

Ian looked down at Blythe's skirt. Her legs were splayed carelessly open, revealing the truth of her earlier claim. His sense of lost opportunity piqued his burgeoning dread. There was something dangerous about that saucer, but he could not remember any specifics.

There is something very wrong here. We should escape

while we can.

But it was already too late. Blythe had captured his hand and was pulling him towards the strange vessel. Others were streaming across the field toward the new arrivals. Families, nature lovers, couples, no one seemed to sense any danger as they plunged ahead. Children ran excitedly out in front of their parents while whining canines pulled their masters forward with a length of leash.

When they passed the last stand of trees and gained a clear view of the saucer, they saw ruddy, four-armed aliens streaming out of a small portal near the bottom of the ship. They carried stereotypical woven picnic baskets lined with red and white checkered cloth, and were spreading out in small groups of two or three not far beyond the perimeter of their vehicle.

"This is incredible! We must get closer!" exclaimed Blythe.

"They could be dangerous."

"Yes their picnic baskets are full of ray guns," Blythe chided Ian.

Ian's stomach was tightening up but he could not stop their progress. There was nothing in his memory to substantiate his concerns.

I know this is not good. Why can't I remember? Why?

They finally stopped just a few feet from the first clique of crimson aliens. Ian watched fascinated as the aliens used all four arms to spread out their picnic goodies on a giant pink blanket.

"They can't be that advanced," Blythe whispered. "They have So-Duh but no orange juice."

How can they have an Earth brand? We don't know who they are!

"Hello, what a gorgeous planet you have. I am Leisure Decoy Two."

241

The alien was speaking to them.

"I'm Blythe, this is Ian. Ian Hesse," she added knowingly.

"Hiss like the noise a snake makes?" asked the alien innocently.

"No, different vowel. Hesse, not hiss," explained Blythe.

"Pleased to meet you both. Would you like a So-Duh?"

It offered both Ian and Blythe a can each with its upper arms. The lower arms continued to extricate and prepare other snacks from its basket.

"Why thank you. I will." Blythe took a can but Ian refused his, shaking his head and keeping his eyes fixed on the alien. "Would you like a chocolate? Have you tried our dark chocolate?" Blythe extended a freshly opened box of Black Dog Extra Dark Chocolates and the alien took one and made a satisfied sound as it popped it inside its mouth. Ian looked away from its teeth.

Black dog, red dog, what am I missing?

"You must stay and join us," invited the alien, gesturing at its own blanket area with all four hands.

Too many hands to keep track of all of them. Not good.

"Surely you would enjoy this, our own extra dark treat." The alien produced a black metallic snake head; a line of black hose extended behind, connecting it to the interior of the alien picnic basket.

Before Ian could protest, Blythe swept her hair away from her neck and the alien clamped the black device below her ear, near the carotid artery. Her eyelids closed and, with an almost sensual sigh, she descended to a supine position. Ian watched in horror as she lay motionless on the pink blanket.

"No! Take it off her!"

Ian turned back toward the ruddy alien expecting to tussle, but everything had changed. The picnic basket was gone and he was now deep in the woods, alone.

Son of a bitch. They took her.

Ian scanned the dense bushes for indications of company. All was quiet. Ian hefted the small slag hammer in his hand. Where had he gotten it?

This must be a dream. There's no continuity and I can't remember normal things.

Strange vocalizations now emanated from further along the path. It was the red aliens again. Ian hid behind a tree and waited for them to pass. It was a group of three, the first two walking together, the third trailing. Each had a pistol, albeit holstered.

As the final silent alien passed, Ian stepped out behind it and landed a hard blow to its head with the blunt end of his hammer. It crumpled. Ian had its weapon out of the holster and in hand before the others realized what had happened to their companion. As they turned back towards Ian, their strange gobbling language registered an uptick in rapidity and loudness. They were not happy.

Ian jumped back into the brush, behind a thick and weathered tree trunk, and stabbed at the safety switch on the side of the blaster.

I know this weapon. Where have I seen it before?

Arcs of light sliced toward him. Ian smelled burnt wood and a branch fell noisily only one arm's length away. The fight was on. Ian hunkered low to the ground and peered out towards the trail.

Where did they go?

Ian noticed his hammer was slick. It was covered with urple blood, the blood of the ruddy Kali-esque alien.

"You won't need those weapons anymore. You are done ere."

The voice startled Ian and he almost fired upon its unlikely source, a man-sized squirrel who had appeared in the bushes close behind him.

"Who are you?"

"You will remember me shortly. The important thing is to not commit any more violence, and to trust me."

"Why should I trust you?"

"Am I armed?" The upright squirrel offered its empty front paws.

"Are we safe here?" Ian peered towards the trail. There was no one in sight.

"You are safe. Come with me." The squirrel turned and began to move forward in a quasi-hopping motion. After each step, it paused and waited for Ian's smaller, slower, and smoother gait to catch him up. They headed uphill, toward the source of aliens, but no aliens were seen.

A grey arch of some alien technology waited for them as they rounded a final twist in the hiking path. It seemed faintly familiar.

This is a trap.

"I'm not going inside that thing."

"You must. It is the only escape from your violent vision."

Talking squirrel. I must be dreaming.

Ian shook his head. "Why would I go in there?"

"You are already inside. That is the *exit*. Please step through." The improbably furry creature focused its implacable gaze upon Ian and waited for understanding to dawn.

This squirrel's persuasion is insistent, and yet respectful.

Ian had little to gain by staying on this unreal version of Earth. He dropped his sticky hammer and stepped into the arch.

244

Chapter Thirty-Nine

Stepping through the arch, Ian was delivered into an absolute black emptiness. The arch had frozen his body, or so he imagined as his body did not seem to exist anymore. His mind was free, but free only to spin its wheels in a profoundly deep and echoic labyrinth. His thoughts seemed to bounce lightly off distant walls.

What is this? There's nothing. I don't think this is good. I can't see because it is dark? Or am I anywhere, maybe just written into the neural networks of Aliens Irreducible, these fiendish things I've never seen before.

Well not all of them were evil. Byrd was cool. I should've never left his planet. But I had to. I know there's something for me back on Earth. Maybe the Centaurans, or DogStar things, or whatever they are, will honour their contract and leave the Earth in peace after five years. Hell maybe they'll share some tech.

I'm dreaming in Technicolor. No I'm dreaming in total freaking darkness. Holy freak, this is not good!

Is there something I can do? Does time pass here? Think of Blythe. Please any God or gods that may exist, let me get back to her, plant me back on Earth, a cosmic seed; I will bear your fruit.

I must be losing it. Correct that. I have already lost it. Lost my life, my wife, my job, my planet. Now, perhaps my sanity. But not yet! Not while I can still control myself and think useful thoughts. Here I have lost my body. I can see nothing, but I believed that squirrel, that giant alien talking squirrel. Why shouldn't I trust it?

I will be out of here in no time and things will get straightened out.

I must be mad to think that.

There is nothing. All is blackness. Not even the random

firings of my optic nerve disturb this visual void. What a terrible thing to be blinded. There's nothing to control my fear now. I can't verify there are no monsters approaching. I can't see that I'm alone and insect-free. At least I have no sensation of skin and therefore no possibility of feeling unknown insects investigating my flesh. It's similar to being buried alive, but I can't detect my straining lungs, can't smell the air recycled into staleness.

Perhaps I'm being punished for my actions on the saucer and this is a merciful death or incarceration.

Maybe this is the end. Perhaps I deserve it after all. I've done little for my planet and my kind. Back when I was a student I used to lecture myself about the hardships I had to endure. If I ate generic yellow cheesy noodles and second rate peanut butter on old bread for a week, I'd just remind myself of all the Nigerian children who spent their days combing through acres of piled garbage with no graduation or escape conceivable. Who was I to complain?

And who am I now to complain, being thrust into this black abyss? Am I in pain? No. I feel nothing. Only my brain seems to exist. So I can't see. Whose fault is that? I made my choice. I took my risk. I entered the arch. I own this moment.

I remember how it ended now. Gale didn't want to know me, the real me. All those years I had suffered with my stutter, never being able to say much at all. I was agreeable because it was just too difficult to disagree, I can now admit.

I saw many a therapist, psychologist, and doctor, but none of the treatments helped. Since puberty, boom, I had a huge avoidance factor for any type of public speaking, and a lot of private conversations as well.

Some teenage boys bemoan the fact they cannot think of something to say, or don't have the nerve to approach a beautiful classmate. I simply could not perform the fluent delivery of any opening remark, no matter how well-formed in my own mind. I was locked out. Locked in an isolation perhaps not entirely different from this one.

The impediment reigned over my life until I completed the Dare to Achieve camp during my first year at DigiFab. It was an extensive executive-style training course where I was sequestered for a week, collaborating with groups of strangers to produce presentations, and in which I had no choice but to participate.

However, the way it was structured, the assignments were quite interesting and fun, and the final solutions creative and engaging, so we delighted in designing and delivering them. I remained in email contact with several of these colleagues as the good vibes from the meeting of the minds had not faded even months later as we conversed, ironically, via email.

I finally had the positive experiences, breath control, and harness on my state of mind to slow down and get any troublesome word out. Better yet, I had seen myself fail but continue without admitting defeat.

Disfluency was no longer defeat; it was merely a brief delay. I now had the ability, well mostly, to take a deep breath, not panic, and get the airways and vibrations cooperating to produce the intended sounds.

Now I could speak to my family, to my friends, to my co-workers, to anybody. It changed my perspective. I was more optimistic and upbeat. This euphoric period lasted only a while.

Soon enough, I found out that people didn't necessarily like the new me, the guy who had questions, feedback, and general opinions. It seems everyone likes to talk, but nobody likes to listen.

I had been unaware of this, being outside of the battle

for verbal dominance for so many years. I just didn't see it. People who talked a lot seemed to me to be interesting and intelligent people. I had long since given up on interrupting them.

Most surprising was how this phenomenon was not limited to insignificant relationships. My younger brothers who forever depending on my ready and steady listening ear were suddenly not taking my calls.

Gale's betrayal was complete. She had used my new voluble turn as an excuse to turn away. How distasteful I had become. My ideas were like weeds in the garden, painful to look upon, not as something delicious and life-sustaining.

It was so disappointing. My greatest triumph had turned into a personal disaster. I should be glad for the black void, except now of course I remember everything.

She grew tired of my two cents. Where before she had spoken 99% of the words, I had unilaterally altered the division to 50% each. This was apparently a deal-breaker. I saw some of her texts to Miguel later and she was back to her 99% style, which seemed to suit him, at least at that time. I have no idea how they are doing now.

Is it that I didn't know her very well, or is it that she didn't know me well? What so hurt me was how, without too much effort, indeed with surprising ease and aplomb, she seemed to know just what to say at each stage of our relationship disintegration, while I did not. Despite having regained physical mastery of fluency, I no longer had the words to express my dismay and pain, so I reverted to my previous almost silent existence.

But it was too late. The damage was done. She had chosen to move on. Can I let her go and move on, myself? Why not? I have Blythe. Well, the Universe has her, I hope. All I have is this void and my endless ticking thoughts.

248

Chapter Forty

Ian fell forward, emerging from the darkness of the arch with a gasp like a man surfacing from deep underwater. Now he remembered everything. He gulped air and waited for his heart to stop racing.

A man-size squirrel stared impassively down at Ian as he lay on the floor. Ian glanced behind himself and confirmed the existence of the arch. As the squirrel began to vocalize a stream of sharp chatter, a small electronic device suspended from a band around its neck provided the translation.

"I got you out of there just in time."

Now Ian remembered this was Nut-beard, his advocate.

"Where did I just come from? I thought I was back on Earth."

"I must apologize but I was legally constrained from warning you about the temperament test. Your hosts, the government of this trade nexus, needed to know just how dangerous you are. The fact that you were apparently willing to kill a DogStar in this simulation does not bode well for your release."

"Willing to kill? I was being attacked! Earth, my planet, was being attacked by these four-armed aliens. And they attacked my female companion. How could I not react in that situation?"

"The appropriate response would have been to invoke the protection of law enforcement personnel."

"Am I not entitled to defend my own life? Don't you take into account my history with these creatures? If you did, then you'd know anything I did was in self-defence."

"That will have to be decided by the authorities. But relax, Ian, I am on your side..."

Ian examined his limbs. He was uninjured and clean. No ill effects lingered from the simulation. He pulled himself into a sitting position.

"I suppose that's the best news I've had in a while. So what is that arch and how did I end up inside it?"

Nut-beard's translator seemed easily able to keep up with his bursts of chatter.

"It is called an Emotional Recovery chamber. It can simulate different realities. In this case it was used to confront you with a specific type of intelligent creature, the DogStars, who you've encountered before, and to see how your subconscious represents them and then how you consciously react to that representation. We use the device for evaluation and identification of criminals and mental defectives. There are also some who use these devices for recreation, but that is not legal on most planets."

"Why not legal? If it's not real, then what harm can it do?"

Ian noticed that Nut-beard was chewing on a large nut it had produced like a magician. Shards of nut flecked the fur around its mouth.

"The things that happen in ER do not have the same reality as things that happen outside it, but they do have an effect on Koryolis, which is a definite cost, a moral or spiritual cost, although those are not the correct expressions. I cannot explain it properly because the translator is in a very basic mode necessitated by our not knowing your true origin point and type. Suffice to say, you should be on your best behaviour when inside an ER chamber.

Here, unfortunately, you slip through a crack in the regulations. As your advocate I am legally precluded from discussing any evaluation or test the authorities want to inflict on you, but being an unknown, you don't have basic information about ER chambers or the K index because of your primitive background."

"I didn't come back right away when I left the arch. I was stuck, disembodied in darkness. What was that?"

"After I left you sleeping in your quarters, an officer of the Trade Nexus Order Enforcement visited you and gave you a drug which induces a state of heightened consciousness while severing all sensory connection with your surroundings. This drug is activated only upon exit from the ER chamber. You would have experienced what felt like an extended duration floating in a black vacuum. From our temporal perspective, this only required a few minutes."

Ian nodded. It had felt like hours to him.

"This pause is intended to allow the guilty to reflect on their crimes, and also to stimulate thoughts which might allow corrective personality development. After that, the officer physically propelled you into the ER chamber where your reactions were monitored."

"So I'll be judged on what I did in the ER chamber, not on what I did in the real world?"

"Your behaviour in the ER is only one facet of our information about you. In no case would it override other significant information. Don't worry about that. I'm certain those results will be excluded anyway because, as I said, you do not have the basic awareness of the ER process as any other citizen would. That is why I appealed to be allowed to enter the ER early and warn you to stop. Now the authorities are aware that you come from a previously ignored planet."

"Ignored? What do you mean?"

"The entire galaxy was surveyed long ago. At that time, your species had either not yet evolved or was deemed insufficiently advanced to be invited to join the space-faring community. Therefore your planet was likely designated off-limits to the commercial and military

251

interests of other species."

"So these DogStar creatures, they're breaking the law by invading my planet?"

"From what you say, yes, I think so. However, there is a difference between a recognized government being responsible for a breach of the Protection of Species Accord and a few rogue spaceships doing so.

In the former case, we can exert pressure to correct the behaviour of the aggressive government. Cases such as these are very rare. I can recall only one instance, and that indirectly, an example from my original training in Interspecies Law."

Nut-beard paused for a moment to swirl a furry paw against its mouth, driving a sizable fraction of the orphaned remnants of his nut snack into its mouth, while loosening the rest to ready them for launch via the pneumatic impulse of its vocalizations. Nut-beard straightened its posture and stared at the ceiling momentarily to ready its reminiscence.

"It was half a galactic revolution ago. The planet of Iron Claw did not recognize the primitive yet intelligent occupants of their neighbour planet, Orange Planet, as it was known. Iron Claw plundered much of Orange Planet's rare minerals and metals.

By the time the Trans-Galactic Tribunal recognized the problem and settled on a course of action, the Orange Planet had already suffered severe environmental degradation. Iron Claw was ordered to repair and rebuild the ecology of Orange Planet but the cost was so great that Iron Claw was driven into economic breakdown. When they could no longer fulfill the orders of the Trans-Galactic Tribunal, Iron Claw was isolated from the community of species through sanctions and blockades.

The unity of their government soon split and Iron Claw descended into civil war. Unfortunately, divisions prevailed and the end result was the total destruction of the Iron Claw planet.

It is a classic morality tale of the strong destroyed by their own reckless ambition. The ultimate outcome was that Orange Planet did recover and evolved into one of the pillars of our galactic community. It is an inspirational case for a young advocate interested in order and harmony."

"So why would these DogStars attack Earth if they knew this history?"

"Well, as I said, the other possible case is that the attack was not sanctioned by any planetary government. If the forces are rogue, there is little we can do in the short term. For documented, long-term abuse of a young planet, there is a process whereby the Trans-Galactic Tribunal can deem the victim world a protected sanctuary and issue an order for active defence of that planet from outsiders.

Of course, this is a resource-intensive course of action which the tribunal would likely only pursue if there were significant strategic or political reasons for doing so."

"So, in the case of an unknown planet, you just let the pirates have at it?"

"If I understand you correctly, then yes, we let them have what is at it. The reasoning is that the Trans-Galactic Tribunal is primarily concerned with pacifying aggression and optimizing relations between inter-species governments, not dealing with rogue criminals. That is usually the purview of the local powers themselves."

"And if there are no local powers?"

Nut-beard flicked its crimson tail from side to side for a moment before speaking again.

"There are some organizations that are interested in such problems."

"Can I contact them?"

"You have more immediate problems. You must think about your own future. We must prepare your defence against the allegations from the DogStar ship."

Nut-beard extracted another nut from who knows where and began to nibble at it thoughtfully.

"The fact that there is no record of your species on the Avian Branch, that's the planet where you boarded the ship you are alleged to have damaged, supports your claim of kidnapping. If you believed you were being kidnapped, and you perceived the innocent DogStars as indistinguishable from the other DogStars, your invaders and fully culpable captors, then self-defence becomes a valid argument."

Minute flecks of nut were riding Nut-beard's breath into the air. Ian perceived a slight odour.

"What worries me most is your status as non-citizen of any recognized government. This means that, even if your defence is completely accepted and you are set free, because there is no one to act as your guarantor or provide for the resources you consume, you would remain in detention aboard this ship until you could be sent back to your home planet.

There is little priority given to such cases and you might well remain here for the rest of your life. Of course, if the DogStars are attacking your planet as you say, then this might be a good thing. It might save your life."

Ian was dumbfounded. Remaining in this admittedly humane cell for the rest of his life was not an attractive option.

"Are you saying that even if I'm proven innocent, there'll be no help for Earth?"

"Your predicament as a displaced entity is distinct from the question of improper interactions between your planet-bound culture and the DogStars. What is more, you really don't want these two issues linked.

254

If the DogStar government requests it, you might be transferred into their custody pending the outcome of an investigation into the piracy claims you've made against some of their citizens. If the piracy investigation reveals the location of your home planet, the DogStars will ensure that your Earth is free of pirates and return you there. While this sounds good in theory, and I believe your welfare would be adequately secured in the care of the legitimate DogStar government, the delay would be no doubt intolerable to you.

Very few DogStar pirates are ever brought to justice because they tend to attack planets that are far beyond the sphere of influence of the transgalactic order. The result would be you rotting in a cell on the DogStar home planet, a significantly less comfortable and agreeable existence than what this trade nexus can provide."

"But I could be returned to Earth eventually, and then the invasion would also be reversed?"

"In theory. That is the stated goal of the DogStar government for such situations. If you look at their actual history, however, there have only been a pawful of cases in which pirate victims were returned home and the victim planet secured.

The most recent case involved a planet called Genorax that had been infested with pirates for several generations of the native inhabitants. Most of the planet was contaminated with industrial byproducts. Also, the crust was severely disrupted by deep mining for minerals. The pirates had forced all the young Genorax into slave labour while the old were slaughtered.

When the DogStars finally abandoned the planet, it was barely habitable and the culture of the Genorax had decayed to a pre-industrial level. The DogStar pirates were punished, but in reality there was nothing that could be

*done to reverse the damage to the Genorax. No. It would
be foolish in the extreme to give yourself into the custody of
the DogStars."*

Nut-beard was shaking its head and motes of nut crumb
flew free. The giant squirrel extracted a small cloth from an
unseen pocket and blew its nose noisily before continuing
the lecture.

*"There may be, however, another possible avenue.
There are certain elements of the Far Galactan civilization
that are very interested in alien justice, and unusual and
complex cases such as yours."*

"Who are these Far Galactans? Is that who controls this
space station?"

*"This trade nexus is one of several special areas in the
galaxy where different civilizations meet and trade under
the protection of the Far Galactans and the Trans-Galactic
Tribunal.*

*Several revolutions ago, long before I was born, the Far
Galactans, or Far Gs as we call them, announced their
presence in this galaxy. They established zones where
representatives of different planets could operate trading
and diplomatic missions under a security guarantee
provided by the Far Gs in the guise of their Trans-Galactic
Tribunal.*

*The tribunal consists of various representatives from
this galaxy plus a quorum of Far Gs. The Far Gs have
enormous sophistication and power, but also an inherent
caution or shyness that keeps most of them far away from
aliens.*

*The Far Gs in the trade nexuses are mostly scientists
interested in exobiology, exopsychology, or cosmic
evolution. They tend to ask more questions about us than
provide answers about themselves. What we do know is
that the Far Gs are immensely powerful but apparently*

benign or at least passive. They are the only species we know that has travelled here from beyond this galaxy. That fact itself speaks of their power. What was your question again?"

"Do the Far Gs own this space station?"

"Yes. I mean the answer is no. This ship was contributed to this trade nexus by my people, the Tree Line Glory. We support the Trans-Galactic Tribunal in enforcing order here in conjunction with the Far Gs, but the day-to-day operations do not require input from the Far Gs.

The Trans-Galactic Trade Nexus Protocols dictate the justice procedures used here, as agreed by the original signatories to the Trans-Galactic Accord under which all the trade nexuses were established. In return for our contribution of this ship and its personnel as stewards of this nexus, we are given a regular allotment of pure hydrogen and oxygen by the Far Gs."

A pinging noise interrupted Nut-beard. The giant squirrel reached around as if to scratch its back, and then revealed a small electronic device. It pinged again. Nut-beard examined the device intently for a moment.

"We have another problem. The DogStars have filed a Motion of Examination. This means they want to take custody of you to establish the veracity of your statements."

"Is that good? Will it speed up the process of stopping the pirates?"

"No. As I've said, the two issues are not connected. They only want to examine the thought patterns surrounding your claim about how you wound up on their ship. What you don't understand is that their interrogation methods can be painful and damaging, especially for species other than DogStars. They conveniently throw leaves upon the idea that their tools are not designed for other species and

then, when something goes wrong, they feign ignorance and claim the accused was either already weak or died in a struggle to escape."

"Sounds like the DogStars are not model galactic citizens."

"The planet of their origin has a harsh environment and their civilization remains a very weak economic entity. There are obvious reasons why so many of them abandon their culture and become pirates. Those that remain behind must submit to the dictates of a cruel hierarchy. You would not last long in their custody. Please give up any idea of fighting for justice for your planet from a DogStar cell."

"I already have. Your advice seems very valuable and I will follow it."

"You are a very intelligent specimen for a primitive alien." Nut-beard blinked rapidly as if re-evaluating its last statement. *"Oh, I'm sorry if that formulation offends you."*

Ian chuckled at the squirrel's obsequiousness. It was the first time he could remember laughing since leaving Earth. He hoped it was not his last.

"I must leave now to consider how to counter this Motion. Please promise to be well-behaved until I return, and do not re-enter the ER even if someone offers to take you there."

Ian promised.

Chapter Forty-One

It was only a couple of hours before Nut-beard returned to Ian's cell, barely enough time for Ian to absorb the information dump his advocate had unloaded on him. It was clear that Ian's future was bound up by a complex network of rules evolving out of agreements that had been set long ago, agreements among entities he little understood or trusted.

Ian's one glimmer of hope was Nut-beard, his unlikely champion, who treated him with respect and apparent honesty. A human lawyer could not have engendered greater trust on Ian's part, although its competence was still a great unknown. The fact that Nut-beard did not seem especially skilled at keeping the area around its mouth free of food particles might be a warning sign that Ian's hopes should remain modest. Or it could just be a bad assumption based upon cultural bias.

At least Ian was out of harm's way, absent from the DogStar saucers, and inaccessible to unpredictable insects from strange planets. Instead, he rested among civil creatures that could understand his language.

Ian took advantage of the shower apparatus in the hygiene nook of his cell. It worked as Nut-beard had promised, and Ian luxuriated in the streams of clean, warm water that issued from the handheld device.

As he towelled himself off back in the main chamber of his cell, Ian reconsidered the best possible outcome of his case: spending the rest of his life aboard the Tree Line Glory's ship in this trade nexus. Nutbeard's people seemed to be sensitive creatures, and his life here would be secure. There might be some kind of contribution an engineer from Earth could provide. And there was always the hope that someday a way back to Earth might be found.

Ian sat on the rest chair beside his sleeping bubble. His legs were still dripping wet, but the warmth of the room rendered him physically comfortable.

If he ever got back to Earth, he would have stories to tell. He could probably write a bestseller about all the strange things he had experienced. Ian dried his legs and balled the towel, carefully tossing it toward the hygiene nook.

But Earth needed him. It needed something. How could he live here and enjoy the intellectual stimulation of new creatures, new cultures and new languages, while his home planet carried the heavy burden of alien oppression? Ian could never be the brave explorer, boldly absorbing new experiences, as long as Earth suffered. He would instead be the nervous refugee, always looking over his shoulder, fearing the return of his tormentors.

Ian's mood took a downward turn. The present was perhaps beyond what he could have asked for, but his future remained inscrutable and ominous.

Nut-beard entered before Ian managed to cover himself.

"Your species' lack of fur is quite extreme. Do you often feel cold?"

Ian turned away and quickly donned the modified DogStar wrap he had been provided.

"On Earth we take great pride in selecting our clothing for visual appeal as well as comfort. There are a lot of different types of clothing we wear because of the range of temperatures in our climate."

"I hope what has been provided meets your aesthetic needs."

Ian shrugged. The replacement DogStar tunic was a bland beige colour, with two sleeves removed and the armholes sewn shut. The stitches were clearly visible, quite possibly an unusual, custom job that provided valuable initial experience for a novice trans-galactic tailor.

"Fashion is not priority for me right now."

Nut-beard chattered briefly but the translator did not elucidate. Ian concluded the non-translated sounds were how citizens of the Tree Line Glory laughed.

"You are well-balanced. You will not be judged by your coverings today. This will not be a fashion battle. But we must be careful of your image. You must remain calm, stand proudly like an innocent citizen, and carefully follow what goes on."

Nut-beard by now understood human nodding.

"Yes, you will be judged today. We must attend the initial hearing today. The Motion for Examination will be discussed and we must argue against having the DogStars take you into their custody. Are you ready?"

"If you think I'm ready."

"There is not much for you to do. You must answer their questions honestly but do not elaborate unnecessarily. When it is my turn to ask questions, then you may answer more fully, knowing that my questions are designed to demonstrate your evolution and morality.

There is one more thing you need to know. A warning. The Far Galactans are not pleasing to the eye. If you react negatively to them or avoid looking at them, that could be misconstrued as guilt. They are very intelligent, but not immune to bias or slights. You must be brave as you look at them."

"What do they look like? Let me guess. Giant insects?"

"No, they are not of the insect family. They are more like fungal sporoids. Imagine a Hoffir gasbag dipped in sewage. If that means nothing, then imagine a compost heap with legs.

Also, when my kind first encountered the Far Gs, our odour suppression technology matured rapidly. Now when we meet them in person, much effort is made to suppress the odour. Unfortunately, some of it is chemical signalling essential to their intraspecies communication, so it cannot be entirely suppressed. You must not cover your breathing holes nor make indications of displeasure if you detect their stench. This is important. If you cannot respect them and be civil, we will not succeed."

"You had me at 'not insects'"

"I do not understand."

"Don't worry. I will control my behaviour. I will respect the judges and give no indication of what I might smell."

"Then we have a chance. Now it is time to go."

* *

Ian and Nut-beard walked the length of the Tree Line Glory ship together, emerging first from a cluster of cells into a medical area, then past the room containing the ER arch and into an access control point where Nut-beard's eye was scanned, and then finally out into a wider corridor where a phantasmagoria of creatures roamed freely.

Mixed into the population were various colours and shapes of Tree Line Glory squirrels, ruddy DogStars, spindly humanoids with opaque black eyes who wore metallic canisters as clothing, a strange lobster-like creature, and even a pair of individuals who seemed entirely robotic. It was possible these latter were organic creatures wearing fully isolating garments to meet their unique atmosphere requirements.

As they walked, Nut-beard explained that they would share the chamber with other cases. As spectators, however, they must not talk to each other once the hearing convened. All translators except those of the judges and the advocate for the current case would be disabled. A quick way to lose your own case would be to interrupt the judges while they were contemplating someone else's, even if you were just

262

whispering last minute instructions to your advocate. Ian again promised to behave.

The chamber for the hearing was long, narrow, and plain. The walls were unadorned, and the style of furniture did not evoke any gravitas. A grid of mostly unoccupied chairs formed an island in the middle of the room.

More seating was available on a set of long benches which spread down one wall. These were already well-occupied by numerous pairs of beings. Most of the advocates appeared to be Tree Line Glory squirrels, or else the squirrels disproportionately constituted the defendants and the diversity of creatures that contributed the other half of each creature pair on the bench were instead advocates.

Nut-beard rested its hind quarters on the bench, extending the queue of creature pairs similarly resting. Ian sat beside Nut-beard, trying to ignore the curious stares of the others. Nut-beard fumbled with its translator. Their eyes met and Ian was about to open his mouth when Nut-beard gave him a warning look and a very human head shake.

Ian closed his mouth and nodded in acquiescence.

Then the judges entered. One was a Tree Line Glory but the other two were Far Gs and, as promised, grotesque. The smell hit Ian almost immediately, like putrescent flesh garnished with a citrus tang. The Far Gs were a slimy, glistening brown, and had little shape. Despite the drab, filthy looking body mass, a ring of translucent skin crowned their ill-defined peaks. Flashes of light escaped the ring, suggesting a turbulent liquid interior.

Ian thought the Far Gs possessed no appendages, but was then surprised to see a tentacle slide onto the table and explore some controls there. The tentacle had developed finger-like manipulators by the time it reached the table. Apparently, the Far Gs simple shape belied their sophisticated shape-changing capabilities.

Now the judges' translator was enabled. Sounds of Tree Line Glory chatter filled the room.

The first pair of creatures rose from the head of the bench queue and stood before the judges. Ian could not determine what was said for the native comments of the first supplicant, a DogStar with a missing arm, were translated only into Tree Line Glory. Nut-beard listened intently, eyes fixed on the judges.

The Tree Line Glory judge made a longish speech and the DogStar's advocate uttered a very brief reply, perhaps a simple assent. Then the questioning began. Each judge had questions for the DogStar with the missing arm. It replied slowly and carefully to each question. Occasionally its advocate would interrupt and there would be some back and forth with one or more of the judges. Despite the language barrier, Ian thought the procedure itself resembled Canadian jurisprudence.

After a few minutes, the questions intensified and the DogStar began to gesture aggressively while answering. Nut-beard glanced at Ian to see if he was evaluating this mistake correctly. The case ended with two very large squirrels escorting the DogStar through the smaller of two doors at the back of the room. It was not the door from which the judges had earlier emerged. The DogStar's advocate then left the chamber via the public front entrance, its head bowed in the shame of defeat.

For the next case, both the supplicant and advocate were Tree Line Glory citizens and the outcome was happier. After only a minute or two of discussion with the judges, both advocate and client rapidly exited via the public entrance, tails twitching with excitement. As the double doors closed behind them, they began to chatter and paw each other.

Several more cases followed. Some clients walked free

while others were directed to the small door at the rear of the chamber. Finally there was no one on the bench closer to the judges than Nut-beard.

The Far G addressed Nut-beard. Ian was close enough now to hear what sounded like a sucking chest wound, or the frantic slithering of an arthropod on steroids, before the judges' translator began to emit squirrel chattering.

Nut-beard switched its own translator on.

"-...the alien of unknown type self-designated as Ian Hesse?-"

"Yes, Judge. I am his advocate."

Nut-beard's translator filtered both Tree Line Glory and Far G into English.

"-We have read your defence. It contains many assertions that have yet to be proven. You state that your client originates on a planet named Earth. However we have no knowledge of any civilized world bearing that name-"

"My client is truthful and intelligent. We communicate using CLLI mode Delta, a generic telepathic protocol for mammalian citizens. He has indicated his home world, Earth, has not yet attained galaxy-class technology. Might I remind the court that some parts of our galaxy have not been surveyed for intelligent life for more than one complete galactic revolution? Therefore it is possible that his species had not yet reached the acceleration point on the intelligent species development curve at the time of the most recent survey. Hence it is entirely possible that his civilization might be unknown to us."

"-No one is asserting your client is an animal. But he is not a citizen and he is not represented by any government. Has the Tree Line Glory ruled on his refugee status?-"

"His status is currently under consideration. The application has been accepted but will not be finalized

until these criminal matters have been resolved. I continue to act as advocate for all legal matters pertaining to my client."

"-Then your paws are full. Let us move on to the Motion for Examination provided by the ranking officer aboard the DogStar ship Responsibility. *They are asserting their right to examine your client for mental aberration, disease, or anti-social tendencies. In the face of your client's not-yet-determined status with the Tree Line Glory, I fail to see an alternative to granting this motion. Do you agree?-"*

"I must object, Judge. This is not acceptable. If responsibility for implementing this Motion is given to the DogStars, then all issues arising from this matter will gravitate into their legal system. To have my client's mental state evaluated based on their DogStar-centric methodology would bias the results and diminish his universal legal rights as the accused."

"-I did not ask if you found this an acceptable alternative. I asked if you agreed that there was no other alternative. Do you understand the difference and, I repeat, do you agree?-"

Nut-beard's tail twitched nervously. This is not a good sign, thought Ian.

"Esteemed Judge, my client was abducted from his home by a group of DogStar pirates who had invaded his planet. He is an innocent, a war refugee. To hand him over to the aggressor entity flies in the face of basic justice."

"-Nonetheless, if you cannot present an alternative, then only the resources of the DogStars can enable the continuance of this investigation, and therefore that is the direction it must go. Do you agree?-"

Nut-beard's tail flicked harder now. It carelessly brushed the side of Ian's face, eliciting in him a faint memory of a long ago pillow fight.

Just as Ian was giving up hope that Nut-beard would speak again, one of the creatures sitting in the public area stood up and activated its translator. As Tree Line Glory chatter emanated from the newly activated translator, a third voice enunciated English from Nut-beard's translator.

"Would it please the court to recognize Elim Icrosod of the Unknown Species Protection Front?"

The Tree Line Glory judge peered across the room at the new speaker. The translucent rings of the two Far G judges flickered briefly.

"-News travels fast. Does the USPF have an interest in these proceedings?-"

"Yes Judge. We would like to offer immediate sponsorship of the alien known as Ian Hesse. We can provide alternate examination and investigatory resources."

Elim was one of the creatures Ian had spotted in the corridor earlier and assumed was either a robot or wearing a spacesuit.

"-The court would have no objection, but both parties to the dispute must agree. You must file your proposed resolution to the Motion by the end of this cycle and both parties will need to reply to it by this time next cycle. We will restart this procedure then. Is this agreeable to the advocate?-"

"I agree, Judge."

"-Very well. We will reconsider the available alternatives next cycle. Next case!-"

Nut-beard turned his translator off and motioned for Ian to retreat the way they had come.

Outside the chamber, Elim introduced itself and explained to Ian that the USPF protected wildlife, intelligent or otherwise, from exploitation by the great space-faring civilizations. Ian's case had caught the interest

267

of their leadership and they did not want him to fall back into the clutches of the DogStars. The USPF believed that, if Ian's story could be verified, the DogStar pirate problem would be subject to much-needed publicity. Elim described the situation.

"These DogStars think they can just sneak over to the far side of the galaxy and do whatever they want to emerging civilizations. The only way to stop them is to expose the harm they cause. You can help us do that."

Nut-beard was grateful to the USPF but uncertain the DogStars would agree to the proposed approach.

Ian shuddered at how close he had come to abject failure in his legal battle. Now he had at least a slim chance for freedom. Things moved fast in trans-galactic justice. Tomorrow, or 'next cycle', he would know if he had any reason for hope.

Chapter Forty-Two

Aboard the DogStar spacecraft *Responsibility*, Ship Supervisor was reviewing its legal options. The Motion of Examination they had earlier submitted, requesting that Ian be handed over to the DogStar legal system for further investigation, was now being modified by a submission from the USPF.

These illogical champions of alien criminals and troublemakers were offering their resources to continue the investigation into the stowaway's reckless actions.

Ship Supervisor thought of all the labour drones back on DogStar. What chance did they have to escape the harsh penury of their existence? Compared to this ridiculous alien, they were leaders, each one sacrificing more for the survival of their species than this one worthless coward.

The two-arm claimed that DogStar ships were attacking its planet and yet it had fled. It had not fought the DogStar pirates. Instead, it had stowed away and then attacked the first innocent civilians it encountered, Ship Supervisor's hapless crew. Only narrowly was disaster averted. If the two-armed alien had continued firing its military weapon, the entire ship could easily have been lost.

Now it wanted a new chance to escape justice. The wrong-headed crusaders of the USPF had latched onto this case for political reasons, making available the organization's resources to prolong the delay of justice. But with every cycle that passed, this story leaked slanderous contamination into new pools of opinion, spoiling the DogStars' reputation.

If Ship Supervisor fought the USPF response to the DogStar motion, further public opinion contamination was inevitable. The small problem of piracy against primitive planets could not be allowed to disrupt the political and economic goals of the DogStar government. The best course of action would be to let the problem, and its public discussion, dissipate as quickly as possible.

The USPF could have the stowaway.

If the two-arm was in USPF custody they would be responsible for any accident that might befall it. Ship Supervisor was well acquainted with DogStars' abysmal record of caring for prisoners. Often prisoners were freed only to immediately die in mysterious circumstances. There was no accounting for luck and if this two-arm was set up for public display, something bad might happen.

Ship Supervisor sent an electronic message to the tribunal. The DogStars had no objection to the USPF driving the investigation into this alien stowaway. Now Ian Hesse was their problem.

* *

Ian was enjoying another shower. The Tree Line Glory ship operated on a diurnal cycle much briefer than that of Earth. Ian estimated it was perhaps fifteen hours long. This did not leave enough time for a proper night's sleep, so Ian had taken to napping. He would nap for a couple of hours, then wake himself up with a warm shower. In this way he maintained a functional, if not comfortable, level of alertness.

When Nut-beard arrived early the next cycle, it softly clapped its paws together in excitement.

"I have very good news! The DogStars have accepted the USPF's bid for examination lead. This means you will be taken into their care, not the DogStars!

I should explain. The USPF is a charitable organization, supported by many planets, and they have deep nut caches. If anyone can prove your story, it is them."

"Does this mean I am free to return to Earth?"

270

"Well, no."

Nut-beard quit clapping, his paws still far apart as if executing an angler's boast.

"We don't know where your planet is. And you are only allowed to go with the USPF because they have posted guarantees regarding your ultimate acceptance of trans-galactic justice. There has been no verdict yet, but with their help, the eventual verdict might be in your favour. If that happens, then your refugee claim will probably succeed and you will be free to live on virtually any planet in the galaxy."

"Any planet? Like Earth?"

"No, I mean any civilized planet. You would be given a translator and enough training to get you started. There are some lovely hominid planets. Perhaps one of them might interest you…"

Ian sat down heavily on the rest chair.

"This is very good news!"

"Yes, I understand. Nut-beard, I want to thank you for all you've done. I'm very grateful but the reality of my situation is still so complicated and my prospect of freedom so far off, that I can't feel much joy at this announcement."

Nut-beard laid a paw on Ian's shoulder.

"If you are innocent, you will go free. It may take some time, but it will happen, so don't lose hope."

It would test Nut-beard's faith in the justice system when, three cycles later, news of Ian's abduction from the paws of the USPF reached the nexus.

Chapter Forty-Three

Ian's second and final hearing proceeded rapidly. The judges quickly confirmed the DogStars had no objection to granting custody of Ian to the USPF. Elim sat beside Ian and rose when the judges addressed it.

"-You understand that the guarantees you have provided today will be forfeited if the accused goes missing?-"

Elim assured the court that it was not the intent of the USPF to subvert justice.

The judges granted a maximum examination period of one hundred cycles, at the end of which Ian would have to return to the Tree Line Glory tribunal ship at Trade Nexus Four. All evidence would then be considered, and a verdict rendered.

Ian was gratified that he would not be compelled to cross the threshold of the small door at the back of the court, behind which a more severe form of incarceration certainly awaited. Today he was free to walk out the public front door of the judgment chamber with his advocate and his USPF ally.

Elim had a ship waiting which would take Ian to a nearby planet with advanced examination devices available. Ian could expect more of the type of testing that he had first experienced as dreams and surreal adventures inside the ER arch. Elim promised the procedures would not be painful or dangerous.

Ian would have felt more assured had he been able to see what kind of creature actually dwelt in the spacesuit that made Elim appear so robotic. Likewise, the metallic tones of its external translator helped maintain his misgivings.

I have picked Door Number Two based only on the process of elimination. I trusted Nut-beard, but can I trust this new creature?

Saying goodbye to Nut-beard was surprisingly hard. Ian shook one of his advocate's oversized paws, but the giant squirrel turned bashful when Ian proffered a hug. Or maybe it thought Ian might have pythonic tendencies. Aliens are always full of surprises.

Elim's shuttle was docked at the far end of the Tree Line Glory ship. As they walked the half kilometre to the docking tubes, the diversity of the population of Nut-beard's city, for it was more city than mere ship, became increasingly evident. Ian wished for a camera; even a few pictures of the riot of species on parade could have enormous scientific and monetary value, that is, if the people of Earth had any interest in aliens after their Centauran' experience.

The shuttle was small but comfortable from a human perspective. Ian was given a very soft berth which could be hermetically sealed with the touch of a button, instantly excluding any external influence. As soon as the ship undocked, Ian took advantage of his private space and napped.

By the time he awoke, there were only stars outside. As he swivelled out of his berth, Elim greeted him with some familiarity, a welcoming empathy, and an activated translator.

"Ian, you have rested for a quarter cycle. Surely now you are well-rested?"

"Thank you. Yes I feel better. The days on the Tree Line ship were very short, much shorter than on my planet."

"While among us, you are free to resume your natural sleeping duration. It is essential for your health. Our cycles are about twice as long as the Tree Line's but you should not attempt to extend your cycle to match ours. That movement of your head means agreement? For a moment, I thought you were going into convulsions.

273

We are now travelling to Nature's Garden, a largely unspoiled planet that is only now being colonized by my kind. There we have the facilities necessary to complete your examination.

Let me explain. In days far past, legal questions could only be resolved through external evidence and logical deduction. Today, we have the technology to peel back the experiential layers of the accused and lay bare the facts of previous deeds. It is time-consuming and resource-intensive to do so, and some alien types are more difficult than others to read, but the underlying truth can usually be uncovered if the accused cooperates.

The USPF has spent a great deal of effort in providing legal examination for certain difficult alien types, as well as the unclassified species such as yourself. To recoup some of our costs, we share our findings with research and health organizations. As well, the governments of many planets provide funding for our work, which is in the general public interest."

"I see," said Ian. "Do you ever take off your spacesuits?"

"No, we do not ever remove our 'spacesuits'. Some of the judges you encountered are what is commonly called 'Far Galactans', but they represent only one phase of our species' life cycle. There is an earlier pre-chrysalis form which requires a methane-rich atmosphere. That is what we are.

When we reach a certain level of physical maturity, we hibernate in a chrysalis and our bodies change to the form you have observed which can sustain itself virtually unaided in an oxygen-based atmosphere. You may call us Young Nebulons, but note that it is we who are young, and not our home, which is a nebula very far away.

I do not think you would like to see a picture of what we

274

look like without our atmosphere suits. To most of the citizens in this galaxy, we are even less attractive than adult Nebulons, the so-called Far Gs.

Most of the crew on this ship are Young Nebulons. One exception is Dr. Manwas. Do not be alarmed at his appearance. He is physically a DogStar, but his parents escaped from that rigid society before he was born and he was raised on Eskaton Prime, a very civilized place. Be assured, he is committed to justice for unclassified species."

Elim summoned Dr. Manwas by touching a few buttons on its sleeve. As the four-armed, ruddy alien entered, Ian tried to appear stoic but the contents of his stomach were performing a zero gravity ballet.

"Ian, this is Dr. Manwas."

Dr. Manwas raised one arm and displayed a pale red, empty palm to Ian, who reciprocated.

"Hello."

"A pleasure to meet you. You are much pinker in person."

"Thank you?"

Elim covered the awkward interval with further exposition of their plans.

"Dr. Manwas will be examining you. He has already studied the legal submissions of your advocate and has our strategy mapped out, what we need to find in your memories and how we'll do it. Would you submit to a preliminary examination by Dr. Manwas?"

"I suppose, but would you stay here with me? I don't think I'm ready to be left alone with a DogStar just yet. No offence."

"None taken and I have no objection. Elim, please stay."

Dr. Manwas' translator sounded less robotic than Elim's.

It motioned Ian to an examination table that folded out of the bulkhead. As Ian settled upon the table, Dr. Manwas requested an exposed arm, took a small scrape of the offered skin, and also sampled Ian's blood with a pencil-like device that somehow extracted several millilitres without breaking the skin.

Dr. Manwas twiddled the pencil-like device for a few seconds before inserting it into a small hole beside the examination table. A flat screen at eye level flashed to life and Dr. Manwas scrolled through the alien script by dragging a finger both horizontally and vertically, as if swimming through the data.

"Your DNA is very similar to ours, that is, to DogStars. The dissimilarities of physical form on the surface are belied by the similarity of our evolution."

Dr. Manwas was smiling at Ian. It was a horrible sight. Never before had Ian seen a DogStar smile. He had been nauseated by a view of their teeth before, but this smile was somehow more grotesque. Like a werewolf winking at you; despite a facade of camaraderie, it did not engender trust. Ian could easily imagine Tycho's arm plummeting into the abyss of that circular gullet. Ian looked away.

"Armless gods! What's this?"

Dr. Manwas bedside manner was lacking.

"What is it?" asked Ian, still trying to figure out how likely it was that the truth would come out of the doctor's disgusting mouth.

"I'm seeing an imbalance in your K index. This is most unusual. You haven't been loitering around anti-matter transducers, have you?"

"I have no idea." Ian turned to Elim. "Is that possible?"

"No," replied the Young Nebulon curtly.

Dr. Manwas expanded on Elim's simple negation of the idea.

"No, that wouldn't do it. It might damage the K lattice, but this is an imbalance, like a pathological growth. This may limit your options in the future."

"What do you mean?"

"You are healthy now, but if you enter a region of space where the underlying K lattice is resonant, the results could be very detrimental."

"Detrimental to me?"

"Perhaps."

The doctor was withholding information. Ian's initial goodwill was giving way to a reactive distrust.

"We will have to be careful where we go. I must analyze the K lattice around Nature's Garden. This may take some time."

Dr. Manwas tapped the screen which promptly went dark, then abruptly turned and left the way it had come in.

Chapter Forty-Four

Ian spent the next cycle learning how to tap-initiate and slide-guide data on a portable data screen Elim had given him. There were many images of the planet Nature's Garden and the name was apt. Not only was the flora lush and varied, but small animals of all shapes and colours were abundant. Without exception, they looked adorably fuzzy and nonthreatening.

Ian wondered if the planet was real, or just a distraction to keep him busy while they spirited him away to his real fate, some horrible finale he dared not imagine.

The food aboard the shuttle was unrecognizable, but quite good. Dr. Manwas had selected foodstuffs most likely to be palatable to a fellow hominid and, with minor exceptions, succeeded.

When Ian emerged from his first visit to the ship's shower facility, he found Dr. Manwas as well as Elim and two other Young Nebulons waiting for him in front of a data screen showing a picture of a very blue planet.

"We are now in orbit around Nature's Garden. Dr. Manwas has assured us that the issue with your K index will not pose any side effects on this planet. We will be landing shortly," emitted Elim's translator.

Ian was relieved the obscure issue, probably a fabrication by Dr. Manwas anyway, would not interfere with their plans to refute the accusations against him.

Even from a high orbit, it was clear the planet was fertile and Earth-like. Ian longed for fresh air and blue sky. Despite the luxuries of the USPF shuttle, living space was quite limited.

Ian was now familiar with all the smells a DogStar could emit. Oddly, the fact that the Young Nebulons were isolated inside their atmosphere suits did not entirely prevent certain

278

odours from escaping. Ian refrained from questioning his hosts how this might be possible.

The other two Young Nebulons were apparently tasked with executing the landing procedure because Elim and Dr. Manwas remained near Ian as he watched the surface of the planet slowly blossom into finer and finer detail on the data screen.

If this is a ruse and I am being led to slaughter, then it won't be much longer.

The landing zone appeared suddenly amid a blanket of greenery. Two large geodesic domes stood in a clearing, perhaps one kilometre square, adjacent to a sparkling lake. The shuttle landed with a barely perceptible bump and the crew hastened about the cabin shutting down or resetting systems.

"You are now breathing Nature's Garden air."

It smelled cool and fresh. Ian had not realized how stale the shuttle had become.

"We will now disembark."

Elim lead the way to the airlock. When they stepped out onto the planet surface, Ian was overwhelmed. He had not stood on solid ground since his decision to enter the second saucer. He stooped to touch the ground. The dirt of Nature's Garden fragmented and flowed through Ian's fingers exactly as Earth soil would.

"Let us show you the living space we have here."

Elim lead Ian and Dr. Manwas into the dome closest to he lake. The building was far more rustic than its geometric shape hinted.

The doors were not automatic and once inside it became evident that the geodesic frame was covered with a thin white material. Even a mildly motivated raccoon could rip ts way through that barrier. The thin white material was also used to divide internal space; it was held taut over an internal frame of tubular members that seemed entirely independent of the exterior structure.

A central room contained hygienic facilities, and a Y-shaped corridor provided access to the private sleeping chambers. Elim and the other two Young Nebulons each had separate quarters on the left side of the Y. Ian and Dr. Manwas would be on the right side.

It was a small facility. With this complement of five, only one chamber remained unoccupied.

Elim indicated Ian's chamber.

"You will sleep here. You are also free to explore the planet in your spare time. There is little on this planet that can harm you, although I caution you not to eat any plants. Nuts, berries, anything. The edge of the lake is exceptionally pleasant and very safe, but if you go deep into the bush you should stay away from insect nests."

Ian contemplated the hammock bed and dirt floor of his chamber.

"These insects, they can't get inside here?"

"No. The wall material provides ventilation but does not allow non-microscopic life to pass. Anything larger can enter only through the exterior door. We keep it closed."

The other dome was disappointingly even less elaborate than the crew quarters. It was bisected into two rooms, both with dirt floors. One room was nearly half-filled with crates of supplies, mostly food Elim assured Ian, a couple of small tables, and no more than six chairs.

The second room contained what appeared to be an ER arch plus a couple of tables strewn with data screens and other less recognizable electronic items.

"This is where we do our work. You will be entering the examination device," Dr. Manwas indicated the ER arch. *"And we will sort and record your memories, but only the relevant memories. Despite the intrusive nature of this type*

of examination, we do respect the ideal of privacy."

The first meal after landfall was exceptional, at least for Ian and Dr. Manwas. The five inhabitants of the planet sat at one table and ate together but while the Young Nebulons squeezed tubes of food paste into holes on the side of their suit helmets, Ian and the DogStar doctor enjoyed various items worthy of chewing. Meat and vegetables were both served. Ian's suspicion that the DogStars were omnivores was swiftly confirmed.

"Are there many DogStars who don't live on the DogStar planet?"

"The Domain of the Invincible Eight Arms consists of two home planets, three planetary colonies, several space habitats, and various missions among the several trade nexuses that the Nebulons participate in. Most of my people, sadly, remain in the thrall of their totalitarian government. There are very few of us who are free.

My parents managed to escape, both mentally and physically, from the domination of the hierarchy. They managed to contribute to the multi-species society on Eskaton Prime. That is where I grew up. There are a few others of my kind on Eskaton Prime, but I am destined to be lonely as no suitable mate my age exists outside the Domain."

"I'm sorry to hear that." Ian could not believe he was sympathizing with this red thing's dating issues.

"Freedom has a price. I will not procreate, but likewise I will not have to raise progeny in an intellectually and socially stifled environment. Nothing exists in isolation, despite appearances. True wisdom is to balance the necessary and the desired with the possible."

"Yes my philosophical friend," Elim interrupted Dr. Manwas' somewhat laconic observations. *"What is there about the medical profession that breeds melancholy and*

philosophy? Could it be the continual exposure to death and suffering?"

"*No, it is only my poor digestion!*" retorted Dr. Manwas, and laughed, its mouth wide and braying. Ian recoiled involuntarily at the sight. "*Besides, I've never lost a patient. I am not a clinical practitioner. I am research scientist.*"

Elim suggested that while the other two Young Nebulons relieve the shuttle of its supplies, it, Ian and Dr. Manwas should enjoy a sunset by the lake shore.

I had suspected I might never enjoy a sunset again, thought Ian.

But I was completely certain that I would never enjoy one with a DogStar as a companion.

Chapter Forty-Five

Despite Ian's misgivings, Dr. Manwas proved to be an engaging companion who relished explaining the work ahead.

"There are five points that we need to establish to form your defence. First, that you are intelligent, albeit a citizen of a world previously unknown to the civilized galaxy. This should not be hard to prove. Certainly you have many memories of your home planet.

Second, we need to show that Domain pirates did indeed attack Earth. Again, simple visual memories will be able to confirm this.

The third point is that the pirate ship kidnapped and transported you to the planet of The Avian Branch. Again, these are relatively easy memories to isolate and document.

The last two points will require more investigative effort, for they require clarification of your intent, meaning your psychological state while undertaking the legally questionable decisions.

Namely, point four, that stowing away aboard the Domain ship Responsibility *was only a misguided attempt to return to your home planet, and that you had no ability to discriminate between the dangerous criminal crew of the pirate Domain ship and the civilized operators of the second Domain ship.*

The fifth and last point hinges on the previous one. While you were trapped on the second ship, you engaged in violence because your own life was in direct danger. We need to prove that you were motivated not only by the general fear of discovery, but a specific fear of imminent demise."

"Will I have to re-live all those unpleasant episodes inside that arch?"

"No, this is not the same as an Emotional Recovery portal. We purposely filter out much of the sensory data. No new experience will be generated. We will simply move forward or backward through time to find the appropriate evidentiary instances. Your job will be to guide us based on predominantly visual cues. Once we have identified the critical moments in time, an instantaneous image of your psychological state will be taken.

You should not be surprised or frightened by anything that happens in the portal. We are gathering evidence by acquiring precise knowledge of the past; we are not testing you."

The sunset on Nature's Garden was spectacular. The yellow star hugged the horizon over the lake for many minutes, the water taking on various warm hues until the blue and purple of the night sky displaced the day with finality.

"You will be going on a journey into the past, but it will be safe and painless. You will share the truth of your experience with us, and by doing so, free yourself from all allegations of wrongdoing. We will begin tomorrow morning."

Elim advised Ian that the duration of the Nature's Garden day was almost twice that of the Tree Line Glory. Ian mentally calculated the night would last fifteen hours. More than enough for a good night's sleep finally.

*   *

When Ian was awakened by Dr. Manwas, it was still dark. At first Ian thought there might be a valid reason for the DogStar's nocturnal intrusion, but this thought rapidly evaporated as he realized the sharp pinch on his arm was an unexpected, non-requested, and probably unauthorized injection.

"Relax, everything will be all right."

284

Dr. Manwas' suggestion did not relieve Ian's anxiety. As he tried to climb from his sling bed, Ian's limbs became increasingly heavy. By the time he had pushed himself clear of the bed, he could do nothing but fall forward into the alien doctor's many arms.

Dr. Manwas continued to whisper phrases seemingly designed to put Ian at ease as it dragged him from the sleeping dome out into the starry night. The sky was clear and moonless. A thick band of stars splashed brightly across one horizon.

"Don't worry. I am here to help you."

Dr. Manwas credibility was negligible so Ian attended his own thoughts.

Somewhere in the galaxy, Earth suffers on without me. Any pinpoint of light that reaches me now from my home, thanks to the relativistic effects of crossing the galaxy nearly instantly, as those saucers must, is from long ago, a happier time, before the invasion, before my coma, probably before the introduction of troublesome inventions like accounting and romantic love. So we're outside. The air is fresh. I can't move. Now what?

Dr. Manwas supported Ian's back with one leg, propping him into a sitting position as his legs sprawled forward on the ground. Ian's head lolled back, his muscles ignoring his central nervous system. The patches of stars were beautiful, thick groupings of more blue stars than Ian had ever seen.

But there was one area that was completely dark, completely circular, and getting larger by the second. By the time it was directly overhead, Ian recognized the approaching spacecraft as a DogStar saucer.

Dr. Manwas gripped Ian's shoulders with its lower two arms and gently guided him into a completely supine position. The saucer was impossibly big now, close enough that Ian feared it might land directly upon them, crushing him like a bug. Was that why Dr. Manwas had stepped a few paces away from Ian and was whispering with no translation available? Was the doctor muttering to itself or was it in contact with this third saucer?

The night air began to appear grainy. Small silver motes danced energetically, the soup of them thickening around Ian as if the stars themselves had come down to smother him in hellfire plasma. Ian felt nothing. His body was completely numb. He could no longer see the starry sky or the horrible round blot above him.

Now Ian was floating in a dull cloud, his body still numb. He felt another pinch on his arm and his eyes grew heavy and he experienced a falling sensation.

At least I can feel my eyes blink and close, and the pain in my arm. At least I am not in that black abyss, without a body and outside of time.

Chapter Forty-Six

Ian opened his eyes. He was inside the saucer, suspended as if weightless, a sliver python symbiote clamped onto his left arm.

Is this the same damn saucer? Did I not break free? Did we not crash onto Byrd's planet, what did they call it, the Avian Branch?

Ian looked about the chamber and could not distinguish it from his very first place of alien confinement.

Was it all a dream? I never escaped at all!? No such thing as Byrd, no second saucer, no tunic, no blobberries. All the pain I felt, dying on that second saucer, all a dream? It can't be. I've never felt real pain in a dream, not physical pain. I was dying of dehydration. I fired that weapon. And what about Nut-beard? Admittedly birds and squirrels are surprising aliens, but can it all come from my own head?

A tear began to leak out of the corner of Ian's right eye.

I'm no farther ahead. All the pain, all the terror. It adds up to nothing. And did they read my mind the whole time? Were they analyzing me, parsing my actions for weakness? Documenting my reactions to add to their field manual on how to defeat humans?

Better they should've killed me. What happens to lab animals after the experiment? Disposal. That's the next step, my last.

Ian's limbs were tingling now, feeling returning. He wiggled his fingers.

How do I know this is not yet another test, another dream they can trespass on. Does Dr. Manwas exist? Or did I dream that creature up? Or did they dream the doctor up and then insert it into my dreams or tests or whatever the hell it was I've gone through?

287

*Is this saucer still in orbit around Earth? What
astoundingly poor luck I have. I'm the intergalactic
Charlie Brown. I spend the last two years in a coma,
experiencing nothing, wasting a chunk of my life, then I
spend how much time I don't know kidnapped by these
monsters, basically stuck in a test tube while they unleash
unforgivable terror and horror on me.*

*I thought I had troubles when I lost my job. I thought I
had reason for self-pity when Gale left me. I had no idea.
The Universe is far more cruel than one can imagine.
Which makes sense else we'd all go mad if we knew what
awaited us at the end of our days.*

*Do I have an appointment with a DogStar scalpel? A
dissection and autopsy might be kinder. At least in that case
you are dead before they begin. This is more like being
buried alive, or a living autopsy.*

Ian blinked against the dewy film between his eyelids.

*No. I will not give up. I've come too far and seen too
much. No, let me assume that everything I've gone through
is real. If so, I've learned a lot about the civil order of the
galaxy, something the DogStars, or Centaurans, or
whatever those odious four-armed creatures are called,
wouldn't want me to know. This means it is not necessarily
just Earth versus DogStar. There are other players, some of
them even ethical after a fashion. I can't assume this is the
end.*

*So this must be Dr. Manwas' saucer. I've been
kidnapped because the doctor is secretly working for the
DogStars, the medical research position with USPF just a
cover.*

*But now what? Do they just kill me, or do they
manufacture evidence to sink my case? What would better
suit them?*

If they implant false memories showing I'm a murderous

288

stowaway or maybe some kind of economic refugee, then the Trans-Galactic Tribunal won't help me or Earth. It'd be better to die fighting these creatures than to let myself be used as their propaganda pawn.

Ian flexed his hands then touched them together. Now was the time to test the usefulness of his memories.

If what I remember is true, then I'm on a third saucer and have a chance. If it's not true, then I'm still on that first saucer and doomed to die alone, fighting these monsters in Earth orbit. Now is the time to try.

Ian touched the silver python head with his right hand. It was warm. His fingers explored the sides and found two small indents just where he expected. Ian placed his thumb and index finger on opposite indents and squeezed. The light on the python head turned from orange to blue.

I am right! My escape did happen! This is the third saucer not the first. Nut-beard and the USPF were real. Earth is not alone against the DogStars!

Ian felt a slightly uncomfortable tug as the tubes disconnected from his veins, retracting into the python head. In a moment, the long black cable was completely detached and began to retreat toward the ceiling. Ian grabbed the python with both hands and let it pull him upwards.

As soon as he had moved a little more than a meter from his position, the weightlessness affecting his body disappeared. Ian's feet swung towards the floor and he released the python. His feet met the floor with little force and he was left standing upright.

Did they put me in an identical room to mess with my mind, or are all their saucers this similar?

Ian moved towards the door and extended his arms to feel around its limits.

The button should be right... here.

Ian's fingers made contact and he squeezed the sides of the double button together. The door opened with a satisfying whoosh.

The antechamber was more packed with equipment than the one on the first saucer, but it was not empty of crew. A DogStar was staring intently at its data screen as Ian stepped inside. The DogStar glanced up calmly and the translator kept pace with the incomprehensible syllables it emitted.

"You are awake! Welcome to the ship Equilibrium, *Ian."*

It was Dr. Manwas. Ian was never so glad to see a creature he despised.

Ian lurched forward and clamped the DogStar's red throat. The translator did not offer output for the doctor's sputtering and gasps as Ian applied more pressure to its red neck.

"Why did you kidnap me? Where are we?"

Ian was asking questions but not allowing any answers. Dr. Manwas' four arms flailed by its sides and spittle flew from his oral cavity. Dr. Manwas eyes shot wildly back and forth, then its arms all stretched forward, trying to reach a button on the wall.

The DogStar did not direct any blows at Ian or attempt any reciprocal strangling. The red thing was acting purely defensively. Ian loosened his grip.

"Why aren't you fighting me?"

"I am not your enemy. I will not harm you."

"That is very hard to believe."

"Nonetheless, it is true."

Ian lifted his hands clear of his adversary and stepped back.

"Why did you kidnap me?"

Two of Dr. Manwas hands rubbed its neck, while the other two settled flat onto its heaving chest. It struggled to regain composure.

"You didn't have to attack me."

"How was I to know that?"

"A fair point. But you must listen to me before you decide what to do."

"So why did you kidnap me from Nature's Garden?"

"To help you."

"But not to help me clear up my trans-nebula whatever charges, like the USPF were planning to do. You described in great detail the steps we were going to take, the proof we were going to offer. How're you helping me by giving up on that?"

"Not all issues can be resolved in a court of law. Your planet is dealing with acts far outside the sphere of galactic influence. You need special help. The USPF is well-intentioned, but quixotic. They might prove your case, but then you will only be freed into a strange culture where your life will have little meaning. You would be a curiosity, not a citizen."

"I don't know. The USPF seemed pretty professional. If they own that whole planet, they can't be that fly-by-night."

"I do not understand the correlation between nocturnal aviation and success but let me assure you that the USPF does not own Nature's Garden. They are allowed to use only a few acres of the planet and not permitted to build permanent dwellings. It is a campground, not a base of operations.

You must understand that the USPF is guided by Young Nebulons and they are just that, young. The Far Galactans are extremely advanced and prosperous. Their young are given free rein to interfere in other cultures as an avenue to higher learning. Your plight is an amusing game to them. They cannot provide justice for your kind."

"Are you saying you can do better, that you can return

me to Earth?"

"My actions in bringing you here have created the possibility for your return. If you cooperate, we can further increase those chances."

Ian appraised Dr. Manwas again. Its three eyes were all fixed earnestly upon Ian. All four palms were now flat and facing forward on open display, hiding nothing from Ian, emblematic of honesty.

Was it a devious monster like all his kind, or was it an individual, worthy of singular appraisal independent of bias? One sign of the doctor's trustworthiness was the fact that no security staff had yet arrived to restrain Ian.

"But this is a DogStar saucer. If you're not working for the DogStars, why're we aboard one of their ships?"

"This was a Domain ship long ago, but no longer. My employers have refurbished it for their own purposes. Come and meet your benefactors and they will explain."

Chapter Forty-Seven

As Dr. Manwas led the way, Ian noted that this saucer was indeed very similar to the first two he had encountered. The circumferential corridor, the blue lights over the portals which opened into weightless inter-level transfer tubes which were the DogStar high-tech equivalent of elevators, the double buttons on every doorway. It all seemed familiar, but not in a comforting manner.

As they made their way towards the top of the ship, Ian's stomach knotted in anticipation. Could he trust Manwas? He and the DogStar were still unaccompanied. Perhaps he could escape. Ian now knew he could overpower the doctor as it was not nearly as strong as the soldiers Ian had encountered earlier.

But it was too late for such considerations. They had arrived. The top level of the saucer was permeated with unpleasant odours that Ian recognized: Young Nebulon leakage, plus the tangy reek of their elders, the Far Galactans.

Dr. Manwas squeezed the buttons on a large set of double doors marked with several cryptic symbols and a few lines of alien script. It was clear the creatures inside were expecting them. The first translator had begun to sound before they had even stepped inside.

"-Welcome Ian! Come in. You are among friends!-"

A Far Galactan, sitting in the middle of the room on an elaborate pedestal, swivelled to face the arrivals. Two Young Nebulons stood, one to each side. The translucent ring around the top of the Far G pulsed again.

"-Yes this vessel was as a Domain ship, but do not despair. We are no friends of the Domain, the DogStars as some call them.-"

"I was just saying that to Dr. Manwas."

"-We know. We saw and heard everything. Your attack and your hesitation. The fact that you are able to distinguish Dr. Manwas and his motives from that of his former government, and also from the rogues who attacked your planet, indicates you have the potential to be a true citizen. You are worthy of our assistance.-"

"You saw the struggle? Then why did you not help him? I might have strangled him to death, then what would you have done with me?"

"-I am aware of everything that goes on aboard this ship. I am neither telepathic nor magical, but we do have a pervasive surveillance system. If you had seriously injured Dr. Manwas, we would have intervened. I doubt you could have caused any damage we could not reverse. Our medical sciences are effective.

Although Dr. Manwas did not complete the examination as was planned on Nature's Garden, we had already come to believe your story. Your actions reinforced the correctness of our decision. We say: 'When you choose to act, you have already judged yourself'. In this case, your actions show a capacity for trust that, in our experience, only accompanies innocence. Because of this, we have decided to help you return to your home planet.-"

"Not to denigrate the trust and innocence connection, but why would you want to help me?"

"-This requires an explanation of who we are. We are not the Nebulon government. We are Nebulons who are interested in justice and are willing to place our own resources at the disposal of those who promote harmony in your galaxy. We are especially interested in young civilizations with potential. These infant planets must be protected from exploitation by rogues.

We have a wide array of strategies to achieve this. Some of them do not fall within the legal framework of the Trans-

Galactic Tribunal system. Therefore we must remain the invisible hand behind certain corrections we initiate.-"

"So you are rogues too?"

"-Perhaps in the legal sense, but not in the moral sense. We strive to help different groups reach a just equilibrium, hence the name of our ship.-"

"Are you saying you can help me return to Earth and also free it of alien occupation?"

"-Those are indeed our goals. Our first step is to determine your true point of origin. For this we must travel to our own galaxy. Our top scientists can answer all questions. Once we know where we will act, we can determine how. Are you willing to work with us?-"

"Do I have a choice?"

"-Of course. We value freedom and cooperation. If you do not wish to work with us, we will return you to Nature's Garden. The USPF will bring in another doctor to examine you and build your defence. This meeting will have never happened.

But recall that even once you are exonerated, there is little hope of your ever returning to Earth, and no hope of helping the Earth.-"

"It seems my life is one test after another. I am no hero, but I can't leave Earth to her fate. I belong there so, if your goal is to return me, I will cooperate fully."

"-You have made a wise decision Ian Hesse.-"

PART 5: THE FAR GALAXY

Chapter Forty-Eight

The crew quarters aboard the *Equilibrium* were more comfortable than the USPF shuttle or the camp on Nature's Garden. The web bunk was designed for DogStars, providing the supplemental width that their extra appendages required. Ian found a large pile of luxuriously soft and thick blankets waiting for him on his bunk. He doubted this was standard issue for DogStar Domain crew members. The chamber itself had four bunks, but the other three were empty.

Dr. Manwas had provided another data screen and Ian again absorbed the pictures of their destination, the far galaxy of the Nebulons. Better still, the doctor was now being very friendly and had also enabled the audio translation on the data screen so Ian could hear the detailed explanations that accompanied each picture.

The Nebulon culture was very old. They populated a mind boggling number of planets around the many stars that comprised the central nebula of their galaxy. It was one of the few known galaxies that did not have a gigantic black hole at the center. The reason for this was unnatural.

Early in their technological ascendance the Nebulons had devised a process to utilize the accumulating matter of their galactic core. While most galaxies had a mass-sucking center that provided the counter force against outward centripetal thrust to keep the spinning arms of the galaxy from drifting or being flung away, the Nebulon galaxy had long ago transformed the burgeoning black hole at their galactic center into a safe and limitless power generation process that accumulated mass in a more controlled manner than that of a natural black hole.

Many of the technical details did not translate well and Ian was left to wonder at the nonsense syllables the translator offered in explanation of the advanced technology.

* *

Even more incredible than the story of their advanced power technology were the pictures of Nebulon cities and their inhabitants. Ian was momentarily dumbfounded at the bizarre pictures of life on a Nebulon home world. He already understood that these aliens had some shape-shifting capability, but the profusion and variation of appendages sprouting from their slimy cylinders was beyond any expectation.

Some Nebulons displayed no appendages, while some bristled like porcupines. Not all appendages were used for object manipulation. Some were strictly sensory. Additional eyes, ears or other sensors that Ian did not understand, and the translator could not convey, were rampant.

If he had not already been exposed to these masters of a far galaxy, his reaction would have been one of disgust and horror. As it was, he was glad the Nebulons were on his side. If they truly were.

One of the squares on his data screen showed what was happening outside the *Equilibrium*. After two cycles in transit, Dr. Manwas interrupted Ian's breakfast to alert him to their progress.

"We are closing on the mothership. You can see it on your data screen under the leftmost blue triangle."

Ian dragged the data square rightward until it stopped, then pushed everything toward the top edge of the viewing surface. A small blue triangle was evident in the bottom left corner. He tapped it.

An immense and luminous gas cloud dominated the

view in front of the *Equilibrium*. Ian was at first unable to distinguish the dark patch near the center of his screen.

"That's the mothership. Once we are aboard, it won't take long to return to the Far Galaxy."

The dark shape swelled to fill the screen. It was round, immense, and nearly featureless. Ian thought the saucer might smash itself against the solid black sphere, but at the last moment a diamond-shaped opening formed and the light spilling out revealed a immense cavity. Inside were nested an array of shuttles and medium-sized spacecraft.

The *Equilibrium* moved carefully through the opening and slid alongside the other vehicles until it found an empty berth. A docking tube slid towards the side of the saucer.

* *

The captain of the Nebulon ship did not smell any better than the captain of the saucer.

Once you've smelled one Nebulon, you've smelled them all, thought Ian.

Maybe that is because each one of them smells like a crowd of Nebulons crammed into a small unventilated room.

Ian noted there were very few Young Nebulons evident on the sphere. Ironically, he was glad to have the familiar if somewhat repulsive face of Dr. Manwas around.

"-We are glad you have decided to join us. I am Captain Alias. Our ship is called the Burden. *May I shake your hand?-"*

Colours pulsed behind the translucent circular band near the crest of the potato-shaped Nebulon and an appendage began to grow upon the side facing Ian. In very few seconds, a well-formed hand extended in Ian's direction.

It looked only a little drier than the Nebulon's slimy trunk. Three fingers and a spindly thumb adorned the solitary hand. Ian extended his own hand and grasped the

298

alien protuberance. It was warm, but better yet, drier than he had anticipated.

"-You are good at controlling your revulsion. That is a sign of wisdom.-"

"Thank you. How did you know my kind likes to shake hands?"

"-Everything that happened aboard the tribunal ship at Trade Nexus Four was observed. You were seen shaking hands with your advocate, the Tree Line Glory named Nutbeard. We also noted a hug.-"

"Oh, that would not really be appropriate in this case, I think."

Ian had disengaged his hand from Captain Alias' grasp and unconsciously taken one step backward. Alias' head band strobed rapidly for a moment and the translator made a deadpan 'ha ha' sound.

"-Ha ha. We will not hug. Pardon my attempt at humour.-"

"Okay. That was funny." Ian agreed, wiping his hand on his tunic.

"-We will not make you shake hands with Dr. Speck Ryzof. She will be your personal physician for the duration of your examination. She is a specialist in mammalian medicine.-"

Another Nebulon rolled forward. A hand emerged from her front and executed a wide wave at Ian.

Is this Nebulon really female or are they just humouring me, wondered Ian.

"-Hello. Pleased to meet you, and please call me Speck.-"

"Call me Ian." Ian waved back before the captain continued.

"-As Dr. Manwas may have explained, we are concerned about the damage the DogStar pirates inflict on

young civilizations. When it came to our attention that there was an unknown type of alien found aboard the Domain 'saucer', as you call it, we suspected the pirates were somehow connected. I have been briefed on the legal documents submitted on Nexus Four.

From that, I understand you claim you were transported directly from your home world, Earth, to the planet of The Avian Branch, where you managed to stow away on a second DogStar saucer, this one operating under the auspices of the Domain and bound for Nexus Four. Unfortunately, the flight information regarding the original saucer is not available to us.

It is not unusual for the Domain to chase after crashed pirate DogStar saucers. They salvage the computational and power equipment and destroy any evidence of malfeasance. The Domain contradicts itself on the issue of its pirates. Officially, they want to destroy the pirates, but unofficially they are happy to simply suppress any information about the existence of that criminal class. So when a pirate saucer crashes, the Domain rushes in to remove all evidence. In this case, that evidence included you and could not be suppressed.

If you agree to work with us, we will locate your planet of origin, insert a data acquisition module inside your brain, and then send you home.-"

"Insert something in my brain?"

"-Do not experience fear. The operation is painless and will not produce any side effects. The device will relay information back to us, information that can be used as evidence of the pirates' actions. Because your planet is not a signatory to the Trans-Galactic Accord, there are impediments to our investigation that your cooperation would resolve. It might still take a lengthy interval to obtain agreement among the signatories that action must

be taken to reverse the occupation of your home by the rogue DogStars, but having the proof, the data you will send us, will be essential.-"

"I understand. If this is what it takes to help Earth, I will agree."

"-My original assessment of you was correct. You are wise. Once again, welcome to the Burden, *our fine ship. Go now with Speck and we will begin.-"*

Chapter Forty-Nine

S peck showed Ian to his new quarters, a roomy chamber with a hammock of webbing suspended on two poles near the center of the room. The hammock looked like it a recent addition. Ian was glad to see there was a hygiene nook similar to the one aboard the Tree Line Glory ship at Nexus Four.

Speck adjusted something on the data screen that Dr. Manwas had earlier provided Ian. Now, Speck promised, Ian had access to the entire picture library of the *Burden*.

"-Something to allay the boredom, when it comes. Boredom is the scourge of the intelligent-." Ian was ready for some shut-eye at that point, but Speck insisted on a quick trip to her lab. *"-Just a quick scan so I can begin my work. It won't take even one hundred breaths.-"*

Speck's estimation was reasonable. In less than five minutes, Ian's scan was complete. Ian was relieved to discover there was no ER arch in Speck's laboratory, only a padded cut-away tube with countless tendrils that appeared limp and harmless until he leaned back as directed.

The tendrils, or tentacles, then came alive and slithered all over his body. Ian started to panic but Speck assured him that nothing would enter any orifice. These were just sensory leads, which was almost the truth. But despite the incipient panic at the strange sensation of a thousand snakes sliding over his body, no harm was done and it was soon over.

Ian greeted his new web bed gratefully and once he lay upon it, sleep came quickly.

* *

When Ian awoke, the impression of the strange dream was still strong. He had been aboard another saucer, a relatively friendly one. Nut-beard was there and they faced an ER arch. Nut-beard recommended that Ian do what he thought best. The specifics were unclear, but its attitude was positive. In this dream, the ER arch was a time machine, and Ian went back to the recently dredged and painful memory of his divorce.

This time Ian was careful. He chose his words sparingly with Gale. Rather than freeing his verbal stream like a dam bursting under a storm swell, he instead opened the sluice gate just enough to let out sufficient rainwater such that Gale would not drown in the flood of his verbiage.

Ian managed her expectations regarding his increased verbal capability by advising her along the way that changes were coming, and he would try not to upset the equilibrium of their relationship.

At first it worked. Ian was buoyant. He had sidestepped fate, and his marriage was saved.

What happened next was a surprising tragedy. Gale began to be distant. As she talked less so he, mindful of their balance of words, also talked less. Soon they were talking only infrequently and superficially. What had gone wrong?

Then came the fateful day. He came home unexpectedly and found her with Miguel in their bedroom. They didn't seem to be talking much either, but their shared activity provoked substantial anguish in Ian.

Despite his efforts to modify his own behaviour, their marriage could not persist; it was over.

What was the meaning of the dream? Was Ian wrong to go back to try to save his marriage? Did the Universe punish the hubris of those who sought to override its cold judgment? Or was this new variation of his history with Gale just an allegory for his current troubles?

Was his subconscious trying to warn him about his new allies? If he led these Nebulons to Earth, would they do as they promised, or would their real agenda be revealed and an even worse fate be unleashed upon Earth?

If he allowed them to implant their instrument in him, would it control him? Would he be giving up all free will? They had promised it was a passive device, something to gather data, but how sure was he that it would not turn him into their robotic slave?

His choices were very limited. He could justify risking his own self, but could he justify risking the fate of all mankind?

These thoughts raced through his mind as he stretched himself in the webbed hammock.

Also, he was hungry.

The whoosh of the sliding door to his chamber startled him, and the fact that Speck rolled up close to him without emitting a word was also a bit disconcerting.

"Good morning. Speck?"

"-Yes it is I, Speck. Hello Ian. I hope you slept well.-"

"Fine. Thank you. Is everything okay?"

"-I have completed my preliminary analysis. There is good news and bad.-"

"Good news first, please, while I try to wake up."

Ian swung his legs around and over the edge of the hammock, enabling him to face Speck directly.

"-I have identified K code markers in your cell formation ice shelf specific to lattice foci-"

"My ice shelf?" Ian rubbed his eyes.

Speck paused as if confused. *"-No, not ice shelf. There is a problem with the translation of technical terms. I will try again.*

I have identified markers in you that I can correlate with characteristics of locales in your galaxy. This means I am very close to locating your star. The remainder of the analysis is automated and should complete shortly.-"

304

"That's great!"

"-Unfortunately, there is also bad news. My scan indicates you are dying.-"

Chapter Fifty

I an eyed Speck suspiciously. The news of his impending death did not make sense. There had been many moments since being taken from Earth when Ian had fully expected to die. This was not one of them.

I've been getting stronger ever since the Nexus. If I was already sick, wouldn't the strain of hiding on that second saucer have killed me? It doesn't make any sense. I finally get to a place where I can eat and sleep in a reasonable manner, and now I'm sick.

Perhaps it's a ruse. Will they try to convince me to self-euthanize next? Will they use my sickness as a lever, holding out on medicine until I agree to whatever it is they really want?

Speck interrupted Ian's thoughts. It was unclear whether she was trying to shake him out of his cycle of morbid reflection or just hasten the conclusion of this difficult conversation.

"-I am very sorry to tell you this. But do not despair. There is a chance we can help you.-"

"What am I dying of? And what can you do about it?"

"-Dr. Manwas earlier detected a disruption in your K index and expressed concern about your landing on Nature's Garden. Do you recall?-"

"Yes I remember. But Manwas also said it wasn't a problem."

"-It wasn't a problem for you to land on Nature's Garden, no, that is true. But what the doctor didn't explain fully is that your problem is aggravated by location. This is somewhat natural and, in the known cases, simply keeping away from certain locations is enough to prevent any symptoms.-"

"Certain locations? What locations are we talking

about?" Ian had a sinking feeling that he was being manipulated.

"-I don't have that information yet. Most probably, it will be somewhere you have already been. Hopefully somewhere you don't want to go, ever again.-"

"What if it is Earth?"

"-Then return may be impossible. But, as you have seen, our technology is advanced. There is a chance we can isolate the gremlin and return you to health.-"

"The gremlin?"

"-No that is not the right word. I do not believe the translator can fully map our language to yours. There are medical and cosmological concepts unknown to you.

I have already discussed your problem with Captain Alias and we have a plan. We are now on course for our, the name will not translate well I am sure, let's call it our specialist planet. There we have equipment which will not only pinpoint the location of your home planet, but also, hopefully, clarify your health situation.-"

"What is this K index thing? I've heard K lattice too. Can you explain these?"

"-I can only try. Imagine trying to explain radioactive isotopes to a student who has no understanding of atomic structure. It would be difficult. In the same way, my explanation will surely suffer.

The K lattice is a layer of reality that underlies the smallest particles, waves and quasi-particles of simple mechanistic and quantum theories of physical reality. In fact, it goes beyond the theory of physical reality in a homogeneous universe, and requires simultaneous and coincident existence of multiple universes, each with complementary physics. This gives rise to the possibility of evil jelly, which can contaminate the K index of a living creature.-"

Ian stared silently at Speck, thinking.

Great. My ice shelf has gremlins and I'm contaminated with evil jelly.

"-Does this make any sense?-"

"Some of it is getting through. Please continue.

"-These other universes all share our K lattice and therefore our jelly, a type of energy, let's say, that can transfer between universes. There have been cases of Nebulons with K index disruption who have survived. K lattice engineering is in its infancy, but there have been some early successes in repairing discontinuities and spillage, often saving those contaminated.-"

"But these have all been Nebulons, not aliens like myself?"

"-I am sorry but I have never heard of a non-Nebulon either suffering from or surviving a K index disruption. But I am not an expert in this area. This is why we are going to our specialist planet.-"

"Is there anything we can do in the meantime to increase my odds of licking this thing?"

"-I do not recommend applying saliva. Really there is little one can...-"

Speck's grunting and wheezing trailed off and the translator fell silent.

"-One thing we can do is apply a magic healing pellet. It will protect you until we get to our destination.-"

Ian detected a slight increase in odour as a small appendage already expressed on Speck's front sprouted several fingers. This arm then reached inside the bag Speck had brought and retrieved a small, beautiful deep blue stone-like object. Speck fiddled with the stone for a second before handing it to Ian. One side seemed sticky.

"-You will wear this. It will moderate any ill effects.-"

Ian pressed the blue stone to his right arm, covering an

old immunization scar.

"Thanks, Speck."

*   *

Dr. Manwas stopped by a few minutes later to console Ian.

"I have heard about your sad news, but I would not worry. There is little these Nebulons cannot do. They travel between galaxies! If not for them, the concept of the K lattice would be unknown to anyone in this galaxy. You are in the best of hands."

What Dr. Manwas said next was of such startling and inadvertent honesty that Ian began to doubt his theory that the whole K index thing was a trap. These smart aliens would not be so careless in synchronizing their lies.

Dr. Manwas was admiring the blue stone on Ian's arm.

"You and Speck seem to be building quite a rapport. Isn't that her one thousand cycle service award you are wearing on your arm?"

Chapter Fifty-One

Nebulon technology was certainly impressive. The voyage to their 'far galaxy' had taken only an additional day. When Ian rose from his web bed and began to ingest DogStar morning foodstuff, the closest thing to human food available on the ship, the piebald orange orb of the specialist planet already dominated the forward view of the ship as seen on his data screen.

Dr. Manwas had thoughtfully dropped another set of specialist planet images into Ian's folder, and Ian sat studying them as he swallowed his wet breakfast cubes.

Before retiring for the cycle, Speck had also activated text-translation software onto Ian's data screen so that he could finally begin to read about, as well as look at, images of the Nebulon civilization.

As far as Ian could tell, the entire surface of the specialist planet was covered with the equivalent of university campuses. Nebulon students came from throughout the far galaxy to live and study together on the planet. Here, Young Nebulons and mature Nebulons studied together.

This was the first time Ian had seen the Young Nebulons without their spacesuits, and he was glad he was seeing only a picture. The pre-chrysalis Nebulon was a spindly, gnarled, and scaly creature with no clear Earth counterpart. It could survive unaided only in the mysterious orange atmosphere around the planet below, while mature Nebulons could also tolerate the quasi-terrestrial atmosphere maintained aboard the *Burden* and the Nexus ship.

Speck interrupted Ian's data browsing. It was time to go to the planet but this time, instead of using a shuttle, they would use direct matter transfer.

"This is the same type of technology that the DogStars used to kidnap me originally."

"- Not quite the same. Our version is much safer, and can be used to effect transfer over far greater distances. It is not a technology we share with your galaxy. I believe DogStars only use their version for transporting cargo and livestock, not personnel.-"

"Good to know."

The Nebulon transporter reminded Ian of Star Trek, except there was no shimmery intermediate state, just an immediate slap of wind in his face. By the time Ian blinked, he was somewhere else.

Ian and Speck materialized in a huge rectangular laboratory. Three walls were obscured with complicated and obviously advanced equipment. Again, Ian wished he had a camera. But the fourth wall was astounding, a dark tunnel, out of which protruded one end of a giant yellow cylinder. It was a new type of alien, an immense brilliant head. It was difficult to look upon, but Ian discerned the features of a face.

"-The Sunface will examine you now.-"

Its eyes were lidded as if in a stupor, and its lips were gently closed but somewhat puckered. It appeared to be metallic or mechanical, but the face was that of a living being, human-like, despite the lack of ears or nose.

"-Move closer. You are expected.-"

Ian closed the distance between himself and the Sunface by half. He was almost close enough to touch it. The eyelids stirred and parted enough to reveal brilliant orange corneas composed of tumultuous lumps of twisting molten lava. Or so it appeared. The Sunface gave off no discernible heat.

It began to speak somewhat slowly, as if the passage of time was inconsequential or malleable.

I have taken you out of the time system to examine you in a more static environment.

The voice was inside Ian's head. He looked back over his shoulder, toward Speck. The slimy brown cylindrical alien was not moving. All the lights on the other three walls were in steady state, not blinking, not changing. Perhaps time had stopped, or slowed to a crawl.

So you are the anomaly in my system. Your travels have been most ... variable. The effects are now foreseen. What changes you will bring to your home and all the corners you've touched!

The Sunface seemed to smile slightly. Ian remained speechless.

An interesting permutation which holds rich promise. You will remain still within until it unfolds. Much can be learned.

"Who are you?"

I am the elder. You have met my spawn. One day they will be as I am. You are the first of your kind I have encountered.

"I'm as surprised as you are."

There is much to contrast our comparative amazement.

"I'm not disagreeing with you."

I fear you have been manipulated by aliens.

"You're definitely onto something there."

You are from Ottawa.

"Yes! You know where Earth is??" Ian's hopes suddenly ballooned. Was his new ally omniscient?

All is clear now. You may rejoin the others.

The lids of the Sunface dropped to cover its amazing eyes, and when Ian turned to face Speck, the room was again alive with the flashing, beeping, and susurration of many machines.

Chapter Fifty-Two

Ian hoped the Sunface had passed more information to the Nebulons than he had divined from it. The significance of the fact that it had gleaned his city of residence as Ottawa was perhaps not so great. It might mean the Sunface knew where Earth was, or it might simply mean it had read the city name from his memory.

Returning to the ship, Ian began to feel less than well. Perhaps his K index disruption had finally started to manifest as an illness. During their time on the *Burden*, Dr. Manwas had taught Ian a game from its adopted home world. But now, even its offer of playing a round of what Ian had dubbed Eskaton Marbles could not stir Ian from his bed.

Dr. Manwas suspected that removing Ian from his home galaxy had exacerbated his condition. But as the doctor no longer had any control over Ian's fate, there was little it could do. Dr. Manwas had made a choice when it effected Ian's transfer from USPF to Nebulon control. Now a sense of guilt and duty, leavened with the empathy the doctor felt for a fellow refugee, compelled it to attend Ian's bedside.

Ian was not in any pain, but neither did he have the energy to vacate his bed. Worse still, he had set aside his data screen. Loss of interest in the outside world was a prime indicator for onset of rapid decline in the sick, according to Dr. Manwas' experience.

But Ian was not so far gone as to be uninterested in what Speck might have uncovered when she rolled in.

"- Ian, I have good news for you. The Sunface has plotted the location of planet Earth. It is the third planet in your solar system, is it not?-"

Ian took a deep breath, as if answering cost him energy he could ill-afford.

"Yes."

"-We were quite sure of it. As well, we now have updated our translators to account for your origin. You should notice a reduction in non sequitur phrases.-"

With some visible effort, Ian pushed himself into an upright sitting position.

"Does this mean I can return to Earth?"

"-Before we discuss that, let me share what we have discovered about the origins of your syndrome. As you are by now aware, there is more to the fabric of the Universe than the physical dimensions and time. There are sublevels based on an unseen microcosm which permeates all existence. We call this the K lattice, K for Koryolis, the name of the scientist who postulated its existence. Every living creature has a K index. Think of it as cosmic DNA, something unique to the individual and something which contains much information about how the individual was formed and how it will progress.

As DNA can be used to predict susceptibility to certain diseases, the K index predicts and indeed controls a great deal more. Even the people on your planet understand that quantum physics implies that the outcome of an event can be altered simply by the fact of it being observed. Likewise with K, outcomes based on probability and rate of transmutation can be manipulated by the interaction of the underlying lattice with the individual's K.

Now in your case, we found the K index has been disrupted, but this was not like any disruption previously documented.

There have been instances of K index disruption caused by proximity to anti-matter transducers, but only if the exposure was prolonged and extreme. Also, in those cases, the damage to the K index was random. Positive and negative effects were balanced and so it was difficult to

314

detect the underlying syndrome.

Now in your case, the damage is symmetrical and precise. This means it is not natural. Clearly, it has been carefully engineered.-"

"Are you saying I've been poisoned? Perhaps by the DogStars when they first kidnapped me?"

"-No, that seems quite impossible. The DogStars do not possess the technical capability to damage a K index so artfully. This skill is beyond even us. I am afraid the evidence in this case points to a perpetrator outside our own Universe.-"

"So extradition will be a problem?" Ian had not lost his sense of humour.

"-That is not the salient issue. Our problem is your rehabilitation, not the culprit's punishment.-"

"I don't understand the motivation. What could be gained by disrupting my K index?"

"-The K lattice extends through all the vast network of related universes. While each Universe is finite, the K lattice itself is infinite. As far as our science can determine, there is a perpetual ongoing transfer of objective karma between the universes.

Objective karma was previously translated as 'evil jelly' and it can be observed as a form of luck, intuition, or any form of congruence between an intelligent life form and its surroundings. The lack of this objective karma can manifest as mutations of physical form, equipment malfunction, spontaneous combustion, illness in animals, including madness and violence.

Someone from far away has created in you a conduit for the transfer of K from your locale to theirs.-"

"They are stealing my luck?"

"-Something far worse, but that formulation does provide some explanatory value. Now we can address your

question about a possible return to Earth.

Your K index disruption is tuned to work in a certain area of the galaxy, close to your home planet. That is where a resonant K node exists. I won't go into details, but this means that the closer you get to Earth, the greater the K transfer is to the other Universe.

Did you notice any strange behaviour in people or equipment near you before you left Earth?-"

Ian recalled the violence and madness that had preceded the DogStar occupation.

"I may have discounted certain things because of the arrival of the Centaurans, I mean the DogStars. But yes, there was a lot going very wrong on Earth at that time. All of it quite near me. Are you saying I was the cause of all that?"

"-Not the cause, the mechanism. You bear no moral burden because you were not aware of, nor responsible for, the K transfer. Now that you do know, however, there is an obligation to protect innocents. This means you cannot return.-"

Ian remained silent. Was this all a giant fabrication to keep him away while the DogStars lunched on Earth's assets? The whole K idea seemed implausible, but then again he had indeed witnessed a great deal of inexplicable violent mayhem during his last few days on Earth.

"-But at the same time, you cannot remain here. This far from your own galaxy, the K conduit will become completely empty, and then you will die. There may be an equilibrium point in space, a location where you are close enough to the K node of your own solar system to avoid death, but far enough away to prevent any ill effects on others of your kind.-"

"A point in space? Do you mean a planet?"

"-Unfortunately no. This point would be somewhere in

316

interstellar space, perhaps halfway between your Solar System and its closest neighbour, Beta Centauri.

Also, at this point, I should notify you that the DogStars have done your planet a disservice in pretending to be Centaurans. As the Sunface discovered, the actual Centaurans have an idealistic society and welcome contact with Earth. There has already been some low-level radio communication between your peoples. This was your first contact with aliens. It would be a shame if the ruse of the DogStars spoiled the chance for cultural exchange between your planet and the Centaurans, the real Centaurans.-"

"Yes, a shame." Ian's concerns were more immediate and personal. "So are you saying that I will survive only if I live in, like, a spacecraft located in deep space, close to Earth, but not too close? Perhaps you have a job for me to do while I sit there?" An edge of anger was creeping into Ian's voice.

"-Perhaps something could be found, but please do not raise your hopes.-"

"I wouldn't worry about that."

"-Good. I regret having to present you these difficult facts. We have uncovered something here today that may impact more worlds in the future. If an individual on Earth was selected to implement this illegal K conduit, then we can be quite certain that more cases will eventually emerge.

I fear that, if we report our findings to the Nebulon Council, you will be sequestered for study and decontamination. Your freedom might be forfeited. That is not a good option for you.-"

"Do I have any options at all then?"

"-I will consult the Captain.-"

Speck rolled out of the room, and Ian was left alone with his misgivings and malaise.

317

Chapter Fifty-Three

As Ian lay exhausted and weak on his web bed, he felt the time drain away and with it, his energy and confidence.

Several hours passed before Ian was summoned before Captain Alias. Dr. Manwas rousted him from his sick bed and even steadied him with two arms as they made their way together to the captain.

Ian marvelled at the idiosyncratic collection of objects adorning the shelves in the captain's private quarters. What appeared to be paintings and sculptures covered most of the two walls flanking what must be a Nebulon bed, a large hybrid between a waterbed and a bean bag chair, an object that might have appeared plush or at least comfortable had it not been covered with a centimetre of slime similar to what covered a mature Nebulon's earth-brown epidermis.

At first glance, the paintings and sculptures appeared to be abstract forms but, as Ian relaxed on a small four-armed chair that seemed out of place in the room, some of the nearest objects resolved into depictions of cylindrical Nebulons. One object was a depiction of three Sunface-like creatures being rather cozy.

The captain did not waste any time.

"-Ian Hesse, I hope you still have sufficient mental and physical function to understand the choice I will give you today.-"

"I have been in much worse shape before," countered Ian. *Although I may have made some bad decisions at that time.* "I'm eager to hear about my choice."

"-Excellent. Let me explain first that there is little we can do to destroy the K conduit that is attached to you. Breaking the conduit would damage both worlds, unleashing repercussions far greater than whatever

*advantage had been obtained by the perpetrators, and
whatever disadvantage had accrued to Earth. Additionally,
it would severely endanger your life. Therefore this is not a
good option.-"*

"Agreed."

*"-This is a new form of inter-universe crime that is
problematic for us. We simply do not have the technology
or understanding to repair what has been done to you.
Some would argue that the only way to resolve the issue is
by terminating your life. I do not agree with this approach.
It is morally repugnant to me.-"*

"I am glad you see it that way."

*"-Of course. As Dr. Manwas has told you, we are
concerned that, if the information obtained by your visit to
the Sunface were to be released to the authorities, you
would be quarantined and studied. While this might have
some potential value for our long-term strategy of
combating this new type of crime, it would do little to
address your own problem, nor that of Earth's, by which I
mean the DogStar pirate occupation. I am interested in a
more immediate remedy.*

*Now as we have previously explained, we are not a part
of the Nebulon government. Therefore I have discretionary
powers that provide us with another option for your return
to Earth.*

*Although we cannot repair your K index, or remove the
K conduit, we do have experimental technology which
might allow you to modulate and direct the flow of K.*

*If you agree, we will implant a small object in your
brain which will allow you to use mental visualization to
control K flow through the conduit. In this way, you will be
provided with a powerful weapon to counter the
occupation. However, the great power that this capability
will provide you does concern us, for power is inevitably*

used by primitives in an arbitrary manner and innocents suffer. But I have given this much thought. If you are not given this opportunity to return, then the pirates will certainly prevail on Earth and many more innocents will suffer. This was not an easy decision on my part, but I believe it is morally necessary.-"

"Black ops necessitated by morality, not political interests. You *are* alien."

"-I detect cynical humour in your comment. But we are not so different. As you would steal food for a starving creature, so we will desiccate a few laws to ensure you remain moist.-"

"I think I understand."

"-There is only one drawback from your point of view. If we implant the control device, then you will be an embarrassment to our government. If ever you leave your planet and encounter any members of the Trans-Galactic Accord, they will hold you for lengthy investigation. Also, remember, if you travel far away from the resonant K node near the Earth, you will weaken and die, as you are doing right now.-"

"I would be very happy to keep your secret and never leave Earth again."

"-It sounds like you have already made up your mind. We can give you only a little more time to decide. It is my duty to remind you that if you remain here in the Nebula, there is a small chance you could yet be cured and become a full Trans-Galactic citizen.-"

"No. I'm not interested in that. I only wish to return home."

"-Obviously I had anticipated you would agree otherwise I would not have made the offer. I congratulate you on your loyalty to your planet. Dr. Manwas will perform the operation and accompany you on the journey.

You leave at once.-"

PART 6: THE BEHEMOTH

Chapter Fifty-Four

I an settled back into one of the shuttle pod's eight comfortably upholstered berths and appreciated the irony of his situation.

Only a few days earlier he had been trapped aboard a ship lousy with hostile DogStars, armed but hungry and dehydrated, with nothing in front of him but almost certain exile and death. Now he rested comfortably as another ruddy DogStar, a friendly one, piloted this more advanced spacecraft for a return to Earth.

Ian was impressed to see the DogStar manipulate the controls. All four hands were in use at the same time. Perhaps the third eye made such a division of attention less noteworthy, but Ian recalled few humans who could operate machinery using each hand independently. And humans had at least one eye per hand. From that perspective, the DogStars were still short one eye, or surplus one hand.

"That is amazing. How you work with all your hands at the same time."

"Is it? It comes quite naturally. Mature Nebulons manifest multiple appendages to operate their spacecraft. As I have no co-pilot in this case, it is necessary for me to emulate their methods."

"Is it difficult to learn to pilot a spacecraft such as this? I mean, did you have a lot of specialized training?"

"Not as much as you might think. This shuttle is quite simple compared to some other spacecraft. Our flight path consists of discrete steps already programmed by the Nebulons. I invoke them in the correct sequence and the ship takes care of the details."

"So if we're blown off course, then we become hopelessly lost?"

"Any particles that might strike us will be either small enough that our anti-gravity shield can successfully repel them, or large enough to trigger automatic evasion. There is no chance of navigational error. There!"

Ian felt a slight lurch as the ship's propulsion system engaged.

"Now we are on our way. It will be about one-half cycle before we reach Earth. I suggest we complete your operation and then you can get some sleep. You have been awake for almost a full cycle."

"Do you have the proper medical facilities on this shuttle? I mean, isn't this an experimental procedure?"

"The device itself is experimental but the operation is very simple. I request that you lay your head flat against the rest surface, facing away from me."

Dr. Manwas moved to the bulkhead closest to Ian and retrieved a small tubular device. Its middle eye narrowed as it focused on the inserter. Two hands held it close to its face while a third made minute adjustments.

"Relax. Don't move now."

Dr. Manwas leaned over Ian and pressed the object near the base of his brain stem. Ian heard a small hissing sound but felt nothing.

"Procedure complete."

"I don't feel any different. How do I access the, how do I control the…"

"Unfortunately there is no way to test the device without proximity to Earth. Once you are in range of the K resonant node near Earth, you will begin to feel a buildup, like heat, in the back of your skull. This is the deficit from the K conduit.

Where previously the deficit would be balanced by

objective karma taken randomly from your nearby environment, you can now instead mentally visualize a band of green light extending from the device in your brain stem to an object of your choice, living or inanimate.

This might take some practice and I suggest you do practice before entering any dangerous situations. Do not become over-confident. Although it is a noted characteristic of K leaks that the source of the conduit is rarely harmed by the direct effects of the transfer, this device will not shield you from other dangers.

Once we approach Earth closely, you must disembark immediately, otherwise this ship will be in danger."

"From the DogStar pirates?"

"From you. I will awaken you when we arrive just outside your solar system. We will have one last, short hop, after which you must depart rapidly."

* *

Ian closed his eyes and welcomed sleep. His brain was ticking over quickly now, with thoughts of Earth flooding back to him. The burden of not knowing when, if ever, he might return was slowly lifting. Instead of contemplating an unimaginable future, now his thoughts were filled with images of blue skies and human faces. In a few moments, he was asleep.

* *

Ian was back in the chamber with the Sunface.

This has to be a dream.

"-No my friend. This is no dream. I am speaking to you from far away. This is our last chance to talk before you realize your destiny.-"

Then you don't mind if I ask a few questions?

"-Certainly. I wish to increase your understanding.-"

Why am I being sent back to Earth really? I find it difficult to believe such a powerful civilization would need

324

me to achieve its ends.

"-There is some truth in that. But not all the truth. You must understand that we are not solely interested in our own goals. We believe you have the right to a planet free from the interference of aliens. You have the right to the struggle for freedom.-"

But why must we struggle? With your powers surely you could free Earth and declare it off-limits without my help?

"-But then we would be the aliens interfering with Earth. We prefer to let you find your own equilibrium against the forces you face.-"

Now that, that is not quite the whole truth. You are cheating by helping me. Why should the humans and DogStars fight like animals when there is a greater power that could help us both? Dr. Manwas is a free DogStar. If all the DogStars became free, would they then still threaten other planets? Why don't you focus on solving the problem at its source?

"-You forget the issue of the K conduit. There are other unseen actors who have forced us to this compromise.-"

Am I then an easy way out for you? I resolve both problems, and I provide an interesting experiment for your cutting-edge brain implant technology. Am I no more to you than an animal in a zoo?

"-It is the nature of primitive cultures to fight over resources but, for ourselves, we must seek to help establish a just and moral existence for all.-"

So sending me back to Earth to wreak havoc is a moral decision? Who is responsible for the destruction I will cause? Myself? Dr. Manwas? You Nebulons?

"-You will bear no moral responsibility. The DogStars are the aggressors in this case and you are only defending your home. We have simply given you a better means of doing so.-"

So I bear no more responsibility than a monkey with a machine gun?

"-I see the primates in your mind. They are your cousins. You are correct. You bear no responsibility, nor do the DogStars for your Koryolis problems; they too are primitive life forms. Do not take this as an insult to your kind.

For my own people, we have several stages of life, three of which you have now seen. We are not Nebulon-centric. I view Young Nebulons, the ones who cannot bear your atmosphere and therefore cloak themselves in atmosphere suits, as similar to Earth primates, DogStars, and indeed all the so-called advanced life forms of your galaxy.

They are not responsible because they lack maturity and advancement. Only we, the more nearly mature Nebulons, currently have the understanding and therefore the responsibility.-"

I don't know. Sounds like a great excuse to treat us as expendable pawns in your moral war against disorder.

"-You misunderstand us.-"

The feeling is mutual. And if this isn't a dream, if you can contact me telepathically over these great distances, why can you not also remotely drive the DogStars from the Earth?

"-You must not reveal our existence to anyone. The secrets of the Nebulons must never be divulged. The implant can be remotely controlled by us to perform other functions.-"

Is that a threat?

"-We do not threaten, only increase awareness. Save your own kind, Ian. Goodbye.-"

Ian looked upon the Sunface. All its features had drained away, but it had become even more brilliant. Its size swelled and he had to look away. It was a blazing sun hanging in a void. Ian felt the heat build inside his brain, but then a veil of cool green gauze descended over him and he felt completely relaxed.

*   *

"Ian, please regain consciousness. We have arrived."
Dr. Manwas was gently poking Ian in the ribs. He blinked, but his eyes seemed dry and his lids met friction.

The starboard side of the shuttle had turned into a giant view screen. A yellow star shone dimly in the distance, brighter than all the stars, but still distant, its shape only a few arc seconds wide.

"That is your home star. When we hop in close to your planet, the matter transmitter will automatically send you to the location you have indicated. There will be no time for questions or goodbyes."

"What do I do?" Ian lifted his feet as if to swing out of his bed.

"No. Just stay in your berth and relax. And Ian, know that I wish you only the best of luck in your battles ahead. You must know that you should not judge my kind based on these parasitic pirates."

"I will not. By bringing me here today, you've shown you're a creature of great integrity and courage. I won't forget you."

Ian offered his hand and Dr. Manwas looked at it uncomprehendingly for a moment before they sealed the deal.

Ian had a few more seconds to admire the shimmering Oort Cloud and his home's interstellar neighbourhood before Dr. Manwas activated the ship for the last leg of the journey. It was over in less than two seconds. Now the Sun blazed with its usual prominence and bulk against the black velvet void, while Earth shone below them, sparkling green and blue. Ian felt a slight breeze and was gone.

327

Gusts of wind buffeted Ian. An empty Robo-Donut coffee cup slid past. The parking lot was empty. It was the middle of the night.

Oh yeah. That was Asia in sunlight I saw from the ship.

There was almost no traffic. A single car approached, a police car. After it had gone past Ian saw its brake lights come on but the light ahead was green. It started to make a U-turn.

I better get out of here. Wouldn't want to be suspected of stealing day-old donuts.

Ian jogged into the back alley abutting the Robo-Donut. One side was a row of houses, the other, two modest-sized apartment buildings. Blythe lived in the nearer one. Ian struggled to remember her apartment number.

She is perhaps the only person in the world who means anything to me anymore, and I don't recall her apartment number.

Ian stifled his disappointment in himself and focused on the problem. He remembered there was a fire escape outside Blythe's window, and she was on the second floor. Also, the kitchen window faced the Robo-Donut. This narrowed the possibilities down to one apartment.

Ian mounted the fire escape and began to climb. Just as he managed to reach her bedroom window, the police car entered the alley.

"Blythe! Wake up! It's me, Ian!"

Ian rapped on the window as the police car's spotlight swung upwards, exposing his indefensible position.

Please be home, please be home.

"Blythe! It's Ian!"

Two police officers had exited their vehicle. Just as Ian thought he might be spending some time answering very difficult questions, Blythe's bedroom light came on.

"Blythe! Open up!"

The shade across her window retreated upward, revealing Blythe in her night gown, carrying a large butcher's knife. She stared at Ian, paralyzed with surprise or perhaps just groggy from sleep interruption.

"Sir! Show us your hands!"

The police officers had their weapons drawn and were slowly approaching the side of the building. Could a taser reach the second floor? Ian did not want to find out.

"It's okay! Just taking a night walk!" Ian yelled down to the police. Blythe put down her knife and opened the window.

"It's okay! We're fine!" she yelled. Then added, "Acute insomnia!"

Ian crawled over the windowsill. He and Blythe stood together, waving and smiling at the officers below.

"Thank you! Sorry!"

The officers lowered their weapons and contemplated the couple for a moment. The officer who had been driving returned their wave, and then both returned to the cruiser. The spotlight extinguished. Blythe and Ian watched the Ottawa City Police vehicle continue down the alley.

"Ian!" Blythe hugged him tightly. She kissed him, and then suddenly recoiled. "Oh God! What have you been eating? Your mouth is horrible!"

"I'm not sure, to be truthful. It's a long story."

The clock beside the bed said it was half past four. They spent the next two hours talking about Ian's adventures.

When he related the story about the Avian Branch planet, and his custodian there, the kindly Admiral Byrd, Blythe laughed. By the time he got to the part about Trans-Galactic Trade Nexus Four and his lawyer, the giant squirrel, she was looking at him oddly. Did she think his brain was scrambled?

Ian truncated his story at Trade Nexus Four. The rest was too difficult to explain. As well, he recalled the admonition to not reveal the existence of the Nebulons.

At six-thirty they ate breakfast. Ian downed a ridiculously heaping bowl of cereal, perhaps half a kilogram, then threw up in the bathroom.

Blythe had to work at eight. There was still much to discuss. Ian cleaned himself up, taking a fresh toothbrush from Blythe's new package of four. Blythe updated him on the local news he had missed.

"Things are getting worse. When you left, the random human-on-human violence dropped right off, but the Cents, that's what we call those three-eyed bastards, they like to intimidate and rule through fear. They think if you kill one human, you motivate everyone nearby. But we're not animals. We *are* motivated, but motivated to kill *them*!

We're organizing a resistance. You remember Zarathustra? He's that homeless guy who was obsessed with you. Turns out he's got a lot of very interesting information about the Cents. We're working with him to formulate a strategy."

"We?" asked Ian.

"You'll get to meet everyone tonight. You stay here and take it easy today."

"Do you really believe everything I told you?" asked Ian.

Blythe pressed herself against Ian and rubbed his arms as if warming him.

"You disappeared from that parking lot. I saw that. You shimmered, and then you were just gone. You left Earth. I'm sure something happened to you up there."

"Just not necessarily what I was telling you."

Blythe smiled into Ian's dark eyes. There was no more

330

time for reassurances. She was expected at work. She kissed him.

"You taste human again."

Chapter Fifty-Six

Ian slept until afternoon. If he had dreamt, he remembered nothing of it. It was the best possible sleep, a restful oblivion. It was well after two o'clock by the time he wandered into the kitchen to make a cup of tea, or 'Earth tea' as he thought of it.

As the tea kettle heated, Ian pulled his pants from Blythe's clothes dryer. They were stained but at least they no longer reeked. Still, he had no shirt. Last night he had been wearing a DogStar tunic. No wonder the police were concerned, seeing such a bizarrely dressed male climbing a fire escape in the dead of night.

He scanned the headlines from the *Ottawa Citizen* news stream. Since that morning there had been an upsurge in violent incidents in his area of Ottawa. A police car had caused a massive pileup on the Queensway in the early rush hour. This was no accident; it had been speeding the wrong way down the freeway but chasing no one. A man had attacked bystanders at a bank and then been shot by police. This occurred only a few blocks from Blythe's apartment.

Ian rubbed the back of his neck. It was sore now, a slow burning sensation that seemed to increase by the second. Were these incidents related to the K conduit? Ian remembered his instructions from Dr. Manwas regarding the implant. He scanned the headlines looking for information on the Cents.

CENTAURAN COMMAND ESTABLISHES HQ
IN OTTAWA WEST

This was what he had been looking for. The Cents had taken over a sprawling building complex in west Ottawa, Nepean really, that had originally housed the flagship

332

telecommunications R&D center for Nortel, the company that had designed Canada's telecommunication infrastructure for over a hundred years, invented digital telephony late in the 20th Century, and then foundered around the millennium due to market bubbles and financial mismanagement.

An elegant glass cupola stood majestic and gleaming above the center of the complex. Was it the Canadian Armed Forces that had taken over the thousands upon thousands of high quality square footage within the impressive glass and concrete complex when Nortel stumbled and lost its footing? It mattered little.

In the last few weeks, the Cents had taken over the complex. Only the UN and other human quislings that required Cent instruction and control visited there now. Security was tight, provided by the RCMP as well as the UN.

Ian focused on the glass tower, imagining a green sheet of lightning moving towards it. In his mind's eye, the tower began to melt, first listing to one side, the hundred of panes of glass transforming into a shower of transparent pellets that rained upon the adjacent duck pond, surprising some Canada geese idling there.

Only a jagged stump now remained on top of the central building. Ian imagined another sheet of green lightning striking the remains of the tower building, its five stories collapsing in upon itself like the World Trade Center towers on September 11, 2001.

When Ian opened his eyes, the pain and burning was gone from the base of his skull. Ian opened Blythe's laptop and checked the CBC Headline News stream. A graphic behind an attractive newsreader female indicated 'Breaking News'.

"-are stunned by a series of explosions that seem to have

entirely levelled Building Five of the federal government's Carling and Moodie facility. The complex houses the command center for the Centauran administration. We have no word on casualties or what could have caused this disaster. Eyewitnesses claim that the glass tower appeared to disintegrate prior to the building collapse.

We have on the line Derek Meddings, senior structural engineer at Meddings and Johnson Engineering. Mr. Meddings, what could possibly explain the type of damage we see at this site?"

"Hello Sandra. Based on the photographs available, I don't think we can explain this type of damage based on structural defect. At first, I thought there was some kind of cascade failure in the structure, but the type of materials used in this building wouldn't support that idea. No pun intended."

"Could a bomb have caused this type of damage?"

"That's not my area of expertise but, if I were to hazard a guess, I'd say no. If explosives were involved, we would expect the force of the blast to throw debris outward. Here we see very little debris leaving the area. It appears that the building fell; it did not explode."

"Thank you for your insight, Mr. Meddings."

"You're very welcome Sandra."

"The Centaurans have sealed off the area and have not reported any casualties as of yet. We will keep you up-to-date on this developing-"

Ian hit the off button.

Oh my God. This implant really works. Does this mean that if I don't use it, it'll randomly create havoc? And if I do use it, I can avoid that?

Ian returned to Blythe's laptop to search for information on additional Cent targets. He soon found it.

The Canadian Forces Base outside Trenton housed many

of Canada's most advanced military aircraft. The Cents were now using its personnel and assets to assist in their mysterious re-direction of Earth's industrial output.

Humans important to the Cents did not travel on commercial planes. All of Earth's military air transport capability was now a chauffeur service for a new elite, the humans who liaised between the few Cents and their vast, new labour force.

Real-time imagery of the base was not available, but Ian did find an aerial view in which the individual buildings were visible. Again he concentrated, forming a sheet of green lightning in his brain and directing it towards first one building and then another.

After imagining three buildings destroyed, Ian realized he could not summon any more green fire. His brain stem was numb and cool, devoid of the heat that had slowly accrued during the night.

Ian was famished. He ate two microwavable meals, one after the other, then felt guilty for depleting Blythe's freezer.

CBC did not report any problems near Trenton. Ian printed a hard copy of the aerial photo, folded and stuffed it into his pants pocket.

I'll try later. I can't let too much of the evil jelly build up inside me.

Chapter Fifty-Seven

Blythe bustled through the door around half past four carrying two reusable bags stuffed full of groceries in each hand.

"Looks like you could really use an extra arm or two today," joked Ian, but Blythe remained mute, a little ashen, and entirely immobile. "Or not. Let me help you unburden."

Blythe's groceries included a carton of blackberries. Ian stuck one in his mouth and was reminded of its corpulent cousin, the blobberry.

He laid the other items out on the counter as she re-arranged her pantry to accommodate the new treasures. Food prices had increased sharply since the Cents arrived. Ian vaguely recalled that grocery day for the divorced man involved throwing out a large amount of uneaten and half-spoiled food during the restocking process. Today however, Blythe threw nothing out, carefully placing the new items at the back of the refrigerator and pantry shelves.

"Did you hear about that building collapse on Moodie Drive?"

"I did it."

"You did what?"

"I made it collapse."

"Did you go out today?"

"No. I did it from here."

Blythe stopped what she was doing and stared at Ian, one arm still obscured by the pantry door.

"What do you mean? How could you do that?"

"I have a special power."

"From those space squirrels?" Blythe's eyebrows were raised.

"No, from some other aliens. They don't look like any

336

kind of animal at all. I really can't say more." Ian pulled the printed aerial photo from his pocket. "These buildings are important to the DogStars, I mean the Cents. I plan to destroy them all tonight. From here."

Blythe looked like she had a question on her mind she was not willing to pursue as she looked from Ian to the printed image of the buildings and back again.

"Don't you believe me?"

"I'd like to."

"Then come on."

Ian motioned her to follow him into the bedroom. He opened the window and crawled out onto the fire escape. She joined him, moving carefully and slowly. Ian felt a little warmth at the back of his neck. It should be enough.

"See the Robo-Donut sign?"

Blythe nodded. Atop a tall pole in front of the Robo-Donut was a large sign, just visible peeking above the intervening restaurant building.

"Keep watching it."

Ian's eyes narrowed and his lips compressed. The front panel fell off the sign, sliding out of view and revealing multiple fluorescent tubes inside. The bulbs exploded and the rest of the sign collapsed, falling inward like a building undergoing controlled demolition. Blythe's eyes were wide as she stared at Ian.

"Let's go inside," he whispered.

She nodded and eagerly climbed back through the window.

As they ate together, Ian explained as best he could. The demonstration had quashed all of her doubts. Now Blythe was doubly eager to introduce Ian to her cell of insurgents.

At half past seven, Blythe unlocked her apartment door. She drew the living room drapes and turned the TV on to cover any sound of conversation. Five minutes later,

Zarathustra entered stealthily, taking care to close the door noiselessly. Ten minutes after that, Dr. Joberkt likewise slipped in.

Blythe made the introductions.

"Ian, you remember Zarathustra? He certainly remembers you."

"I'm sorry. I don't think we've met." Ian shook Zarathustra's rough hand gently.

"No, perhaps not, but I've been, how should I say it, *stalking* you since the first days of the invasion. You see, the Cents aren't the only aliens on this planet. My brain was used as a hard drive by another set of aliens, and the information they kept in me was you. All about you."

"As wild as that sounds, it must be true. Sorry for interrupting, I am Dr. Joberkt. I've examined Zarathustra claim and he does indeed possess medical information about you that he couldn't possibly have gotten from any earthly source." Dr. Joberkt shook Ian's hand and continued. "He also possesses information about our attackers that no one else seems to have. Zara?"

"Yes, I do. These aliens aren't from Beta Centauri at all. That's disinformation. They call themselves DogStars, although they are estranged from their original home world. Also, the saucers we see above our cities aren't real. They're an illusion. There are only two actual saucers, and they're in a much higher orbit than where these fake saucers appear."

"Actually, there's just one saucer now," corrected Ian.

The others were momentarily speechless.

"I must apologize to you Ian," said Zarathustra.

"Why is that?" asked Ian.

"When the information about you was first deposited into my brain, I thought you were collaborating with the invaders. I intended to hunt you down and kill you. It was

338

only later, when additional information was given to me, and I realized a second set of aliens were involved, that I understood you were a victim of their manipulation, just as I was. Also, at the time, I was off my meds so I didn't interpret a lot of things correctly."

"Who do you think this second set of aliens is?" asked Ian.

Has Zarathustra been in contact with the Nebulons? wondered Ian.

"I don't know their identity, but I know they mean us no harm. I believe they're trying to reverse the harm done by these so-called Cents. They've given me information that'll help us terrorize and repel our attackers."

Dr. Joberkt interrupted again. "Last time we met, we worked out a series of targets based on Zara's information. The Cents are vulnerable to carefully targeted attack. Their chain of command is their weakest link."

Now Blythe interrupted the doctor. "And Ian can provide us a means of taking out those links."

"Are you volunteering as a suicide bomber?"

Before Ian could answer Dr. Joberkt, Blythe spoke again.

"No, no. Ian has a special power. He was modified during the time he was held in the saucer, and now he can destroy things with his mind. Today he destroyed that building on Moodie Drive the Cents were using as their HQ. Also, he imploded the Robo-Donut sign up the block. I saw him do it just by staring at it."

"Is that what happened? They've got the whole parking lot cordoned off, wrapped with police tape. There's practically a battalion of police out there. If this is true, then you better refrain from using your power again. We don't want the authorities to put the two incidents together."

"I think I have to use it. If I don't, it'll build up and then spill out, destroying things at random."

"We can certainly find uses for your talent. As I said, we have a list of targets."

"You mentioned a vulnerability in the Cents." Ian had turned to question Zarathustra. "What is it?"

"These creatures are very hierarchical and totalitarian. They have many workers and few leaders, and their leaders don't allow dissent or questions. They don't tolerate any information that flows upward through the hierarchy if it hasn't been specifically requested. The leaders pride themselves on their contingency planning and strategy. Basically there're two types of roles in their society: the theorists and the actionists.

The theorists sit at the top of the hierarchy. They request information, plan, and make decisions. The actionists are the lower class. They follow orders. Thinking is not tolerated among them. There's some mobility between the classes but it's based on seniority, age, and loyalty more than merit.

This leads to their vulnerability. If we take out the leaders, they will *not* be quickly replaced. And with the theorists out of the way, the actionists will be unable to implement the five-year plan. I believe they'd withdraw from Earth and their regrouping would take a long time.

Whatever plan they might devise at that point could very well *not* include the occupation of Earth. In other words, the goals of the new leadership, when it eventually emerges, would not necessarily follow that of the previous leadership."

"So," summarized Joberkt, "We have targets, and now we have a weapon. The question, Ian, is can we begin tonight?"

Already Ian had begun to feel the now familiar warmth building in his brain stem.

340

"We must."

As the discussion turned to specific targets, Ian disclosed that his built-in weapon had limitations. He had to be able to visualize the target, a picture helped, and he had to know the location of the target, so the green fire would be unleashed in the proper direction. As his targets were all individual Cent leaders who were continually on the move, a kill from a remote location would be impossible.

"If we knew the location of the real saucer, Ian could target it, couldn't you?" asked Blythe.

"Yes. That could be very effective. Most of the leadership must be on the saucer. That could be the *coup de grâce*," agreed Ian.

Joberkt was shaking his head. "I've got some friends in the military. The decoy saucers don't have radar images and the real saucer, well, it would be a needle in a haystack trying to find it. And the military is tightly controlled now. Anyone caught anywhere near the, uh, haystack would be killed. I do have some sources in the university's astronomy department. They could look for the real saucer optically, but that could take a long time. And there's no guarantee. It's a long shot."

"If I knew where the real saucer was, I think I could damage it. I know what they look like. I was on one when it crashed on another planet. So assuming the last saucer looks the same … perhaps just the location would suffice," mused Ian.

"This is very promising. I'll talk to my sources and prod them into action. We'll find the location of that saucer. In the meantime, we do have some Earth-based targets."

Joberkt looked at Ian expectantly and Ian nodded solemnly.

Chapter Fifty-Eight

Ian and Zarathustra were the mission team. The objective was an enclave of Cent leadership that had commandeered the Canadian Security Intelligence Services complex in East Ottawa.

Ian drove Blythe's car to the shopping mall nearest the CSIS complex and parked. Zarathustra retrieved a backpack from the back seat; it contained some tools, plus a change of clothes and a balaclava for each of them.

Ian instructed Zarathustra to stay close, but remain as unseen as possible, trailing directly behind him. Ian worried about friendly fire. Of course unfriendly fire might also be a big problem, so Ian wanted to shield his navigator as much as possible while having him close to his ear.

"There is an emergency door on the side. This leads directly up to where the four Cents should be." Zarathustra's information included detailed blueprints of the target buildings, some of which had never been released to the public, another indication that his alien source was valid and his information accurate.

Their faces were already covered as they left the public road and approached the forbidden grassy annex to the CSIS complex. How to squelch any alarm? They needed a diversion. Ian stared at the architecturally impressive glass atrium of the formal entrance at the front of the main building. He imagined a sheet of green lightning smashing it. A river of safety glass pellets formed as the glass walls collapsed. Alarms sounded.

The complex was surrounded by cameras on poles. Ian melted some which covered the approach to their destination, as well as a few others to muddy his intentions. When they reached the emergency exit at the extremity of the targeted wing, Ian rapidly melted the hinges of the door and then used a crowbar from Zarathustra's backpack to yank it out of its frame.

Inside, the alarm was louder. A small cadre of night shift workers were fleeing down the stairs directly towards the intruders. Ian sent a small green lick of fire to the group and they dissolved into a quarrelling mass, pummelling and strangling each other. One of the group jumped over the railing and fell a few meters onto a lower landing. Zarathustra had not seen such bizarre and random violence since the days just before Ian had disappeared.

Truly within this Saxon are the seeds of time's end.

Zarathustra's hallucinations and delusions were, for once, grounded in firm reality.

They duo ascended rapidly. Ian melted the door lock mechanism at the summit of the stairwell, and then they were truly inside the top secret facility. A long corridor faced them. To one side was a vast cubicle farm; on the other, a series of closed doors with only a numeric designation affixed to each.

"This way," hissed Zarathustra, pointing the other way. "We are looking for 504.021. End of this corridor, second last room."

The top floor was mostly deserted. Ian noticed one worker peeking up over the half wall of her workspace, but she looked so petrified to see the two intruders that Ian didn't send any green death her way.

Focus on what is ahead. Faster.

The second last door at the end of the corridor was marked with the number Zarathustra had provided.

Perfect.

Ian tried the doorknob and it turned freely. He pushed the door open and was confronted by two guards carrying small automatic rifles.

"Who are you?" they demanded, levelling their weapons

at the unexpected visitors.

"I'm here to help," explained Ian as he pushed a small green flame into their minds. They fell on the floor writhing, their weapons forgotten.

"The inner office," Zarathustra whispered urgently from behind Ian.

Ian sent a thick green wave at the door opposite him. It exploded inwards, showering their next objective with molten metal. One Cent was already dead from the explosion before they entered. Two others were stunned, sitting on the floor.

Only a single Cent remained composed, sitting behind a desk and raising its alien pistol at them. Before it could react, Ian sent another wave through the room and the eyeballs of each Cent melted out of their heads. It was done.

"You got all four!" Zarathustra thumped Ian on the back, and then suddenly lost his giddiness. "Time to get out."

Back in the corridor, Zarathustra redirected them to another stairwell. They descended rapidly and emerged into the cool night air on the far side of the wing.

As they crossed the grassy field on the other side of the complex they could see a stream of vehicles pouring into the large empty parking lot in front of the complex. They reached the road just as a police car screeched to a halt in front of them.

"Get down on the ground! Do it now!" shouted one officer who was already standing behind her open car door, pistol drawn and pointed in their direction.

I'm sorry.

As both Ian and Zarathustra raised their hands, Ian sent a ball of green fire at the vehicle. It exploded, throwing the officer to the ground. Before another car arrived, Ian and Zarathustra had uncovered their faces and walked through a

344

crowd of people who had gathered on the main road to watch the spectacular fire now raging throughout the CSIS complex.

Humans: four. DogStars: zero.

Chapter Fifty-Nine

Ian slowly approached the saucer, ensuring each footfall landed soundlessly. The Cent's attention was fixed on the mass of wires and tubing in the open panel in front of it. One arm lazily scratched its back, one shielded its eyes from the overhead sun, and the other two were deep inside the saucer panel. Ian was barely one meter behind it.

Green Green. Fire.

Nothing happened. Ian could hear the Cent's aggravated sigh. The repairs were not going well.

What's wrong with my power? Am I out of jelly?

Any moment now the Cent might turn around. Ian knew he could not win in hand to hand combat with such a creature.

Plan B.

Ian pulled the slag hammer from his makeshift tunic pocket and struck the back of the Cent's head with the pointy end. It staggered backward and then collapsed with a gurgle. Ian pulled his hammer free of the Cent's skull and wiped it clean, leaving purple streaks on his victim's tunic. He spotted an identical hammer hanging from a loop near the fallen Cent's waist.

Just a worker.

A tsunami of nausea and panic rose in Ian's mind.

It carries a tool used for constructive work, now used for murder. Not a military weapon. Never before have I killed a creature in anger. Isn't that correct? These are not monsters; they are individuals.

Ian stared at his hammer. Back in Byrd's atrium he had used it to kill a spider. He had bashed holes in Byrd's walls to help him climb free, but then had returned to the atrium.

A movement near the Cent's body startled Ian. A large hairy spider was crawling out from under the corpse. Ian shuddered and stepped back.

There is no reason to kill it.

Around the arc of the saucer's hull, Ian spotted another Cent, immersed in its maintenance work as the first had been. Ian thought to move stealthily towards it, but hesitated instead.

* *

"Your move."

Ian stared at the pieces on the chess board. He was now in a black chamber, sitting on a stool, staring down at a chess board on a small table.

"Your move," his opponent repeated. "My knight is vulnerable."

Indeed Ian could easily take out the black knight but what were the ramifications?

Is it a trap, a manipulation to force me into trading more valuable pieces for lesser? Should I take the bait?

Ian tried to read his opponent. Its skin was red, teeth sharp and eyes malevolent. Horns graced its forehead. A devil. But it had three eyes. It was a Cent.

"Your time is limited, Ian."

The Cent was Dr. Manwas, but it had none of the collegial and affable manner of the alien physician.

"You must make your move."

It smiled horribly and Ian fought the urge to flee. This must be a different Cent. Why would he be playing a game with such a creature? Hadn't he already escaped Byrd's planet and returned to Earth? What was wrong with his memory?

* *

The sound of the alarm clock brought relief from these dreams.

"You stay." Blythe pushed herself out of the bed and forced Ian back onto the mattress in the same motion.

"Rest." She slipped on her night shirt and left the bedroom.

Details of the two dreams swirled in Ian's conscious mind like water down a drain. Already the images were fading.

Ian retained one impression: himself staring down at the purple-bloodied hammer and assuring himself he had never struck out in anger before. It was not true. Ian realized that he didn't know if his original attacker, the one who had put him in a coma, had survived.

I hope he survived. His only fault was being in the wrong time and place. The first victim of the K conduit scam.

Then, the actual details of the previous night returned to him. He had killed four Cents, but how many humans? One of them was a police officer. Was she also hurt?

Was the dream trying to help him forget the trauma of last night's battle at the CSIS complex? It didn't work. Ian's stomach knotted at the violent memories.

I am not a villain.

Ian realized he could no longer afford to harbour animosity for anyone; things might go very badly if he should lose focus and aim his green ire at an unintended target. Going forward he would have to be constantly aware that his thoughts could have deadly consequences.

What have I gotten myself into? Well to start, let's be fair to myself: I didn't get myself into this. Yes I did agree to Speck's terms, although it was under the duress of those exigent circumstances.

He closed his eyes and tried to calm his racing brain.

I am back on Earth. I am safe. Well, more or less. I have escaped all the horror of my long kidnapping.

Those birds on that Avian Branch planet – they don't really look like any Earth birds. I think my brain re-interpreted my sensory input to make them related to adorable Earth fauna and therefore, more recognizable, perhaps friendlier, and certainly less scary. Thinking of them now, I realize just how far from reality was my perception.

Same for the Tree Line Glory aliens; they did not actually resemble squirrels much at all. But seeing them as they actually were had the potential to generate a lot of horror. I guess my brain had to do something to stop my revulsion, else my fears might have led to catatonia or some final violent act. But it had worked; I had stayed calm through it all really.

Framing my situation in acceptable terms made all the difference. One cannot sit idly and think, oh, I have been abducted by a slimy abomination and still cogitate properly.

The delusion of the fuzzy animals was just an easy way for me to accept and deal with the unknowns that confronted me. Sometimes it takes a long while but eventually you gain the perspective to see things as they really are. It is not an easy process.

This applies to my own life as well. In the proper perspective, Gale is not the monster I make her out to be. Her betrayal was not malicious. Now I can accept my divorce.

Gale made her choice based on her own feelings and I can't fault her. It was not her doing that I gained my speech impediment, nor that I lost it. I had made such a big thing of it, my stutter. Throughout my cosmic travels, I had formed allies with various aliens, and all without the spoken word! Has my life of limited fluency prepared me better for these challenges than the loquacious would have been? Perhaps. I have survived. I am here. It is not all bad.

Gale and I had a good thing, originally. It didn't require too many words. What are words anyway? Just fake little plastic models of reality that think they have hard edges and are true categories, but are leaking meaning all around them, on every front, and shift and change over time like the non-compliant dynamic little wit-bags they are.

But still. It is what we have. There is the case of something is good enough.

So then we had the benefit of 'improved' communication, and it fouled the soup.

I understand that I really had changed. It was not just that I could speak, but the knowledge that I could speak, and my availing myself of it, made me into a different person. I changed right away, a new star gone nova, brilliant for a time.

I was elated, and perhaps I lost focus on her. That must be how she felt. It was an amazing time in my life, the glory before the long fall, her leaving me, the divorce, and my stagnation at work, my loss of interest.

I thought if this woman who claimed love for me, suddenly now really does know me and does not love me anymore, then did she ever really love me, or was it some kind of illusion? There are many possibilities I guess but all that matters is she is gone.

Now I understand it was not just her. I had changed. I was not the same guy she selected. How can I fault her for crying foul at a bait and switch such as my transformation?

Yes, Gale had a co-dependent nature that was no longer being assuaged. Her dominant streak had run out. There I was, commenting and opining with impunity. It was a nightmare for her! I can accept that now, but I do so without devaluing myself. I don't suit her pathology, but remain highly functional.

I forgive her. I wish Gale happiness. I can move on. I can find real love.

Ian remembered sitting with Blythe, asking why she had saved him during the attack at the hospital. She said that she remembered when he arrived they had no next-of-kin contact info for him. To get past the narrow-minded computer disallowing an intake without a contact number, the doctor on duty had input the morgue number. Blythe was touched by this, and it made her keep a close eye on him.

When everything was falling apart as the Cents invaded, she felt she could not leave him behind. Clearly, she liked the way he looked as well.

Ian recalled that, at that time, his contact should have been his best friend Orestes. After the divorce, however, everything was wiped and Ian did not add anyone. His parents were long gone and his two younger brothers were narcissists, or at least egocentric, and could be counted upon for nothing more complicated or time-consuming than to pull the plug.

Ian received no visitors during those two years.

Perhaps that doctor did the best thing.

Ian had always worked things out on his own. He had not had the advantage or luxury of hashing out his ideas in front of a receptive audience. His stutter saw to that.

What had he made of his life?

Maybe a lifeboat but not a ship to take me somewhere, or to travel at ease and in comfort.

But I survived! I even did a bit more. I learned. I loved. I adapted. Survived, maybe not thrived optimally, but somewhere in between.

I have hopes for an adaptive outcome. Now I know who I am. Now I know that Gale was not a good match. But Blythe!

Today, I have the power and the vision or light to go forward. Power in darkness is chaotic. You need to see

351

where you can go.

Now Ian was ready.

"You want some breakfast?" Blythe called from beyond the half-closed bedroom door. When Ian emerged, he could see she was eating toast slathered with peanut butter. A plastic container of cherries sat on the table. Her laptop was open and a news video was running.

"You're famous," she smiled.

"-cannot say who might be behind this audacious attack but one thing that is certain is the targets were not only Centauran, but human as well. The burnt-out shell of a police cruiser was towed from the area, and Ottawa City Police have already issued a statement indicating at least two of their officers were killed in the attack. Police are not releasing any other details, but anonymous sources have revealed that certain elements of this attack tie it to the destruction of the Department of National Defence's Moodie facility and the collapse of several buildings at CFB Trenton. In other news-"

Blythe hit the mute button.

"Not too hungry. Bad dreams."

Blythe came around the table to tangle Ian in her arms.

"Don't feel bad. This is war. You're a hero. You're not a …" Blythe paused as if the need to lick her lips overrode the priority of pronouncing the missing noun.

A murderer?

"You're not guilty of anything except trying to save the world. Now, don't go anywhere today. You just stay here, and stay clear of the windows."

Blythe's work shift was imminent, so she had to leave Ian alone and hiding in her apartment. Ian eventually ate a few cherries and began to read the coverage of his mission's results.

A grainy security photo, no doubt greatly enlarged and

cropped, showed Ian and Zarathustra wearing their balaclavas and striding away from the compromised complex. A large reward was offered for their identities.

Ian racked his memory for details of their incursion. He had worn gloves but hardly touched anything, maybe two doorknobs. The masks kept any stray hairs from escaping.

They won't find any DNA.

Ian closed Blythe's laptop and put the cherries back in the fridge. A loud thump and the sound of shattering glass came from outside. Ian moved to the window and peered out from between the closed drapes. Next to the Robo-Donut parking lot exit, a small, black car sat gouged and wrecked, straddling the middle of the road. A brilliant coppery SUV had plowed into the side of the smaller vehicle. Now the two drivers were wrestling on the pavement, oblivious to the traffic backing up around them.

Ian felt his neck. It was warm.

So soon?

Ian yanked the aerial image of the Trenton base from the back pocket of yesterday's pants and then dropped them back onto the bedroom floor. Ian directed some green ire at several other buildings depicted on the hard copy.

Slowly, the warmth at the base of his skull subsided.

Chapter Sixty

Clerk Two almost wished to be back on the home world, living the life of a simple actionist. The clerk remembered days spent with work crews, the songs they sang and the jokes they shared.

There were no songs on this ship.

The clerk had risen far above the social weaknesses of the work gang to become a pirate and a theorist. It always suspected itself was an individual outside the moral order and therefore had aspired to leave what it saw as a suffocating role upon DogStar Prime. Although there had been few times it had regretted that decision, today was one.

Things had not gone well with the Earth project. True, they were transporting large quantities of precious minerals and metals to the huge sub-light freighter parked at the gravitational equilibrium point that trailed Earth on its journey around the Sun, but there had been significant problems.

First, the loss of their second command ship had been a near-fatal blow, taking almost a third of their personnel with it as it crashed on the Avian Branch planet. Personnel were replaceable, to some extent, but the equipment and weaponry of that ship would certainly be missed.

There was only one DogStar saucer left and, not knowing what had gone wrong with the other, Clerk Two's usual high confidence level was becoming more and more a smokescreen and shield against criticism. Clerk Two was faking it, and had begun to suspect that the other theorists on their single remaining command ship were likewise only providing the appearance of operational certainty.

Ridiculous as it seemed, Clerk Two could now admit, if only to itself, that there existed the possibility that they might never leave this planet alive.

The second problem was that, somehow, the laughably two-armed creatures on this planet had struck back with a cunning and powerful weapon of unknown design. DogStars had died on this backwater planet.

Its report would not be welcomed by its superiors and Clerk Two had recently allowed itself to accept that most of the pirate theorists were rapidly-promoted actionists who suffered over-confidence and rarely distinguished between the messenger and the message. An unstable hierarchy allowed more mobility for those seeking to climb it, but while that ascent could be exhilaratingly rapid for the ambitious, so too the descent was often a quick path, often ending in an airlock send-off.

Clerk Two entered Ship Supervisor's chamber.

"My esteemed leader, allow me to report, if it should please you."

"I doubt your report will please me, but I will listen to it now."

"Thank you, dear leader. I regret to report additional building collapses at the Trenton base."

"Were these not inspected and reinforced after the first incidents?" Ship Supervisor was speaking much too loudly for Clerk Two's comfort. Violence of expression leads to violence of arms, it recalled the truism from one of their forbidden poet's suppressed works.

"Yes, most valued one. Much work was performed in the last cycle to reinforce the areas used by our personnel, but these have collapsed as well. I am concerned that we are dealing with a new type of weapon, one we did not suspect the two-arms possessed."

"That is unlikely, Clerk Two. These creatures' technology is simple."

"Your statements are accurate, as always, our jewel of

command, but the facts are plain. Repeated analysis of the damaged materials shows a type of metal fatigue inconsistent with the time-frame or any possible stimulus. We might assume the source of the damage was a weapon operated from far away, something initiated by advanced equipment operated by an intelligence from a far more advanced area of the cosmos.

However, we have no indication of such a force being present in this stellar neighbourhood. We also have new reports of specific attacks occurring nearly simultaneously in the city called Ottawa, one of our three main command and control centres for this planet.

Most distressing is an attack that killed four of our most senior staff, using the same technology, and this time, definitely in the hands of the two-arms. We have a picture of the attackers fleeing their target."

Clerk Two showed Ship Supervisor the grainy blowup of the two balaclava-bearing Canadians.

"There is no weapon apparent on them," noted Ship Supervisor.

"Yes. No equipment at all."

"Sir."

"A thousand pardons, your brilliance. No equipment at all, sir."

"If this city, Ottawa, were to cease to exist, we might silence this strange foe. Do you agree?"

"Yes, my esteemed leader." Clerk Two's internal alarm bells were clanging. Did Ship Supervisor actually ask its opinion? "However, it will take some time to remove our equipment and personnel from the blast zone. As well, extra efforts will be required to re-coordinate the two-arms from a new location."

"How long?" Ship Supervisor's third eye narrowed suspiciously.

"One cycle to remove our local operations, and another two cycles to restore them elsewhere, worthy one."

"Very well. One cycle from this moment, we will destroy Ottawa. You may begin the process to relocate our operations now. Now." Ship Supervisor was already looking at its chronometer when it uttered the second *now*. Clerk Two backed out of the chamber while simultaneously giving thanks for its orders.

Clerk Two's first step was to call all DogStar crew currently in Ottawa back to the remaining ship. The clerk would need technical assistance readying the antimatter bomb.

Chapter Sixty-One

After Ian had finished flattening, or attempting to flatten (only the news media could confirm it), the military buildings at CFB Trenton, he felt drained; he retreated to the bedroom, to lie in its dim and safely disconnected space, the sounds and fresh air from the outside world flowing in through the fire escape window.

Someone on Blythe's side of the building had a bird feeder. Behind the swell and ebb of automotive rancour, a steady, more natural sound wormed its way into his attention foreground: birdsong. One bird's series of escalating and nuanced riffs was particularly impressive. This non-human music relaxed Ian.

Ian knew that birds were the descendants of those few creatures to survive the asteroid holocaust that had truncated the dinosaur era. He now imagined that the birdsong was a long-lost warning, passed on by their ancestors, the meaning of which was now lost to the singers: beware of fiery rocks falling from the sky.

Ian recalled a nature film about a type of bird that killed or drove away other birds by destroying their eggs and taking over their nests.

How could beautiful creatures with such sweet song be so cruel? Was it an illusion of Nature, their beauty and their cruelty? Or a trick of human expectations or prejudice? Humans certainly had the same capacity for aesthetic brilliance and bloody mayhem. Perhaps one should expect better from us, the purportedly more intelligent creatures. Although, one could extend that argument to claim that aliens with intelligence superior to humans should also be morally superior.

Ian recalled early assertions by UFO aficionados that, because of their advanced civilization, visiting aliens would never attack Earth.

That didn't pan out too well.

Ian's experience told him the Universe was full of creatures who had their own interests and their own ethics, some of it very alien. Monsters were sometimes swayed by pity. Sometimes angels were deranged. Even cannibals had their own table manners.

Occasionally well-intentioned rules got in the way of honest creatures thrown into unexpected circumstances. Good and evil could not describe all the behaviour Ian had witnessed.

Nor does it describe what I have to do.

But the scales of justice were returning to equilibrium. Ian reviewed all the creatures he had encountered, weighing their actions against his own interests. The final sum was surprising.

Most of these creatures exhibited great care in their dealings with me. Perhaps the early UFO aficionados were correct. We need only fear the rogues of the galaxy.

Ian recalled how Byrd had captured him, brought him to safety, and given him food and water. And how the strange creature had eventually helped him back to where he had been found. Ian had been set free.

A memory of a distant afternoon returned to Ian. He and Gale had built a box for a wounded sparrow that, having knocked itself senseless on the kitchen window, was subsequently found lying inert on the lawn. They had provided it a small cloth bed and a water dish.

Within an hour, the bird recovered and flew away, unhurt. Ian and Gale congratulated themselves on protecting it from predators and even healing it. Certainly they had done less.

But they had done something. Perhaps the bird realized they were not its enemy. Or perhaps it was glad to escape the excited monsters who had touched it with odd-smelling hands.

From Ian's new perspective, the Universe had generously re-paid his actions of that long ago afternoon.

* *

Ian must have fallen asleep. He was shocked awake by the slamming of the apartment door. Before he could rise, Blythe was sitting next to him.

"The Cents are leaving Ottawa!"

Ian was too groggy to respond coherently, but he thought he had heard correctly. Then, as suddenly as she had appeared, she was gone. Ian heard her fingers tapping on her laptop keyboard.

"Did you say…?"

"Yes. It's very strange. It's just a local thing. There's a lot of buzz on the net. The UN doesn't know what's happening. Their liaison here is in the dark. The Cents are no longer talking. They're just ignoring everyone and leaving. Nobody knows why."

"What do you mean, a local thing?"

"It's just Ottawa. At their other HQs, in Seoul and Bonn, it's business as usual. Maybe you've driven them out!"

"I don't know about that. This could be very bad. If they are withdrawing, they could be planning an attack. Maybe they've put the clues together and they know the source of their new problem is here. They could be preparing to nuke us."

Blythe leaned back from her laptop.

"You're right. This isn't good news at all. Although, Dr. Joberkt was pretty excited about it. He's gone to see his friends at the university.

He says they should've regained access to the orbital telemetry data. When the Cents arrived, his friends had tracking data on those first ships, but then they either went into hiding, were imprisoned or worse. The Cents didn't want anyone figuring out those hundreds of giant saucers were illusion."

Blythe's phone jangled.

"Hi. Okay. Yes I know where it is. We'll be there in ten minutes."

* *

Getting into Blythe's car made Ian nervous because it had been the getaway car for his CSIS mission. Dr. Joberkt had summoned them to the Thirsk Observatory at Carleton University. It was only a ten minute drive and the Cents had bigger problems to worry about than this possibly infamous vehicle.

The observatory building was a modern glass cube with a satcom tower on top. There was no dome, and no large telescope. The facility provided a base for astronomers to contact other observatories throughout the world and in orbit, and to crunch their data with its considerable dedicated computer assets.

Dr. Joberkt was on the roof with a grey-haired woman who was dressed somewhat shabbily, *à la* academic chic.

"Ian, Blythe, this is Dr. Olivia Ryan."

Pleasantries were briefly exchanged. Dr. Joberkt seemed stressed out, as if trying to beat the clock. A small telescope sat atop a portable tripod. Dr. Ryan was reading data from her portable data device.

"Declination 20 degrees, 31 minutes, 59 seconds."

"Check." Dr. Joberkt adjusted the telescope carefully and then turned to address Ian.

"It's still daylight, but I don't think we have much time. The only explanation for the Cents abandoning their operations in this city is that they intend to destroy us. We have to act first.

Dr. Ryan, at great personal risk to herself, has been

361

searching for the locations of the Cent ships ever since they arrived. Her results are quite surprising, and even encouraging. Olivia, do you want to tell them?"

"Yes. As you know, the saucers we've seen hovering over cities are entirely insubstantial. Only through careful filtering and cross-referencing of various data steams was I able to uncover this truth. There were only *two* actual saucers, and these were in a very high Earth orbit. Even better, one of the saucers disappeared about two weeks ago."

My kidnappers.

"So, now there's only one saucer left. It appeared over the eastern horizon one hour ago and will be directly overhead in another ninety minutes. We have just plugged its co-ordinates and trajectory into this hobby telescope which is now tracking its progress across the sky."

"But it's still daylight outside. How can you see anything through that telescope?" protested Ian.

"No, you're quite right. This is an optical telescope and the Sun is not going to set for several hours yet. We won't be able to see the saucer," replied Dr. Ryan.

"Ian, you shouldn't need to see it. You know what it looks like," interjected Dr. Joberkt.

"I know what the *other* saucer looked like. Are we assuming they're the same?"

"I would say we are deducing, tentatively, not assuming," amended Dr. Ryan.

"Olivia has already confirmed that the two saucers have identical shapes and very similar mass," explained Dr. Joberkt.

"The delta is less than one tenth of one per cent. Not significantly different." Dr. Ryan shook her head for emphasis.

"So *you* know what it looks like and *we* know where it

is. That should do it.

It shouldn't be more difficult than your Trenton attack. But I think we need to act now. I suspect the Cents will initiate their attack as soon as they are directly overhead." Dr. Joberkt moved away from the telescope eye piece. "I suggest you use the telescope to visualize the saucer in the correct location." He waved Ian towards the telescope.

Ian gazed into the patch of sky where the telescope pointed. It was blue. He hunched over the eye piece and peered through it. A circle of blue.

There is a saucer out there. It looks like this. It is right there.

Ian imagined a sheet of green fire reaching into the sky, escaping the atmosphere, finding the twin saucer and smothering it. Ian sent another sheet. Then another. There was no way to tell if it was working. Ian continued his efforts until his occipital lobe of his brain was numb.

Out of jelly.

Ian sat down abruptly, and rubbed the back of his head. "That's all I can do."

The other three scanned the sky for any sign of success. The sky was a flawless blue dome, a beautiful and pleasant summer evening, worthy of a last day.

"There!" Dr. Ryan pointed. A dot of light, out of place in the blueness. It brightened, then elongated, moving west.

"A shooting star?" asked Blythe.

"Ian is our shooting star," quipped Dr. Joberkt. "This is much better!" Then he laughed. Blythe had never heard such a horse bray come out of the reserved doctor. She smiled in surprise.

The dot was moving more quickly. Now there were more dots, each one starting a new path tangential to the original. The saucer was breaking up.

"You did it!" Blythe dropped to her knees and hugged

Ian, who was still sitting on the ground, his forehead shiny from effort.

"Incredible." Dr. Ryan looked at Ian as if he were a cosmic dust cloud that had spontaneously re-shaped itself into a facsimile of the Turin Shroud image. "Just incredible."

Chapter Sixty-Two

From the *Ottawa Citizen* news stream the next morning, also known as Earth Freedom Day:

FREE AT LAST!

Yesterday at 5:19 pm EST, a falling star was seen by millions as it crossed the sky above central and eastern Canada. The significance of the event was not understood until three hours later when Environment Canada officials announced the object had been tracked to its impact crater in Nunavut and verified to be the primary spacecraft used by the Centaurans. The cause of the crash is not known, or perhaps has not been released by the military.

A statement released by eNATO Brigadier General Ellyn Habbakuk last night confirmed that Centauran forces had withdrawn from their Ottawa HQ for unknown reasons earlier that afternoon. Just prior to the crash of the Centauran space vehicle, the sixty-four 'flying saucers' that had hovered over national capitals throughout the world simultaneously disappeared. General Habbakuk revealed that these saucers were holograms, a ruse created by the invaders to instill fear and elicit obedience.

Our special report provides detailed coverage on the aftermath of the Centauran withdrawal, including our prognosis for international relations in the shadow of the unprecedented debacle of unconditional surrender by all the major nations that occurred when the invaders arrived.

*　　*

From the *Ottawa Sun* news stream, one week later:

OUR LAST TWO CENTS

We won't be seeing too much of our four-armed friends anymore. German authorities in Bonn today handed over two surviving Cent soldiers to eNATO for "examination and execution". Chancellor Bilderberg rebuffed the concerns of human rights organizations stating "human rights do not apply to non-humans". Later in the morning, demonstrators clashed outside the eNATO mission on Bornheimer. No arrests were made, but some protesters were seen being treated for tear gas exposure.

Four Cents were killed by police forces in Seoul the morning after Earth Freedom Day was declared in North America last week, lowering the worldwide total of despised enemy survivors to these final two.

* *

From The *Ottawa Citizen* website, eight days later:

INVADERS MISIDENTIFIED,
eNATO OFFICIAL CLAIMS

Dr. Leonard Joberkt, acting chair of the eNato Reboot Committee, commented today that compressed-wave communication with Beta Centauri should "continue to be pursued". The aliens who enslaved Earth earlier this month were "not from Beta Centauri".

Dr. Joberkt refused to elaborate, citing a military secrecy doctrine, but reiterated that the invaders were not the entities behind humanity's initial radio contact with extraterrestrials almost thirteen years ago.

* *

From the *Ottawa Citizen* news stream, eleven days later:

UN FUNDING FOR LANDMINE REMOVAL
LANDS IN OTTAWA

The UN Office of Post-Conflict Assistance today announced a new $300 million contract with a private Ottawa firm to remediate landmines and other unexploded ordinance in Korea.

Jin Lee, High Commissioner of UNOOPCA, said "this involves experimental technology that we are hopeful will be much more effective than the current methods which generally pose grave risks to field personnel. The new technology is classified, but I can assure you this will be money well spent."

Details regarding ownership of the contracted company, 8513498187 Ontario, were not available.

Chapter Sixty-Three

Ian liked his new military-issued tablet. The application SkyEye was like a Google Earth from the far future. He could zoom in to any point on Earth and examine details as small as three centimetres across.

And the information was in real-time! Ian could call for an updated image as often as he liked. His tablet was the only authorized user of SkyEye. The computational resources required to perform this feat were housed in military labs spread around the world.

All Ian had had to do to obtain this wonder was promise to behave, provide a complete debriefing on his off-planet activities, swear himself to eternal secrecy, and accept an astronomical up-front bonus and salary.

Ian studied an obscure corner of Korean geography. The vast field was empty, a few brown scruffs of grass over dry, untended soil. It was a forsaken trapezoid of land amid a rapidly developing border area. Ian zoomed in on a tiny plot, the next square along the strip he was currently scrubbing.

Green jelly seeping in here.

Ian updated the image and was satisfied to notice several new craters in the ground. He counted the marks and added the total to his spreadsheet. The engineer in Ian liked to have a concrete measure of his success.

Ian did not think of Blythe. It would be extremely dangerous to let his thoughts wander during working hours, but he was contentedly in love. He had found it true that you develop intense bonds with those whom accompany you through adversity. There was something easy and obvious about their relationship.

His work was boring, but necessary, and not just for those whom lived near unexploded ordinance. Ian knew he needed to drain the jelly every day, otherwise a dangerous buildup would manifest in horrors very close to home. His work provided a creative outlet for that destructive energy.

Ian moved to the next plot and concentrated again.

Just a tiny flicker of fire. Droplets of green striking the ground one per square centimetre...

Ian refreshed the image, counted the new pockmarks, and verbally updated his spreadsheet yet again.

That's five hundred so far today. Five hundred lives or limbs I have saved.

Ian did not like to think of the collateral damage he had caused in the war against the Cents. He preferred his role as saviour of the innocent.

THE END

ACKNOWLEDGEMENTS

A heartfelt thank-you for the editorial and emotional support during the writing and revising of this manuscript:
Lois Crowe,
Lucie Kearns,
Pattie Balcom.